THE
NIGHT VOICE

THE NIGHT VOICE

A Novel of the Noble Dead

Barb & J. C. Hendee

A ROC BOOK

ROC

Published by New American Library,
an imprint of Penguin Random House LLC
375 Hudson Street, New York, New York 10014

This book is an original publication of New American Library.

First Printing, January 2016

For more information about Penguin Random House, visit penguin.com.

LIBRARY OF CONGRESS CATALOGING-IN-PUBLICATION DATA:

Hendee, Barb.
The night voice: a novel of the noble dead / Barb & J. C. Hendee.
pages cm.—(Noble dead; 11)
ISBN 978-0-451-46932-8 (hardback)
I. Hendee, J. C., author. II. Title.
PS3608.E525N54 2016
813'.6—dc23   2015029616

Printed in the United States of America
10 9 8 7 6 5 4 3 2

Penguin
Random
House

THE
NIGHT VOICE

PROLOGUE

Light, salt-laden winds blew in over the evening ocean, where an aging man with white-blond hair sat leaning against the bare base of a tree. His hair might have once been even closer to white, and it now showed darker streaks, making it more white-gray than white-blond.

Only a few noises reached him from the little seaside town a short walk inland. He never looked back and only stared out over the water, as if he already knew every sound that he heard.

A pale glimmer like an old worn road of light ran from the shore beyond his outstretched legs and tall boots to the horizon, where the sun had sunk beyond sight and the ocean. He was quiet and still, for he was not truly looking for anything out there. Lost elsewhere in thought, perhaps he didn't hear ever-so-soft footfalls among the trees. If he did, he didn't show it. More likely, he knew those sounds as well as those of the town.

The dark, small form was lighter of foot than almost anyone else.

"So . . . where's that husband of yours?" he asked wryly without stirring.

The short one among the deeper dark of the trees halted with a sigh.

"Oh, Father!" she whispered in exasperation. "One day, I *will* sneak up on you."

He laughed, though it was a tired sound. "Not in this life, my little wild one."

When she stepped nearer out of the trees, she was no more than a shadow, indistinct in a long robe and deep cowl. The closer she came, the more the light showed her sage's robe of deep forest green. That in itself was strange, since no known order of sages wore that color.

Inside the cowl's depths, twilight might have sparked a more brilliant, verdant green in her large, almond-shaped eyes. Those eyes were not unlike his, though his were the more traditional amber of their people. She slowed to a stop a few steps off and behind on his right, and he still stared out across the waters.

"I came as soon as I received your message," the daughter said softly, taking another step. "You did not go with Mother . . . to see *her.*"

"No point," her father answered with a slight shake of his head. "*She's* already gone by now, and so your mother was enough."

Silence lingered briefly.

"You did not want to go?" she asked.

"Of course I did!"

Finally, he glanced away from the light upon the water, but he still didn't look up at her. She felt his sadness, for she shared it for the one who had passed away. Too short a life had ended, even for a human woman, an old friend to them all.

The daughter looked closely at her father's sad and coldly angry profile. Even in the dark, she saw the lines of age on his face.

"At least she was happy again, for a while," he added. "I'll give *him* that, and she deserved it."

Another long silence, and then . . .

"She was your friend as well as Mother's," the daughter insisted. "You should have gone. I would have, but I thought to come here first."

At first, he didn't answer. "Your mother needed to go alone this time," he said quietly. "It's the last time. And you don't know everything . . . about how it might end."

CHAPTER ONE

Ghassan il'Sänke was powerless to stop the motion of his legs. He strode down the darkened streets of Samau'a Gaulb, the main port city of il'Dha'ab Najuum, the imperial city of the Suman Empire. Trying to exert his will for perhaps the hundredth time, he screamed out with his thoughts, for even his voice was not his to command.

Stop!

As always, it had no effect.

Trapped, he was merely a passenger . . . a prisoner within his own flesh taken over by a thousand-year-old specter.

Khalidah now ruled his flesh.

Ghassan's body walked past people on the street who barely glanced his way. To them, he would appear mundane. Beneath the hood of a faded open-front robe, his short chocolate-colored hair with flecks of silver was in disarray. Strands dangled to his thick brows above eyes separated by a straight but overly prominent nose. Though he had once worn the midnight blue robe of a sage in the order of Metaology, now his borrowed clothing—a dusky linen shirt and drab pantaloons—was no different from that of a common street vendor.

His body turned into a side alley. His head swiveled as he—as Khalidah—looked around.

Spotting several barrels halfway down the shadowed alley, he went and crouched down beside them. His left hand reached inside his shirt, and his fingers gripped the chain of a medallion, which he drew out. Panic—no, terror—flooded him, and he screamed out again.

No!

"Buzz, you little brain fly," Khalidah whispered with the domin's own voice, and then came the command, cutting like a knife in only thought. *Be silent!*

Everything before Ghassan's mind's eye went black with pain. He felt the specter squeeze the medallion and focus his will to make the connection to the one other who carried such a medallion. All Ghassan could do was listen.

My prince . . . my emperor, are you there?

Ghassan heard the answer, another cruelty of awareness dealt by his captor.

Yes, Ghassan. I am here.

Ghassan's impotence smothered his pain in despair; he was trapped in the prison of his own mind and unable to protect his prince.

The former imperial prince, Ounyal'am, had been elevated to emperor pending his coronation. Still, and as always, he trusted very few people. He trusted Ghassan almost absolutely, and Ghassan had taught him long ago how to use the medallion so they could communicate in the secrecy of thought from a distance.

Ounyal'am was likely in his private chambers, believing he conversed with his mentor. Instead, he touched thoughts with the thousand-year-old specter of the first sorcerer to walk the world.

Ghassan struggled for one instant of control over his flesh—and he failed again against the will of Khalidah. He would have wept in the dark if he could have as his prince—his emperor-to-be—asked . . .

Is all well, domin?

*   *   *

Gripping the medallion, Khalidah exerted more of his will to suppress Ghassan il'Sänke. That it took a little effort surprised him, but only for a passing thought. Of any body he had ever inhabited, he had never been forced to work at all to keep its original inhabitant trapped.

Still, taking il'Sänke had been a great blessing, for the renegade domin possessed the trust—the friendship—of the emperor-to-be. And he answered back while still allowing the domin to hear.

Yes, my emperor . . . simply busy. And what of you?

Ounyal'am's answer took a moment.

Funeral arrangements for my father have been finalized. The palace is overrun with nobles and royals. I did not think court plots would ever become so thick . . . and open.

Khalidah had seen the result of the impending funeral in the city as well. Many areas had become overcrowded. Temporary housing had grown scarce.

And your coronation plans . . . and wedding? he ventured.

Another moment's hesitation passed. *Both progress, but there has been some upheaval since I announced my chosen bride.*

Well, the young fool should have expected that. A'ish'ah, daughter of the general and emir Mansoor, was too cripplingly shy to fit the role of first empress. Worse, the most powerful families of the empire had all vied to place their own daughters at the side of Ounyal'am. His announcement must have come as quite a slap to their faces.

Of course there would be a backlash.

Khalidah had no interest in whomever Ounyal'am married and had asked only because il'Sänke would have. The new emperor's trust must be maintained as a potential resource. Now it was time to press on to matters of more interest.

After recent events, Khalidah began, *have restrictions on movement out of the city been eased?*

Yes, as other matters have taken precedence.

Have any reports of concern come from other parts of the empire, perhaps from the eastern desert?

No . . . why? Is there something to be concerned about?

With a quick twinge, Khalidah grew cautious. Had he gone too far—been too specific—in his questions?

Like the captain of your private guard, I have always feared an assassination attempt. More so now before your pending coronation. Your death is the only way left for others to wrest authority over the empire. I protect you from without as your bodyguards protect you within the palace walls.

Yes . . . yes, of course. But no, I have not received reports of interest since my father's death.

Very good. And then Khalidah considered another ploy, to keep Ounyal'am not only ever dependent but also useful. *But too little news can be a warning. An empire that is suddenly quiet is one to watch closely for the slightest oddity. I will be in contact again soon . . . my emperor.*

Good night, Ghassan.

The medallion cooled in Khalidah's grip as he rose, dropped it inside his shirt, and strode toward the alley's open end. It was time to return to Ghassan il'Sänke's hidden "sanctuary" shielded from all senses by the ensorcellments of the domin's eradicated sect. There hid a collection of people equally useful.

Magiere, the dhampir, rested in secret with her half-elven mate, Leesil. There was also a young foreign sage, Wynn Hygeorht, and her own companion, Chane Andraso, a vampire. Then there were two elven males, one young and naive, and the other elderly, able, and disturbingly with a mind that seemed impenetrable so far. There was a mixed-blood girl who was more baggage than anything. But the worst were the two nonhuman, nonelven *creatures* among the others.

The pair of majay-hì—Fay-descended wolves—had yet to sense Khalidah, likely because of the living flesh he inhabited. He had seen their kind begin to appear near the end of the war a thousand years ago.

Still, Khalidah almost could not believe his twisted fortune and thought it was not all luck. In the end, it was a great opportunity.

This group had attempted to kill him, and that unto itself was amusing. They believed they had succeeded, never suspecting that he had fled his previous host before death for the flesh of Ghassan il'Sänke. Even if they ever doubted his destruction, he was in the last possible host they would think vulnerable to "the specter."

Khalidah felt il'Sänke thrash against his greater will, which was all the more satisfying. Of course, he should not chuckle to himself while walking the streets. It would look odd.

The domin's assembled group had to be controlled—guided—in their task of gathering his god's greatest treasures: the anchors of creation.

One each for the five metaphysical elements, they were now merely called "orbs." These powerful devices had been created more than a thousand years ago by a god with too many names.

Fáhmon, the Foe or Enemy . . . *Kêravägh*, the Nightfallen . . . *Keiron*, the Black One . . . *in'Sa'umar* . . . the words in the dark . . . *il'Samar*, the Night Voice . . .

No, perhaps not names but titles. Even more had come and gone to be forgotten by most, but he remembered them all. And the last held the false affection of a slave's eternal fear of his master.

Hkàbêv . . . Loved One . . . Beloved.

That title made him burn inside. Even true love betrayed countless times could become hatred equally passionate.

Centuries ago, Beloved had lost a great war upon the world and retreated into a hidden and dark dormancy. Now this god had awakened, calling its servants—slaves—to regather its prime tools, the "orbs."

Khalidah clenched his hands—il'Sänke's hands—as he quickened his pace. He would bring the orbs to Beloved . . . but not as his god wished.

Now deep into the capital's east side, he turned down a dark, lampless side street past three shabby buildings and stopped before the fourth's crooked door. Its once-turquoise paint was pale and peeling. So many cracks had spread over so many years of heat and dry wind that they were visible in the dark.

In this decrepit tenement's top floor was a set of hidden rooms where il'Sänke had given sanctuary to Magiere and the others. The place had been ensorcelled by the domin's sect of sorcerers among the metaologers of the Guild of Sagecraft's Suman branch. The same sect had kept Khalidah imprisoned for more than a century before he escaped and killed all but Ghassan il'Sänke. They had a few other such places throughout the capital and even in other cities of the empire. If he chose to walk up to the top floor, at the end of its passage he would face the phantasm of a window—that was actually a secret door.

Though the window appeared and felt quite real, the scant number of people who knew the truth might explain it as an illusion. Khalidah knew this was not the case, as there was no "illusion" to be dismissed. A phantasm lived—became real—to the senses of whomever it affected. And all were affected when the passage's end came into their awareness, their sight, or even just their touch, should that place be too dark at night to see clearly. Only several small pebbles ensorcelled by the sect allowed a bearer to experience, touch, and open the door that was hidden there.

Khalidah remained in the street, staring at the crooked, bleached, and peeling front door. With a blink, he slipped into a cutway between the buildings and entered the alley behind the tenement. In another blink, the dark behind his eyelids filled with lines of spreading light.

A double square, formed in sigils, symbols, and signs, burned brightly; then came a triangle within the square and another triangle inverted within the first. As his eyes—il'Sänke's eyes—winked open, his incantation in thought finished faster than a catch of breath.

Khalidah's hearing magnified instantly.

A few blocks away, he heard a scratchy-voiced woman berating a monger for trying to cheat her over a jar of olives. Though distant, many footfalls, mewling mules, goats, and haggling and bargaining accosted his heightened hearing. He shut all of this out, and then heard a thundering buzz nearby.

A fly swarmed too near him.

With a flash of a fingertip, he killed it without looking, but what he could not hear irritated him even more. Yes, he heard voices and movements inside the lowly tenement, but he heard nothing from the hidden rooms at the end of the top floor. The ensorcellment upon the sanctuary was stronger than expected.

"Ah me, my dear domin," he whispered aloud, though it was not necessary for il'Sänke to hear him. "Such great effort and yet for nothing."

Khalidah exerted his will, broke through, and, tilting up one ear, he heard . . .

"Chap, where's the last of our cheese?" Wynn asked, digging into a small canvas sack. "Did you eat it? All of it?"

Chap glanced over without lifting his head from his forepaws and watched Wynn invert the sack and shake it to see if anything fell out. She was dressed in a loose shirt and pants, having left her midnight blue sage's robe crumpled on her bedroll. Wispy light brown hair, still uncombed, hung around her pretty oval face.

"Well, did you?" Wynn pressed, dropping the sack.

He knew what she saw when she looked at him: an overly tall wolf with silver-gray fur and crystalline blue eyes, the ears and muzzle just a little long for its kind. That was because he was not a wolf.

Chap did not bother answering.

Eight people and two majay-hì, he being one of them, had been living on top of one another in two rooms for days and nights on end, and this state of affairs was taking its toll. They were safe for the moment but trapped in hiding. Their current quarters had passed from feeling overcrowded to outright stifling.

There was little enough comfort these days so, yes, he had eaten the cheese.

If there had been any more, he would have eaten that too!

Chap surveyed his surroundings for the . . . uncountable time.

Shelves lined three walls of the main room, all filled with scrolls, books, plank-bound sheaves, and other academic paraphernalia. This was no surprise in a place once a hideaway for a sect of renegade metaologer sages who had resurrected the forbidden practice of sorcery.

Cold lamps provided light, and one rested on a round table surrounded by three chairs with high backs of finely finished near-black wood intricately carved in wild see-through patterns. The lamps' ornate brass bases were filled with alchemical fluids producing mild heat to keep the crystals lit.

The right side of the main room's back half, just beyond a folding partition, was covered in large, vibrantly patterned floor cushions. Farther right was a doorless archway into another room with two beds. Fringed carpets defined various areas throughout the place.

For two or three people, all of this would have been a welcome luxury. For eight people and two majay-hì, it was cramped, cluttered, and becoming unbearable. There were also packs and sacks filled with personal belongings everywhere . . . aside from two large chests in the bedchamber.

"Chap, answer me!" Wynn insisted.

"Oh, leave him alone," Magiere growled. "We can buy more cheese."

Chap's gaze shifted to her standing in the bedchamber's opening. Just behind her, Leesil was fussing with something unseen.

Magiere was tall and slender with smooth skin pale to the point of seeming white. Her long black hair hung loose, but the lamps here did not provide enough light to spark the bloodred tint in her tresses. She wore the tan pantaloons favored by the Suman people and a blue sleeveless tunic. These were a stark contrast to her usual studded-leather armor and dark canvas pants.

"Don't snap at Wynn," Leesil admonished her, as if more tension were needed. "If Chap's been rooting around like a hog again, *I'd* call him out."

Magiere half turned on her husband but apparently bit back whatever retort came to mind.

It was an excuse for another bit of petty bickering after being stuffed away in hiding for too long.

Chap rumbled with a twitch of jowls but did not lift his head.

Leesil was only slightly taller than his wife. His coloring was the sharper contrast. White-blond hair, amber irises, tan skin, and slightly elongated ears betrayed his mother's people, the an'Cróan—"[Those] of the Blood"— or the elves of the eastern continent. His father had been human. Leesil too wore tan pantaloons, but his tunic was a shade of burnt-orange.

And as to the others present . . .

Wayfarer, a sixteen-year-old girl three-quarters an'Cróan, sat in one high-backed chair at the table, mending a torn blanket. Unlike Leesil's, her hair was a rich brown, and in any direct light, her eyes were a shade of green. Chap was fond of her and, shy and quiet as she was, she clung to him the most, though she had come to look upon Magiere and Leesil almost as new parents, or at least as accepted authority figures.

Osha, a young full-blooded an'Cróan with the height as well as the white-blond hair of his people, sat across from the girl, fletching an arrow. He had proven himself an exceptional archer, though how he had come by that skill was not a subject to raise with him. Vigilant in guarding all with him, he caused little trouble, with one exception: he was obsessed with Wynn.

Any feelings Wynn had for him, she did not show. That situation bore watching, considering Wayfarer's mixed feelings for Osha. And if that was not bad enough . . .

Chane Andraso—a Noble Dead, a vampire—stood near Wynn, as dour and sullen as always. Though he was barely tolerated by anyone here besides her, they had all been given little choice in tolerating his presence. He resembled a young nobleman, with red-brown hair and with skin nearly as pale as Magiere's. His white shirt, dark pants, and high boots were well made, if well-worn. And he, like Osha, was obsessed with Wynn.

Chap's gaze shifted slightly right, and he failed to suppress a snarl. Sitting cross-legged on the floor below the one window at the back left of the room was Brot'an—Brot'ân'duivé, "the Dog in the Dark." That aging elven master assassin was one of Chap's greater concerns.

Coarse white-blond hair with strands of darkening gray hung over his peaked ears and down his back beneath his hood. Lines crinkled the corners of his mouth and his large amber-irised eyes, which rarely looked at anything specific but always saw everything. The feature of the man that stood out the most, if someone drew near enough to look into his hood, were four pale scars—as if from claws—upon his deeply tanned face. Those ran at an angle from the midpoint of his forehead to break his left feathery eyebrow and then skip over his right eye to finish across his cheekbone.

Brot'an claimed to be protecting Magiere, but Chap knew better. Brot'an always had an agenda and would place it over the lives of anyone if a choice had to be made. He had proven this more than once.

Needless to say, Chap was in a very foul mood.

He might hate Chane for *what* he was, but he hated Brot'an for *who* he was.

As Chap's eyes continued drifting—to the cramped room's one other occupant—his feelings grew more complicated. The other tall but charcoal black majay-hì lay on the floor beside Wynn, where the troublesome sage still knelt with the upturned cheese sack.

Chap's own daughter, Shade, refused to acknowledge his existence for the most part. She was not without good reason, but tonight he chose not to think about that. Instead, he swallowed down his pain and turned his attention back to Wynn, speaking directly into her mind as he could do only with her.

Now that our host has stepped out for a while, perhaps it is time to talk . . . of something other than cheese.

Wynn slapped the sack onto the floor and turned toward him with an angry frown. But the frown faded, and she did not argue, only letting out a tired sigh.

Their "host," Ghassan il'Sänke, had gone out on an errand, and time without his company was rare.

She nodded. "Yes . . . we should."

"Should what?" Magiere asked, and then looked to Chap, knowing something had passed between the two.

Chap often spoke to Magiere, Leesil, and Wayfarer by calling up words out of their own memories—something Wynn quaintly called "memory-words." How he communicated with Wynn was not based on pulling up broken, spoken phrases. She was the only one to whom he could *speak* directly in thought—after she had fouled up a thaumaturgical ritual while journeying with him in the past.

"What's he babbling into your head now?" Leesil asked, pushing out of the bedchamber and past Magiere.

"We should settle some important things while Ghassan is away," Wynn said to the two of them.

All annoyance faded from Magiere's pale face. "I don't know what. Unless you've come up with an idea for a hiding place we haven't already discounted."

Wynn shook her head, and Chap let out a long exhale.

They were not hidden away in this place by choice.

Several years ago, the four of them had found themselves embroiled in a desperate search for five "orbs" or "anchors." Some believed the Ancient Enemy had wielded these devices a thousand years ago in its war on the world. Servants of the Enemy had hidden them centuries ago when the war had ended. The Enemy's living and undead minions had now begun surfacing to seek the devices for their master or perhaps just for themselves.

The orbs could never be allowed to fall into such hands and had to be rehidden.

The first two that Magiere had located were those of Water and Fire. Chap alone had hidden those far up in the icy northern wastes of this continent. Wynn, Shade, and Chane had located the orb of Earth, and Chane had taken it to the dwarves' "stonewalkers," so that it might be safely hidden away in the underworld of their people's honored dead. More recently, Spirit and Air had been recovered, and both of those orbs were now in chests inside this bedchamber.

This was the problem Chap and the others faced.

Wynn pushed tiredly up to her feet. "I agree with Wayfarer's suggestion that we take the orb of Spirit to the lands of the Lhoin'na. That is at least . . . something."

Yes, it was. The Lhoin'na—"(Those) of the Glade"—were the elves of this continent. No undead could walk into their lands because of the influence of Chârmun, the great golden tree in their vast forest, who was thought by some to be the first life of the world. As the anchor of Spirit seemed most useful to the undead—as a possible tool—Wayfarer's suggestion had been considered seriously.

Magiere did not want either orb out of her sight. She was waiting for a plan for the orb of Air before any action was taken. Chap had another dilemma, one he could not speak of to anyone, not even to Wynn.

When he had been up north, burying the orbs of Water and Fire, he had sensed something inside them: the presence of the Fay—or rather that a singular Fay presence might be trapped inside each orb.

The Fay were the source of all Existence. He had been part of them, it, the one and the many, before choosing to be born into the body of a majay-hì pup and later walk his current path.

Now that he was in the presence of the two final orbs, he longed to privately test one of them. Would he be able to commune with the Fay as a whole, or even with the single Fay imprisoned inside any one orb? The physical proximity of both orbs taunted him, but trapped here with the others, he never had a private enough moment. He might never find that moment until Magiere decided it was time to move the orbs from this sanctuary.

Wynn faced Magiere. "If I can't come up with something soon, do you have any ideas?"

"Maybe . . . something."

At this from Magiere, for the first time all day and night, Chap's mind went blank. He stared at her, waiting.

Magiere was frustrated by their failure to think of a suitable hiding place for the orb of Air, though in truth, she wasn't overly concerned. The orb was in their possession, and that mattered the most. All five had been found, three safely rehidden, and there was a plan for the orb of Spirit. She and those she loved were in one piece and still breathing.

All in all, everything could've been worse.

Yes, Leesil had been somewhat snippy, but even he'd seemed more at ease in the past half-moon. The end was in sight, and once they'd hidden the last two orbs, they could go home. That was all he'd ever wanted.

Glancing around the room, Magiere realized everyone was watching her. "I could take the orb of Air out to sea and drop it at a depth where it could never be recovered."

Leesil's amber eyes widened slightly with hope. "Yes, that would do."

She knew he was overly anxious to have this all finished. Most likely he would have jumped at any suggestion. The others didn't appear quite so convinced. And at least with Chap and Wynn, there had to be some agreement before they—she—did anything.

"Why you?" Chane asked in his harsh, rasping voice.

Magiere choked back a retort. He had no place in this and was here only because Wynn insisted on keeping his company.

Leesil and I . . . would go . . . with you—

Those broken phrases out of her memories came from Chap. Of course he and Leesil would go with her. That was a given. Of late, her dhampir half had grown harder to control when she was pushed to her limits. More often, it had taken over and she'd lost herself. Only Leesil and Chap could bring her back under control.

Before she could respond to Chap, Brot'an rose straight up and stepped closer.

"What of the orb of Spirit?" he asked flatly. "While you are at sea, will some of us take it to the Lhoin'na?"

That was the crux of the problem; Magiere had no intention of trusting anyone else with an orb. She tilted her head up slightly to look him in the eyes.

Aside from being a former member of the Anmaglâhk, a caste of assassins among the an'Cróan elves, he was also a greimasg'äh—"shadow-gripper"—and a master of their ways. She wasn't intimidated by him or by how he tended to use his height to intimidate others.

"No," she answered. "Leesil, Chap, and I will take both orbs, drop the one of Air at sea, and then take Spirit into the Lhoin'na lands."

"And what about the rest of us?" Wynn asked.

Magiere would trust her life to Wynn, but not the orbs, not with Chane around.

Wayfarer dropped her head, her face hidden by dangling hair.

Magiere suspected the girl assumed she would take part in delivering the orb of Spirit to the Lhoin'na—as it had been her idea. That wasn't going to happen.

Osha's expression flattened. He'd followed Wynn here and often seemed uncertain of his place in this larger group. He rarely caused trouble but too often agreed with whatever Wynn wanted.

"Can the three of you protect two orbs?" he asked, suddenly stern of expression.

This took Magiere by surprise. Of late, Osha's grasp of languages other than his own had improved a bit, but asking a forceful question wasn't like him. She didn't like being questioned, not now. Still, she held her temper. This was too important, and any flash of anger would just start another heated argument.

"Yes," she answered carefully, remaining calm. "The three of us can travel faster by ourselves, and we *can* protect the orbs."

Wynn's brow wrinkled, and then she sighed in resignation. "I suppose that is best. A small group is less likely to attract attention, and you three are . . . able in that regard."

And the most trustworthy, Magiere thought with a quick glance at Brot'an, though she didn't say it.

Brot'an's expression was unreadable. Likely, he wasn't going to let this drop so easily but would bide his time.

"So we're really going to do this?" Leesil asked. "Get these last two hidden?"

"And then what?" Wayfarer asked softly, her head still down.

"We go home," Magiere answered, and stepping closer, she put a hand on the girl's shoulder. "And that means you too . . . with us."

The girl was an orphan, thrust by circumstance into the care of Brot'an. Magiere had no intention of leaving her with him.

Wayfarer looked up, eyes wide, but then glanced at Osha.

"So," Wynn said, cutting off any more from Magiere, "how do we begin? I suppose we find a ship? Did you plan to simply slip up on deck one night and drop the orb over the side when no one is watching? We'll need to book passage for three on a vessel making a long voyage in a straight run with few if any stops. That is the only kind likely to head out into deeper water for speed."

"No," Magiere answered, "I was thinking of our manning something smaller by ourselves. We wouldn't need to sail far before—"

The sanctuary door opened, cutting her off.

Domin Ghassan il'Sänke stepped in. He was tall for a Suman, with dusky skin and peppered hair. Though he'd been more than useful in recent days, Magiere didn't trust him any more than Brot'an—maybe less.

He took in the sight of the gathering, and the sudden silence as well. Clearly, he could tell he'd interrupted some discussion.

"Have I missed something?" he asked.

Magiere let out a long breath. There was no sense putting this off. "We're going to hide the orb of Air. So we'll be relocating both orbs soon."

"You might hold off," he said sharply.

Magiere was taken aback.

Ghassan rarely showed anger, though he had a barbed tongue. His tone wasn't lost on Leesil either.

"What do you mean?" Leesil demanded.

Ghassan ignored him and remained focused on Magiere. "I mean that something has happened that might prohibit moving the orbs . . . or make the task too dangerous."

"What is that?" Wynn asked.

Magiere could almost feel Leesil tensing as he stepped near, shoulder-to-shoulder with her.

Ghassan remained fixed on her as he went on. "I have spoken with the new emperor. He related reports of strange movements in the east. Bands of unknowns have been spotted in the desert but only at night. When approached, they fled and vanished, even in the open. There was also mention of bodies found . . . torn apart, partially eaten to the bones, or merely pale and desiccated in the heat and—"

In midsentence the domin scowled, flinched, scowled again, and appeared to turn menacing. Then some sudden shock spread over his dark face, as if a thought came to his mind that startled him. All of this quickly vanished, and he was calm and attentive again, as if waiting for a response.

Magiere was too puzzled and wary to say anything.

You will stop! Ghassan ordered with every particle of will he could gather.

He tried to seize control of his body, or at least his own mouth and tongue, and failed. The ancient specter had been distracted, focusing hard on his lies to Magiere and the others.

Ounyal'am had related no such reports, and the specter's blatant lies were intended to keep Magiere from relocating two orbs . . . and to keep those devices within its reach. But Khalidah had not been ready for such a sudden assault from within.

For the first time, Ghassan had felt his captor's hold falter amid distraction. Ghassan had seized that moment, which passed and was now gone. Pressing down wild hope and desperation, he quickly refocused.

A second push to seize control drained him utterly without effect.

Enough, you little gnat, Khalidah hissed within their shared thoughts.

Ghassan flinched as everything went black, and he no longer saw through his own eyes. Raking pain like claws tore down his back in the darkness, then down his chest, and then his face, and he screamed.

Be silent, be still . . . or you will be gone entirely.

At those words in the darkness, a shaft of light came a stone's throw away, as if shining down from somewhere above. In it stood a dimly lit and spindly figure in a dark robe coated in scintillating symbols, which undulated with the cloth as the figure stepped nearer. The face seemed marked and withered.

I tolerate you only for the memories you have that are useful to me.

And closer still, those marks on its old face of wrinkles, narrow chin, and pinched mouth were patterns and symbols inked upon pallid skin. But its large, sunken eyes—the irises—were as black as the ink . . . black as the darkness all around Ghassan.

Annoy me again, and you will be the last of our kind, our art, as I was— am—the first!

The light vanished. Once again, Ghassan was pressed down into the darkness.

Lost in the dark of his own mind—his prison—for a moment he curled up and wept. But for one instant only, he had almost seized control in Khalidah's distraction amid fear and anger.

And then Ghassan heard another voice, as if the specter let that one in to taunt him.

"What are you saying?" Wynn asked.

*   *   *

Leesil couldn't believe what he was hearing, and he feared what was being implied. Small bands in the desert seen only at night? Bodies eaten to the bone? Pallid corpses as if drained of blood? He stared at the domin, but Ghassan's dark brown eyes fixed on Wynn.

"I am saying the Ancient Enemy may be awakening," the domin answered. "It is calling to and sending out those who still serve it."

Leesil went cold and then hot in a flash. Everything was almost over and done . . . They would soon be going home.

Magiere took a quick step toward the domin.

"That's all you have?" she snarled at him. "All the more reason to get the orbs out of reach!"

Chap was suddenly at Leesil's side but raised no memory-words. Of all the times he'd blathered into Leesil's head, this wasn't a time to say nothing. Wynn appeared too stunned to speak as she backed up a step on Chap's other side. Then Shade closed to the outside of Wynn, and all of them just stood there.

"Domin . . . ," Wynn started, using his old title. "The new emperor told you of this? Is he sending soldiers? What is he doing to help the nomads or tribes out there? Is anyone going out there to confirm this?"

"None at present," Ghassan answered. "The reports are too scattered, and he would not understand what they mean as we do. With the coronation pending, there are many nobles, dignitaries, and the royals of the seven nations gathering in the imperial capital. Their security takes precedence."

"And what exactly do you think it means?" Leesil asked, feeling his self-control slipping away.

"I told you," Ghassan answered calmly. "Except for the undead, what creatures drain their prey of blood or eat them while alive?"

Leesil had never heard of any flesh-eating undead, but that was a minor thing at the moment.

"And when have you ever heard of any traveling in packs?" Ghassan continued. "Undead are solitary creatures for a reason—to avoid exposing themselves for too many deaths at a time in a given place. And why would one or especially more be in a desolate area with so little to prey upon? They are gathering and not by their own choice. The Enemy is awakening . . . and it may have even become aware of orbs close within this land."

Osha, Wayfarer, and Chane had not moved, but Brot'an now crossed the room slowly.

"If that is indeed the case," he said, "we cannot drop the orb of Air into the sea. Nor can we hide the orb of Spirit with the Lhoin'na."

Magiere turned to him. "Why not?"

"Because we may have need of them," Brot'an answered. "We may need all five. What other weapons or method might destroy so powerful a being, finally? If not, how long before this happens yet again? I will not tolerate that for my people, let alone any other."

Leesil felt a knot in his stomach. What was happening here?

"I fear Brot'an may be correct," Ghassan added, lowering his head and meshing his fingers together.

"No!" Magiere nearly shouted as she lunged a step toward Ghassan.

That caught Leesil's whole attention, for this was now getting dangerous. Before he made a grab for her, she twisted on Brot'an.

"We don't know anything other than secondhand rumors!" she went on. "You're both guessing, and even if such rumors were true, it's more reason to hide the orbs where no one finds any or all of them again." She turned back to Ghassan. "That's when it's finished . . . when I'm finished!"

Though panicked that Magiere might lose control, Leesil couldn't help hoping she was right. But the knot grew in the pit of his stomach.

"For safety's sake," Brot'an added, "we must gather all five orbs to be ready for any contingency. For anywhere that any of us have gone in hiding them means someone may have been followed . . . to a place where one or more orbs are now unguarded."

Leesil knew the second part of this statement wasn't true. Two of the orbs had been hidden in a way that they would never be found, and the third was guarded by the stonewalkers.

A low, rumbling growl built up, and Leesil glanced down at Chap, but the dog still hadn't called up memory-words in his head. Leesil began to fear that Chap might even be considering Brot'an's mad notion.

A long moment passed.

Leesil stood there, watching Ghassan in silence and waiting for Magiere, Chap, or anyone to say something.

"Magiere?" Wynn began, and half turned to glance up at Chane, who had his hand on her shoulder. Did she expect answers from the vampire?

Magiere shook her head. "I can't listen to this anymore, and I can't—" Breaking off, she strode for the door out of the sanctuary.

Leesil followed her, as he always would.

CHAPTER TWO

Wynn watched Magiere and Leesil walk out.

Then she flinched when the door slammed shut, and as the sound faded, Ghassan's whole sanctuary fell into silence. The domin's revelations had left her reeling. She knew things couldn't be left like this, but no plans or decisions were possible without Magiere and Leesil—especially Magiere. She glanced down at Chap.

"Come on," she half whispered to him. "We'd better go after them."

"Not alone," Chane rasped, stepping closer.

Wynn struggled for the best response. Though she would welcome his company, Magiere, Leesil . . . and Chap most certainly would not.

"No, it's all right," she said, and then looked down to Shade. "Sorry, but you stay too."

Chane scowled. Shade rumbled and twitched one jowl in clear disagreement. It was hard to tell what the dog disliked more, staying behind or being forced to.

Wynn started for the door and paused before Ghassan.

"You handled that badly," she said, and then turned her head toward Brot'an. "Both of you. Chap and I will go after Leesil and Magiere . . . alone! The rest of you stay here until we get this sorted out."

With Chap waiting at the door, she hurried onward before anyone could think to argue. Chap had been uncharacteristically silent, which worried her, but there was no way to keep him out of this.

Once outside the sanctuary, she pulled the door closed and watched it vanish. Suddenly, she faced only a dead-end wall with an old window. The battered shutters were open over the alley below, as if the rooms she'd just left didn't exist and the dingy passage ended at the tenement's back wall.

The phantasm placed upon the sanctuary by Ghassan and his eradicated sect of sorcerers had kept everyone within safely hidden. He'd given her an ensorcelled pebble that would allow her mind and senses to evade this defense. She'd rarely had to use the pebble, as someone inside could hear her knock and open the door from within. But this end wall and its window, so real to all senses, still made her shiver.

"You lead," she told Chap. "See if you can pick up a scent."

She expected him to answer into her head—to at least say *something*—but he didn't.

Instead, he turned away silently, and Wynn followed him all the way down the passage and then down the far stairs. At the bottom, he veered away from the front door and headed toward the back door that led to the rear alley. Maybe he'd smelled something to lead him that way, though Wynn couldn't see how amid the stench of the old tenement or the decrepit district around it. Chap paused at the door, waiting until she opened it.

Wynn peeked out both ways, and there were Magiere and Leesil just to the left. They were both crouched down, leaning back against the alley wall and talking too quietly to hear.

Chap pushed out around Wynn's legs, and thankfully neither Leesil nor Magiere frowned at the interruption. Leesil was closer, and he eyed the door after Wynn followed Chap, perhaps wondering whether anyone else was coming.

"Just us," Wynn said quickly.

Leesil locked eyes with Chap, so the dog must have said something to him in memory-words. Even in the darkness, Wynn saw strain—pain—spread across Leesil's face. Magiere's expression was blank, almost cold, and she wouldn't look at anyone.

"We're not going back in there," she whispered, almost echoing Chane's rasp.

Chap circled around and dropped on his haunches beside Magiere. Although Chap was Leesil's oldest friend, since before Leesil even knew he was more than a dog, lately Chap had been much in Magiere's company—and confidence. At least since their time in the prison below the imperial palace.

Wynn crouched beside Leesil and leaned out to keep sight of Magiere. "Staying out here won't change anything."

Of course this was obvious, but she hated being the voice of reason in forcing Magiere and Leesil into something they didn't want to do. Wynn had been stuck in this position too many times over the last few years. At the same time, she understood why they—especially Leesil—had to get away from Ghassan and Brot'an. She found some relief in that herself, but their situation was growing more awkward and tense.

"You don't agree with Brot'an, do you?" Magiere asked. "You don't want to regather the orbs?"

Wynn clenched her jaw.

"I don't *want* any of this," she answered as calmly as she could. "But you heard Ghassan. The Forgotten War started somewhere near what is now the Suman Empire. If anything he heard is even partly true . . . I don't think we can ignore it. Do you?"

No one spoke.

Leesil hadn't said anything since Wynn stepped out into the alley, and that made her feel even worse. At times, going through him to get to Magiere was the easier way, but not this time and not when it was about this. He'd always hated what they were doing concerning the orbs, finding, attaining, and hiding them, even more so after Brot'an reappeared in their midst. This time, things would have to work the other way, with convincing Magiere first. So why wasn't Chap doing something?

"You think it's that easy?" Magiere nearly hissed.

Wynn stiffened upright at the threat in her voice, but Magiere was fixed on Chap. Wynn expected Chap to snarl or snap in response, but he didn't. He sat, focusing on Magiere's face until she finally dropped her head onto her pulled-up knees. Leesil didn't move.

At least Wynn now knew Chap was trying. When he took something seriously, everyone else had better pay attention, and hopefully Magiere would.

"What do you think we can do about it?" Magiere whispered without lifting her head.

Wynn now wished she were the one who could talk into Chap's head. He looked right at her, and huffed once for "yes." It was less than a blink before she guessed it was her turn, so she readied for an onslaught before answering.

"We have to do as Brot'an suggested, at least as a contingency. The orbs might be the only weapons powerful enough to use against the Enemy, if it comes to that. What would become of the world—again—if that thing, whatever it is, really is awakening? If so, we don't have anything else but the orbs."

"No!" Leesil shouted.

As Leesil turned on Wynn, Magiere gripped his upper arm and jerked him back. Chap snarled, rose on all fours, and bared his teeth at Leesil. Wynn sat there on the alley floor, shaking.

Magiere had always been the volatile one.

Yet now it was Leesil tipping on the edge of reason, panting in anger. And Wynn couldn't blame him, for there was a part of her beneath reason that wanted to just go away and hide where no one could find her.

Leesil wrenched his arm out of Magiere's grip and settled back against the alley wall.

"Stay out of my head!" he snapped, though he didn't look at anyone.

He didn't have to. Chap sighed and turned from Leesil to Magiere.

"We gather nothing," Magiere said, "until we know what's happening out there . . . in the east, in the desert."

A voice in every language Wynn understood filled her head.

She is right in one part. More answers are needed.

At these words, Wynn kept quiet, fearing any hint of a silent exchange might set Leesil off again.

But I will gather the other orbs, Chap went on, *and you will go with Leesil and Magiere. As for the others . . .*

Chap's head tilted upward, and Wynn followed his gaze up the back wall of the tenement. All she saw was a dark hint of that one disturbing window frame. He continued to speak to her, and occasionally, she couldn't help nodding.

Magiere managed to remain sitting there in the alley, though inside she'd felt she might rip apart. Chap and Wynn were clearly plotting and planning, though there was little to hear other than Wynn's occasional acknowledgments.

Leesil ignored everyone.

Magiere couldn't stand the thought of disappointing him again.

They'd been on the verge of being done and going home. How much farther could she push him before she lost him entirely? When she glanced over at him, there was Wynn still sitting beside him, but entirely fixed on Chap.

What were those two up to?

Leesil finally turned his head, but his eyes narrowed at Wynn.

"Look at you," he said. "Look at what you've done, though it's bad enough with him," and he cocked his head toward Chap. "I'm getting tired of the mistakes, blind leaps, and—"

"You think you know everything I've been through?" Wynn cut in. "Just because I told you the short version?"

"I know you took up with that *thing* up there," Leesil shot back. "Chane's no better than whatever is out in that desert."

"You don't know that either!" she countered." I don't make assumptions on what little you've told me, so don't you ever talk to me like some—"

"Enough, both of you," Magiere ordered.

Everyone fell silent again.

Whatever cracks Magiere felt in her resolve, she saw the same widening among all of them.

The rest . . . should be . . . said . . . to everyone.

Magiere looked into Chap's eyes, though in the dark she barely saw their crystalline, sky blue color.

I do not . . . wish . . . to explain . . . more than once. Do . . . you . . . still . . . trust me . . . in this?

And what if she said no? She didn't know whether losing Leesil or letting the world burn in another war would be worse right now. She couldn't make the choice herself.

"Yes," Magiere answered weakly.

Back in the sanctuary with everyone gathered, Chap braced himself as Wynn laid out the plan as he had instructed. As he expected, Leesil was the first to slip into an outrage.

"Did messing with the orbs make you stupid?" Leesil panted, turning from Wynn to Chap. "You're taking *him*"—he jutted his chin at Chane—"to get the orbs you hid up north in the wastes?"

Chane appeared shocked as well. Magiere fixed Chap with a glare, her breath visibly quickening. Wayfarer and Osha were equally stunned, though Osha's rapid blinks betrayed doubt that he had heard correctly. Brot'an stood by the rear window and expressed no reaction at all.

Ghassan put one hand thoughtfully to his mouth. "Why Chane and the elder majay-hì?"

To Wynn's credit, in speaking for Chap, her voice barely wavered.

"Because Chap is the one who hid the orbs of Water and Fire. He won't divulge their location to anyone. No one can force that information from him. Chane gave the orb of Earth to the stonewalkers for safekeeping through one of their own, Ore-Locks." She turned to Chane. "Neither Ore-Locks nor his sect will relinquish it to anyone but you . . . and maybe not even you without some convincing."

Chane's shock passed, replaced by suspicion. "And where will you be while . . . if I take this lengthy journey?"

Chap tensed, ready to act.

"With Leesil and Magiere, and Ghassan and Brot'an," Wynn answered, "scouting in the east."

Osha went rigid, but it was Chane who stepped in on her. "Out in the desert, with possible packs of undead? I will not leave you to that!"

Chap snarled, clacked his jaws, and drew everyone's attention. The idea of traveling alone with that undead repulsed him, but he was equally disgusted by the vampire's belief that no one else could protect Wynn. None of them could afford to be so overprotective anymore.

"This has to be done!" Wynn insisted, not backing away from Chane. "You and Chap are the only ones who can gather the three hidden orbs. Once you reach the wastes up north and are back on land, you'll travel by night. The two of you can move faster on your own."

She paused and addressed everyone in the main room.

"The rest of us will take the orbs of Spirit and Air across the desert. We'll head east along the base of the Sky-Cutter Range. Once we get far enough, we'll start scouting for any sign to verify that these reports are true." She faced Chane once more. "Please, do this for us, for the world. Ore-Locks won't give the orb to anyone but you . . . not even me."

Chane stared at her but said nothing more.

Chap grew uncomfortable at the clear connection between those two. His stomach rolled every time Wynn said "please" to that monster. Still, there were larger issues at stake, and he studied the others.

Leesil had withdrawn, settled in a chair at the table, and turned his back on everyone. Magiere was visibly tense—no, taut and stiff—as if holding herself in. Wayfarer looked uncertainly from Osha to Magiere, then to Leesil, and finally back to Osha again. Shade pressed in against Wynn as if fearing someone would suggest they be separated.

Brot'an had still not reacted at all, and as to Ghassan . . .

The fallen domin watched Wynn expectantly. With a brief glance at the others, he finished on Magiere, and his gaze lingered too long for Chap's comfort. The one person Ghassan did not look at was Chap himself.

"There will be a lot to prepare," Magiere half voiced, turning to Chap. "You're going to need chests for the three orbs. Plus gear and supplies for traveling up north. Same but different for the rest of us heading into the desert."

She appeared no more enthused than anyone, but at least the discussion had turned to something useful.

"We'll need to gather any coins we have," Wynn added, "and separate local currency from the rest to use for important things, like passage for Chap and Chane. The logical order would be for the two of them to retrieve Chap's orbs first and then stop at Dhredze Seatt for Ore-Locks's orb on the way back. It's going to be a very long journey . . . and the same for the rest of us."

"How will they find us upon their return?" Wayfarer asked.

Chap was surprised she'd spoken at all, and at "us," he winced. She turned to him with open worry on her young face. She was as attached to him as to Magiere or Leesil, but her question was based on an assumption that had been put off until now.

"There is a better path than traveling all the way back to here," Wynn answered, and then once again addressed Chane. "On your way back, disembark at Soráno, travel inland to the Lhoin'na lands and down to the way we took into Bäalâle Seatt . . . on the north side of the Sky-Cutter Range. Once through the seatt, you can meet up with us on the range's south side."

Chane did not nod or otherwise agree in any fashion.

Though Chap certainly did not relish passing through a lost dwarven seatt partially destroyed a thousand years ago, he saw no faster alternative to rejoin the others, and time itself was their first enemy in all of this.

"So we're actually doing this?"

Chap swung around at Leesil's harsh words.

Leesil sat at the table, all of its other chairs still empty. Then he added, "Instead of hiding the last two, we're gathering all five?"

Chap longed to call up memory-words to explain yet again that they had no choice. But there were no words that could ever take away Leesil's pained disappointment.

It was Wynn who turned to Leesil, speaking in a clear but quiet voice. "We can't stop now, or everything we've fought for . . . all our efforts will have been in vain. Our aim was always to save the world, not just to hide the orbs. We've believed all along that hiding the orbs would accomplish that, but now we see what really has to be done. I know you thought we were near the end . . . that our struggles were almost over . . . but we have to finish this." She paused. "We must."

Leesil listened but didn't respond.

Magiere stood watching Wayfarer.

Magiere—and Leesil—had come to care deeply for the girl. They would not want to take her into the desert and further danger.

Chap had known this even before they returned to the sanctuary tonight, so he had made another suggestion to Wynn based on things she had told him. In turn, he had instructed her regarding what should come concerning Wayfarer's assumption about traveling with Magiere and Leesil.

Before Wynn could say anything further . . .

Enough for now. Everyone needs time to absorb all of this. Find something to distract them for a while.

To her credit, Wynn did not acknowledge that he'd spoken to her. Instead, she headed across the room.

"It's getting late, and we haven't eaten, though we're still out of cheese," she said rather pointedly. "We have jerked goat meat and figs, some olives and flatbread, so we should put something together for supper."

Once she took charge, all discussion of journeys ceased, and again Chap watched as Magiere's worried eyes strayed to Wayfarer.

Wynn reached for the canvas sack she'd dropped in one chair and then heard someone closing from behind her.

"I'll put the blankets away and come help you."

It wasn't the voice Wynn had expected, which was Magiere's, and she spun to face Wayfarer. The girl sounded quietly agitated, and Wynn suspected Wayfarer merely sought any distraction from the heightened tension in the room.

Before Wynn could reply, the girl rushed off toward the bedchamber. She wanted to follow, but that would've looked too obvious, and she turned to the others.

"Osha, could you pass out these figs?"

Chane drifted to the far end of the front bookshelves near the door and stood staring at her. Shade joined him, and this made Wynn feel worse. She couldn't deal with either of them right now. Osha came over, took the figs without a word, and began handing them out. Everything had turned awful, and it wasn't even close to over yet.

"I'll get the jerky," Magiere said.

Wynn nodded and kept her expression still, or so she hoped, but her thoughts wouldn't let go of something else Chap had suggested—insisted—while they were in the alley. It wasn't that she disagreed; no, quite the opposite. But there was more to do, more to prepare, before it came out to the entire group.

Wayfarer was unsuited for a long desert trek, let alone what might be found at its end. Of course Magiere and Leesil knew this, but they would both be unwilling to let the girl out of their sight—more so when it came to where Chap wanted to send the girl . . . along with Osha and Shade.

Wynn couldn't catch her breath in thinking on what those last two might say or do when they heard.

It is time, while the girl is alone.

She stiffened at Chap's words in her head. Crouching by her shopping bags, she wondered how she might slip into the bedroom without the others noticing. There seemed no way to avoid it, and when she finally rose . . .

Wayfarer reappeared in the bedchamber's archway. Slender as a young willow in a smaller version of clothing Magiere and Leesil had adopted, she wore a red sleeveless tunic with her tan pantaloons.

"Wynn," the girl called hesitantly, "could you help me with the blankets?"

That was a transparent excuse. Wayfarer had handled bedding on her own more than once. However, it *was* an excuse for Wynn not to have to sneak away. She went to Wayfarer, but the girl didn't turn into the bedchamber.

Wayfarer leaned closer and then hesitated. Up close, the girl's eyes were a dark, shadowy green in the dim light.

"Bring Chap," she whispered.

Wynn hesitated. Looking back, she found Chap watching them both. The others were still passing around food, and then Chap was right next to Wynn before she said anything. He'd either caught something in her thoughts or perhaps saw Wayfarer's hesitant whisper.

Wayfarer grabbed Wynn's hand—rather bold for the shy girl—and pulled her into the bedchamber. Chap followed.

It was a simple room with two beds. Several packs and a travel chest sat near one wall. Two additional chests—both containing an orb—were positioned between the beds. Wayfarer hurried to the travel chest.

"I need to show both of you something," she whispered, kneeling down and pulling out a book, which she held before Chap. "Do you remember this? I—I took it. I know it was wrong, but I could not bring myself to put it back."

Wynn approached. "What is it?"

Before Wayfarer could answer, Chap did so into Wynn's mind.

A book she found in the library at the Guild of Sagecraft's annex in Chathburh. It is filled with information and illustrations pertaining to Lhoin'na artisans. I did not know she had taken it.

In spite of everything that had happened tonight, Wynn was a little shocked. "Oh, Wayfarer. It must be returned."

The girl blushed in embarrassment. "I felt . . . compelled . . . because of something I found in it." The girl paged rapidly through the book, passing many hand-drawn illustrations, some tinted with faded colors, until she stopped at a detailed illustration.

"This is a story," she explained, "about five finely crafted urns stolen by outsiders. A group of the Lhoin'na guardians called 'Shé'ith' went after the thieves to retrieve the urns."

Wynn frowned. "Yes, I know the Shé'ith, but what does . . ."

She lost that thought when she looked more closely at the illustration. Something there, and she wasn't yet certain what, fixated her. Three elves with long hair held up in topknots rode horses galloping at high speed. She made out the fleeing band of thieves, smaller in the image's background. The riders had to be Shé'ith. Their intimidating leader held an unsheathed sword swung back, low and wide, as if ready for a strike.

Wynn's gaze locked on that sword.

Compared to the rider's grip, its handle was long enough for a second hand. The blade was slightly broad, though not like Magiere's falchion. It was straight until the last third that swept back slightly to the point. Small details were hard to make out, but it looked like the crossguard's two struts swept back at the bottom and forward at the top.

It seemed familiar, though Wynn couldn't place it.

Wayfarer quick-stepped past Wynn and Chap to the doorway, peeked out once, and then put a finger over her lips. She rushed to the far bed and knelt, then slid out a long and narrow canvas-wrapped bundle from beneath the bed.

Wynn's jaw dropped at what Wayfarer was doing.

She knew what was in that canvas, though she'd never seen it firsthand. Osha had once described it to her, and Shade had shown her a flicker of a memory stolen from him.

The Chein'âs—"the Burning Ones"—who lived in the earth's heated depths, made all weapons and tools of white metal gifts for the Anmaglâhk. Those in turn were the guardians of Osha, Brot'an, and Wayfarer's people, the an'Cróan. Osha had once been Anmaglâhk, but he had been called to the Chein'âs a second time.

They had violently stripped him of gifted weapons and tools when he refused to give them up. They forced a sword of white metal on him among other items, and he was no longer Anmaglâhk. Osha reviled that blade so much that, to the best of Wynn's knowledge, he had never opened the canvas wrap himself. Brot'an had taken the blade to be properly fitted with a hilt before they had left their people's territory.

Wynn didn't believe Wayfarer knew the sword's whole story. Osha didn't willingly speak of that terrible experience and had told Wynn only under duress.

Wayfarer reached toward the bundle.

"No!" Wynn whispered, even more shocked at this invasion of Osha's privacy.

Without even pausing, Wayfarer ripped loose the twine to expose the sword. Chap pushed past Wynn to stare at the blade, and the plain sight of it hit Wynn with a sharp realization.

It looked exactly like the sword of the Shé'ith in the book's illustration.

"I recognized it," Wayfarer whispered. "Anmaglâhk do not carry swords, but Shé'ith do, and the Chein'âs gave this one to Osha."

So the girl *did* know the story, at least in part. This bothered Wynn for some reason, as it meant Osha had shown Wayfarer the sword itself. That was the only way the girl could have made the connection.

"Do you see what this means?" Wayfarer asked. "The sword must be a link between Osha and the Shé'ith."

Wynn didn't know what to think. And why should it bother her that Osha shared more with Wayfarer than with her?

Pushing this last concern aside, Wynn wondered if she could perhaps use what Wayfarer had just related to progress the discussion toward what Chap had earlier requested . . . no, commanded.

It appeared that Wayfarer could catch the conscious memories of the majay-hì with a touch. There was only one other person Wynn knew who could do this. And Wynn didn't count herself, as her own ability to do so with just Shade was different.

So far, Wayfarer's ability had been tested only with Chap and Shade. They were both more directly Fay-descended than any other majay-hì, possibly back to the first of their kind. This still left Wynn wondering about the girl's name given by the an'Cróan ancestors.

Sheli'câlhad—"To a Lost Way."

Poor Wayfarer had cringed from that second name, especially after the one given her at birth—Leanâlhâm, "Child of Sorrow." Then Magiere—with Leesil and Chap's help—had given the girl a third one: Wayfarer.

Perhaps "To a Lost Way" meant something other than what the girl and others thought. In the forests of the Lhoin'na, Wynn had met someone utterly unique, or so she'd thought back then.

Vreuvillä, "Leaf's Heart," who was the last of their ancient priestesses, was called the Foirfeahkan. She ran with the majay-hì who guarded the Lhoin'na lands. On Wynn's visit there, she had more than once seen the priestess touch a member of her large pack and then know things she couldn't have experienced herself.

Yes, what must be done might be easier now. So finish this.

Wynn wasn't so certain as she dropped her gaze to meet Chap's stare. The girl's strange gift was too close to that of the wild woman of the Lhoin'na forests. "To a Lost Way" could apply to the calling of the last of the Foirfeahkan.

Wayfarer looked between the two of them in puzzlement. "Well?" she whispered. "Do you see where Osha needs to go?"

There was a hint of challenge in her question. Before facing Magiere and Leesil, Wynn had to get Wayfarer to understand another possible meaning for a reviled name.

Not long ago, the girl had suggested to Magiere that Osha and Wayfarer herself take the orb of Spirit into Lhoin'na lands while Magiere and Leesil dealt with the other orbs. Oh, yes, Wynn had heard about this from Chap.

Now everything had changed. The orbs were no longer to be hidden, and no doubt the girl assumed she would be going with Magiere and Leesil. Yet Wayfarer still had reasons to separate Osha from the others . . . or rather from Wynn.

"Osha needs to meet the Shé'ith," the girl said emphatically, "and perhaps learn why he was given a weapon like theirs. The Chein'âs are one of the five ancient races, possibly the oldest one, so there must be a reason."

Wynn almost couldn't believe what she was hearing. The girl's own notion was halfway to what Chap wanted. For one, he did *not* want the girl traveling with Magiere in the desert, hunting possible groups of undeads. He wanted her safe, and she could not journey to a place of safety alone. But there was more . . .

Chap's eyes had narrowed on the girl. That Wayfarer still waited for a response meant that Chap also hadn't given her one. Wynn grew angry, for obviously he was waiting for her to do it.

The coward!

Chap turned a sudden glare on Wynn.

Wynn glared back before turning to Wayfarer, and then she thought of something to make her point more clearly than words.

Stepping to the bedchamber door, she called, "Shade, come in here."

Wynn turned back before Shade entered, but Shade stalled in the doorway at the sight of her father, Chap.

"In . . . now," Wynn whispered.

Shade's jowls wrinkled at that, though she padded in three more steps before stopping again.

"I have something to show you," Wynn said to Wayfarer, and then leaned down to touch Shade's back as she closed her eyes.

There was one relevant past moment she shared in kind with Shade. Majay-hì, who used memory-speak among their own kind, had far more vivid powers of recollection. Wynn knew so from having shared in Shade's memories of what they had experienced together. She opened her eyes to meet Shade's crystalline, sky blue ones watching her without blinking.

"Show her," Wynn said, cocking her head toward Wayfarer, "and be nice about it."

Shade wrinkled her jowls again as she turned toward the girl.

Wayfarer backed up against the bedside. "What are you doing?"

"Something words can't do as well," Wynn answered. "Don't be afraid. Shade has something I want you to see . . . experience . . . and it is nothing frightening, I swear."

Shade crept in on Wayfarer and stood waiting. When the girl finally reached to touch the side of Shade's face . . .

Wynn couldn't help but remember once more.

When she, Shade, and Chane, along with Ore-Locks, had gone to Vreuvillä's home in the forest, the priestess had stopped and tensed for an instant. A circlet of braided raw shéot'a strips held back her silver-streaked hair. That hair was also too dark for a Lhoin'na, let alone an an'Cróan—just like Wayfarer. She was also deeply tanned from her life out in the wild. Standing there in her pants, high soft boots, and a thong-belted jerkin, all made of darkened hide, she was small for her people. She looked like some wild spirit embodied in the flesh of an elf, neither truly Lhoin'na nor an'Cróan.

Though there were faint lines in her face, she did not move or act like an old one, yet her very presence carried the weight of long years. One of the pack who flanked her drew near, and in the same instant, she looked down . . . and touched that silver-gray female.

Vreuvillä's large amber eyes lifted again, though her long fingers still combed lightly between the tall ears of the silver-gray majay-hì—and it followed her gaze. She stared beyond Wynn as her nostrils flared once, as if she were both seeing and smelling something that wasn't there. Something had passed between the priestess and one of her pack.

Wayfarer cringed back against the bedside, staring at Shade. And those bright, fearful eyes turned on Wynn.

"What—what—," the girl stuttered.

"Osha isn't the only one," Wynn began, "who has a reason to go to the lands of Lhoin'na. You are not as alone—or as 'lost'—as you thought. That isn't what that name . . . that other name . . . might mean."

Wayfarer peered cautiously at Shade without a word.

That is enough for now.

Wynn looked to Chap.

We tell Shade last, once Wayfarer and Osha accept what they must do. I will see the three of them partway there, and thereby keep our youngest ones out of harm's way. That leaves us both with one less worry.

One less but not none, Wynn noted as she thought of whom she had to face now in all of Chap's scheming. Magiere and Leesil, in being forced to accept Wayfarer's being sent away, would be only slightly worse than Shade for being sent off with the young pair. And at the thought of dealing with Magiere next, Chap went on . . .

It will not be your last time. While I am away, it falls on you to keep Magiere and Leesil from recklessness, to keep them safe as long as possible.

Wynn felt so tired. All she wanted to do was curl up in a bed and sleep, but that was not going to happen.

What had the Chein'âs really intended for Osha by giving him a weapon of a make from a land halfway across the world? And why in the same place where there was a woman who potentially had the same ability as Wayfarer, who bore a hated name given by ancient spirits of another of the five races? Those thoughts gave Wynn a quick chill.

In all of this, both Osha and Chane would be away for a long while. She still couldn't see what to do concerning their feelings for her—and hers for them. At least she could escape that, but not forever. If there was a forever.

Whatever came in the end, it would be Magiere and possibly Leesil who would have to face the final challenge. But with all others involved, someone had to get them that point.

That fell upon Chap . . . and Wynn.

CHAPTER THREE

Four nights later, Chane stood on the docks of the Suman Empire's capital port, preparing to board a ship for a long journey in the company of a majay-hì who hated him. Osha, Wayfarer, and Shade were joining them on the voyage as well, though they would go only partway to another destination. Somehow—and Chane was still not quite sure how—Wynn had convinced Osha to accompany Wayfarer to the forests of the Lhoin'na.

Even on the docks, the hot and dry air was thick with the scents of spice, brine, people, and livestock. Most of the dusky-skinned citizens walking near the piers wore light, loose-fitting cloth shifts or equally loose and light leggings or pants. Wraps in varied colors and patterns upon their heads were done up in short or tall, thick or thin mounds. Some people herded goats or carried square baskets of fowl.

A large Numan vessel waited thirty paces down the dock from where Chane stood. He still could not believe what he had been forced into accepting.

Everyone who would remain behind for the desert search had come to see off the others. This was not a night like any other, past or yet to come.

The decision had been made—or forced—to gather the three hidden orbs. From then on, every spare moment had been filled with preparations.

He and Wynn had had no time to speak of anything that mattered to them, to him.

Wynn had soon realized that Chane would encounter issues in communicating with Chap along the way. The only reason that Magiere and Chap could exist in close proximity to Chane was because of the arcane "ring of nothing," as he called it, that he wore on his left hand. As a dhampir and majay-hì, hunters of the undead, they were driven into a hunting rage if they neared anything undead.

Chane could be seen, heard, and touched by natural means, but anyone with the ability to sense his "unnatural" state could not do so while he wore the ring. Even his thoughts and memories were shielded from invasion. Only the ring kept his nature from breaching the tentative truce with Chap and Magiere.

However, it also kept Chap from speaking to him through memory-words.

Chap could express "yes," "no," and "maybe" by a series of huffing sounds. One huff meant "yes," two meant "no," and three meant "maybe." This would hardly be enough for the two of them to create or agree on plans while traveling.

By way of answer, Wynn procured a thick goat hide. She wrote the Belaskian alphabet in the center and then created rows of commonly used words at the top and bottom and down the sides. Chap would be able to point to simple words or spell out more complicated ones, and in this way, they would be able to communicate. Apparently, Magiere and Leesil had used something similar in the past called "the talking hide," before Chap had learned to call up memory-words.

Chane now carried the new hide in his pack.

Three moderate-sized chests had also been procured to hold the three orbs to be recovered. Passage had been purchased for them to travel north on a route that stopped over at the Port of Soráno, where Wayfarer, Osha, and Shade would disembark to head for the lands of the Lhoin'na.

Chane would sail onward with only Chap.

What little coin was left had been divided two to one, the greater part for himself and Chap.

It was all so cut-and-dried.

Wynn stood facing him on the dock and had not said a word so far. She was so short—or he was so tall—that she had to lean her head back to look up at him. Her pretty, oval face surrounded by wispy light brown hair always made him ponder how much of his existence . . . how *he* had been altered by this woman whom he loved. And now she was sending him away while she went off with Magiere and some of the others to scout eastward into the great desert.

She had done so by playing his love for her against his better judgment. Her words still haunted him.

Please . . . do this for us . . . for the world.

For "why," she was right, but for "how," she was wrong, and he should never have consented. Now it was too late.

Wynn was one of the few who both cared and had placed herself in position to take action against large forces and events almost no one else could foresee. She had asked for his help, and he could not refuse her.

"Chane," she said, and that one word always left him vulnerable to her.

In her eyes, he saw himself as no else did. He wanted to *be* what she saw. She did not see him as a killer or a monster, though he had been—perhaps still was—both. To her, he was a companion who had fought at her side. She saw him as strong and resourceful and necessary.

He could do something for her now that no one else could.

Ore-Locks won't give the orb to anyone but you . . . not even me.

Yes, one orb had been left with the wayward stonewalker and his brethren for safekeeping. Perhaps not a friend, but at least a comrade, Ore-Locks was the true inheritor of the orb of Earth. No one else could ever dare ask for it.

"It's been so long since we were apart," Wynn said.

Hearing her words took away his own. All he could say was, "Be safe."

Reaching out, she touched his hand. "I need to tell Shade good-bye."

He nodded as she turned toward the younger majay-hì.

"Take this."

The sudden other voice startled him, and he turned his head quickly.

Ghassan il'Sänke held out his hand, and Chane looked down. In the ex-domin's palm was a tiny nondescript pebble.

"Keep it with you," il'Sänke said, "on your person at all times."

Chane's eyes narrowed in suspicion. Likely, none of them would ever return to the ensorcelled sanctuary hidden in the empire's capital.

"Why?" he asked.

"I am the one who placed the ensorcellment upon it, so that it could be used to open the hidden sanctuary doors. I therefore have a connection to it and will be able to gauge your general distance and direction. It will be easier to find and meet you when you and Chap return to this region."

Chane still hesitated; he did not like being "tracked."

Il'Sänke glanced toward Wynn, who was kneeling before Shade. "How else will I—or she—find you along the foothills, mountains, or a vast desert?"

With some reluctance, Chane took the pebble, knowing he was being manipulated.

When Wynn turned from Chane, she forced herself not to look back, or she might say something she'd later regret. There were others watching that she also had to face. All of this was harder than she'd expected.

It could be a whole season—maybe more—before she would again see those who had traveled at her side for so long. Parting with Chane was especially difficult.

There was nothing else to be done. They all had tasks to complete.

Shade stood waiting, eyeing Wynn fiercely with her hackles slightly bristling. Wynn knelt down on the dock and took Shade's charcoal-colored face in her small hands.

"Please, sister," she said quietly. "Don't make this any harder for us both. You have to watch over Wayfarer . . . and Osha."

Shade remained silent for a long moment, and her hackles stiffened upright as she gave a rising growl. One memory-word exploded in Wynn's mind.

—No!—

Shade pressed her whole head into Wynn's face.

— . . . Not go!— . . . —Wynn cannot be . . . alone— . . . —. . . unsafe . . . dangerous—

Shade's grasp of words was far less developed than Chap's, even though she'd been the first to figure how to single out words from Wynn's memories and use them to "speak." Unlike Chap, Shade could do this only with Wynn and only when they physically touched.

Wynn had not expected another outright refusal immediately before boarding. She wasn't angry. How could she be? Shade wasn't being overprotective here, as she sometimes could be. Of course, Wynn would be at risk without Shade—or Chane or even Osha.

"You must go," Wynn whispered, glancing at Wayfarer, who was thankfully occupied in checking the contents of her pack. "Wayfarer needs at least one majay-hì who will be *on her side*, no matter what."

Closing her eyes, Wynn recalled a night not too long ago, when Wayfarer, Chap, Magiere, and Leesil had been freed from a whole moon's imprisonment. Upon emerging, the girl had leaned on Chap, unable to walk on her own. In remembering, Wynn reminded Shade of that moment.

"She will need you," Wynn whispered into Shade's ear, "as I have needed you . . . and your father."

Shade jerked back with a snarl, but Wynn didn't let go of her.

Wynn had hoped this journey might bring some understanding in a daughter for why a father had both abandoned her and through her mother sent her away from her home. Wynn said nothing more about it, as it would do no good here and now. As with everything else, she could only hope.

"Take Wayfarer to Vreuvillä," Wynn added, "and guard her. Only you can do this."

Shade's neck muscles tightened under Wynn's hands, though she did not pull away.

"I will miss you, sister," Wynn murmured. "Until I see you again."

She could at least say such things to Shade, if not to Chane . . . or Osha. And she rose quickly before any tears fell, prepared to face the last one.

Osha eyed her, his expression full of pain and maybe spite. He turned his back to her and crouched to fuss with the luggage for the journey.

Wynn clenched her jaw, breathing hard to hold back more tears. And when her sight cleared . . .

Magiere, farther down the dock, turned to look back, her pale face emotionless.

"Boarding has started," she called. "Sailors are coming for luggage."

Leesil stood a few paces short from her and hadn't said much in the past four days. Chap stood beside him and, thankfully, refrained from any more snarling at Chane. Wynn knew the situation went against all his instincts, but it was his plan.

Three pale-skinned sailors came trotting down the dock.

"Anything else?" the lead one asked in Numanese with a glance at the three chests.

"Just those," Chane answered, as he always carried his own packs.

Magiere strode over to embrace Wayfarer, whispered something in the girl's ear, and Wayfarer held on until Magiere had to pull free. Osha came and took Wayfarer's hand to lead her after the sailors carrying the chests. Chane followed them with a last slow nod to Wynn, which she returned, and he called to Shade.

Shade lingered.

Wynn nodded with a weak wave to push Shade onward and then dropped her gaze. She couldn't watch any longer.

There had been painful partings in the past among all of them. Two groups who'd grown to depend upon and trust those with them had been split and mixed in ways that would make trust among some of them almost impossible. More than just sorrow now weighed upon everyone.

It was the worst of partings in Wynn's whole life.

It will not get better, but you can face it, little one.

Wynn raised her eyes to meet Chap's. He hadn't called her "little one" in years.

I trust you most of all. Watch yourself until I find you again, but watch those two most of all.

Wynn looked to Magiere and Leesil.

No . . . the other two.

Wynn hesitated but did not turn. Somewhere behind her, Ghassan and Brot'an stood waiting. They were the only two, besides Chane when he was wearing his ring, from whom Chap could never see any surface thoughts.

Chap huffed once at Wynn, and she barely had time for a wave before he trotted up the dock after the others who were boarding the ship.

Khalidah returned to the tenement with Magiere, Leesil, Wynn, and Brot'an. Upon reaching the warped front door, he led the way in without pause and upstairs to the top passage, where he stopped before the paneless window at the far end. Khalidah closed his grip hard on one of Ghassan's pebbles.

The shadowy form of a heavy door overlay the window.

He twisted its lever handle, and, as he opened it, the door became solid and real to all present. He held it open and ushered everyone else inside.

The first to enter was the dhampir, and he purposefully avoided eyeing her in any conspicuous way. But the last to enter gave him reason for a second glance. Brot'an's—Brot'ân'duivé's—first step through the doorway was almost hesitant.

It was so brief that anyone else might not have noticed.

For Khalidah, once leader of the triad called the Sâ'yminfiäl—"Masters of Frenzy"—under Beloved, very little of true use escaped his notice. More so where enemies were concerned. The elder "shadow-gripper" took one quick glance at the door's frame as he entered. Perhaps a slight frown crossed that scarred face, and his large amber eyes narrowed for an instant.

"Well, it's done," Leesil said.

The half-blood and the dhampir both looked drawn and weary as they stepped to the table, but they didn't yet sit.

"Yes," Wynn said, "and there's no turning back."

She began fussing about for a ladle to dip water from one of the large jugs. The sage would likely be making tea, though no one had asked for such, and it was rather late. Brot'an was the first to settle in a chair, and he sat waiting.

With three people and both majay-hì removed, the main room looked far less overcrowded. Not that Khalidah planned to join them at the moment.

"I must go out," he said in Ghassan's voice, and at that he felt the domin squirming in his—*their*—mind. "I need to report to the prince . . . to the new emperor that I will be leaving soon."

Wynn's brow wrinkled as she turned. "You haven't told him yet?"

"No, and I thought to wait until the journey was imminent. You should all rest while you can, and I will let myself back in."

He left and pulled the door closed before that annoying little sage pestered him even more. The false window overlooking the alley reappeared.

Khalidah strode down the passage, down the stairs, and out into the night streets. Of course he was not going to report to the new emperor. That was simply the most believable excuse for what he must now do.

A different meeting had been arranged.

While he walked the night streets, his thoughts lingered upon one left behind in the sanctuary, the only one who truly troubled him.

Try as he might, not once had he penetrated the thoughts and memories of the scarred greimasg'äh.

That both majay-hì minds had been impervious as well was no surprise, but the elder elf was another matter. Each time he had tried to slip into Brot'an's mind, he found his efforts obscured by shadows.

It was like knowing there was movement somewhere within a maze of black gauze curtains. Each time he sensed movement therein, and swatted aside another drape of night fabric, he faced only more of the same.

Khalidah was suddenly aware of how quiet and still Ghassan il'Sänke had become.

"Oh, tsk-tsk, my domin," he whispered inwardly and aloud. "Do you truly think there is some hope in the scarred one? Quite the opposite."

Walking deeper into the city, he navigated toward a less-populated area composed mainly of shops long closed. There, he slipped into a cutway between an eatery and a perfume shop and stepped out in the back alley for a strange gathering.

Khalidah's gaze fixed first on a man standing apart, as if pretending he had no connection to the others. He was tall and well formed, and his face was so pale that it appeared to glimmer even in the dark. Except for his head, nothing more of him was exposed, from his black gloves and leather-laced tunic to his dark pants and high riding boots. Oh, and then there was a wide leather collar of triple straps buckled around his neck, as if he needed that extra support to keep his head erect.

Sau'ilahk eyed Khalidah in turn without a word, both of them hiding in stolen flesh, though at least Khalidah's own was still alive. Fallen Sau'ilahk had once been first and highest of the Reverent, priests of il'Samar, Beloved, during the Great War. Actually, he and his had been simple conjurers, though he too had been betrayed by Beloved.

Khalidah knew the story, or at least the important parts, which were all that mattered.

Sau'ilahk had begged his god for eternal life; he should have asked for eternal youth instead. Only one would have given him true immortality and kept his beauty unmarred by age. Forced to watch his own body decay and die, he still gained his eternal life, of a sort, as an undead spirit. The wraith, Sau'ilahk, had only regained flesh most recently.

Poor, poor priest, high or not, undone by boundless vanity and assumed synonyms.

Khalidah was careful not to smile. The ex-priest was not to be trusted any more than when they had hated each other in their living days. Now a mutual hate for their god was greater than that, and Sau'ilahk's hate could be useful.

As to the other one who had come for the gathering, Khalidah's gaze shifted as a small, semitransparent, and glimmering girl-child in a tattered and bloodied nightshift stepped toward him out of the alley's darkness.

Light from a streetlamp at the alley's end both illuminated and penetrated her. Her visage was that of the moment of her death, including her severed throat. She stopped beyond arm's reach and peered up as if he were an undesirable necessity.

Behind her came a litter with two large side wheels rolled by a pair of muscled men—both animated corpses. At the sight of Khalidah, the men rocked the litter forward until its front end clacked on the cobble. Lashed to the litter was a preserved corpse held erect by straps.

His hands, folded and bound across his chest, were bare, exposing bony fingers and nails elongated by withered, shrinking skin. He was dressed in a long black robe, and where his face should have been there was a mask of aged leather that ended above a bony jaw supporting a withered mouth, likely more withered in death than in his last moment of life.

There were no eye slits in his mask.

Somewhat like that of the ex-priest in stolen flesh, the corpse's neck was wrapped in hardened leather to keep its head upright. Unlike Sau'ilahk, this creature was from the current era though still pretending to serve Beloved.

Ubâd, a filthy necromancer, could not move and had trapped himself somewhere between life and death. The only way he could speak was through his conjured slave, the ghost girl.

Khalidah knew little more, but he needed to know only that Ubâd had also been betrayed by Beloved. How unfortunate not to see the hate in his face, as in Sau'ilahk's.

"You are late," the girl said too articulately for her apparent age. "Do not keep me waiting again."

Khalidah sighed. "My time is limited." Raising his gaze to the corpse, he added, "So do not waste it with petulant complaints."

Slowly, Sau'ilahk stepped nearer. "Why are we here, mad one?"

"To see the end of our *beloved* affair, of course," Khalidah answered. "Which has become stale and tasteless . . . no, moldy. I guess—I *know*—it has for you."

Sau'ilahk remained silent a moment, and then said, "Get to the point."

Khalidah's self-satisfaction remained. "I have the dhampir. And even now those who follow her are gathering the anchors of creation."

He let those words hang to savor his triumph, his superiority.

Sau'ilahk's expression filled first with shock, and then a shadow of doubt. "Is this true?"

"The vampire and gray majay-hì sailed tonight," he related. "They travel north to the white wastes of this continent for two orbs. Upon return, they stop at the last seatt of the Rughìr, the dwarves, for the third in hiding. They claim they know the route from the north side of the Sky-Cutter Range that emerges on the south side through—"

"Through Bäalâle," Sau'ilahk whispered.

Khalidah smiled. "Oh, yes, a great loss in the war that was . . . more for me than you. I convinced the dhampir there are reports of undead heading eastward in the great desert. She and those remaining behind will travel there with me, bringing the orbs of Spirit and Air as we 'scout' to verify these reports." He paused for effect. "When the vampire and the elder majay-hì rejoin us, all five orbs will be in my possession."

Sau'ilahk's expression hardened. "This vampire . . . Is he called Chane Andraso?"

Khalidah shrugged. "Yes."

Taking a few quick steps closer, Sau'ilahk nearly walked through the ghost girl. "He is mine to kill, as is the small sage!"

"And I take the gray majay-hì!" the ghost girl added, sounding bitter and unhinged.

Khalidah was certain of the necromancer's and Reverent One's hate for Beloved, though theirs would never match his. As with the vampire and the two majay-hì—and Brot'an—it had been impossible to read the thoughts of his conspirators. It had not occurred to him that they might harbor petty, personal grievances.

Well, this too could be useful, if it kept them focused and distracted in the end.

Dramatically, he shrugged and spread his hands.

"As you both wish, so long as these desires can wait. Playing my part as the fallen domin is still to your advantage. Wynn Hygeorht trusts Ghassan il'Sänke more than she admits. Where she goes, Chane and both majay-hì will eventually follow. You two will play your parts until I say otherwise."

Sau'ilahk tilted his head. "And what are our parts?"

"Bait," Khalidah answered. "The dhampir expects to find undead to the east, though the others each hope in different ways that she will not. I will instruct how you will fulfill that expectation as we proceed."

As an undead, Sau'ilahk would need to feed as he traveled, though *how* would be uncertain. There was not much to feed upon in the desert and mountains, as Khalidah knew well, so what was found needed to serve for sustenance as well as another purpose.

"What of Andraso and the gray majay-hì?" Sau'ilahk challenged. "They are beyond being monitored. You have no way to know if they return early, or at all, or with or without the missing orbs until they arrive."

Khalidah raised an eyebrow. "And what makes you think I have not accounted for that?"

"Have you?" Sau'ilahk pressed.

"I have dealt with it," Khalidah countered. "I will always know their direction and general distance."

He was not about to elaborate or share information concerning the ensorcelled pebble he had given Chane Andraso. Better to leave his confederates in the dark—and ignorant of the pebble's other potential uses. Besides, as Ghassan had ensorcelled the pebble, it was forever connected to his mental presence. So long as Khalidah kept that presence alive and imprisoned, he as well controlled the pebble.

It gave him more power over the pebble's bearer than Chane knew. Well, if and when the lowly vampire ever removed that irritating brass ring.

The ghost girl eyed him. "Once the orbs are gathered, you know Beloved's last resting place?"

The answer required great care. He had seen it, and he suspected so had Sau'ilahk, but the range was vast and a thousand years had passed. The images were vague.

"Even if not," he began dismissively, "once the orbs are gathered, dear Beloved will certainly call us. We, as our god's most potent—and *obedient*—supplicants, will bring the anchors to our god. And then . . ."

The rest need not be said.

Khalidah knew more than these two about orbs—the anchors. He had learned through success as well as defeat and failure nearly ultimate. As leader of the triad, the Sâ'yminfiäl, whom the dwarves had called the "Eaters of Silence," he had been at the fall of Bäalâle Seatt in using the anchor of Earth.

He still remembered the roots of the mountain suddenly blowing apart around him. He remembered the agony of being simultaneously burned, torn, and crushed. His last willful act at the instant of death was to tear his own consciousness free.

Neither priest nor necromancer could have done so, yet it gained him too little and too much . . . for Beloved abandoned him to his fate. Centuries passed before any living being with the necessary mental capacity had wandered near enough for him to seize, and it was longer still in that longest starvation until he found something else upon which to feed. And then, captivity again by il'Sänke's hidden sect, trapped in the pure darkness of an ensorcelled, brass sarcophagus for so many years.

Neither of these two corpses in this alley knew such suffering . . . or the absolute purity it brought. And Beloved would never expect open betrayal either. His god believed him cowed in fear and reverence.

To kill a god meant to become a god. And again there would be only one, only him.

Oh, but he had savored this too long.

Reaching inside his cloak, he withdrew a medallion hanging on a chain and held it out to Sau'ilahk.

"What is it?" the dead priest asked without taking it.

"A communication device, invented by my current host and his dead peers. I took it off one of them and wear one myself. Wear it against your flesh."

Sau'ilahk only watched him and did not move.

Further explanation followed another sigh and tsk-tsk. "Anyone with your arcane . . . background should have no trouble mastering it. If you feel it grow warm, I am attempting to contact you. Hold the medallion, and my thoughts will reach you. If you wish to contact me, hold it in your hand and focus upon me in your thoughts."

Sau'ilahk still hesitated. "What do you mean, your thoughts will reach me?"

Khalidah wanted to sigh. "It is much like speaking, though either of us only hears thoughts the other wishes to share. We must be able to locate each other. Take it!"

Sau'ilahk hesitated again but reached out and took the medallion.

Khalidah glanced from the ghost girl to Ubâd. "You will all leave for the desert tomorrow night . . . and I will instruct you as opportunity permits."

A brief silence followed, and the ghost girl answered, "Yes."

Trapped inside his own body, Ghassan raged in panic, though no one but Khalidah would hear him. The only answer he received was to feel his own face smile softly. Then his body turned and stepped back along the cutway out of the alley.

CHAPTER FOUR

Days slipped into nights, until Chap nearly lost count as various ships carrying him and Chane sailed north up the entire continent. One evening, as the sun dipped lower, he stood on the deck of a small ship in the chill air and looked out at a snow-crusted shoreline.

All land in sight appeared glazed, frosted, or frozen, but he knew where he was, as he had been here before. He focused on a coastal settlement ahead along the shore.

"White Hut!" a sailor called from the bow.

Dusk was near, though the captain would not force him to disembark until Chane awoke. Though it had grated on Chap at first, he had grown reluctantly accustomed to playing Chane's "dog" after so many days and nights.

In the early part of the journey, he had wondered how Chane would manage long-distance travel since he fell dormant the instant the sun rose. Yet this had proven surprisingly easy. Chane simply told any vessel's captain that he suffered from a skin condition and could not be exposed to daylight. Odd as it sounded, no one questioned him. Some, such as the first mate of this ship, had even expressed sympathy.

The journey so far had passed without incident. From the Suman port, they sailed directly to Soráno, where Chane had proven useful. He already knew where the caravaners camped beyond the city and quickly found one group loaded up for a journey to a'Ghràihlôn'na—"Blessed of the Woods"—and the central settlement of the Lhoin'na.

Chane had offered both Osha's and Shade's services as caravan guards in exchange for passage. He paid Wayfarer's fee in coin.

While Chap would never admit it, he would not have managed this so easily on his own. After that, all that remained was a somewhat painful good-bye to Wayfarer and to Osha as well. His panic at leaving them to a foreign people and land did not pass quickly. He had to trust that Shade and Osha would guard the girl as much as possible in whatever she would face. He still believed her safer in this than in following Magiere and Leesil.

Parting from Shade had been painful in a different way, and at best civil.

There could be no reconciliation after what Chap had done to his unborn daughter, left behind long ago, and the only glimmer of what little trust might now exist between them was one he had not recognized at the time.

Often during the voyage's first part, Wayfarer could not stand remaining in the cabin she shared with Osha and Chap himself. Shade always slept in Chane's cabin. One day, Chap had gone up on deck to find Osha sitting on the cargo hatch's edge with Wayfarer at the rail nearby.

Shade was there next to the girl.

With her forepaws on the rail as she too looked out over the water, she must have heard or sensed something. Shade glanced back once at Chap and returned to watching the ocean with Wayfarer. At least Shade had accepted the girl as her new charge, but something more did not occur to Chap until later that day.

Shade had left Chane unguarded.

Whether she believed her father would not act against Chane, or that no one would, considering he was now necessary, Chap would never know. Chane did check in with everyone whenever he rose after dusk. Those were tense times at best, but there were others late at night that only Chap noticed.

While he lay half asleep on the end of Wayfarer's bunk, he had often heard Chane's cabin door open. Then came bootfalls in the outer passage . . . mimicked by a set of clawed paws.

Chane did not need to be guarded at night. That any majay-hì kept company with an undead was unsettling. That she, his daughter, did so by choice burned him with anger and pain, but he swallowed both and kept silent.

Later, upon seeing the young trio off with a caravan, there had been little more than plain acknowledgment from a daughter for a father; more than she had ever shown him, though less than he wanted.

Then . . . when Chap had reboarded with Chane, it was just the two of them. They took to one cabin so as not to waste what coin was left. They had little to say to each other and even more limited methods with which to say it. Along the journey north, it had been necessary to change ships twice.

Chane had proven himself frugal, retaining enough coin for their return journey. Before leaving the others, everyone had shared and separated their differing coins. The total proved worrisome until Ghassan contributed a surprising amount, which he claimed comprised the secretly amassed reserves of his sect. Magiere could be prideful over anything she considered "charity," but even she said nothing when all was thrown in and divided.

Along the journey, Chap had watched Chane carefully, ready to take him down if he showed any inclination to feed upon the ship's crew. This never happened, though, which left Chap wondering about how often a vampire needed to feed. Perhaps they could survive for longer periods than he would have thought. He had no intention of asking. Wynn had once assured Magiere that Chane fed only on livestock. Neither Chap nor Magiere believed this, and there was no livestock aboard the ships they occupied.

Now he stood on deck as White Hut came into view.

The sun dipped below the horizon as the vessel anchored offshore from the trading station, as there were no docks. Shortly after, the aftcastle door opened.

Chane emerged in a heavy cloak. Sometimes it bothered Chap that he no longer felt any instinctual impulse to snarl in the undead's presence. Because of Chane's brass ring, it was also unnerving not to sense when Chane came near unless Chap saw, smelled, or heard him approach.

"We have arrived?" Chane asked as he approached the captain.

Captain Nellort was a bulky, grisly man who wore a variety of patchwork furs. Strangely enough, he smelled worse when he was not bundled up.

"Yes," he confirmed. "It's White Hut."

"Will you be sailing onward?"

"No, this is our last landfall," Nellort answered. "We never go farther north than here."

Chane hesitated, and Chap grew anxious. They needed as quick a return as possible once the two orbs were recovered.

"Why not?" Chane asked.

The captain pointed ahead. "Winter's coming. The sea will start to freeze for leagues out from shore. Only Northlander longboats travel where nothing but the ice shifts and flows . . . and can crush anything that can't be dragged over the top of it."

Chap let out a hissing breath, though no one noticed. If only they had headed north at least half a moon earlier. Now they would have to find yet another ship . . . or rather wait for one to head up north this far.

Chane nodded to the captain. "I need to hire a guide, sled, and dog team."

Chap turned a quick glare on Chane. Had the vampire bothered to ask him, *he* could have provided this information.

"Well, White Hut's the last stop up here," Nellort said. "You might find a guide and team still willing to head out. You'd do best to look for a Northlander. Most speak passable Numanese, though you'd be wise to keep two eyes on any you hire."

Chane merely nodded.

Then he commandeered a few men to assist him and went below while Chap remained on deck. Sailors were already stacking crates along the deck to off-load before the trading post's skiffs arrived, and none looked his way. They had already grown accustomed to him not bothering anyone. By the time Chane returned with the two men, he had both his packs and hauled one empty chest. The sailors brought the other two, and Chap spotted the longboat skiffs coming closer. The captain put Chane and Chap on the smallest to be put ashore before the cargo was loaded.

With two square sails furled to single cross poles on stout masts, the long boat felt narrow and wobbly compared to a Numan ship. It was still easily half the length of the vessel they had left. When the prow nudged to a halt on shore, Chap leaped out, clearing any water. Chane followed and then helped to off-load the chests.

And there the two of them stood as the longboats went back out for cargo.

Chap looked up at Chane with a quick rumble, as if to ask, "Now what?"

Dropping to one knee, Chane dug through a pack and withdrew the rolled goat hide covered in letters and words Wynn had inked on it. Chane rolled out the hide.

"How did you, Magiere, and Leesil hire a guide?" he asked.

This method of speaking was slow, but it worked. Chap pawed out the answer.

Main big hut. Ask.

Chane looked toward White Hut. Even from a distance, both of them could see a plank over the door with unrecognizable characters. Black smoke rose from the haphazard chimney made from large bits of now-blackened bark. The rest of it was a dome of sod, as if it had been dug into or made into a large hillock.

"There?" Chane asked.

Chap huffed once for "yes" and began pawing at more words and letters. Chane again followed along.

"How will I carry the chests?" he asked, and then peered along the shoreline. "Wait here."

Torches and two lanterns were enough for both of them to spot two boys skipping stones out into the ocean. Chane approached them and held out a coin, likely a Numan one. He pointed back to the chests near Chap, mimed the act of picking something up, and pointed to the large sod dome with the bark chimney.

The boys exchanged a few words, the taller one smiled and reached for the coin, and Chane raised it out of reach. He twisted aside and extended his other arm toward the chests. The slightly shorter boy rolled his eyes and led the way.

Neither balked at the sight of Chap, as they likely saw him as only a big sled dog. Most of those were descended in part from wolves. The boys each hefted a small empty chest, and Chane slung both packs over a shoulder as he grabbed up the third one by an end handle.

All four made their way toward the main hut.

Once inside the sod dome, the boys were paid, and they hurried back out.

Though it was not cold inside, Chap shivered. Memories of everything that had happened the last time in the wastes rose up. On his previous visit, this place had been the beginning of a long nightmare.

Oil lamps upon rough tables made a glimmering haze in the smoky room. Stools and a few benches surrounded these on the packed dirt floor between the long, faded plank counter atop barrels and the crude, clay fireplace in the back wall.

The whole place was crowded.

Perhaps thirty people, mostly men, all dressed in furs or thick hides, sat, stood, or shuffled about. More than a few sucked on pipes or sipped from steaming clay and wooden bowls or cups. Most wore their hair long, and it shimmered as if greased. All had darkly tanned skin for humans.

The sight of every one of them made Chap cringe, for one that he saw only in memory was not present. Would he find . . . *see* that one—that body—when he went for the orbs?

Chap quickly pushed this aside, not wishing to think of that name, let alone a face.

No one looked much at him though many glanced sidelong at Chane, who looked out of place with his near-white skin and red-brown hair. A few glanced toward the place's entrance as if the boys were still there. Perhaps Chane's transaction in coin rather than trade with those two had drawn attention.

Chap stepped forward, gauging the men at the tables. Chane followed a half step behind and let him take the lead here. Finally, Chap fixed on a lone man smoking a long-stemmed pipe and taking short sips from a dark clay mug.

He was perhaps thirty years old, though he looked worn for that age, with a round face and thick black hair. He wore a shabby white fur around his shoulders. His boots were furred but well-worn. A heavy canvas pack was propped against the legs of his chair, immediately within reach. He was obviously used to being on the move.

His hands were calloused and scarred.

Chap dipped the man's mind for any rising memories. At first, he saw nothing . . . except maybe an echo of himself. Then came an image of dogs running ahead of a sled.

Chap huffed once for "yes," and Chane stepped immediately ahead.

"Pardon," Chane said. "Do you speak Numanese?"

The man looked up from his mug. "Some."

"I wish to hire a guide with a sled."

The man studied Chane's face.

Chap had known Chane back when his skin had not been quite so translucent. His eyes had once held more color too, a deeper brown as opposed to their light brown, almost clear appearance now. The longer he existed as an undead, the more these changes became apparent.

Chane ignored the guide's scrutiny and held up a pouch. "How much?" he asked, implying he already knew the man's trade. The man set down his pipe and gestured to a chair across the table. Chane sat. Chap positioned himself at the table's open side between the two.

"I am Igaluk," the man said. "How far inland do you travel?"

Chap and Chane had discussed this at length while on the last ship.

"Five days inland, southeast, and then five days back," Chane answered.

Again, the man studied him. "So you know exactly where you go?"

"Yes."

"Then why do you need a guide?"

Chane's expression didn't flicker. "I do not. I need someone with a sled and dogs." He paused long enough to drop the pouch on the table with an audible chitter of coins.

Chap wrinkled his jowls, for that action and small noise would attract unwanted attention.

"And someone who does not ask many questions," Chane added.

Igaluk shrugged. "I can take you."

When discussion turned to price and needed supplies, Chap turned his attention to the rest of the room in watching for undue attention by anyone present. One awkward moment pulled his attention back to the bartering.

"Tomorrow . . . night?" Igaluk asked sharply.

"Yes, as I said," Chane countered. "Shortly past dusk."

This was followed by Chane's familiar explanation of a "skin condition." There was the added complication that he also required a thick canvas tent with an additional tarp over it, which went well beyond the normal. When traveling on ship or in civilization, protection from sunlight was not difficult. The wilderness was a different matter.

These odd requirements made Igaluk's dark brow wrinkle, though in the end he agreed.

With a nod, Chane rose. "I will meet you here, outside, tomorrow after full darkness."

He turned toward the counter, and Chap followed. Chane then stopped to crouch as if picking something off the bottom of his boot. Glancing aside, he looked into Chap's eyes.

"I will purchase the tent myself," he whispered. "Then we set camp away from this place. Once daylight comes, you must keep watch and make certain no one approaches . . . us."

The bizarre nature of their situation suddenly struck Chap. He was to spend the following day guarding an undead—the same as . . . the same one as his daughter.

With no other choice, he huffed once. As Chane rose and stepped to the trading post's counter, to acquire what he needed, Chap's mind drifted to the nights ahead. He knew precisely where he had hidden the orbs of Water and Fire. Something else might still be there as well. For in hiding those, he had done something unforgivable.

He had needed to take the body and mind of his last guide on that journey. Without hands of his own, there had been no other way to bury the orbs in secret. He now clung to that necessity—that justification—to do more and perhaps worse than was necessary.

Far to the south, Leesil crept along the nighttime sands of the Suman desert just below the foothills of the Sky-Cutter Range. They'd left Magiere, Wynn, and Brot'an back at camp at least half a league behind, as only he and Ghassan needed to reach a well the fallen domin claimed he knew of. They both carried two large, empty waterskins.

Stealing water out here was more than thievery, worse than murder. It meant the deaths of many in taking something that so many needed to survive. They would both be killed if caught, and although Leesil knew they had no choice, he didn't like this. He also didn't like depending on anyone except Magiere or Chap . . . or even Wynn, sometimes.

Worse, without Ghassan, he wouldn't have known what to look for, and he still wasn't certain. Wells were always hidden in some way as the most precious possession of a family, clan, or tribe. These peopled killed any but their own in order to get more if they ran out. Or at least that was what Ghassan had said. And yet the ex-domin knew where to find such, or at least where to look.

"There," Ghassan whispered, pointing over the rock crest behind which they crouched.

Leesil looked carefully but spotted nothing.

"That cluster of small stones," Ghassan added. "See how three larger ones are on top . . . and would not be naturally? Someone put them there and kicked dust and dirt on them to hide any sign of the change."

Once Leesil saw this, he recognized it for what it was. He and Ghassan had been forced to steal from eight other wells along the journey. Somehow—though Leesil didn't know how—their luck had held. The key to thievery was to know what you wanted, take it quickly, and then get out.

Leesil didn't hesitate.

With one last look about, he vaulted the rock crest, scurried light-footed down the gradual slope, and then ran for the three stones and crouched low. After another look around, he began removing stones, finding only dirt beneath them. For an instant he even thought of using the cold-lamp crystal Wynn had loaned him.

He wasn't that desperate yet, for the light might give away their position.

Carefully, he began spreading and probing the parched, dusty earth with his fingers. And there was something there. He felt a hard but flexing semi-smooth surface and brushed part of it clear. Though it was hard to see in the dark, this wasn't the first time he'd touched that kind of hardened leather.

Leesil found the edge of the thick, leather plate and flipped it quietly off to stare down into a black hole in the packed earth. There was no rope, bucket, or urn to lower. That would've made it easier for thieves. Or at least any who found this place and were unprepared.

Leesil softly clicked his tongue three times. The domin rose from hiding beyond the crest and hurried toward him. Leesil began unwrapping the leather-braid rope from around his waist.

Before he'd even finished, Ghassan bound the rope's loose end to one waterskin's loop handles. He then dropped a stone into the skin's wide mouth to help it sink. Once Leesil finished unwrapping the rope's other end, Ghassan dropped the skin into the hole.

Leesil lowered the rope until its tension slackened for an instant and then let it sink.

"Keep watch," he whispered.

He was well armed, and Ghassan had his own methods of defense. Between the two of them, they could probably handle six or seven men. The danger was in being caught by a larger number. And out here, any group they'd spotted had been larger than that. They'd hidden from all of them.

In the desert, there were no stragglers or twos and threes. Larger numbers were the only way to survive.

The skin quickly grew heavy and was hard to draw up. Ghassan assisted him, and once the first skin was out of the hole, he tied it shut below the handles with a leather thong. And the next—and the next—skin was lowered.

Ghassan rose slightly and watched all around as each skin was dropped in. They both wore light, loose clothing, including dusky muslin over-robes and similar cloths bound around their heads to drape down their backs. This helped them blend into the landscape unless they moved suddenly.

Leesil's mind flowed backward as he felt the last skin reach the waterline.

This journey already felt too long. They'd been delayed in the imperial city while Ghassan fussed over choices of supplies and necessities, particularly food that would last in the heat.

They'd also purchased tents, blankets, lanterns, and oil, even though most of them carried a cold-lamp crystal. On the day of their departure, Ghassan had told them to meet him outside the city, and then he'd vanished. Upon arriving at the agreed meeting place, Leesil, Wynn, Magiere, and Brot'an ended up waiting longer than Leesil liked.

When the ex-domin finally arrived, he was leading two camels. In a rush, they'd strapped the orb chests and supplies on the beasts and set off immediately after dark.

Leesil had always wondered exactly how Ghassan procured those expensive pack animals, but he never asked. At least they hadn't had to carry the chests and supplies themselves.

The days that followed became monotonous amid the constant tension of trying to track something—without really knowing what—while not being seen or tracked themselves. And even when they'd gotten across the blistering sands and reached the foothills of the Sky-Cutter Range, there wasn't much relief to be had.

The heat, even after dusk in the shadow of the peaks, kept increasing the farther east they went. They slept at midday, avoiding exertion, and then again at midnight. This kept on until Leesil lost count of the days and nights. And even so, by Ghassan's reckoning of the new emperor's reports, they hadn't gone far enough east to scout for anything.

Along the seemingly endless slog, Leesil often wondered about Chap, his oldest friend, as well as Wayfarer and Osha among the elves. It still seemed madness that they'd split everyone up this way.

Leesil hauled up the last filled waterskin. While he rewrapped the braided rope around his waist, Ghassan tied shut the last skin and checked the others. There was nothing left to do but take up two each and sneak away for the long trek back to camp.

Leesil peered all around in the night. It appeared no one had seen or heard them . . . again.

Ghassan started off, taking a few steps and looking back, but Leesil lingered looking—and listening—all ways in the dark.

"Well?"

The domin's sharp whisper shook him into action, and he stepped off under the straining weight of two full waterskins. This was the ninth well they'd raided without being spotted or caught, and yet they weren't even as far east as they needed to be.

Leesil began wondering how long this much luck would last.

Chane jogged beside the rushing sled with Chap out ahead and Igaluk running behind with the dog team's reins. In this way, the only weight the dogs pulled was that of the supplies, equipment, and empty chests loaded on the sled.

The ground was frozen hard with enough crust and snow in most places for the sled. Winter up here came early, and the air was frigid.

Chane wore multiple layers beneath his cloak and hood along with gloves and a heavy, furred coat. Though he did not feel the cold, he was still susceptible to it. Without a beating heart, there was a greater risk of freezing than for a living man. Once, on a journey into the eastern continent's Pock Peaks, he had been careless.

One of his hands had begun to freeze solid.

He never forgot that night and remained vigilant. Four nights had passed, and halfway into the fifth, each night seemed colder than the last.

A few times, Chap had changed course out ahead and altered their path. Each time, Chane instructed Igaluk to follow. If this seemed bizarre to the guide, he said nothing and had so far lived up to his bargain without unnecessary questions. But the days held even greater concerns for Chane.

He ordered Igaluk not to enter his tent, citing a need for privacy. Chap had always been on watch just inside the tent's entrance, but this gave Chane no ease—quite the opposite.

Shade filled his thoughts in the moments before he could hold off dormancy no longer. The two of them had become trusted allies, even when separated from Wynn. And now, instead of her, he had an enemy who had hunted him more than once, lying within his tent and watching over him as he fell dormant and helpless each day.

When Chane rose again, the nights were always the same.

Chap was still watching, as if never having gone to sleep, and Chane's thoughts turned to Wynn. He imagined her in the desert with the others—with Magiere—hunting for unknown undead. He shared that fear with no one here, and something more now plagued him in this fifth night.

He was hungry . . . again.

Chane had promised Wynn that, so long as he wished to remain in her company, he would never again feed on humans. Since then, he had fed on only animals, usually livestock. Then another change came, but he had not told her of this one.

In their search for the orb of Spirit, they had traveled to the keep of an isolated duchy without knowing what they would find. In a single night, they learned of an orb hidden in the keep's lower levels; the orb was being guarded and used by a wraith who was an old threat to Wynn.

The wraith, called Sau'ilahk, used that orb to transmogrify a young duke's body.

After a thousand years as an undead spirit like no other, Sau'ilahk regained flesh.

But only for one night.

Chane's only companion in the final hunt had been Shade. When they caught Sau'ilahk in the guise of the duke's flesh, the wraith struck down Shade, and Chane thought her dead. He lost control, pinned the man, bit through his neck, and bled him to death. He fed from a body possessed by a thousand-year-old spirit who had served the Ancient Enemy.

Since that night, he had felt only a twinge of hunger a few times.

Those quickly passed, and he had feared and then hoped this change might last. While on the sea voyage north, he had felt that twinge twice again. Perhaps it had lasted a little longer than before, but now . . .

It would not stop, and it was more than a twinge.

There was no livestock out here; there were only the dogs needed to retrieve the orbs.

Running beside the sled on this fifth night, he was too preoccupied, and Chap's sudden bark startled him. He did not see Chap halt out ahead until Igaluk pulled his team to a stop with a harsh exclamation.

Chane ignored the guide's barked demand and ran onward, dropping to one knee near Chap.

"Why have you stopped us?" he whispered. "Are we . . . there . . . here?"

Chap huffed twice for "no."

Chane was lost for an instant, and as he was about to go for the talking hide, he understood.

"Somewhere nearby," he whispered.

Chap huffed once and looked toward the sled.

Chane immediately got up and trotted back. He began digging out a pick and shovel they had procured in White Hut.

"What are you doing?" Igaluk asked, wrapping the reins on the sled's handle as he stepped closer.

"You will wait here," Chane ordered.

Before the guide could respond, Chane slipped the shovel's handle through the end handles of two empty chests. He left the third chest in the sled and grabbed the shovel in the middle to lift both chests. Then he dug out the talking hide, stowed it under his coat, and took up the pickax as Igaluk stepped even closer.

"Why?" the guide demanded. "Where are you going?"

Chane ignored the questions. "I will be gone for a while, perhaps most of the night, but I will return. That is all you need to know. And you have our . . . my belongings as security for my return."

Without waiting for more arguments, Chane turned and headed for where Chap stood waiting.

"Go on," he ordered.

Chap started off, and Chane followed, focusing on nothing but Chap. He paid some attention to the night landscape around him, mostly as a way to ignore the hunger. A long while passed before Chap slowed to a halt, as did Chane. When Chap still lingered, slowly looking about in the dark, Chane set down the chests strung on the shovel's handle. And still Chap hesitated.

"Are you lost?"

Chap snarled in answer for Chane's question. No—and yes—would have been the truth. He had purposefully taken a different path from when he had first hidden the orbs. It was not a matter of the guide seeing the hiding place that would never be used again. It was the orbs themselves that he wanted no one else to see . . . and perhaps a secret more personal.

Now that he had a moment to get his bearings, he knew where to go for his first stop, and he lunged off across the snow-crusted ground. Sometime later, he slowed to a trot, for he could *feel* what he sought. Then he realized that he heard only his own steps and slowed to look back.

Chane had come to nearly a complete stop and set both chests on the ground. In the dark, it was hard for Chap to be certain, but it appeared Chane stared somewhere ahead as one of his hands worked at the other. Chap glanced back ahead as well.

Something gray in the night rose high out of the snow: a dome of granite with one side sheared off. And then Chap felt his hackles rise out of control. He heard something drop behind him, but before he could turn, rage swallowed him, followed by the urge to hunt.

"They are here."

It was all Chap could do to suppress a howl as he swung around at that rasping voice. He fixed on Chane, whose hands were bare, and all Chap wanted was to pull that *thing* down and tear it . . . him . . . apart.

Chane quickly slid the brass "ring of nothing" back on his finger, but Chap still stood with teeth bared, eyes narrowed, hackles stiffened, and ears flattened. A peeling hiss like a cat's warning escaped Chap's clenched teeth with every breath steaming in the night air.

"My apologies," Chane said quickly. "I needed to know . . . if I could feel them, like the others."

That was half of the truth; what he needed was to kill the hunger.

It faded as before in the close proximity to an orb, more so now that there were two. And even more in the instant he removed his ring. He had needed to have that sharper flood of relief. A thought occurred to him. Perhaps the reason he had not felt hunger for so long had been less about feeding upon the duke's body than about traveling in the presence of the orb of Spirit when he accompanied Wynn south.

On this journey north, he and Chap had been sailing without an orb, and his hunger had slowly returned. Now that he was near an orb again, the hunger was gone.

Chap watched him expectantly.

Chane hesitated but then turned his gaze from Chap and crouched to pick up the ax and the empty chests strung on the shovel's handle. Even as he rose—slowly—he did not look at Chap until he was ready to move on.

With a last grating hiss, Chap turned onward toward the huge half dome of granite.

Chane followed at a suitable distance in regained ease and clarity.

When Chap stopped before the sheered side of the granite dome, he turned and eyed Chane. Then he clawed at the crusted snow.

Chane hesitated again. This was Chap's prearranged signal for a need of the talking hide when they were alone. Here and now did it mean something else? Was he to start digging on that spot?

With a low growl, Chap took two steps and clawed again on a different spot.

Chane set down his tools, pulled out, and unrolled the hide on the ground. Chap began pawing the letters and words.

You dig. I return soon.

Chane looked up from the hide. "Where are you going?"

Chap turned away and ran off around the granite.

Chane almost called out, not that he could have shouted with his maimed voice. He still quick-stepped back the way he had come to see Chap vanish into the sparse trees, and he stood there even longer in hesitation.

Sooner or later, Chap would return. He would certainly not wish to leave the guide waiting too long into the night. Nor would he leave two orbs in the lone hands of a longtime enemy.

With a grating hiss of his own, Chane turned back to start with the pickax.

Chap raced through the trees, though in the dark everything looked much the same. It took longer than he wished to search out what he sought.

There was no need for concern about Chane and the orbs; the undead's obsession with Wynn and her wishes would keep the vampire obedient. Still, Chap was torn between turning back and going onward. He had to know—to find—one more certainty, now that he had returned so close to the place of his greatest sin.

He kept running in the freezing night.

To hide the orbs of Water and Fire, he had been forced to do something unspeakable. No one—not even the guide Leesil had hired for him at that time—could ever know the orbs' last resting place. If only it had been their last place.

Once, he had existed as part of the eternal Fay. When he was born into flesh, his kin had removed many of his memories of his existence among them. So many that only later had he suspected what they had done to him. Upon finally confronting them, he had attempted to fathom what fragments he was missing.

Among those had been the notion of a first sin—their sin . . . his sin.

So horrified by it, they had not wanted even him to remember it.

Upon creating Existence itself, a place to "be" other than in their timeless and placeless existence, they had learned they could "be" anything they perceived within this new existence. He had only suspected what that meant. His suspicion must have built itself upon something hidden deep inside from when he had been part of them that they could not extract.

Chap had led that first guide, named Nawyat, and his dog team well past a spot he had chosen along the way. Then he stopped as if for the night. This guide had been simple, kind, and even strangely charmed by a dog—a wolf—like no other.

It had been so easy to abuse simple Nawyat's trust.

Chap invaded and took control of the man's flesh while temporarily abandoning his own. He needed hands to dig frozen earth and to bury the orbs in secret. And when he had returned to camp . . . returned to his own body . . .

Nawyat lay within the tent, staring blankly up at nothing. He barely breathed.

Try as Chap had, he could not find one memory in the guide's mind. He lay there beside Nawyat, trying again and again to find something of the man inside that husk of flesh. With Magiere and Leesil waiting down the coast, he was forced to leave.

He had enacted the sin, the first sin, of the Fay: *domination*—utter and complete—in mind, body, and his own eternal spirit.

Chap halted and stood in the same clearing where he had stolen Nawyat's flesh. The place was bare, filled only with crushed snow. He could not even see sunken lines where a sled might have passed more than a season ago. Chap raced about, tearing up crust with his claws in search of any sign of that previous camp he had fled.

He couldn't find anything.

He had broken with his own kin, the Fay, upon learning how much had been torn from him at his birth into flesh. Piece by piece he put together that they had wanted him to be simple, controllable, and viable as a tool. Had he agreed to this before separating from them?

His only purpose had been to keep Magiere—through Leesil—hidden away from her own nature, origin, and purpose.

Now he could not hold in his shuddering whimpers as he looked wildly about the empty clearing. Had Nawyat ever come back to his own flesh, or had that flesh simply perished, still empty in this place? Could a mortal's mind and spirit ever return once its body was taken by an eternal Fay? Had someone found and rescued him, perhaps for him to only fade and die later? Had he been found only to be buried in hiding and have all of his possessions scavenged?

Chap would never know.

He stood there alone, quaking in the frigid darkness. Cold ate all the way into his spirit, but even that was not enough to numb the pain, to drive out the shame . . . and his sin.

The one thing he had done that no one else would ever know.

Raising the pickax, Chane slammed it down again, breaking deeper into the cold-hardened earth. He took up the shovel and began digging again. He tried to call on his inner strength, to let that chained beast—monster—inside him partially awaken.

It did not.

There was no hunger to call it in the close presence of two orbs he still had not found. There was only his own anger to keep him going, as the hole grew.

Where was Chap? Where had that cursed majay-hì, bane of his life, gone to now?

He neither slowed nor rested until his shovel struck something hard, and it twisted in his grip. He stopped and squinted down, but the pit was already knee-deep or more. Not enough moonlight for even his eyes reached its bottom through the tall trees.

Chane leaned the shovel into the crook of one elbow to tear off his gloves and dig into a coat pocket. He pulled out the cold-lamp crystal Wynn had given him and stroked it harshly three times down his coat. It lit up instantly, and he crouched to claw at the pit's bottom with his other hand.

His fingernails grated across something harder than frozen earth. Setting the crystal up on the ledge of the hole, he crouched again and began scraping away more earth with both hands and the shovel's head.

Finally, he saw the lightly dimpled but smooth gray-black of an orb. Before long, he had freed it and lifted it, only to nearly drop it.

There at the side of the pit stood Chap.

"Announce yourself next time," Chane rasped, expecting a response of spite in return.

Chap made not a sound, dropped his head, and stared into the pit. Then he looked to the orb in Chane's hands.

Its central ball was made from a dark material, char in color rather than black. The surface looked like chisel basalt though it felt slightly smoother than such stone.

Atop it, now that Chane had righted it, was the large head of a tapered spike that pierced through the globe's center. Spike and orb looked cut from the same piece of stone with no indication that they could be separated. But the spike's head had a groove running around its circumference that would fit the knobs of an orb key or handle, or what some thought looked like a dwarven neck adornment, called a thôrhk.

Chap huffed for attention and lowered his head to look down into the pit.

Chane did not need to ask. He set the orb on the pit's ledge and crouched to dig out the next one. When finished, he climbed out and pulled on his gloves and stood there with two orbs at his feet between himself and the majay-hì.

It took far less time to load the orbs into the chests, lock them shut, and gather the tools. All that remained was to haul the chests one by one a reasonable distance from the pit. So Chane did this with Chap guarding the second one that remained behind. Through all of this, Chap made not a sound nor showed any desire or need to communicate.

His absolute silence unnerved Chane. They had what they had come for, so should not Chap express some relief? Once both chests were together again, far from the open pit, the question remained as to which one of them would guard the orbs while the other went for the guide and sled.

Chane had his answer when Chap climbed up and settled to straddle both chests.

CHAPTER FIVE

Khalidah and the others had walked for half of the night, another night after many along the desert's fringe below the foothills. In the predawn darkness, he noticed Wynn dragging one foot after the other as if she could barely remain upright.

The sage had shown surprising stamina, but of the five of them, she was the least suited to this seemingly endless trek. More important, since their routine midnight rest, Khalidah had pondered how to preoccupy Magiere and the others so that he could attend to a private task. Wynn's exhaustion provided the remedy.

In one blink, the dark behind his eyelids filled with lines of spreading light. A double square formed in sigils, symbols, and signs. As his eyes opened, they fixed that pattern upon Wynn Hygeorht. All it took was a soft command at the edge of her consciousness.

Sleep.

She collapsed face forward onto the sand.

"Wynn!" Magiere cried.

She and Leesil ran for the sage, and both crouched as Leesil rolled Wynn over.

"She's breathing all right," he said with exhaled relief. "But she's done in."

He scooped her up in his arms and rose as if she weighed nothing. Magiere stood up beside him. The worry on her face was clouded by thinly veiled anger.

During the days, Magiere's hair and skin were still a baffling sight. They had been under a desert sun for so long, and yet her skin retained its pale color. Bloodred tints were always visible in her black hair as well.

She was most certainly marked by Beloved.

In the dark, these traits were not so noticeable.

"Find a place to set the tents," Brot'an called out, still managing both camels' leads. "We will make camp early."

Khalidah still found the hulking, scarred elf an enigma.

Though Brot'an claimed to simply be assisting in Magiere's search, Khalidah did not believe so and never would. Too often, he caught Brot'an eyeing Leesil. No, that one had another agenda as yet a mystery. But he had revealed something useful earlier on.

Khalidah had been unable to penetrate the master assassin's mind to any depth, just as with both majay-hì now conveniently elsewhere. There was one anomaly that also matched the same in those annoying beasts. Brot'an had been affected exactly like all the others by the ensorcellment embedded in Ghassan il'Sänke's sanctuary.

That could be very useful, eventually. He felt Ghassan begin to rage again, but he only smiled briefly.

"I will find us a place," Khalidah called.

He headed into the foothills. Quickly enough, he spotted one taller hill on the right that would block the sun once it rose . . . for a while.

"Here!" he called back.

Soon, the others were busy setting up tents and tending to Wynn—even the aging elf. As they worked, Khalidah studied all of their belongings and supplies as if searching for something.

"Our water is low," he said, and Leesil looked up for an instant. "If I can find a hidden well, I will return for assistance."

No one questioned this, as all were too concerned for the sage, and so he slipped away. But Khalidah only searched for a place out of their sight, in case someone followed him too soon. Alone again, he crouched and prepared for another "peek" at Chane and Chap's position.

The pebble he had given Chane was common knowledge to all involved. It had been meant to help them all find one another again. However, "finding" Chane was what the pebble could do for him. And he had his own vested interest in the success of the vampire and gray majay-hì.

Beyond gathering the orbs through these fortunate and unwitting companions, he had his own search to complete. His first goal was to learn where Beloved awakened. Until that was confirmed, along with the gathering of the orbs, he needed to foster Magiere's belief that all "anchors" were necessary to face their "Ancient Enemy." The others would follow her, willingly or not.

But he—not they, or even Magiere—would be the one to finish Beloved.

In ancient times, he had known the whereabouts of Beloved's hiding place to the far east. That had been a torturous thousand years ago, perhaps more, and the exact details had long since faded from memory. For now, he did not want Magiere finding such a place until all five orbs were present.

Khalidah blinked, and noted the much lighter sky. He had lingered too long and turned to his reason for slipping away. Closing his eyes, he blanked out all thoughts but one.

The pebble.

There was no sensation of crossing great distances; he instantly touched it with his emptied mind. Space and time meant nothing, and it was almost as if he were *there* . . .

Everything suddenly appeared darker than where he had settled in the foothills.

He was standing nearby but unseen next to Chane, though Chane was running.

A sled drawn by dogs raced through the near dark and tall trees and over snow-crusted earth. Chap was barely visible, running on the sled's far side.

A dark-skinned man bulked up with heavy furs ran behind the sled, gripping its reins and occasionally shouting to the dogs in a strange, awkward language.

At first, Khalidah thought they were in search of the two orbs hidden in the wastes.

"Chap!" Chane tried to shout in his rasping, broken voice. "Find a clearing . . . quickly."

The majay-hì bolted ahead into the trees, distracting Khalidah for an instant.

"We stop," Chane added. "Set camp fast!"

Khalidah glanced aside in time to see the sled driver nod. Then he noticed the faint lightening of the darkness. Dawn would be coming, though later than here where his body sat among the foothills.

Then he realized the sled was aimed westward rather than inland.

It was burdened with three chests, as expected, but as he looked closer, two had locks on their latches. The third was not locked.

Hope expanded within Khalidah, for two out of three to be locked implied only one thing.

Chane and Chap had already recovered the orbs of Water and Fire. They were returning to the coast—and in their haste, pushing the limit of Chane's safety against the dawn.

Amid relief—and hesitation—Khalidah opened his eyes to dawn in the foothills of the Sky-Cutter Range. He would check on the undead and the dog again in several days, but for now he sat there on the edge of ecstasy.

To kill a god was to become a god . . . at least in the eyes of one's inferiors.

Without warning, a hissing voice rose in his thoughts and eradicated his joy.

My servant.

It had been so long since he had heard it that he froze, unable to answer immediately.

Yes, my Beloved?

You guard the dhampir as instructed?

Khalidah weighed his answer carefully in keeping his thoughts shielded. He knew that his god believed him to be bringing the child of its making— Magiere—for some purpose only it knew. As of yet, though, Khalidah had not uncovered that purpose, and Beloved had not been forthcoming on precisely where to bring her.

Yes, she is in my company, Beloved. He wavered, uncertain, and then thought a sliver of truth was the best lie. *I have two of the anchors in my possession. Three are still being gathered. I thought to wait until all five were in my possession before asking where to bring all with the dhampir to you.*

Khalidah lingered, waiting for a response, and . . .

That is acceptable, servant.

Yes, Beloved, as is my joy in serving my god.

No sooner had those carefully contrite words passed through his thoughts than he heard one final command.

See that you do not fail . . . again . . . as in Bäalâle.

Khalidah swallowed down spite with fear as silence filled his mind. He hated groveling to this betrayer but comforted himself in knowing he would have his revenge. Briefly touching the chain around his neck, he wondered about contacting Sau'ilahk for a location report, but he had already been gone for too long and stood up to return to the camp.

When he rounded the tall hill, a shadow fell across his path.

Khalidah looked upslope as Brot'an descended to face him. The elder elf studied him.

"You were gone so long, we grew concerned," Brot'an said.

Khalidah kept his expression passive. Leesil was the one who accompanied him on water raids, and he knew the half-blood was beginning to grow suspicious as to why they had not been spotted, let alone caught, even once. Of course, Khalidah had used his sorcery to hide them from anyone's awareness, and his own power exceeded that of his internal captive, Ghassan il'Sänke.

Might Leesil have mentioned his suspicions to Brot'an?

"I am safe, as you see," Khalidah said with a warm smile. "I saw no one else in my search."

"Did you find water?"

"I fear not. Is Wynn better?"

Brot'an did not answer at first. "She is awake and coherent."

Khalidah brushed past, eager to end this conversation. "Then let us return."

He led the way, but even more than before, he felt a need to know the assassin's true agenda here.

Several evenings later in White Hut, Chap sat alone outside the tent on the fringe of the settlement. Inside, Chane sat alone with all three chests, two containing orbs. They had been unsuccessful in attaining passage south, for no new ship had arrived . . . until now.

Chap lingered in watching an arriving vessel until certain it had anchored and longboats were headed out to exchange cargo. Then he whirled, nosed through the tent's flap, and snatched up the talking hide in his teeth. Chane had his full attention before he even dropped the hide, clawed it open, and began pawing out the news.

Chane ducked out of the tent to take a look before Chap finished.

Chap followed and had barely stepped outside when Chane rushed back into the tent to begin their preparations for departure. It did not take long.

"I need to hire a few boys to help carry the chests," he said.

Though the thought of this delay tried Chap's patience, he knew it was necessary that they transport everything to the shore at once. Whether this ship granted them passage or not, they had to be ready and waiting.

Soon enough, Chane returned with three strong-looking boys. Chane carried the chest with the orb of Water. One of the boys carried the empty chest, and the other worked together to half carry, half drag the chest with the orb of Fire—as it was heavy and their going was slow. Chane never let them out of his sight, but in the end, he set his orb on the shore for Chap to guard and jogged back to carry the orb of Fire for the final stretch.

Once on shore, all three boys ran as soon as they were paid.

Chane then spoke briefly to a sailor in a longboat, and when that boat was emptied, he climbed in and rode back over the waves toward the ship to see if he might arrange for passage.

Chap remained behind to guard the orbs, and while waiting alone on the beach, he had too much time to think as he sat between the two locked chests. He had not realized how much the sight of them being unearthed would haunt him . . . as if the memory of Nawyat were a ghost he would never escape.

He almost wished he could open one of those locked chests. While in the simple guide's body, in handling the orbs, he had to remove the man's glove. He had touched an orb for the first time with his own . . . with Nawyat's flesh.

There was a presence trapped inside each one—a Fay, singular, like himself. And still he had not stopped. He buried alive two of his kin in a frozen grave. At the time, he had told himself that all he had done had been for the good of the world. And now?

Now he had taken company with a Noble Dead, gone into the northern wastes, and unearthed the same orbs. And again, he believed this was necessary.

He could not call it right or good—only necessary.

How many more great but lesser sins would he bear next to Nawyat?

Closing his eyes, he pictured Magiere, Leesil, and Wynn, who trusted in him, and yet he no longer truly trusted himself. He did only what he hoped was right in the end even though many things he had done felt wrong.

Questions built like whispers in the depths below his thoughts.

There was only one—and the many—who had answers: his kin, the Fay. Part of them—like himself—had somehow been trapped inside those orbs. If he touched one again, could he find answers?

To do so he would need to have Chane unlock the chests, and Chane would want to know why. Chap could never tell any undead what was hidden inside the orbs.

A rhythmic splash shook him to awareness, and he looked out over the water. The longboat was returning to shore, and quickly enough, Chane leaped out to rush up the frozen beach.

"The ship sails south at dawn," he rasped. "Let these sailors load the orbs. We need to board now."

The longboat's prow ground to a halt on the beach, and two sailors hopped out to approach.

With some reluctance, Chap huffed once at Chane in agreement. He did not like the idea of letting the sailors handle the orbs, but even if Chane loaded all the chests onto the longboat himself, it would still take several men to get them onto the ship.

Chane lifted one chest himself. A young Numan sailor gripped the handles of another one and attempted to heft it up. Chap had worried about this. Although the orbs were about the size of a helm, they were unnaturally dense and heavy.

"What have you got in here?" the sailor asked, trying a second time with more effort.

Chane glared at the man without answering. The sailor said nothing more and managed to lift the chest with both arms while his companion carried the third, empty chest.

Moments later, they were on the water, and then it was not long before they boarded the ship . . . with a darkened, bloodstained deck and huge hooks on chains coiled along its side.

"Whaling vessel," Chane said in a half whisper.

They were shown to a cabin below and provided with help to get all their belongings stowed safely inside. Upon entering the cabin, Chap could not help wrinkling his nose. The entire place stank and felt too closed in. However, Chane's normally stoic expression vanished, replaced by some mild relief.

Chap looked the cabin over. Without a small, wide-based lantern set upon the floor, the place would have been dark, for there was no porthole.

Still, Chap understood. Chane must have dreaded those days lying dormant with nothing between himself and the sun but the tent. Chap pushed such thoughts away, for after all, the vampire had died years ago and now existed in an unnatural state. Such *things* deserved no understanding or consideration.

They passed the night in silence.

When the sun rose, Chap managed to lever the door's handle with his teeth while Chane lay dormant, and he slipped out into the passage, pushing the door closed behind him. That he had to guard the nature of Chane from discovery did not mean he had to sleep anymore in the monster's presence. He felt the ship move and headed up on deck for a quick look.

When he climbed the steep steps and looked out across the deck, a few sailors paused to look over. They gave him no further notice and went back to their duties, and he walked over to the starboard railing. Rearing up with forepaws on the rail, he looked out over the sea. They were not far enough north to have to deal with breaking through frozen water, but large flats and chunks of ice were visible.

Now that he was alone again, Chap's thoughts turned to their next destination: Dhredze Seatt.

He had never been to this dwarven city before, and Chane had. Not only had Chane spent time in Dhredze Seatt, he apparently had connections to several religious figures living in a local temple. Even more unthinkable, he was . . . connected to one of the stonewalkers, a guardian of the honored dead.

How any of this had come about was still baffling, but the end result was that Chane would be leading the way through the seatt, and Chap was going to have to trust him to deal with the stonewalkers in order to retrieve the orb of Earth. Trusting—and depending—on Chane in any capacity went against every instinct inside him.

And yet, there was no choice.

Dropping his paws from the rail, he heard a crack as the ship's prow broke through an ice floe.

Wynn walked as straight and rigid as everyone else into dusk. Today, they had started walking in the late afternoon once the sun dipped low. She was still embarrassed by having fallen unconscious a few nights ago. Maybe the others watched her or not; either way, she wasn't going to let that happen again.

Leesil had joked that it was dumb luck that no one else had gone for a "sand dive" on the trek. Wynn didn't laugh and only flushed.

Without Shade or Chane, she had no one with whom to betray a hint of doubt or weakness. Why was that? It hadn't always been so with Magiere and Leesil, but it was now. So she pretended her collapse never happened, wouldn't speak of it, and pressed onward.

And why hadn't she awakened when—according to the others—she'd hit the ground face-first?

That wasn't right, and it was suspicious.

Tonight, she brought up the rear and watched her companions ahead. She couldn't help thinking that the five of them were a bizarre quintet.

Brot'an nearly always led the two camels, and walking behind those was not pleasant. By nature, camels were often bad-tempered, though they obeyed the master anmaglâhk. Ghassan walked beside the animals in comfortably long but slow strides. From what Wynn knew, he had spent part of his life in the desert. Magiere and Leesil were six or seven paces ahead of Wynn and off to the other side. But they were always close together, which made Wynn even more uncomfortable.

At times, she had reconsidered the sleeping arrangements.

With only two tents, she shared one with Magiere and Leesil, while Ghassan and Brot'an took the other. This had simply . . . *happened*. By now Wynn couldn't help worrying about Leesil and Magiere's lack of privacy.

Eight mornings past, as they began to set camp before another burning noon, she'd mentioned that they might prefer to sleep by themselves. This implied she would rest in the other tent.

Magiere scowled. "You . . . in a tent with the domin and Brot'an? I don't think so!"

While Wynn appreciated her friend's protective nature, she still couldn't help feeling like an interloper. She never thought she would miss another night in that overcrowded sanctuary, but at least there she had slept on the floor with only Shade watching her.

And she missed Chane.

Now trudging after the others, Wynn wondered if they would find anything to support the reports Ghassan had received from the new emperor. What if they found nothing, no matter how far they went? Had it been a mistake for Chap and Chane to go after the other three orbs? Were they risking something worse by bringing all five together . . . perhaps for nothing?

When the choice had been made, she'd been certain; now her doubts continued to grow.

Brot'an's sudden halt caught her off guard. She wasn't the only one to take more steps before stopping.

"What is it?" Magiere asked, circling in.

Ghassan had frozen as well, while Leesil glanced back and held out a hand to Wynn.

"Come on," he said.

At another time, she might have been annoyed at his "older brother" attitude. Now she didn't mind and quick-stepped forward to take his hand. Together they gathered with the others, but Brot'an still gazed ahead. Then he pointed.

"There—ground level at the base of that hill."

Wynn squinted. Encroaching dusk often made anything at a distance difficult to see. As her eyes adjusted, she saw what appeared to be a set of legs, half covered, as if the individual they belonged to had burrowed into the sand.

Leesil released Wynn's hand and pulled at a cord around his neck, drawing an amulet from inside his shirt. It had once been Magiere's, gifted to him.

Wynn stared at the rough crystal that would glow in the close presence of an undead. It was still dull and lightless.

"Magiere?" Leesil asked.

She shook her head. "I don't sense anything."

"Neither do I," Ghassan added.

Wynn wasn't certain exactly what he might sense. "So, we are alone?" she asked.

No one responded, and she decided to take action, for they needed more light. She drew the cold-lamp crystal from her pocket, rubbed it between her palms, and a soft light grew within it.

"Stay here," Magiere ordered, pulling her falchion from its sheath.

"No," Wynn answered.

Ghassan ignored them both and stepped onward, followed by Brot'an and the camels. Leesil loosened a tie on a winged blade strapped to his thigh but didn't pull it out. Once again, Wynn brought up the rear as they approached.

Ghassan, in the lead, stopped. Everyone else slowed in coming up next to him. And they were close enough, the crystal's light . . .

Wynn put her other hand over her mouth.

The legs weren't attached to anything.

The sand was dark around their ragged stumps, as if those legs that been torn off rather than cut with a weapon or even bitten through by some unimaginably large predator.

Leesil rushed ahead and around the hill's nearer side.

"Wynn, you stay there!" he called before vanishing from sight.

Over the recent years, Wynn had seen more bodies than she could count. Something about this sight struck her cold, and she didn't move. Then Brot'an tossed the camels' leads to the domin and headed off after Leesil. At that, Magiere went as well. Ghassan remained with Wynn, and her mind flashed back to waking up after her collapse.

She was not going to be treated differently on this journey. Before Ghassan could stop her, she trotted off after the others, and he made no protest. When she glanced back, he had abandoned the camels to follow her . . . around the hillside.

She stopped.

Magiere, Leesil, and Brot'an were crouched at different places in an area about thirty paces wide between the first hill and a higher one farther toward the range. Brot'an showed no emotion, as usual. Leesil looked stricken and Magiere wary.

Wynn counted six arms and three torsos scattered about among what looked like pieces of goats.

Leesil rose slowly, drawing both winged punching blades, and upon spotting Wynn . . .

"I told you to wait!"

She approached slowly, though her eyes were pulled to the sight of one torso with the head still attached. Bile rose into her mouth.

"They're dried . . . and weathered," she said quietly. "They have been here at least a day, maybe several."

Leesil, still angry, looked down at the half body. "Yes."

Wynn tried to feel nothing as she studied the scant blood-soaked sand. "There isn't enough blood. This body . . . part of it . . . must have been moved from elsewhere."

"The same with the other pieces," Brot'an said flatly, still crouched off to the right over another torn leg.

Magiere paced an arc around Wynn as she took in the whole scene, and Ghassan stepped forward to stand over a torso. No one spoke for a moment, and Magiere's face was unreadable . . . disturbing for all lack of emotion. But at least she had not given in to her other half.

Everything had possibly changed now, if any of this had been done by the undead. And yet no vampire or wraith would have fed this way.

But there was *something* out here.

"We must bury them before they attract scavengers or predators," Ghassan said.

Wynn looked to him, but he only studied the hills toward the range's peaks. He was right, though she couldn't bring herself to respond.

"Three people alone is odd," he added. "Few live out here, only nomads, and they travel in large groups, as always."

Again, Wynn had no response.

"It appears we have come far enough," Brot'an said, rising. "We should set up a longer-term camp and begin scouting."

Yes, that was why they had come so far—to scout for a migration or gathering of the Enemy's servants. But why here?

She looked around and saw nothing. Perhaps there was something, some hidden place, deeper into the foothills.

"Two of us should always remain at the camp," she said, "to guard . . ."

She didn't want to say "the orbs." Not here, so close to . . . whatever.

"Three can scout," she added, "while two guard our possessions, and we should set the camp someplace where we can see anything that is coming."

Such calm planning while standing among dismembered remains struck her as surreal. Yet, this was what their existence had become.

"Out of the taller hills but still hidden," Magiere said.

Wynn looked up and nodded. When Magiere turned to walk out of this place, Wynn followed, though the others lingered behind. When both women rounded the first hill, and the camels were in sight, Magiere slowed, shifting closer to whisper.

"One of us—you, me, or Leesil—must be among the two who always stay behind."

Wynn blinked, then nodded slowly, though she didn't look back to see if Brot'an or Ghassan had followed as yet.

CHAPTER SIX

Evening settled over the little port below Chemarré, "Sea-Side," the western settlement of Dhredze Seatt, home of the dwarven people across the bay from Calm Seatt, Malourné.

Chane descended the whaling vessel's ramp, carrying the chest for the orb of Water with Chap close behind him. Two sailors followed, one struggling with the chest for the orb of Fire and the other hauling the third empty chest and Chane's two packs. All four made their way down the dock to the waterfront, where the sailors relinquished their loads and returned to the ship.

With no business at the seatt, the whaling captain had stopped only for his two passengers. Of the three other ships in port, two were stout dwarven vessels with names painted in Dwarvish, while the third was a three-masted, Numan merchant vessel called the *Kestrel*.

The small port below the sheer mountainside had not changed since the last time Chane had seen it. Other than a few small warehouses, the buildings were squat, sparse, and deeply weathered, and there was only one inn. The shoreline beyond could never be called a beach; even in calm wind, small waves pounded and sprayed the jagged rocks.

At the sound of snuffling, Chane looked down.

Chap raised his head, his eyes peering up—and up—the cliffs. From down here, close to the base of the peninsula's peak, it was impossible to see much, especially at night.

"We will take a rolling lift up," Chane said. "Then you will see the outer . . . lesser part of Chemarré."

Glancing down at the three chests, he felt at a loss. There was still a long journey to their final destination. While some called Dhredze Seatt kingdom-like or the "city" of the dwarves, each of its settlements with its many under-levels could easily rival any small to medium city throughout the Numan lands. Dhredze Seatt was the last known living place of the Rughìr'thai'âch or Rughìr, the "Earth-born" or the dwarves.

Chap stepped in, nosed one of the chests, and looked up as if to say, "How?"

Chane's thoughts raced for how to carry all three chests where they were going . . . to the mountain's far side in Cheku'ûn, or "Sea-Side." Even that would not be the last stop, and hiring bearers for every leg of the journey was not wise. Eventually someone would be curious about a man with this much luggage traveling alone with a dog.

Dropping to one knee, he faced Chap. "We have to hide the orbs here."

At first, Chap did not react, and then he snarled and huffed twice for "no."

Chane bit back a sharp retort and tried to explain himself. "After the lift, we must take a tram through the mountain, arriving in a station deep behind the largest market cavern in the whole seatt. Then we make our way outside and up to the temple of Bedzâ'kenge—'Feather-Tongue'—in the Bay-Side settlement. That is where we seek Mallet, head shirvêsh of the temple, who knows me and is my contact with Ore-Locks in the underworld of stone-walkers."

Chap had ceased snarling but still glowered at him.

"I cannot carry all of this myself, nor do I think we should hire help. The dwarves are a curious people. But there is a safe place here near the port. Only stonewalkers know of it besides Wynn and me . . . and she would agree with me."

Chap's left jowl curled at that last comment.

"We can move more quickly this way," Chane rushed on, "and have fewer concerns. When we again take to the sea, sailing south to Soráno, the chests will be close at hand aboard a ship, but we must hide them for now."

Chap was silent and still for a long moment, then turned his head and tilted his nose toward Chane's first pack. Chane retrieved the talking hide and rolled it out, and Chap began pawing it.

Where?

"I will show you. It is where Wynn, Shade, and I first breached the underworld." At another rumble from Chap, he added, "It is not easy to find for those who do not know it exists. I swear the orbs will be safe."

When Chap did not argue or respond, Chane slung both packs over his shoulders. He stacked the chests with the orbs of Fire and Water and attempted to heft them both. At first he struggled to even stand.

Together, they were almost too heavy even for him. Once standing, he could barely see over the top chest but thought he could at least get far enough down shore to be out of sight of the port.

"Leave the empty chest here. It will be easy enough to carry with us."

Without waiting for agreement, Chane made his way through the port to the shoreline.

Salt water crashing on the rocks soon enough sprayed his boots and then his pants as he carefully worked his way north, blindly but carefully traversing the uneven rocks underfoot. He did not—could not—look back to see how Chap fared. Instead, he looked for the familiar landmark: a long rock backbone hiding an inlet below the mountain's sheer side.

Finally, he spotted it.

Setting down the chests, he slipped and dropped hard on one knee. After a moment to clench away the pain, he pivoted to see a not quite thoroughly soaked majay-hì.

"Wait here with the orbs," he said.

At best, Chap might have sighed, though the surf's noise drowned this out.

Chane needed to make certain the tunnel was still there. For all he knew, the stonewalkers might have sealed it after it had been breached by an undead, a precocious sage, and a black majay-hì. After climbing up the rock backbone and down its other side, he reached into his pocket for the cold-lamp crystal Wynn had given him. When he rubbed it against his cloak, the friction ignited its soft glow, illuminating the inlet's overhang but not the dark space beyond it.

He worked his way along the cliff wall and under the overhang. Nothing he did now could be seen from the shore. Soon, he found the round opening at the back of the overhang, no more than a shadow in the rock until he stepped directly in front of it. He had to duck to step inside.

The curved floor inside was smoother than the inlet's bottom, for the tunnel was fully round like a great stone pipe piercing the mountain's base. It had been excavated long ago, and algae and remains of other dried growths spread halfway up its curved sides.

He could stand upright, though his head brushed the tunnel's top, and the path widened farther in until he could touch either side with outstretched hands. The gradual incline increased imperceptibly, until he no longer walked in shallow water, and then he saw a grate—or rather a gate.

Vertical bars filled the tunnel from top to bottom, their frame mounted in the circumference by massive rivets. The last time he came here, he had bent several bars to gain access; now those were straightened with no sign they had ever been otherwise. Regardless of safeguards restored, all that mattered was that the tunnel's mouth had not been sealed and the chests could be placed high enough to remain above the high tide.

Chane returned to the shore and found Chap still waiting . . . and still glowering.

"It is as I remembered, except for some repairs," Chane said. "We can store the orbs within the tunnel, out of sight, as no one comes here."

Though he sounded confident, something else troubled him. The tunnel had originally served as a passage to the locked chamber of a half-mad prince, both protected and imprisoned by the stonewalkers.

Now though, the stonewalkers had no reason to come out to the tunnel's mouth. Chane pushed these concerns from his thoughts.

"Wait a little longer, and I will show you," he said to Chap.

Holding the cold crystal in his teeth, he hefted the chest with the orb of Fire and returned to the tunnel's first gate. There he placed the chest and hurried back to Chap for the chest containing the orb of Water.

"Come," he said.

Chap followed, and by the time they reached the gate, the dog was fully soaked. He approached the bars, cocking his head in sniffing, and even bit on one, as if to test it. Then he peered between the bars up the tunnel.

As Chane set down the second chest, he found Chap watching him and rumbling softly—clearly not liking this arrangement.

"If you have thought of something better," Chane replied, "then say so."

He already knew the answer.

Chap huffed twice for "no."

"You could stay here and guard them yourself . . . while I go on alone."

Chap only growled.

Chane turned back to leave the tunnel. He had taken only three steps when he heard the matching click of Chap's clawed strides.

Chap followed Chane back down the rocky shore to the port. His instincts tried to pull him around to go back after the orbs, not that he could have without Chane. And he was not letting that undead go after the third without him.

It took little time to reach the port now that Chane was unburdened. The vampire stopped long enough to retrieve the third chest and then continued through the port to the far end. He turned a corner inland, and as Chap followed, Chane was already climbing a ramp up to a gate.

As Chap approached, a wild-haired dwarf in a knee-length, black-furred vest strutted out of a nearby booth. In truth, Chap had little experience with dwarves. Contrary to tales on the eastern continent, they were not diminutive. Though shorter than humans, they look almost twice as wide. This full, black-bearded one's head reached the middle of Chane's chest.

He appeared undaunted by the tall, pale human before him and grunted in Numanese, "How far?"

"To the top," Chane answered.

Confused, Chap looked upward, for he saw no other choices in the dark. He did not like facing the unknown in any dealings with Chane, who seemed to know exactly what he was doing.

The vampire set down the chest, pulled out a faded pouch, and opened it. He removed two large, thick rounds of iron with holes in the center. There might have been some form of engraving or stamp on them, but Chane dropped the pieces into the attendant's broad hand.

The attendant's bushy eyebrows lifted. He quickly stowed the coins in a pocket Chap hadn't seen in the thickly furred vest and then stepped rather lively to the "lift" gate and pulled it open. Chane picked up the empty chest again, balancing it on his left shoulder in order to keep his right hand free.

"Nonstop to the top, sir," the dwarf said with a quick bow of his head.

Chap's ears pricked. He did not see how bits of iron warranted such a change of demeanor, let alone bypassing any supposed stops on the way up.

"Thank you," Chane replied, stepping to the lift's gate, turning around, and waiting as he eyed Chap without emotion.

Chap's irritation got the better of him again. No, he would never admit openly that Chane was . . . useful. He stepped up under the gaze of the attendant and onto a thick wooden platform framed by huge wheels. And as soon as he was on the floor's thick timbers, he heard the gate shut . . .

"Brace yourself," Chane rasped as he grabbed hold of the rear railing with his free hand.

The lift lurched upward, and Chap quickly spread all fours. He did not wonder how the attendant had signaled whatever machinery above raised the lift. He wanted to snarl at Chane for not warning him better as the lift gained speed—and more speed—and crags and gashes of the mountain rushed by.

After that, all that Chap could do, besides brace himself, was try to swallow his stomach back down . . . again and again. He wanted to close his eyes but dared not as he needed to see what was happening around him. A loud racket rose louder and louder under the platform from the immense wheels on the lift's two sides.

He barely noticed any of the small settlements bypassed along the way. The vibrations alone threatened to empty his stomach and . . . and something else he had not lost control of since he was a puppy.

"Not far now," Chane rasped.

The last thing Chap wanted was assurances from that *thing*.

The lift finally approached the top and began to slow, but at the roll over the lip of the mountain shelf, the lift suddenly rocked.

Chap lost control.

When the tram finally stopped, Chane was staring at him. The undead cleared his throat uncomfortably while looking away and then hurried to open the front gate himself as a rotund attendant arrived.

Chap just stood there, shaking in sickness . . . and shame.

He shook off each back foot with every step as he left a puddle behind.

The rotund and somewhat grimy lift master snarled at him, "You filthy mongrel."

Chap hung his head and hunched his shoulders. He wobbled down the ramp, still trying to shake off his rear paws, and did not look back toward what the lift master would have to clean up.

Chane stood ahead on the immense landing of Chemarré, looking the other way toward a large opening into the mountain. All around them, the roads appeared to flow in steep runs between sharp turns. All ways were bordered by various buildings of stone built with thin-line fitted blocks or carved from the mountain's native rock.

Chap hesitantly looked around the landing and spotted the lift's crank house and a huge enclosed turnstile driven by mules. He did not see how the lift had achieved such speed, and he looked again to the enormous open arch in the mountainside.

Orange-yellow light glowed from within.

"We're at Chemarré's way station," Chane said, heading for the arch.

Feeling even more at a loss, Chap followed. The entryway was not as large as he had first thought, but it was still immense. Ahead was a vast tunnel with central stone columns so big that two, or even three, people could have hidden behind one. On the right was another opening to another space.

There were numerous people about, heading this way or that. Most were dwarves in various attire, some in armor and a few with huge dogs that sniffed in his direction. There were some humans among them, and most of these were dressed as prosperous merchants, vessel captains, or other traders a little more wild and rough looking.

Chane headed for the central tunnel and into that other side archway. As Chap followed, he stopped at what filled his sight.

Two tunnels, each the width of three roads, ran directly into the mountain. Triple sets of twined steel-lined ruts in the granite floor ran into each of these.

At the near ends of the ruts stood platforms of stout wood planks and timbers, like the docks of a harbor. One platform was crowded with dwarves and humans jostling to board and find seats in a string of open-sided cars. A half-empty string of the same stretched out beside the other platform.

"Trams," Chane said quietly, "to get through the whole mountain to the other two settlements."

Those trams of connected cars, constructed of solid wood painted in tawny and jade tones, rode on steel and iron undercarriages. Their wheels were shod with steel. Rows of benches faced ahead inside each car, separated by a narrow walkway down the center. Passengers were protected on the outside by waist-high rail walls. Each car was roofed, but only their fronts contained a full wall and a door, probably to break rushing winds once the tram gained speed.

The very thought made Chap grow queasy again.

"Apparently, majay-hì have difficulty with dwarven travel," Chane said. "Though not quite father like daughter."

This time, Chap did snarl.

A wide, bearded dwarf in a plain leather hauberk stepped to the nearer platform's edge and cupped his mouth with large, sinewy hands.

"*Maksag Chekiuní-da!*" he boomed, and then, in Numanese, "Leaving for Point-Side!"

After this, he trundled along the platform, shooing lingering passengers into the cars.

"Not ours," Chane commented.

No sooner had the last passenger settled than a cloud of steam billowed around the tram's lead car, making it impossible to see clearly. Chap barely made out its front, which seemed to end in a point.

The steam lit up with a bright glow from within. Its front point burned like one of the massive pylon crystals along the main tunnel. Whatever crystal rode on the tram engine's front had to be so much larger. And its light pulsed in a slow rhythm.

A sharp explosion of steam belched from the lead car's undercarriage, and the glow brightened to a steady, hot yellow.

The tram's whole chain of cars inched forward with a metallic scrape of wheels along the ruts. In moments, it picked up the speed of a trotting horse. As it bore into the tunnel, the sharp glow in the lead lit the way, and Chap heard its wheels' rhythm building steadily. Within a few breaths, it vanished from sight.

Chane stood watching after it as well.

"Crystal power . . . some kind of arcane engine," he whispered, and then pointed to the other platform. "That will be ours."

Chane stepped ahead, but Chap lingered. This was going to be worse than the lift up the mountainside. Reluctantly, he followed.

Another stationmaster, a female, walked the platform and herded passengers into the cars. The Cheku'ûn, "Bay-Side," tram filled quickly.

"Here," Chane said, entering a car and dropping onto the nearest empty bench.

Chap crept in, resisting the urge to growl at other passengers. The female dwarf—still directing people—glanced at him.

"How long to Cheku'ûn?" Chane asked her.

"No stops on this run," she answered in a deep voice, "so by Night-Summer's end."

She went off to the next car in the line, and Chap was left wondering what that time frame meant. He glanced up at Chane.

"The trip will take about a quarter night," Chane explained.

Chap grew even sicker. He had hoped to finish their task here and be gone with the third orb by dawn. That was not going to happen, and he sank onto the tram's floor as Chane piled his packs and the chest on the empty side of his bench.

The car lurched, and Chap could not hold back a whimper.

Chane would never admit it, but by the journey's end, he felt sorry for Chap. As the tram pulled into Cheku'ûn station, Chap was still flattened upon the floor with drool dripping from his jowls. Shade had also grown ill to the point of vomiting during her first tram ride.

However, she had never urinated all over a lift.

"It will pass soon," Chane said shortly, slinging both his packs and then balancing the chest again. "Your daughter suffered worse on these vehicles, but she never left Wynn's side."

Chap looked up in a mix of wariness and puzzlement.

Chane could not suppress another flash of pity for the majay-hì, but without further comment, he rose and followed other passengers off the tram into another way-station cavern. When he glanced back, Chap was trying to wobble around the thick legs of dwarves hurriedly disembarking. Chane waited.

Once Chap stumbled down the platform's ramp, Chane led the way through an arch in the right stone wall, down several crowded passages, and out into the almost impossibly enormous market cavern of the Cheku'ûn. When he paused to check on his companion, Chap's ears flattened as he stared all around the place.

A thinned forest of sculpted columns the size of small keep towers rose to the high domed roof of this smoothly chiseled cavern. Even at night, the chaos of vendors, hawkers, peddlers, and travelers echoed as the dome caught all noise and rained it down on everyone.

All forms of goods were being carted to and from and traded at stalls and makeshift tents. Dwarves and humans of varied shapes and sizes, and perhaps a Lhoin'na quickly lost in the crowd, bartered for everything from meat pies and tea to small casks of ale and sacks of honey-coated nuts.

In the avenues between columns, large glowing crystals steamed atop stone pylons. Smoke from portable braziers and steam escaping around crystals filled the great cavern with a hazy orange-yellow glow. Directly across the vast place was another opening so tall one could see it clearly over the crowd.

"There," Chane said, lifting his chin. "Let us leave this chaos."

He stepped off to break through the crowd with an occasional glance back to see that Chap followed. He towered over nearly everyone, even the human merchants and travelers, and more than a few people glanced their way as they passed. Chane ignored them and strode straight for the archway. Once outside in the cool night air, he heard Chap take a deep breath and release it.

Here, they had a full view of the stone city built on a mountainside. The main road snaked tightly upward between buildings of stone and scant timber. Moonlight barely revealed slate, tile, stone, and a few shakes or plank roofs. Only short and steep side streets aimed directly upward, and most were built of wide stone steps and multiple landings. All of it was behemoth-like—rather like the dwarves themselves.

Dwellings and inns, smithies and tanneries, and other shops spread out, around and above them in a muddled maze.

"It can be daunting at first," Chane said. "I remember my first time."

As soon as the words escaped his mouth, he would have flushed with embarrassment if he had had warm, pumping blood to do so.

Why should he care if the majay-hì was daunted?

Chane strode up the street's gradual slant, deeper and higher into Bay-Side and to one of the few places where he was known and welcomed. That in itself was strange for him.

He was rarely welcomed anywhere but the temple of Bedzâ'kenge—"Feather-Tongue."

Dwarves practiced a unique form of ancestor worship. They revered those of their own who attained notable status in life, akin to a human hero or saint or rather both. Any who became known for virtuous accomplishments, by feat and/or service to the people, might one day become a thänæ—one of the honored. Though similar to human knighthood or noble entitlement, it was not a position of rulership or authority. After death, a thänæ who had achieved renown among the people through continued retelling of their exploits over decades or centuries, might one day be elevated to Bäynæ—one of the dwarven Eternals.

These were dwarves' spiritual immortals, the honored ancestors of their people as a whole.

Feather-Tongue, their paragon of orators and historians, was the patron of wisdom and heritage through story, song, and poem. From what Chane understood, for as long as any history remembered, the dwarves kept to oral tradition rather than the literary ways of humankind. In that, at least he saw Feather-Tongue as the paragon of paragons.

Chane paused briefly at an intersection. Looking up a stone staircase, he spotted a tan banner hanging above a wide oak door. The banner depicted a map, and the shop was a landmark he remembered.

"Nearly there," he said.

They climbed past the mapmaker's shop and several others, all the way to the main street's next switchback. At the next intersecting stairway, Chane turned upward again but stopped halfway to let Chap catch his breath on a landing with a sculpted miniature fir tree in a large black marble urn. He pressed on to the next switchback of the main street.

Across the way was a familiar structure emerging from the mountainside.

Its white marble double doors were set back beneath a high overhang supported by columns carved like living trees. He peered up the steps rising to the temple, where its frontage emerged from the mountainside and twin granite columns carved like large tree trunks framed the landing's front end. Even so, the structure hardly seemed large enough to house its shirvêsh, but he knew this to be an illusion.

A heavy oblong arc of polished brass hung between the front columns like a gateway. Suspended from the roof's front by intricate harnesses of leather, its open ends dangled a shin's length above the landing's floor. Its metal was formed from a hollowed tube and not a solid bar.

Chane stepped up to it, grasped a short brass rod from a bracket on the left column, and struck it against the great brass arc. Though he knew what to expect, his whole body clenched as a baritone clang assaulted his ears. He rang twice more as Chap flinched beside him. As the third tone faded, one of the doors began to open.

A solid, white-haired dwarf leaned out and peered at the duo upon the landing, his face rather flat and wrinkled like a half-dried white grape. Wavy hair flowed down and broke over his wide shoulders, becoming one with his thick beard in front, though no mustache sprouted below his broad nose. He was dressed in brown breeches and typical heavy dwarven boots, and his muslin shirt was overlaid with a hip-long felt vestment of fiery burnt-orange.

Recognition dawned in the old one's widening eyes. "Chane Andraso?"

Chane bowed his head slightly. "Forgive me, Shirvêsh Mallet. I know it is late, but may we enter?"

"We?" Mallet muttered, glancing at Chap before ushering them both inside. "Where are Journeyor Hygeorht and her charcoal companion?"

Chane did not know how to answer; the truth would take too long if he dared speak of it at all.

"She is well but overly occupied," he answered, hoping it was true as he entered with Chap. "She has sent me here in her place for something important."

Glancing down, he found Chap studying the entryway's mosaic floor. Colored thumbnail tiles created the image of a stout, dark-haired, and bearded dwarf bearing a tall, char-gray or black staff. He wore a burnt-orange vestment like the elder shirvêsh and appeared to step straight out of the floor from the open road leading away from a hazy violet mountain range. This was Feather-Tongue.

When Chane looked up, he found Shirvêsh Mallet studying him.

"And why did the young miss send you?" the dwarf asked.

Time was short, and Chane took the straightforward approach. "I need to speak with Ore-Locks. Would you please send for him?"

From anyone else, this would have been a shocking request, but Ore-Locks himself had made this arrangement.

Shirvêsh Mallet blinked twice, frowned, and sighed. "Come to the meal hall. At this time, it is the most private place in the temple."

Chap grew anxious over lost time after Shirvêsh Mallet finally left them alone in the meal hall. It was nearing the mid of night, and Chap wasn't certain what to expect next. As Chane dropped his packs, Chap went over and pawed at the one containing the talking hide. Chane knelt to dig and roll it out. Chap began pawing words and letters, but his questions took a while even with the skipping of unnecessary words.

If stonewalkers in underworld, how long till O comes?

"A little while," Chane answered. "I do not know how contact is made, but Ore-Locks will hurry in, knowing I am waiting. He has several . . . ways to do so."

Chap pawed again.

Ways?

Chane shook his head. "It is easier to wait and see."

Growling, Chap was about to argue and changed his mind. Since he had learned to use memory-words to speak to Magiere, Leesil, and some others, the talking hide now felt slow and clumsy.

Chane rolled up the hide and put it away, and they waited in silence.

Chap had no way to gauge the creep of time. It seemed quite long before he heard heavy booted footsteps echoing in from the outer passage. He barely got up, watching the way in, when three dwarves entered.

The first was Shirvêsh Mallet.

The second was a dour stranger. Though his head would only reach Chane's shoulder, he was nearly twice as wide and three times Chane's bulk.

Wild, dark-streaked locks hung to his shoulders, framing the hard line of his mouth within steely bristles of a beard. Over his char-gray breeches and wool shirt, he wore a short-sleeved hauberk of black leather scales, each scale's tip sheathed in ornately engraved and polished steel. Two war daggers in like-adorned black sheaths were tucked slantwise in his thick belt.

Then the third dwarf stepped into plain sight.

Chap had briefly met Ore-Locks Iron-Braid in Calm Seatt before everyone had split up in search of the last two orbs. The stonewalker wore his long red hair tied with a leather thong into a tail hanging over his collar. Unlike most male dwarves, he was clean-shaven. Though he appeared much younger than the dark juggernaut, he too wore the black-scaled armor and two daggers of his caste.

"I will leave you now," Shirvêsh Mallet said politely. "I can see you have much to discuss." With that, he left.

Chane turned to the elder dwarf in visible surprise and perhaps some anger. "Master Cinder-Shard, I did not send for you."

"No," the dwarf answered. "And yet I am here."

Chap was instantly on guard. He'd expected some resistance from Ore-Locks about turning over the orb, but the presence of this other man was completely unexpected.

Chane tensed all over, and then Ore-Locks stepped around Master Cinder-Shard to approach.

"It is good to see you," he said, "though I know you would not have come nor called for me without a serious reason."

Chane's tension eased slightly. By shared trials and battles, the young stonewalker had become something close to a friend. And Chane did not have many friends.

"It is good to see you as well," he answered, "and I—"

"Enough niceties!" Cinder-Shard barked. "Why has a . . . Why have *you* returned here, and how does one of your kind hold influence with a head shirvêsh?"

His gaze flicked toward Chap, and his eyes widened a little.

Chane followed his gaze. Did Cinder-Shard recognize a majay-hì?

That stood to reason, considering the master stonewalker was friends with Chuillyon, the white-robed sage of the Lhoin'na . . . and a notorious liar.

Cinder-Shard's focus shifted to Ore-Locks. "I hope you had nothing to do with this."

Ore-Locks hesitated and then straightened. "Yes, I did."

Cinder-Shard's face tinged red.

Chane saw no way to be diplomatic. "I need the orb of Earth," he said bluntly. "And there is good reason."

At this, Cinder-Shard's reddish tinge went gray, and even Ore-Locks was silenced in wary shock.

Chane had not expected to deal with the master of the stonewalkers, and he felt somewhat blindsided. He had to regain control quickly and raised a hand to forestall outrage or arguments.

"I will not explain here," he said, and nodded to Chap. "This majay-hì and I traveled a great distance, and we fear minions of the Enemy could have followed. We need a place they cannot go . . . or hear . . . before anything more is said."

Expressing such concerns was risky, and it might simply cause Cinder-Shard to retreat beyond reach and order Ore-Locks to follow. The last time Chane had been here, he, Wynn, and Shade had been followed by the wraith, Sau'ilahk.

In hunting them and an orb, Sau'ilahk had infiltrated the underworld.

Although this was not Chane, Wynn, or Shade's fault, their own actions had led to the havoc and loss caused by the wraith. In the aftermath, further safeguards had been implemented below. The underworld of the dwarves' most honored dead was still the most secure place in the seatt. It had to be.

Cinder-Shard's expression was flat. He shifted his weight from his right foot to his left, and then his left shifted back a few inches and planted. His large right hand rose to settle around the hilt of a battle dagger.

"You . . . among the honored dead . . . again?" he said. "Your kind . . . with an anchor of creation?"

Chane almost reached for his own sword, anticipating an attack. And if possible, he chilled slightly at this particular opponent.

"Master," Ore-Locks said, turning quickly. "No matter what else he may be, he is no liar. And he was there to help in retrieving the orb."

Still, Cinder-Shard fixed only on Chane.

"And in the end, the orb is still *my* charge," Ore-Locks added.

At that, Cinder-Shard's gaze shifted to the youngest stonewalker.

"I know all of us, with you, are jointly responsible for the orb," Ore-Locks went on, "but I am its inheritor, so named by its all-eater guardians."

Chane remained watchful but remembered what had happened. In

Bäalâle Seatt, the forgotten resting place of this orb, there had been all-eaters—dragons.

They had guarded the orb through generations since the seatt's fall at the end the Great War. One of Ore-Locks's ancestors, and brother of Feather-Tongue now among the Bäynæ, had been the one to collapse the seatt with the aid of those dragons' ancestor. That act had blocked the Enemy's forces from using Bäalâle as a way to easily flood into the north.

The few who escaped the cataclysm, including Feather-Tongue, did not know this truth.

They knew only that one of their own—assumed a "fallen" stonewalker—had seemingly aided the Enemy.

Feather-Tongue's brother, Byûnduní, "Deep-Root," was forgotten. In his place, only the false legend of Thallûhearag, the "Lord of Slaughter," was remembered by the dwarves. And Deep-Root was now among the Lhärgnæ, or "Fallen Ones," who were the malevolent counterpart to the dwarves' Bäynæ.

Ore-Locks and his family were the descendants of both brothers.

Chane grew uncomfortable as well as fearful. Though the connection of Ore-Locks's family to Thallûhearag was known by very few, they had still lived for generations in a poor state devoid of honor among their people. The orb of Earth was perhaps the only, smallest evidence of the truth for one day to come . . . which Chane now needed to take away.

Ore-Locks spoke quietly. "Master, I vouch for Chane Andraso's word and honor. Please hear him out."

Cinder-Shard did not answer at first. His dark eyes lowered to rest for a moment on Chap. Then he spun, headed for the exit, and barked only one word.

"Follow!"

Chap felt swept along on a journey that he did not fully understand. Through Wynn, he did know some of the story of finding the orb of Earth. It appeared that the aftermath was more complicated. And it wasn't until after a short but harrowing lift ride ended with a swift walk through the peak's top settlement that his puzzlement became irritation.

Why were they going *up* in order to go down into some "underworld"?

The four of them finally entered an empty but immense open-air theater, and Cinder-Shard had not said a word along the way.

The elder stonewalker turned at the first side passage.

They made their way down corridors behind the theater's stage, turning at intersections, descending ramps and stairs, and twisting and winding so much that Chap worried he would never find his way out. They finally rounded a corner that aimed straight at a deep archway blocked by tall iron doors . . . without handles.

Chap saw no other opening along the corridor to where it ended in a left turn.

He peered around one side of Ore-Locks, studying the iron doors. He did not see even a keyhole or empty brackets for a bar. How would the stonewalkers open these?

Master Cinder-Shard barely paused and then walked through the stone wall beside the arch.

Chap hunched and retreated with a snarl. Chane did not react at all, but Chap was once again becoming fed up with surprises.

"Wait a moment," Chane said without even looking down.

Standing frozen and lost—and angry again—Chap heard grinding from somewhere. The iron doors split along their center seam, and they were thicker than any Chap had encountered. In sliding away into the walls of the arch, they revealed a second set, which also split and slid, and then a third set.

It was a bit much for even Chap's paranoia, and as the last set separated . . .

Master Cinder-Shard stood on the other side, no less dour than before.

The aging master had passed through the wall and somehow opened the doors from the other side. It appeared "stonewalker" had a very literal meaning, and Chane must have already known by his apparent disinterest in the sight. Wynn might have been considerate enough to mention this.

Upon entering the next room, Chap wondered how the triple doors were controlled from within. All he noticed was a three-by-four grid of what appeared to be square iron rods on a ledge. Behind this were small round and possibly metal vertical struts inside an opening in the inner wall.

Master Cinder-Shard strode toward the chamber's center, leaving no chance for further inquiry. And any such questions vanished from Chap's thoughts.

Embedded in the chamber floor's center was a perfectly round mirror big enough to hold a wagon. But that mirror was made of metal . . . white metal, rather than glass. How did the stonewalkers, let alone any dwarves, know and use the white metal of the Chein'âs, who made Anmaglâhk weapons and tools?

More and more questions mounted, with no chance to seek answers to any of them.

There was another hair-thin seam dividing that great disk in the floor. No bars, locks, latches, or handles of any kind could be seen.

Chap almost invaded Cinder-Shard's thoughts and memories to learn more. He held back for fear of disrupting the elder stonewalker's reluctant agreement so far. But he would certainly question Chane at length later.

"Ore-Locks . . . ring!" Cinder-Shard barked.

Chap's ears pricked up, but before he could wonder, Ore-Locks crossed the chamber to grip a rope and unwind it from an iron tie-mount on the wall. He heaved on it with all his weight, and the chamber resonated with one deep tone, as from a bell.

Ore-Locks released the rope, and a now-familiar grinding grew in the chamber.

Chap crept to the white metal portal's edge. His ears flattened, and he backed away as the floor portal's center hairline split. Its halves slid smoothly away beneath the chamber's floor, and then a stone platform rose to fill the opening. It stopped at floor level.

Cinder-Shard, Ore-Locks, and Chane stepped onto the platform. Chap watched them and gave a low growl.

"Chap," Chane said.

Still growling, Chap inched forward—he was sick of these dwarven contraptions—literally sick. Touching the platform with his paw, he tested it and then stepped on it.

He clenched all over, waiting for the inevitable. Two breaths later, the platform began to drop, slowly at first and then picking up enough speed. He could feel his fur lightly rustled by rushing air.

He felt as if he were falling down the perfectly round shaft, and he could not help closing his eyes. That did not help his stomach, and the sense of falling went on and on.

A sudden lurch almost made him vomit. Fortunately, he had not eaten yet. The platform began to slow—and slow—until he cracked one eye open. He quickly shut it again on seeing the shaft's stone wall passing upward. And the sudden thump of hitting bottom was worse.

He heard two heavy steps of boots and still could not open his eyes. He would have faced feral vampires in a bloodbath rather than another night like this one.

"Chap?" Chane rasped.

When Chap finally opened his eyes, Ore-Locks had paused in a stone passage ahead to look back. Cinder-Shard strode onward, and Chane still stood waiting on the lift.

Chap wobbled out into the passage and heard Chane follow as Ore-Locks headed onward. Worse, from what Chap saw, they would have to take that lift out again soon. Much of the night had to be gone by now.

Down the way, the passage split in three directions. Ahead, it appeared to lead into a cavern with a low ceiling. Phosphorescence flooded out of there, providing some light, and they must be deep below the mountain for that to occur. In spite of his sickness, Chap's curiosity was piqued.

Cinder-Shard stopped short of the cavern opening ahead.

Peering toward the greenish phosphorescent glow, Chap tried to see into that cavern. He made out stalactites and stalagmites joined together in concave, lumpy columns. However, Cinder-Shard stepped in front of him like a wall and looked beyond him. Chap glanced back along the dark one's gaze at Chane.

"This is as far as you go," Cinder-Shard warned. "Now . . . why are you after the anchor of Earth?"

It puzzled Chap that the master of stonewalkers knew and used the term "anchor" rather than "orb."

After a pause, Chane began to explain their reasons for coming. He spoke of retrieving the orb of Spirit, how he learned that Water and Fire had been hidden in the northern wastes, and then traveled to the Suman Empire for the recovery of Air. He told them of rumors of the Ancient Enemy's servants gathering in the great desert's east. And finally, he warned that this last could be a forewarning of the Ancient Enemy's reawakening.

The orbs were needed as the only possible protection for the world—the only weapon against their creator.

Chane did not mention that he and Chap had already recovered Water and Fire from the wastes.

Master Cinder-Shard listened in silence.

"The orb of Earth is now needed," Chane finished. "Without it to complete the five, there is no potential weapon to use against the Enemy."

There was one other detail that Chane had not mentioned.

None of them actually knew how to use the orbs as yet.

When Chap looked up, Ore-Locks was watching his master's face intently, but Cinder-Shard still had not spoken.

Ore-Locks became visibly anxious. "Master, I—"

"I will guard the anchor on this journey," Cinder-Shard cut in. "You will remain here."

"No," Ore-Locks answered, and this one word echoed off the stone walls.

Cinder-Shard turned his coal black eyes on his subordinate. "You have wandered enough for a lifetime."

"I will be the one to go," Ore-Locks insisted.

Cinder-Shard's expression shifted to fury. "It is enough that you left to follow the misbegotten little human sage who brought that thing"—he pointed to Chane—"out into the realm. This is too important . . . too dangerous . . . for your recklessness."

Ore-Locks stalled. Perhaps he had never argued with his superior before, though he had gone behind the elders' backs in some things, Chap knew.

"I was entrusted with the orb at Bäalâle Seatt." The young stonewalker's voice carried an edge. "I am its sole keeper, its inheritor, and without Chane, that might not have happened. Do not think you can usurp me in this, in disregard of the all-eaters . . . Master."

Chap had not even considered the possibility of a stonewalker accompanying them, and he did not care for the idea now.

Cinder-Shard appeared about to retort when Chane interrupted.

"Ore-Locks speaks the truth, and as much as I respect you, Master Cinder-Shard, this is ultimately his decision, and I will follow his wishes."

"I will not be countered!" Cinder-Shard barked. "Not by something like you."

Chap sensed a crisis building. What if Cinder-Shard refused to release the orb? Could Ore-Locks get to it himself? Or was it hidden where only Cinder-Shard knew?

There could be no chance of losing it now, and Chap locked his eyes on the dark, grizzled dwarf. He was uncertain if memory-words would even work with a stonewalker, but he had to try. Cinder-Shard's contention with Ore-Locks had already evoked conscious memories of past arguments.

—*Give the anchor . . . to Ore-Locks . . . and . . . send him . . . with us*—

The master stonewalker jerked out one blade in a back step, but he eyed Chane. Chap heard Chane draw a blade as well. Ore-Locks immediately stepped between them, blocking Chap's sight line to the elder stonewalker.

"Enough!" Ore-Locks shouted, unaware of the cause. "Both of you, put your blades away. Chane . . . now!"

Chap glanced back once with a snarl and a huff for "yes."

Chane glanced down once, eyes narrowing in suspicion—then widening in realization. He slipped his shorter blade back into its sheath.

Chap pushed around Ore-Locks's legs before the young stonewalker realized. He focused on Cinder-Shard with another snarl and clack of teeth.

—Look . . . down . . . not . . . to Chane—

Cinder-Shard did so, and his brow furrowed with confusion.

—I am majay-hì . . . and . . . more— . . . *—I . . . protect . . . the anchors—*

He paused to let the realization sink in as to who actually spoke.

Cinder-Shard's confusion melted into visible shock.

—Give . . . the anchor of Earth . . . to Chane . . . and send Ore-Locks . . . with us—

Cinder-Shard still stood his ground with blade in hand, and his scowl returned. He slowly looked from Chap to Chane. Shock plus doubt returned when he met Chap's eyes once more.

"You travel with him?" He pointed the dagger toward Chane. "Knowing what he is?"

—He is . . . useful . . . and . . . another guardian . . . for . . . the anchors—

Cinder-Shard's frown deepened again. He finally looked up and waved Ore-Locks out of his way. With hesitation, he slipped the broad-based dagger back into its sheath.

"This majay-hì somehow speaks in thoughts, in voices, from my past," he said directly to Chane, though Chane said nothing. "He expects me to do as suggested, and he claims that he protects the anchors . . . as in more than one."

Yes, Chap had made that slip in desperation and anger, and he still saw it as necessary. Both sides here needed a show of trust to end this conflict, and he had chosen to be the first. How could stonewalkers trust them—trust him—if he did not trust in them?

Chap huffed once at Chane to confirm Cinder-Shard's words.

With a slow nod, Chane turned to Ore-Locks. "We have already traveled to the wastes and recovered the orbs of Water and Fire. We have hidden them nearby and will carry them south . . . with yours."

"Here?" Cinder-Shard demanded, as if nearing patience's end. "Where?"

"At the mouth of the old tunnel that once led to the prince's cell."

Cinder-Shard's gaze wandered in an expression of open panic.

"You must let me do this, Master," Ore-Locks said.

Long moments of silence followed.

"How will you travel?" Cinder-Shard finally demanded of Chane.

"First by sea, though we have yet to find outbound passage," Chane answered cautiously. "We only need to go as far as Soráno, and then by land."

The master stonewalker hesitated again, and then spoke directly to Ore-Locks. "The *Kestrel* is in the harbor. I will make certain the captain gives you passage."

Ore-Locks released a sigh of relief, and Cinder-Shard leaned down toward Chap with a wrinkled brow.

"Considering the topic at hand," he said, "I can only guess sending the two of you together is another twisted jest by Chuillyon."

Chap had no idea what that meant, and when he looked to Chane, the undead's jaw clenched. Whoever this Chuillyon might be, Chane knew of him or her.

"Take these two out the aqueduct tunnel," Cinder-Shard instructed Ore-Locks. "Retrieve their anchors and take them to the ship. I will have dealt with the captain by then . . . and I will arrange to have the anchor of Earth stowed in cargo."

Before Chap could even wonder how the master stonewalker could accomplish all of this so quickly, Ore-Locks heaved another sigh of relief.

"Yes, Master," he said, "and thank you."

Chap did not care to leave this place without the third orb. But so far, regardless of a temper and a quite sensible hatred of the undead, it seemed unlikely that the master stonewalker would break his word.

"Give me the chest," Cinder-Shard commanded.

Chane did so, along with the third lock and key.

What mattered most to Chap was that he had succeeded here—even though Chane's presence had been both a help and a hindrance. And the other problems, such as passage, had been solved. There was one more minor relief as well.

Chap would not face another cursed lift or tram to leave this place.

CHAPTER SEVEN

Magiere trekked through another desert dawn and deeper into the foothills, which had grown higher the closer she traveled toward the main Sky-Cutter Range. She had only Ghassan and Brot'an for company. Wynn and Leesil had remained in camp with the orbs.

"We should turn back," Ghassan said, glancing toward the eastern, lightening sky.

"A little farther," Magiere countered, pressing on in the lead.

She felt torn at going back after having found nothing again. Finding anything to support Ghassan's belief in the Enemy's reawakening seemed slimmer and slimmer by the day.

She'd lost count of the nights since they'd found the bodies, or parts of the bodies, and there was no way of truly knowing what had happened to those people. The nights now repeated the same choice: who scouted and who stayed behind. Any who went out had to cover as much new ground as possible before returning at dawn . . . to collapse in exhaustion. They had already moved camp, always eastward, numerous times to expand the search.

Along the way, more time was lost in finding wells and stealing water for both themselves and the camels. Food stores held up but were dwindling. Everyone was tired of jerked goat meat, cracked flatbread, and dried-up figs.

Magiere never said so aloud, but she wondered if any of this would amount to anything. Leesil said less and withdrew more each day, and she couldn't offer him a word about when all this would end.

It couldn't end yet. They had to continue eastward.

Magiere stopped and half turned.

Brot'an, like the rest of them, wore a long cloth tied over his head, stretching down his back and overhanging his eyes, even at night. The light-toned muslin made his tan face look even darker. They still often traveled in early daylight or even in the later afternoons to escape the worst heat. Sleeping midday was necessary to take cover from the burning sun.

"What do you think?" she asked.

No one fully trusted Brot'an, but she depended on his judgment in scouting. He seemed to know exactly how long it would take to return to camp, no matter where they went.

"A bit farther, if you wish," he answered. "From here, we would make it back to camp well before midday."

Nodding, she turned onward around another hill instead of over it. A warm breeze blew across her face . . . and she froze.

She smelled blood—a thick scent—and turned her face into the breeze. Without thinking, she bolted upward for the top of the hill. Something more had been changing in her the farther east they went.

There had always been times when her senses sharpened. This had always come with the rise of her other half. But lately . . .

When she gained a vantage point, she pulled her falchion and froze, looking downward.

"Magiere!"

She heard Brot'an's sure steps racing upward behind her, followed by Ghassan's. When both joined her, they too looked down at the remnants of a massacre.

Magiere had almost known before she saw it. There had been other moments like this, not foresight but, well, maybe fore-sense. If Chap had been here, and thankfully he wasn't, he might have known. Leesil and the others didn't know about her growing ability, and she kept it that way.

Now hunger did widen her sight.

Bodies were strewn about at the hill's back base, most with limbs flayed out where they'd dropped. As to the blood scent, Magiere's sight widened further at the sight of torn-out throats.

One boy was short of manhood. Three others were children.

Four people in faded and semitattered robes and head wraps moved through the bodies. They rarely paused. One veiled woman knelt and hunched with her head nearly on the chest of a small body. The other three were men, two young and one with a steel gray beard.

Magiere rushed down without thinking.

Four more people peeked out around and over lower boulders where they had hidden. These looked panicked. One shouted out to the searchers, and a young man among them pulled a long, curved knife.

"Sa'alaam!" Ghassan called from behind.

Magiere had picked up enough common Sumanese to know he'd shouted the word for "peace," but it struck her as a poor choice. How could these people be at peace among their dead with strangers suddenly descending on them? She swung wide from the boulders before reaching the gulley's floor.

Brot'an was only an instant behind her. He ignored the men and studied the scene without reaction. Ghassan skidded to a stop with both hands up as he faced the men.

"Desert nomads," Ghassan whispered. "Let me deal with them."

When he stepped away, something else struck Magiere. The one word Ghassan had spoken stalled most of the survivors, but all of them watched him carefully as a second man pulled out a curved knife almost long enough to be a short sword. He barked something like a question.

Magiere couldn't follow the man's words. Even Brot'an frowned slightly, and his Sumanese was better than hers.

"A different dialect?" he murmured.

Magiere looked back to the bodies and began to count—eleven.

Ghassan talked quickly with the survivors, always keeping his hands out and visible. The two young men did most of the talking or questioning, while the stern and haggard old man listened and watched. The three women—one still bent over a body, one peering from around a boulder, and another clutching tightly an elder boy—were all silent.

Ghassan continued speaking to the men.

"What are they saying?" Magiere demanded. "What happened here?"

When he glanced at her, every muscle in his face looked tight.

"They say they were attacked before dawn," Ghassan began, "by madmen . . . with the teeth of animals. They were too fast, too strong to fight, when they started to slaughter people and . . . eat them."

Magiere's brow furrowed in confusion with one quick glance at the nearest body, a man, probably in his twenties, though dried blood obscured his face.

"I do not think they understood at first," Ghassan added, "that it was blood, not flesh, their attackers were after."

That made sense to anyone with sense.

Too often, those who knew of the undead thought that everyone else did as well, as if such things were commonly known. In truth, the undead were few, rare, and that was their advantage.

Yes, Magiere had seen otherwise, but that didn't count.

Sometimes they came because of her and what she was. In a large world, there were unlimited new places to hunt, filled with unwitting prey. And the cunning ones kept it that way, even killing off the reckless among their own kind.

She closed her eyes and didn't listen as Ghassan struggled to learn more from the survivors. This time, the monsters had come in numbers, disregarding secrecy. Frenzy marked their starvation, and no undead needing to feed on life would willingly come to such desolate, lifeless places.

Magiere no longer doubted Ghassan's reports from the new emperor.

Opening her eyes, she called out, "How many attacked them?"

Ghassan glanced back at her but didn't answer. He returned to conversing with the two young men as the old one watched and listened to everything. Ghassan's tone grew sharp and fast, and a young one answered him in kind.

"Ghassan, what are they saying?" Brot'an called out.

At that, the trio of men and even one woman looked at him.

Ghassan spun around, glaring. Who wouldn't be angry in the face of all this? Magiere certainly was, but the domin rarely betrayed his thoughts, let alone his feelings.

"Answer Brot'an," she told him.

"I am trying to gain information," he said, his voice strained. "Something with a bit of sense, but they have little of that!"

This didn't seem believable for the amount of back-and-forth between him and the others. Then again, she knew sages too often thought the learned— educated—were so much clearer and informed than anyone else.

She waited for his frustrations to get the better of him, and Ghassan took a long, tired breath as he stepped toward her.

"Forgive me. I am unsettled." He paused an arm's length away and lowered his voice barely above a whisper. "They say it happened quickly in the night. Some managed to run and hide. Any who stayed to fight were found dead. It happened very fast."

"How many came at them?" Magiere asked.

"Six . . . to nine . . . or something in between." He shook his head. "Too many different answers to be certain."

She'd never known vampires to travel in numbers greater than three, and those were rare. They weren't social creatures. Any undead disliked sharing territory, but out here . . .

"That is all," Ghassan finished. "They cannot describe their attackers beyond 'mad' and 'strong' or 'beasts in human form.' And I think it unlikely they will let us help bury their dead."

He stepped even closer to whisper softly. "We are lucky they feared attacking us upon sight, likely because we came near dawn. That may change. We should leave to return to camp and move it immediately."

Magiere didn't like that. She'd had to walk away from victims too many times. What she wanted most was to try to track the undead who had attacked here. If they'd managed to get high enough in the rockier terrain, Brot'an might still track what she couldn't smell or feel at a distance. But then her gaze shifted in looking over the domin's shoulder.

The two younger men stood close to the elder, speaking quietly. And the gray-bearded old man watched Magiere and her companions without blinking.

"We leave now," Brot'an said.

Magiere bit down the instinct to argue with him, and she still felt Ghassan held something back. Her only certainty was the proof of why Ghassan had brought them eastward.

She dreaded wiping away any doubts Leesil had left.

Chane stood on the deck of the *Kestrel*, watching the main pier of the docks below Chemarré.

On the previous night, Ore-Locks had led him, Chap, and two other stonewalkers to carry the two hidden orbs to the ship. By the time they arrived, all had been arranged exactly as Master Cinder-Shard had said.

The third orb—Ore-Locks's orb—in the third chest was waiting in the ship's hold.

Neither Chane nor Chap had liked the idea of leaving the orbs out of their sight, but it seemed better than trying to stow them in the one cabin they all shared.

Still, Chap was down in the hold for now, refusing to leave the orbs unguarded until the ship left port and they were out to sea.

The only thing delaying their departure was Ore-Locks.

Upon getting them settled aboard the *Kestrel*, he had claimed that he had several matters to attend to back in the seatt. Of course Chane understood this, as Ore-Locks was about to leave his current life behind and venture off on an extended journey with no set time to return. He must have duties and responsibilities among the stonewalkers. Or at least that was what Chane assumed . . . though he now grew anxious while waiting.

The vessel itself had been a pleasant surprise, roomy and clean, and their cabin sported two comfortable bunks. The captain had not appeared pleased at last-minute passengers, but he said nothing and was civil about all arrangements. Even Chane's offer of coin for passage had been refused. It still seemed strange, even suspicious, that Cinder-Shard, master of the dwarves' underworld, had such influence among the living, especially among nondwarves.

Movement at the pier's landward end caught Chane's attention—and there came Ore-Locks striding toward the ship.

Even with his face shadowed by the large hood of a traveler's cloak, there was no mistaking him. Chane stepped out to head toward the ship's ramp, where two sailors also stood waiting.

When Ore-Locks finally came up the ramp, he stopped and pushed his hood back, revealing dark red hair now hanging unbound over the shoulders of his iron-colored cloak. He no longer wore his caste's black-scaled armor, though he still bore its twin battle daggers tucked into his wide belt. He was dressed plainly in brown breeches and a natural canvas shirt . . . beneath a burnt-orange, wool tabard.

In their previous journey together, Ore-Locks had donned that same vestment to disguise himself as a holy shirvêsh of Bedzâ'kenge, Feather-Tongue. Back then, he had also carried the traditional iron staff of that order, but not tonight.

Instead, he wore a sheathed sword on his left hip.

Shorter than Chane's longsword, which was made of prized and mottled dwarven steel, Ore-Locks's weapon was nearly twice as wide of blade. No, he had not brought the nonlethal staff—metal, wood, or otherwise—common to many shirvêsh orders. He had come prepared for battle and war, and he glanced down, following Chane's stare.

"Not big enough?" he quipped.

He always had a dry, caustic manner if and when he showed humor at all.

"Not for you, certainly," Chane answered.

Perhaps he felt something to which he had never become accustomed except with Wynn, and later with Shade. It was rare—no, unique—that he wanted company from anyone else. This long journey with Chap had been more difficult than he imagined, for as a natural enemy of the undead, Chap hated him. The majay-hì could not be blamed for that, based on what Chane was . . . and more, what he had once been before Wynn.

Chane offered his hand to Ore-Locks. Though the young stonewalker hesitated for an instant, he took it.

Khalidah had been furious upon returning to camp with Magiere and Brot'an that morning. Yet he kept his feigned air of concern as Magiere and Brot'an reported to Leesil and Wynn what they had encountered.

In truth, Khalidah had no concern over the survivors. The reckless slaughter was another matter.

Leesil listened to the news stoically, and, of course, the sage asked every question imaginable, including putting up a moment's fuss over how to help the survivors. The half-blood said nothing.

When she exhausted her questions, a moment of silence followed. Magiere's expression grew even more tense, as if what they had found and the repercussions were beginning to sink in. Looking at her face, Leesil came to life. He grasped her hand and dragged her off to the tent they shared with the sage. Wynn took a step after, paused, and then followed them.

Rest was short that day, and Khalidah roused everyone in the afternoon. They moved eastward, but as the sun touched the western horizon, he suggested they stop and set up a new base camp from which to explore this area.

While the others were busy with this, he excused himself to scout for water.

Once out of sight of the camp, he strode back into the foothills. His restraint against rage faltered. Dropping to a crouch, he jerked the medallion from inside his shirt and gripped it tightly.

Sau'ilahk!

A one-word answer took too long in coming.

What?

Where are you?

A moment of silence followed, and then . . .

We are camped a quarter league ahead of you to the east beneath a jagged foothill with an overhang.

Wait there.

He released the medallion before he could be questioned and rose to stride back toward the foothills' edge above the open desert. When certain of not being seen, he paused again with fear feeding his rage.

He hoped his rage was justified and that his fears were unfounded.

A small buzz rose inside his mind . . . Ghassan was once again trying to pester and confuse him.

"Shut up, you little insect!" he hissed.

Concentrating, he allowed an immense tangle of signs, sigils, and symbols to appear over his sight, and he lifted himself on his will. His body rose just high enough that his passage would not stir a trail of dust and sand in his wake . . . as he shot through the dusk toward the east. It was not long before he spotted the landmark of craggy foothills with an overhang.

Touching down lightly, he banished all glowing symbols from his sight and broke into a run. As he rounded the hill below its overhang, the ghost girl with her severed throat stood in his way, watching him.

There in the camp beyond her was the necromancer still strapped to his wheeled litter. Ubâd was tilted upright, as if awaiting the arrival between his two corpse attendants. Nearby stood Sau'ilahk, arms folded, his pale skin still vivid in the twilight, though his blue-black hair nearly melded with the encroaching darkness.

Khalidah strode straight through the ghost girl, his gaze locked on Sau'ilahk.

He rarely used physical force, for he did not need to do so. There were so many better methods at his disposal. Yet now he could not stop himself. Grabbing the front of the false duke's shirt, he shoved Sau'ilahk back into the rocky hillside.

Before the wraith-in-flesh even righted himself among the sliding stones, Khalidah shouted, "What are you playing at, you self-righteous priest?"

Sau'ilahk straightened to full height, cold and quiet in a returned glare, and Khalidah suddenly second-guessed his action.

The priest's . . . the wraith's body was dead, unlike his own, but it appeared to be quite physically strong, and Khalidah had no idea of what else Sau'ilahk might be capable.

"Do not touch me again," Sau'ilahk warned in a threatening whisper. "And what are you talking about?"

Pressing down tangled fear and fury, Khalidah fought for calm.

"You know! I told you to leave hints . . . a bit of bait to keep Magiere here until the other orbs are brought. I did not tell you to slaughter a pack of vagrant nomads. And how did you convince them of greater numbers?" He pointed to Ubâd's male servants. "Did you use them? Or has that dead necromancer created a few more ghosts?"

Sau'ilahk's brow furrowed in confusion. He did not even glance at Ubâd. Then the ghost girl suddenly appeared between them.

"What is this?" she lashed out at Khalidah. "We have not changed our position since you contacted us the night before last."

Khalidah stiffened. As angry as he was at the idea of Sau'ilahk's giving in to an urge of excess, the alternative was worse, as he had no control over it.

"We have *not* moved," Sau'ilahk added.

Khalidah turned away. After a moment, he related the scene of slaughter, still not truly believing the denials—the feigned ignorance—of his confederates. For if Sau'ilahk was not the culprit, and the story of the survivors was true in another way, then the ruse Khalidah had used to lead Magiere on was no longer a ruse.

Beloved was calling its servants.

This meant their god *was* on the verge of reawakening.

Choices now became few: dangerous, and worse.

Magiere might stop scouting for proof and turn to find Beloved if more random events spurred her on. If groups of the undead and their like were now truly scurrying to the east . . .

Khalidah was not ready for this. Three orbs were still not in his possession. His only controllable allies were this miscreant High Reverent One and a necromancer with no true life to lose. And both were as starved for revenge as he was.

None of them trusted one another. In life, Sau'ilahk had made no secret of how much he despised the Sâ'yminfiäl, the Masters of Frenzy or Eaters of Silence. The feeling had been mutual between the sects.

And now Ubâd would know that both Sau'ilahk and Khalidah despised him. Compared to them, he was a rebellious child for all of their centuries of suffering and enslavement. From what Khalidah understood, Ubâd had been taken down by a single majay-hì and not even by the dhampir herself.

Yet, all three of them had their own uses in this matter.

All three labored toward the same goal.

As Khalidah finished recounting the morning slaughter, Sau'ilahk had been as silent as the corpse master.

"If this is true," he finally said, "if a horde is being gathered, then what of our own plans?"

"Nothing has changed," Khalidah answered, "though it will make my dealings with the dhampir more difficult."

"Lies from the master of lies," the ghost girl countered for Ubâd. "The closer she comes to so many prey, the more she will want to hunt."

"Then I will keep her from them," Khalidah replied. "I will not allow her to find the resting place of Beloved yet . . . of anything gathering there."

"Where are Andraso and the majay-hì?" Sau'ilahk asked. "How much longer until they return with the other orbs?"

At least this turned to better news with which to pacify his inferiors.

"They have acquired all three remaining orbs," Khalidah assured. "They now sail south for Soráno."

"That is still a good distance," Sau'ilahk cut in. "Can you keep the dhampir in control until they return?"

Khalidah did not bother responding and turned to give instructions.

"Leave a few more hints for her," he said. "And perhaps next time, something to give the little sage pause. Make Wynn wonder if the past returns to . . . haunt her . . . oh, restless spirit! Wynn's fears are shackles upon the dhampir as well."

Sau'ilahk's eyes narrowed, and he nodded once.

Khalidah did not need to feed so long as he was in proximity to orbs, but in part, he envied the priest, for his body—Ghassan's body—still required food.

"It is more difficult to find desert denizens than imagined," Sau'ilahk said. "And less so living ones the farther east that we go."

"I have faith in you," Khalidah answered dryly.

Sau'ilahk sneered and turned away.

Trapped within his flesh, Ghassan il'Sänke found that his panic grew. He was party to every action, every word that Khalidah spoke, and yet he was powerless. And he felt himself becoming weaker, fading a little more each night. It had become difficult to remember certain things too far in the past.

Somehow, some way, he had to warn Wynn Hygeorht. She was the only one who might recognize something from him, not from Khalidah.

CHAPTER EIGHT

Aboard the *Kestrel*, Chane came to a decision halfway to Soráno. He had been preparing to try something and believed he was ready.

Chap and Ore-Locks had adapted to living on his schedule, sleeping through the days, though they were always up before he rose at dusk. They also chose to spend a fair portion of time on deck, which gave Chane some much-desired privacy.

He carried two packs wherever he traveled. The first contained his personal possessions, spare clothing, and now the talking hide for Chap. The second was old and faded and a guarded treasure.

That pack and most of its contents had once belonged to Welstiel Massing, another vampire, Magiere's half brother, and son in life to a vampire once a vagrant noble. Welstiel had also been an arcane practitioner of thaumaturgy by artificing, specifically alchemy. And his subtle skill with both pushed the limits of Chane's minor knowledge of conjury.

When Welstiel died, Chane had taken his pack. A number of objects inside it had proven invaluable in his own experiments. The pack also now contained texts Chane had stolen from a monastery of healers on the eastern continent.

The most critical one for this night was *The Seven Leaves of Life*.

Chane was obsessed with one page in that volume, though its instructions were archaic and obscure. It described the making of a rare and potent healing concoction. During his stays with Wynn at the Calm Seatt branch of the Guild of Sagecraft, he had privately discussed both the ingredients and the creation process with Premin Hawes, head of the branch's order of Metaology. Most of the ingredients were herbs, easy to obtain, but two were unknown to him until Hawes translated and explained them.

Muhkgean was a mushroom grown by the dwarves. Ore-Locks had once helped him gain those mushrooms, and they were harmless.

The other had not proved harmless, at least for him.

Anamgiah, the "life shield," was a white flower found in the fields outside the Lhoin'na forests. Later, he had learned the same grew in the lands of the an'Cróan on the world's far continent, where it was called *Anasgiah*. Even raw, those opalescent blossoms had healing properties. And so much more when combined correctly with the other six ingredients.

When he had recognized those blossoms upon first visiting the Lhoin'na lands with Wynn, Shade, and Ore-Locks, he had been stunned. He should have never gathered them by hand, and he had nearly died the last time upon barely touching their glistening petals.

But now he had them in his possession, dried, wrapped, and stored in the second pack well away from contact with his skin. Over time, he had collected the other necessities for the formula. At last, he had everything, or so he hoped.

Before rejoining Wynn, and hopefully Shade—and before any of them faced the Ancient Enemy—he needed to be certain of saving either of them, should the worst come. His own body was nearly indestructible. Wynn's was not, and even Shade had her limits.

However, instructions to make the potion appeared deliberately vague.

This elixir was powerful enough to be feared in the wrong hands, and he had reasoned why. A tyrant or butcher of the battlefield could be nearly untouchable with the ability to heal the gravest wounds in short order. And from what Chane surmised, this elixir might as well be protection against poison, venom, disease . . . anything that caused living flesh to fail.

He studied the page with a translation that he and Hawes had made, pausing on the word "boil" and not for the first time.

This suggested water or liquid; every concoction he had ever read of related to nonliquids used thrice-purified water as the medium. He suspected the same herein, though like many things in the fields of hidden knowledge and practice, it was not explicitly mentioned by the author.

Chane picked up a copper bottle but did not remove its matching stopper. He gently turned it, feeling its contents slosh. He had taken great pains to make as much thrice-purified water as he could.

From the journey's earliest part, he had caught clean rain in a bowl held out the cabin's porthole whenever he could, and he stored the rainwater in a glass vessel.

When he had enough rainwater, he sterilized an empty copper bottle with wood alcohol, pouring that out to save, and blowing out excess fumes, and then carefully inverting the bottle over the flame of a candle.

Any ignition had been extinguished.

After this, he prepared an oil-fueled burner with several *Anamgiah* accoutrements. He took up the glass vessel filled with rainwater and the copper one he had sterilized. Upon filling the copper bottle with rainwater, he replaced its stopper with a ceramic elbow-shaped pipe.

He set the glass bottle under the elbow's other end.

Steam rose into the ceramic elbow and dripped into the glass bottle's mouth. It took a while, and the process had to be repeated twice. In the end, he had less than a third of the original water, now thrice purified. He stored this in the sterilized copper bottle.

On the night the *Kestrel* docked at Chathburh, less than halfway to Soráno, Chane steeled himself to attempt making the elixir from *The Seven Leaves of Life*. He feared failure, for there would be no chance to replenish the two most important ingredients, but he could no longer put off the attempt. When he,

Ore-Locks, and Chap went up on deck, he waited for Chap to wander off toward the forecastle.

Chane pulled Ore-Locks aside. "Do you trust me?"

Ore-Locks blinked and frowned. Neither had ever asked such a pointed but general question of the other.

It was a long moment before Ore-Locks nodded. "Yes . . . I do."

Equally surprised by the answer, Chane realized he trusted Ore-Locks enough to share part of the truth.

"I need time alone in the cabin to make something for Wynn's protection—and maybe others'—should the worst come."

In spite of his prior claim, Ore-Locks frowned. "Make something?"

"Medicine," Chane answered, for this was partly true, though if successful, it would be more than that. "No one else should know for now, and Chap does not trust me enough to stay out of my way. Can you keep him from the cabin for as long as possible?"

Ore-Locks's frown deepened, and he growled, "Very well."

About to leave, Chane then wondered what the errant stonewalker might be able to do about Chap. Asking would waste time, so with a nod, he hurried for the aftcastle door. The last thing he did was to borrow a bucket of cold seawater from a deckhand.

Once inside the cabin, Chane bolted its door from inside and set to work.

He had attempted something similar only once before.

Welstiel had possessed an elixir that allowed a vampire to remain awake during daylight, though it had to stay out of direct sunlight. When Chane had stolen the pack after Welstiel's death at Magiere's hands, he had found a small amount of this elixir in the pack.

And there were journals and notes as well.

After obtaining a key component—a poisonous flower called *Dyvjàka Svonchek* or "boar's bell"—he had later managed to re-create that elixir by using himself as a test subject. The process was unpleasant and dangerous, but he succeeded after multiple attempts and gained the advantage of guarding Wynn constantly during some of their worst times.

Unfortunately, he had used up all of that elixir, and there had been no opportunity to procure more boar's bell.

Now he was to try something he could not test on himself, for it would contain extract from *Anamgiah* blossoms. The result would be "deadly" to any physical undead. There would be no room for mistakes, no way to test it, and no certainty of success until it was needed.

Chane slowly opened Welstiel's faded pack.

One by one, he took out the components, tools, and necessities and laid them out upon the floor. A clear glass vessel was among them. After this, he prepared the oil-fueled burner. Then he took up the copper bottle filled with thrice-purified water.

Opening *The Seven Leaves of Life*, he turned to the correct page and laid the book out on the floor. With the copper bottle wedged between his folded legs, he began to powder and prepare the ingredients. Again, he guessed— hoped—the list in the book represented the proper order for adding ingredients. For such a concoction, adding all at once did not make sense; this was not some cook's soup. For each ingredient added, he applied heat to the copper vessel and then poured a tiny amount into the glass one to examine it.

Twice the water was cloudy; twice he reapplied heat. More puzzling was how the water eventually turned clear again after the first two ingredients. He took this as a sign of correctness for all others that followed . . . until the last two.

Chane glanced at those two still wrapped in folded paper. Opening the first, he uncovered the dried *Muhkgean*, strange gray mushrooms with caps that spread in branched protrusions. Though now withered, each branch's end splayed and flattened in a shape like a tiny leaf. He powdered the mushrooms with a pestle and mortar.

Quantities for ingredients were another guess, and so far with measures, he had assumed all ingredients were added in equal quantities. He did the same with a pinch of powdered *Muhkgean*. But no matter how often he checked and reboiled the mixture . . . something had gone wrong.

Chane sat staring at the cloudy, slightly grayed water, caught between panic and anger at failure. Had he used too much or too little of the mushrooms? Had he done so with one or more of the other ingredients? There was not enough left of some to try again. And how much longer could Ore-Locks keep Chap from returning to the cabin?

Panic and frustration turned into desperation as Chane stared down.

The tiny leaf-shaped petals of dried *Anamgiah* had lost almost all of their opalescence, though they were still pure white. There was nothing he could do now but finish.

He took out a pair of small tin tweezers from among Welstiel's tools and carefully pinched dried petals to grind with mortar and pestle. Even dried, he dared not touch them with his own flesh, so measuring an "inch" on the tip of a knife made him freeze up for an instant.

Chane tilted the knife's tip over the copper bottle. And just before he placed the copper vessel back upon the tripod above the flame . . .

Hope failed him, and neither fear nor rage could bring it back. There had been too many variables in the process.

All he could do was continue.

Up on deck, Chap strolled about in the fresh air. It was far better than being cooped up with his traveling companions. Eventually, he elicited one too many annoyed glances from the crew members rushing about in their duties, so he turned back from the bow.

Then he noticed Ore-Locks was alone, and he paused. Chane often spent some of his waking time belowdecks, but not usually so early in the evening. Where had he gone? Ore-Locks was turned away to the near rail, looking out to sea, and Chap decided to go below and see what Chane was doing. He headed toward the aft doorway.

"Majay-hì."

Chap halted and looked to the dwarf. Ore-Locks rarely spoke to him, and he had little idea what to even think of the young stonewalker.

In a few overheard conversations with Chane, Ore-Locks had sounded displeased when he learned they would be stopping at the city of the Lhoin'na before the long trek to Bäalâle Seatt. It seemed the stonewalker had a deep mistrust of anything he considered to be "elven." Worse, Ore-Locks's attitude made it plain that he considered Chap to belong in that category.

Chap watched as the dwarf left the rail and came toward him.

"Majay-hì," Ore-Locks repeated, "my master said that you spoke into his thoughts with words out of his own memories, and in the voices of others in his past. Can you do so . . . with me?"

Chap's surprise—and suspicion—grew as the dwarf continued.

"Chane said you cannot speak to him because of the ring he wears. Is this also true?"

That Chane and Ore-Locks had discussed this was another surprise. Chap had never spoken directly to the vampire and did not wish to do so, ever. He could only imagine what atrocities Chane had committed in the past that might rise out of his memory. The cries of his past victims were the last thing Chap wished to use for a voice—of words—with that *thing*.

Or did Chane ever even think of the slaughter he had left in his passing?

Still, Chap did not answer Ore-Locks.

Until recently, Chap preferred to keep his new ability to himself. His way of communicating with Wynn was unique. He had limited the other, newer method to Magiere, Leesil, and Wayfarer. Only desperation had pushed him to use "memory-words" with Cinder-Shard and reveal himself as more than he appeared to be.

He did not like letting that secret out.

"As we will travel," Ore-Locks went on, "with other challenges to meet and who knows what else . . . perhaps it is best if you and I could speak? Or you with me, that is."

Chap sighed, for it was certainly sensible and practical. And in this case, there was no secret left to be kept, though he wondered why Ore-Locks had waited until now.

—*What . . . would you like . . . me . . . to say?*—

Ore-Locks's eyes widened, blinking rapidly, until he swallowed and cleared his throat.

Chap wanted to roll his canine eyes. But someone knowing he could do this and experiencing it firsthand were worlds apart.

"By the ancestors!" Ore-Locks whispered.

—*Did you think . . . your master . . . lied . . . about me?*—

"No, no . . . but . . ." and then came a furtive glance toward the aftcastle door.

Chap stiffened. After this mostly one-sided conversation, something else occurred to him.

—*Where . . . is . . . Chane?*—

And again, Ore-Locks appeared startled, but not in the same way.

Chap turned and dashed for the aftcastle door.

In the cabin, Chane heated and reheated and visually tested and retested the concoction. Each time he poured the tiniest drop through a piece of silk as filter and into the glass, it was still clouded. He had then rinsed the glass bottle and tried again—and again.

He knew he had been down here alone for too long. Soon enough, Chap would notice and become suspicious.

If Chane was caught, he would have to explain, though Chap would not believe anything he said. There was too little—or rather no—personal trust between them.

Chane studied the next droplet in the glass flask . . . still faintly gray.

Very well, if the majay-hì caught him, so be it.

He poured as much of the droplet as he could back into the copper bottle, stoppered it, and set it on the tripod to heat again. This time, he did not watch, dropped his head and closed his eyes, and silently counted off the time. He listened for the warning soft hiss to make certain the fluid did not come to a full boil.

A snarl and slam shuddered the cabin floor.

Chane stiffened upright as it happened again. He watched the door buck and heard its bolt rattle. Heavy bootfalls quickly grew louder in the passage outside. Then the growling, rolling snarl turned to a half howl.

He knew that sound. He had heard it more than once in being hunted by Chap.

"Enough!" Ore-Locks shouted out in the passage. "You will draw the entire crew!"

Chane snatched up the brass bottle as he rose and snuffed the burner. He could do nothing about the smell of smoke in the cabin. He heard and then felt the sizzle of his own flesh from the scorching copper bottle and swung it behind his back as he stepped to the door. Just before he grabbed the bolt, the door bucked so hard, he heard its planks start to crack.

"Please desist!" Ore-Locks snapped, and then said more loudly, "Chane, it is over. Open the door!"

Chane pulled the bolt, and the door slammed into him. He barely righted himself in retreat. Chap lunged in, fur on end, ears flattened, jowls pulled back, and teeth exposed in a long rumbling hiss. And Chane set himself for a fight.

His gaze flicked once to his swords tucked under the right-side bunk.

Ore-Locks took only one step into the doorway, and Chap looked back once with a snarl. Ore-Locks barely raised open hands in yielding, and Chap turned on Chane again. Sniffing the air and everything on the floor, Chap inched forward but never took his eyes off Chane.

Chane felt the bottle's searing heat spreading in his whole hand.

Chap's head flashed around at Ore-Locks and quickly back. Ore-Locks stiffened in a flinch and blinked twice, and looked at Chane.

"He . . . demands to know what you were doing," Ore-Locks said.

Chane looked back to Chap. Perhaps growing pain spreading to his forearm got the better of him.

"No," he rasped.

Chap snarled and lunged, Chane dropped to a crouch ready to counter, and Ore-Locks rushed in behind Chap.

The dwarf tried to grab Chap's tail and only half succeeded.

Ore-Locks barely closed his big hand when Chap turned and snapped. Chane almost lunged but stalled, uncertain whom to go after. Ore-Locks jerked his hand back.

He glared at Chap, stuttering, "You . . . you . . . *yiannû-billê*!"

Chane did not react. Hopefully Chap did not understand that racist comment, but when Chap's growl sharpened, Chane knew better.

Ore-Locks quickly raised a booted foot and slammed it down.

Even as Chap quickly retreated, Chane felt the whole cabin shudder.

"And what do you think *you* can do about it?" Ore-Locks snarled at Chap.

The dog must have said something into the dwarf's head. Chane could not guess what, and before he tried . . .

"I do not need to wait for port," Ore-Locks ranted on. "All I need to do is take *my* orb and drop over the side to sink. Try to follow through stone at the ocean floor, if you can."

That panicked Chane. He could not fail Wynn like this, even for perhaps his only other friend.

"I am tired of both of you," Ore-Locks grumbled, and then eyed Chane. "And you need to stop baiting the majay-hì with your secrets!"

That as well frightened Chane as he looked between his cabin mates. When his gaze returned to the dwarf, Ore-Locks's narrowed eyes were not looking directly back; he was looking much lower.

Ore-Locks thrust out his hand. "Give it to me."

Chane hesitated.

"Now!" Ore-Locks added.

Chane did not like this. He had multiple reasons for not wanting anyone else—especially Chap—to know what he had been doing. Even Wynn might not have liked it, considering he had again been using Welstiel's tools.

Ore-Locks thrust out his hand even farther.

With a soft exhale through his teeth, Chane relented and held out the copper bottle.

Ore-Locks took it, held it up, eyed it with a scowl, and then eyed Chap. He suddenly pulled the stopper and put the bottle to his mouth.

"No, do not!" Chane rasped.

It was too late, and Ore-Locks tipped the bottle slightly. He smacked his lips once, ran his tongue over them, and wrinkled his broad nose, as if he had smelled something unpleasant. He tilted his head as if some puzzled thought occurred to him, and then looked down at Chap.

"There," he said, "I am fine . . . See?"

Chane was not so certain, though he had seen dwarves drink wood alcohol that would kill a human. The elixir had not clarified, which left him worried about unknown effects upon even one of them.

Ore-Locks slapped the stopper into the bottle and tossed it at Chane, who caught it in another rush of panic. It felt nearly full.

"You two settle this matter, once and for all," Ore-Locks warned.

He turned out of the cabin, slamming the door.

Chane was alone with Chap. The majay-hì climbed up on the far bunk, lay down, and glowered in silence. Chane settled on the other bunk above where his swords were hidden.

"I am not the only one with secrets," Chane said. "What were you doing when you ran off into the trees and left me to dig up two orbs?"

Chap did not move or even blink. He made no sound at all, nor did he do anything to indicate that Chane should pull out the talking hide for a response.

Chane finally dropped his gaze to the copper bottle in his hands, one of which still stung from being seared. From what he felt of the bottle's weight,

Ore-Locks had taken no more than a sip, but that still worried Chane. He bent over to pick up the glass bottle and the scrap of silk, and filtered a tiny amount of the concoction into the glass bottle.

For an instant, what he saw did not make sense, and when he had poured every bit of the mixture into the glass bottle, he could only stare.

The liquid was now entirely crystal clear.

Not long past sunset, Wynn watched as Magiere, Leesil, and Brot'an set off on another scouting trip. Dinner—or perhaps breakfast—tonight had come as a relief.

Ghassan had somehow caught and killed a sizable desert lizard. He had also been saving the best chunks of coal from previous fires, and soon had a low-flamed heat ready for cooking. And meanwhile, he dressed down the lizard. The creature provided nearly as much meat as a chicken.

Everyone was beyond tired of eating dried stores. Though none had ever eaten lizard before, it proved quite tasty—either because it was or because they were desperate for anything other than their normal rations. There was a time when Wynn ate only vegetables and fish. Now she ate whatever was available.

Once the trio passed beyond sight, she turned to Ghassan, who had remained behind with her to guard the orbs. There had been some tension between him and Magiere, as Ghassan wanted more proof of any supposed gathering of a horde before they turned to hunting their real quarry's hiding place.

Wynn wished they knew more about this Ancient Enemy—il'Samar, Beloved, and any of too many other names. All they really understood was it was a being or person of great power who had waged a great war across the world, created the first of the undead, and then for unknown reasons withdrawn into hiding.

Even this much was speculation based on what she'd gleaned from ancient texts. Now, apparently, it was reawakening after a thousand years.

Magiere was driven to find it.

And things were moving out there toward . . . wherever . . . in the east.

Ghassan urged caution until all five orbs had been brought together. He felt that more information should be gained first. Were most of the gathering servants vampires? Or were some more powerful, like the wraith, Sau'ilahk?

Magiere saw little point to learning any of this, and for her, finding the location of the Enemy was all that mattered. After a heated debate, she and Ghassan had compromised. Scouting trips would continue, but if she came across any undead heading east, she and those with her would try to trail them to their final destination, and hopefully to Ancient Enemy.

Night after night, Magiere came across only a few bodies.

Wynn was nearly always left behind at camp. With her shorter legs, she only frustrated Magiere and even Brot'an with their long strides. Lately, Ghassan had been the other one most often to remain in camp.

Wynn had grown more and more concerned about Leesil. He never joked or teased her anymore. He'd become even quieter than Brot'an, and that by itself was the most disconcerting change.

Now Ghassan sank down cross-legged before the tent he shared with Brot'an. Wynn knew he preferred being out under the night sky unless he was asleep. She looked up, for though it was full night, the desert was clear to see beneath a brilliant silvery moon.

"Ghassan," she began slowly, "do you think we would need all five orbs, should Magiere find the Enemy?"

She expected resistance, but she thought she saw him stiffen where he sat. "Why do you ask?"

Wynn hesitated, wondering how far to take this. "Magiere has only opened the orb of Water, and not fully. I wasn't with her, but I know what happened. All moisture in the area rushed into the orb in a storm. The potential destruction . . ." She faltered, uncertain how much farther to go. "It barely started before the spike was slammed back into the orb, closing it. And I know something of how the orb of Earth was used to bring down Bäalâle Seatt."

"And what are you suggesting?" Ghassan asked.

This was something she wouldn't dare say to the others.

"We have the orbs of Air and Spirit in our possession," she began again. "I don't know what Spirit will do when it's opened, but Air could create a similarly destructive storm to Water. If—if we trap the Enemy, and one of us gets close enough to open the orb of Air . . ."

She couldn't say it aloud. Knowing Ghassan, she didn't have to. Yes, that suicidal move might be enough to either kill or trap the Enemy again . . . along with whoever tried to use the orb of Air.

"I am surprised to hear such a notion from you," Ghassan said.

His abrupt dismissal annoyed Wynn. She shifted where she sat near the dying coals of the fire to look right at him. She could not see him clearly, but she saw enough by the moon's bright light. He was watching her intently but calmly.

"Why?" she asked.

His head tilted down, one of his hands moved slightly, and a whisper of some kind escaped his lips.

A faint glow caught Wynn's eyes halfway between herself and him. A stone first appeared to have a glimmer around it, as if dust-mote fireflies began to swarm. The glow grew, softly at first and then brighter and brighter—from the stone itself.

Wynn inched back a little. How had he done this?

"Listen!" Ghassan commanded. "We do not go recklessly stumbling into the lair of the Enemy and attempt to open one orb. If one can cause cataclysmic destruction by itself, do not assume five would be fivefold worse. The Enemy created the five anchors for a reason. That is the answer we must uncover first, before any needless rush or wasted life—yours and others'."

"And who will use all five, if we learn how? You?"

"Unless you would like to try."

At the start of this journey, they had intended to gather the orbs as a last option, should the Enemy be proved to be reawakening. If that terrifying reality came, she had envisioned at least a few careful experiments to see how the devices might be used together. Now she wasn't sure at all if anyone should know that secret . . . and live to tell it.

And she hadn't known how set Ghassan was on the original, final option.

"What if Chane and Chap fail?" she asked. "Or they don't return at all?"

Ghassan lifted his head and fixed on her in the half dark under the moon. "Chap and Chane have not failed."

Wynn balked for a moment. Ghassan appeared to close his eyes and bowed his head, and he remained that way for too long. This gave Wynn further pause before she asked anything more.

"How could you—?"

"The same way that I knew you were in the alley behind the sanctuary . . . on the night I needed your help to persuade the others to hunt the specter."

Wynn swallowed in confusion and almost challenged him again. Then she knew how *he* knew that Chane and Chap had succeeded. Relief flooded her in knowing they were safe.

"The pebble, the one you gave Chane."

Ghassan raised his head again and nodded once.

"You could know this? From so far away?" she asked.

"Even now they are on a ship nearing Soráno. And they have the final orb and its stonewalker guardian as well."

"Ore-Locks? He's coming with them?"

Ghassan nodded again. "You understand my reason for checking on them?"

She did, yet he seemed different from the man she'd once known, and she looked again to that still-glowing rock between them.

Ghassan was a sorcerer, a practitioner of a reviled magic. His focus was upon that of the mind, its powers, and its manipulations, though he had employed guild thaumaturgical alchemists in Calm Seatt to make her sun-crystal staff. Causing a rock to produce light was psychokinetic at a physical level, or at least that was how she would describe it from studies in the sciences.

She had never seen him do so before. It left her wondering about the sun crystal. He had once used that to track her into Bäalâle Seatt?

Had sorcery been involved in what he had contributed to the sun crystal's making?

"And now I need your help," Ghassan said, almost tiredly.

Wynn was afraid to even ask. "What help?"

Ghassan lay in the dark of his own mind, his own flesh not his anymore. In one instant of pause during conversation with Wynn, the specter had turned inwardly upon him.

Though he had no flesh within that darkness, he now lay shuddering as if burned and beaten to his own last breath. And the specter—Khalidah—had found and taken what he needed.

. . . *The same way that I knew you were in the alley behind the sanctuary* . . .

The specter had not been there in that moment; that had been Ghassan himself. Khalidah had taken that memory from him to once again deceive Wynn and to regain her trust in using hope against her. Khalidah wanted those orbs more than she knew, and yet . . .

Ghassan's false breath caught in realization as much as agony.

Khalidah was afraid to face the Enemy as yet.

He—the specter—did not yet know how to use the orbs.

How could that be possible? There were two nearby, and the specter could have even put Wynn into a natural slumber, so that he might delve those devices through sorcery. There was only one reason that had not happened.

Khalidah already knew his sorcery would not work on an orb.

Oh, yes, he might lift one by his art while in a chest, or perhaps even directly, but he could not examine and find the secrets of the orbs themselves through his art.

Were the orbs impervious to the other two magical arts as well?

If they were proof against thaumaturgy and conjuring, how had they even been made? Such defenses so ultimate could not have been applied to them during or after their making. As to during, for what they could already do, such work would have been almost impossible.

No one could truly know how they had been made, what they were—except perhaps the Enemy.

Ghassan's mind blanked in trying to see how to use this. He stored it away as one other thing took hold of his awareness. The specter had to come at him to find something to convince Wynn that she still spoke to Ghassan himself. Khalidah had to come and tear that out of him forcibly.

The specter had not found that on his own, as he likely could have with past hosts.

Again, Ghassan did not see the use of this . . . not yet.

Upon disembarking in Soráno, Chap found his relief at having solid ground under his paws wiped away everything else for a moment. The sea voyage was over, and now they would travel inland to a'Ghràihlôn'na to find Wayfarer, Osha, and Shade. At that thought, he found himself looking forward to company besides Ore-Locks's and Chane's.

The three of them walked the port city's streets after obtaining a stout, strong mule on which to lash two of the chests. Ore-Locks carried the third, as three orbs might be too heavy, even for a mule.

Although Chap and Chane had stopped briefly here on the way north in dropping off the younger trio, Chap had remained on the docks that time, while Chane had gone in to make the caravan arrangements.

But now Chap walked through the evening streets of the port city, running necessary preparations for further travels through his mind. Reaching the Lhoin'na lands was not even half of the journey ahead. Being lost in such thoughts, he was halfway through the city when he slowed upon noticing a young woman in a long, saffron-colored wrap gown passing by. As he took in her olive-toned skin, light brown hair, and roundish face, he halted completely and looked about.

Nearly everyone here looked like Wynn!

Fine boned, though round cheeked, the people of the Romagrae Commonwealth weren't as tall as the Numans of Malourné, Faunier, or Witeny, nor quite as dark-skinned as the Sumans. Nearly all walking past wore pantaloons and cotton vestments or long wrap dresses of white and soft colors. But they all had olive-toned skin with light brown hair and eyes.

Chap knew Wynn had been left as an infant at the gates of the guild's Calm Seatt branch. He now wondered if her parents had come from here, and how she had ended up being abandoned so far north. Some answers were never found, but still he wondered.

Thinking of her filled him with sharp urgency to move onward.

Soráno's streets were clean, most cobbled in sandy-tan stones, and small open-air markets were all along the way. There were many solo stalls, tents, and booths here and there. Almost any necessity—and some minor fancies—were available within a short walk from every side street. Everyone appeared to be some kind of merchant or farmer or crafter or artisan, and all appeared to have the freedom to set up "shop" wherever they pleased. The result was somewhat overwhelming.

Arrays of olives, dried dates, fish, and herb-laced cooking oils were abundant. Of course, though, it was past dusk, and many vendors were now closing up for the night.

"They are a friendly and polite people," Chane rasped. "But do not wander off. It disturbs them when animals are seen unattended."

Chap refrained from making a sound. Yes, he had forgotten that Chane had been here before with Wynn and Shade. He also did not like how "thick"

Ore-Locks was with Chane; the young stonewalker was not to be trusted too much because of that.

Still, Ore-Locks now had his uses.

—*What now?*— . . . —*A caravan?*—

Ore-Locks paused in the street, looked down at him, and then to Chane. "The majay-hì asks if we should seek a caravan headed our way. I pondered the same thing."

Chane turned, halting the mule. "What other choice is there?"

"We both know the way. I say we buy a wagon and team for ourselves."

Chap thought that sensible enough. Much as the orbs were locked up and well guarded, he did not care for the idea of traveling with them among strangers.

"I would agree," Chane said, "if we had enough coin left."

Ore-Locks shook his head slightly and waved off the objection. "I have coin. Master Cinder-Shard made certain before I left."

Both Chane and Chap blinked in surprise.

Ore-Locks shrugged. "It did not come up until now."

After another pause, Chap offered a single huff.

"Very well," Chane said. "We are all in agreement . . . for once."

As with most needs in this place, it was not long before they found a stable. They summoned the owner from within a small sandstone domicile attached to it. Ore-Locks took to doing the talking with the middle-aged man before he even stepped out.

Chane glanced down at Chap and whispered, "If you have never before seen a dwarf haggle, you may as well sit. This could take a while."

And it did. The poor stable master began to grow red in the face amid the bargaining.

Chap sighed at almost the same instant as Chane.

"Wait here," Chane whispered, dropping the mule's lead next to Chap. "I will go back to the main street and find supplies before all of the vendors are gone."

He walked away before Chap could consent. And by the time Ore-Locks finished, the poor stable master looked exhausted. That was how Chap felt in just sitting there while pinning down the mule's lead with his rump.

Chane returned with an armload of goods as Ore-Locks gave in on trading both the mule and money for a wagon and two bay mares, as well as full harnesses and several folds of canvas in the bed. Even so, when the dwarf produced a pouch with strange silver coins, each had a hole punched through its center.

The stable master balked at the sight of those, until he bit each one—several of them twice—to test their metal.

"That was still quite an amount of coin," Chane observed as they loaded the stores, chests, and all of their belongings into the wagon.

Ore-Locks merely grunted and shrugged, heaving another chest onto the wagon's bed.

"You know my people value iron more," he said. "Or even copper, tin, and steel. And I did not want the poor man to have a stroke on the spot."

"Do we leave tonight?" Chane asked, pausing and looking down at Chap.

As curious as the city was, Chap worried what might have become of Wayfarer and Osha—and his daughter, Shade—in all of this time. And after that, there was still more distance to cross beyond the forests of the Lhoin'na.

Chap huffed once in agreement. The sooner, the better.

CHAPTER NINE

O sha once again headed toward the barracks of the Shé'ith on the outskirts of a'Ghràihlôn'na, the great city of the Lhoin'na, though he did not want to. His days here were like a mist-laden sleep caught between a dream and a nightmare. And he could not awaken until Leanâlhâm—Wayfarer—chose to let him, wherever she was. He so rarely saw her now.

The two of them and Shade had traveled with a caravan as far as a fork in the inland road, where they were directed to take the northward path. Leaving the caravan, they had traveled on foot. Where that path finally broke from the woods, they halted before an open, grassy plain.

Tan stalks with traces of yellow-green gently shifted in the breeze. For a moment, Osha had forgotten his bitterness at the sight of the forest beyond the plain.

The trees were so immense; perhaps more so than in the homeland he had lost. Welcome as the sight was at first, it then left him so sad. It was not his home, that of his people. Wayfarer had finally pulled him onward with Shade lagging behind, and they took a few steps along the road through the plain.

The sound of hoofbeats grew louder before Osha stopped and spotted three riders headed their way at a gallop. He pushed Wayfarer back behind him as Shade rounded forward on his other side.

The two rear riders held their reins in one hand and gripped long wooden poles in the other. The leader appeared to hold only a bow in his free grip.

Osha quickly shrugged his own bow off his left shoulder and into his hand, but he did not draw an arrow yet. As the riders raced nearer, he made out their hair and eyes.

Oversized and teardrop-shaped—like those of his own people—their amber-irised eyes sparked now and then in the light of the falling sun. Their triangular faces looked much like those of his own people, though perhaps not as darkly tanned. Instead of white-blond hair, their sandy and wheat-colored hair was pulled up and back in high tails by single silver rings at the back crown of their heads. They had the same ears as his own kind.

Garbed in tawny leather vestments garnished with swirling patterns of steel that matched the shoulder armor, each bore a pale golden sash diagonal over his chest. When they were near enough, Osha saw the long, narrow, slightly curved sword hilts protruding over their right shoulders.

Shade rumbled, and Osha dropped his other hand to shoo her back.

He knew exactly who these riders were by the illustration in the sages' book that Wayfarer still carried. However, to see the Shé'ith with his own eyes was something else.

The riders neared to a stop before all three dismounted. The two leveled their poles as the third, the leader, closed in. Any stern challenge on that one's face faltered at the sight of the trio before him.

Osha could understand that. To have two foreign "elves" arrive in the company of a majay-hì would be startling—certainly not a common sight. He expected suspicion, harsh questions, and no immediate belief of the answers. It would have been the same from the guardians of his own people—the Anmaglâhk—before Brot'ân'duivé and Most Aged Father seeded war among the caste.

But there were no questions, not at first.

The leader, whom Osha would later know as "Commander" Althahk, stared at a black majay-hì with strangers who looked much like his own people. After one wave of his hand, the other two raised their poles, dropped the butt-ends on the earth, and stood waiting.

"Are you in need of assistance?" he asked.

Or at least that was what Osha could make out.

He had trouble following the strange pattern and pronunciation of some words. But he had expected a different dialect and did his best to communicate. It was not long before he, Wayfarer, and Shade were escorted along the road. Althahk walked beside them, leading his horse, and sent the other two Shé'ith back to patrolling.

Such a welcome was perhaps a relief to Wayfarer, though Shade seemed indifferent. To Osha, it meant little. And yet it was the beginning of his seeing the stark differences between these people and his own.

Althahk took them onward to the city. As they finally passed through a living arch of two trees grown together high above, the sight beyond almost made Osha think of turning back.

Cleared stretches for paths were "paved" with packed gravel and stone slabs. Gardens and alcoves of flora flowed around countless buildings—rather than living-tree homes. Tendril vines with glistening green leaves and flowering buds climbed immense trees . . . with more "made" structures and "made" walkways in their heights.

Earthbound buildings constructed of cut timber and stone were startling compared to the one port settlement of his own people. The an'Cróan did not build cities; they lived in—with—their land and did not dig, chop, cut, and change it like this place. He could understand and accept that humans did so, but not people supposedly like his own.

As Osha walked the main path, Wayfarer whispered to him in pointing out countless gardens overladen with heavy blooms. Every bit of space possessed nurtured—controlled—areas that stood out from their surroundings as . . . unnatural.

When Althahk paused and pointed down a side path—another with stone paving—he mentioned finding them lodging. Instead, Osha asked to speak to him alone and told Wayfarer and Shade to wait. He stepped off before the commander even acknowledged the request, though Althahk caught up quickly and redirected him down another side path.

Osha looked around for anyone who might be watching and then pulled the long, canvas bundle off his back and unwrapped it.

Althahk stared without expression.

Osha had already learned his sword was like that of the Shé'ith, though his was made of Chein'âs white metal the commander would have never seen before. He did not know how these other guardians of another people earned their weapons. That was, if they earned such things at all.

Althahk raised his eyes to Osha. "What is this?" he asked. "And where did you get it?"

Osha did his best to explain without revealing much concerning the Anmaglâhk, the Chein'âs, the Séyilf, and . . . too many other things.

Althahk listened in silence and remained so for a while after Osha finished. If he was not satisfied, it was difficult to tell.

"What do you seek here?" the commander then asked.

This was the moment Osha dreaded. It was difficult to even say, as he held up the sword.

"To remain among you—the Shé'ith—long enough to understand what this means."

The large eyes in the elder's face were too much like those of the great and most honorable Sgäilsheilleache, Osha's deceased teacher.

"That is wise," Althahk finally said.

After this, Osha explained Wayfarer's purpose in coming here. On that same day, the commander took them deep into the forest.

At one point, Shade stopped, looked all around, and then sank on her haunches and began to howl. When Osha asked the majay-hì to stop and move on, Wayfarer grabbed his arm as she looked all around the forest. The girl trembled with fright but stood her ground as if waiting.

"The sacred one knows who is coming," Althahk said. Raising his eyes from Shade, he gazed in only one direction.

Osha followed the commander's gaze and heard noises in the undergrowth immediately.

A steel gray female majay-hì shot out of the undergrowth and halted.

Osha remained perfectly still, even as Wayfarer stepped around behind him. Were the majay-hì here as different as everything else in this land?

The female studied everyone tensely, as if prepared to act. She was obviously the scout, for Osha could hear the rest of the pack moving all around but out of sight. And Wayfarer pressed up against his side so that he could feel her trembling as she watched the steel gray female.

He knew what she feared from all of that one's kind except for Shade and Chap—she feared that they would sense her human blood and reject her as not one of "the people." She had once told him this fear in secret.

The female swung her head to look back into the brush-thickened trees.

A wild-looking woman pushed out through the leaves with another majay-hì, a mottled-brown male, at her side.

She was small for either a Lhoin'na or an'Cróan, and little taller than an average human woman. Her hair was dark brown—like Wayfarer's—but with silver streaks. Those locks were bound back by a circlet band of braided green cloth, which might be made of raw shéot'a by its dull shimmer.

Osha did not know Lhoin'na knew how to make such cloth.

The woman's complexion was dark enough to be that of an an'Cróan. This had to be the one that Wynn had called Vreuvillä.

"Leaf's Heart" was the last of the Foirfeahkan, whatever that meant. Osha had never heard of such a caste, clan, or calling. There was no such word among his own people.

More majay-hì began coming into sight all around the clearing.

The woman settled a narrow hand upon the head of the mottled-brown male, and she looked down at him as if startled. When she raised her wide eyes, they shifted to someone slightly to Osha's left.

On instinct, Osha swung his bow arm back to push Wayfarer farther out of sight.

The wild woman's gaze hardened at him but turned again to Wayfarer.

Vreuvillä's wild eyes widened and became glassy, as if tears might come. Her lips trembled once. Osha had seen that look on others, those who found something they thought gone forever. He did not like that look aimed at Wayfarer.

Neither did Shade, who crept out with hackles rising.

Vreuvillä's pained and relieved gaze dropped to Shade with puzzlement and then . . . recognition. Her frown returned as she looked to the commander with a slow sigh.

"How often do you let fate shove you about?"

That was the strangest question Osha had ever heard.

"I could hardly resist," the commander answered, "as you would know."

At the hint of a smile altering his stern expression, Osha glanced back to Vreuvillä and felt certain she did the same for an instant. There was something more than mere familiarity between these two.

What was happening here?

Vreuvillä looked once more to Osha's left.

"Please . . . come out," she said softly.

Softness was not something Osha expected from this woman. He felt Wayfarer shift outward around his side. He tried to hold her back, but she grabbed his arm and held it off. At the sight of her, the woman slowly approached.

Osha watched carefully as Vreuvillä reached out, touched Wayfarer's arm with only her fingertips, and closed her eyes so slowly, she might have been falling asleep.

When she opened them again, she whispered, "You wish to stay?"

Wayfarer nodded. "For a while."

It troubled Osha to leave her with a strange woman and a pack of majay-hì. But this was why the girl had come, supposedly, and at least Shade would be with her. With one glance up at him, Wayfarer stepped off and followed the wild woman. Shade caught up, pushing in front between Wayfarer and Vreu-villä.

Both girl and dog looked back at Osha more than once.

He suddenly could not tolerate this. But at his first step, a grip closed tight on his bow arm.

"No, not yet," Althahk warned, all hint of humor gone. "Come with me."

Osha returned to the city and spent a restless night in an inn. The following day, Althahk took him to the barracks and introduced him to a group of five: three men and two women.

"This one will train with you," he told them.

Without question, they accepted him.

The first day had involved nothing but a long walk through the forest. They finally camped somewhere on the forest's edge beneath its immense trees. At least with those sentinels, though even taller than the ones of his homeland, he had one more moment of ease . . . until he looked to the open, grassy plain beyond. It seemed like the same one he had first crossed upon entering this land.

And there were horses out there grazing.

When he asked about them, the smallest of the trainees—later known to him as Yavifheran—answered, "For later, when they think you are worthy."

That set him on edge, and he eyed the horses: only five, as his inclusion in this group had been unanticipated.

There was not one day that followed when he was free of guilt over leaving Wayfarer and Shade with that unknown woman. And he felt more guilt than any sense of peace he felt with these others out in the wild. Though his skill was poor as compared to others of the caste, his anmaglâhk training aided him in what "games" were played for stealth, surveillance, hunting, and tracking.

From early on, not one of his new companions could match him with a bow.

More than one asked why he looked hesitant before—and angry and sad after—he fired an arrow and never missed his mark. He could not answer, for they would never understand. Praise for his skill only made this worse.

By looking in their eyes, he knew not one of them had ever killed in battle.

Especially not Siôrs, who was lighthearted and not a deep thinker. But of the five, Osha found Siôrs's company a tonic sorely needed, for Osha himself had come to think far too much. Unfortunately, this broad-shouldered Shé'ith trainee also gave Osha new turmoil. Siôrs was forceful in teaching Osha the horse, and then the pole . . . and finally the sword.

Each proved difficult for different reasons; the last was the worst, but riding came first.

The idea of sitting on the back of and attempting to control another being was abhorrent to him. That "she" had a name put upon her by someone was troubling, even though he had become accustomed to such things in the human world. This was even worse when Osha realized she was something *more* than the horses he had previously encountered.

En'wi'rên—"Wild-Water"—threw him off violently the first three times he hesitantly tried to mount her. The last time he hit the earth, she came at him. He rolled and scrambled away as her fore-hooves slammed and broke the forest floor, though nowhere near enough to have struck him.

She stood there, threw her head, and snorted.

"Oh, blessed green!"

Osha started at that moaned shout. There stood Siôrs among the others, all watching him.

"Stop treating her as if she will break!" Siôrs called with too much drama.

Even reed-thin Mehenisa looked astonished—or aghast. By her slight build, anyone might have thought her unsuitable to such a rough life. Ulahk and Kêl, cousins by human terms, were trying and failing not to snicker. Yavifheran, the youngest member, if judged by his size, watched with more disapproval than anyone else.

"Do you think the commander would send us out with untrained companions?" Siôrs asked as if the answer were obvious, and he flipped a hand toward En'wi'rên. "She is already a warrior and guardian, a full and true Shé'ith because—"

Yavifheran backhanded Siôrs across the arm, and Siôrs stopped short, as if he had almost made a slip.

Osha was too stunned by something else to give that much thought. A horse, not only named, held equal—no, superior—status among those present who trained to be Shé'ith?

Then who was En'wi'rên's true rider?

"Show her respect, not your doubt!" Siôrs barked at Osha. "She has earned that more than any of us. Mount her knowing she will be there—always!"

As if to illustrate, he turned, charged straight at the horse, and leaped in the last instant.

Siôrs's hands braced on the horse's back as he vaulted and swung one leg over to land astride En'wi'rên's back. Though she shifted, clearly that was a brief adjustment for the sudden passenger. Siôrs never even touched the reins.

"See?" he said, spreading his arms wide. Siôrs then swung his far leg over, slid off the horse's back, and landed lightly on his feet.

En'wi'rên looked at Osha with her big black eyes, snorted at him, and shook her head.

Osha burned with embarrassment and stifled anger.

But it was the last time he disrespected En'wi'rên, no matter how much he abhorred riding another being. It was not that last time he fell, though that came later—again and again—in training with the pole or "mercy's lance."

He had difficulty learning to both feel and anticipate how En'wi'rên compensated for his mistakes while sparring on horseback. Most of his first falls were not from being knocked off her by an opponent's lance across his midriff. He tried to pay more attention—to *listen*—to what she taught him in her movements. Less often did she have to save him, if possible. And then he still took a lance across the chest too many times.

En'wi'rên always stood silently, waiting each time until he picked himself up.

The worst came last, when he finally held that sword forced upon him. It was like touching the very thing that had taken everything he wanted when he had become Anmaglâhk. It was an unnatural, hateful thing; the seeming purity of the white metal blade mocked him. Everything about its use made this worse.

He understood striking from a distance with the bow, and even the return of the same from an enemy. With a small blade, though he could match few of his former caste, and never his teacher, the great Sgäilsheilleache, he also understood the bone knife's hook, the stiletto's hidden flash and speed, the strike and sweep of leg and arm, hand and foot, so close to an opponent that they were one.

But the sword . . .

Constantly shifting at a distance beyond touch and yet well short of an arrow's flight seemed impossible to master. How many times did he suddenly freeze in finding Siôrs's sword—or that of one of the others—resting flattened upon his shoulder near his neck?

Too many times to count.

What little peace Osha found in the forest began to wither.

At night, in trying to sleep, he was too often tortured by thoughts of Wynn. Not only for the pain of wanting her and the pain of her sending him away, but in imagining her in a barren desert and in danger without him.

As well, he wondered what had become of Wayfarer and Shade.

There had been times when Wayfarer had sent Shade to find and assure him. Even fewer times had the black majay-hì agreed to guide him to Wayfarer, and always in a place that could not be where she stayed with that wild woman. Even when he did manage to see Wayfarer with Shade's assistance, she was slowly becoming someone he no longer recognized. She treated him more and more as almost a stranger.

Several times, he left the others on foot to try to find her himself, though he never succeeded, and when he returned . . .

The others' worry, irritation, and anger were quite open. That cut him more than expected, and he did not know why. After having once abandoned her to Brot'ân'duivé and the others, he should have been relieved if not glad of her growing self-reliance. He was not.

There came a time when only Shade seemed glad to see him, and she was the only one he saw. Those were the only moments he found peace anymore, for she lingered longer and longer with him when Wayfarer did not come. The sight of a black majay-hì coming for him, and shying away from anyone else, puzzled the other trainees, though they never asked about this.

Finally, a dawn arrived when Osha tried to count how many had come and gone in the time of his training. He could not. Another dawn came when the others decided—or knew—it was time to return to a'Ghràihlôn'na. The journey back took longer than it might have, for the horses—including En'wi'rên—were gone that morning when he rose. Perhaps that had been the signal to the others.

It was dark by the time they arrived in the city, and Osha wondered what he would do now. All of his new peers had families here, and he had no one.

"You will stay with me," Siôrs said, as if it were fact. "My mother loves guests."

Osha did not know how to refuse politely. He had grown fond of Siôrs but would not be comfortable in an unfamiliar Lhoin'na family. He was still trying to find the right words as they approached the barracks when Althahk came striding out of the large stable nearby.

The commander's expression was so stern that the entire group stopped and bowed their heads.

"Osha!" Althahk barked, ignoring the others. "Come!"

Osha blinked, startled, uncertain how to respond. After a quick glance at Siôrs, who only shrugged, Osha hurried after the commander. Althahk had already turned toward the stable, his boots cutting the ground in long, hard strides.

Osha grew more alarmed in catching up. Before he could ask, they reached the open doors of the stable, and the Shé'ith commander stopped.

"*These* claim an acquaintance with you," he said. "I know two of them, and I told them it could not be true."

Lost and confused, Osha peered into the stable. Chap and Chane, as well as a red-haired dwarf, were all standing before the backside of a wagon with three chests in its bed. The dwarf was familiar, for Osha had met him briefly in Calm Seatt when he assisted with their original escape from that city. He could not quite remember his name, though the dwarf appraised him with thinly veiled dislike.

All the recent past days and nights of training vanished in an instant as Osha saw the three chests in the wagon. Full reality returned as he looked to Chane, who nodded once.

"You know them?" Althahk demanded.

"Yes," Osha answered. "Yes . . . I know them."

"Go and collect Wayfarer and Shade," Chane said without greeting. "Chap and Ore-Locks will go with you. I remain to guard . . . our wagon, and as soon as we resupply, we are leaving."

Osha went numb amid confusion. It was not that he wished to stay, but as of yet, he had gained no answers to his questions:

Why had the Chein'âs forced the sword upon him?

Why had they linked him to the Shé'ith?

Chuillyon sat feeling sorry for himself at his usual table in a public house on the edge of a'Ghràihlôn'na. Once he had been the head of a secret order of the Lhoin'na branch of the Guild of Sagecraft. He had dressed in white robes and commanded subtle but real power. He had been a great scholar . . . and more.

Now he sat drinking wine each night at the same table. Perhaps as a vain tribute to his former life, he wore a long black open robe over his simple pants and tunic. Black as the opposite of white was too much irony, though likely no one else would see it that way. No one noticed him much at all, for he always remained aloof.

How long had it been since he had chosen to secretly chase after Wynn Hygeorht into the bowels of lost Bäalâle Seatt? He had gone without permission or even guild knowledge, and one of his own acolytes had been killed. Another acolyte from a different order, but devoted to him, had been gravely injured. And upon his return, Chuillyon had been stripped of all positions and cast from the guild. Though he had mentally accepted this outcome, he had certainly never come to terms with it.

Then, an echo of Wynn Hygeorht had appeared two moons ago. He had been out walking in the city when that arrogant Althahk came in without his companions, but with three others.

Shé'ith always traveled in threes when ranging in their duties. Althahk alone escorted two foreign "elves" . . . and a charcoal black majay-hì.

Shade, unique upon sight as Wynn's companion, was utterly unmistakable to Chuillyon.

He remained frozen in place, watching from a distance. What was Wynn Hygeorht's wayward majay-hì doing here—and without the troublesome if endearing little human sage?

Strolling behind and off to the side, he closed on them enough to hear what might be said. The tall male and the short female spoke quite strangely. They were not Lhoin'na, which meant they had come a long way from that *other* place so few knew of on this side of the world.

But he knew.

Oh, yes, Chuillyon had occasionally traveled that far, considering that Chârmun, the great sacred tree of his people, had a "child" in the an'Cróan's ancestral burial ground. Yes, this was simple enough information to acquire if one knew what he could do and how.

Wynn Hygeorht as well had spent several years on the eastern continent, though he had not known her then.

Chuillyon had long foreseen the growing darkness ahead. In concern, he had counseled sages, nobles, and royals secretly. Warning signs both light and dark heralded its coming nearer. And considering Wynn's black companion was involved and now here . . .

He followed the trio that day, remaining out of sight as they first entered the forest. To his confusion and shock, Shade and the girl went off with Vreuvillä, that mad recluse who worshiped Chârmun and lived among majay-hì. But not before he caught a glimpse of the strange girl's eyes.

Even from a distance in the forest's shadows, those eyes were a strange, vibrant green instead of proper amber. After Shade and the girl were gone, the commander escorted the lanky young male to the barracks of the Shé'ith, where he was sent off with initiates likely in training.

None of this made any sense.

However possible, Chuillyon spent as much time as he could spying on them. Not so much with the girl, for it was quite difficult to get close with a pack of majay-hì always about. He did learn their names—Osha and Wayfarer—though at least once, the young male made a strange slip and almost called the girl something else.

And as with the girl's eyes, there was something strange about the young male as well.

Osha apparently possessed a Shé'ith sword not given to him by the Shé'ith.

Every time Chuillyon learned another tidbit, it gave him fits of aggravation. Not quite as bad as with Wynn Hygeorht, but still . . .

Tonight, at the inn, he stared into a full goblet. He had not taken a single sip.

The obvious was unavoidable if he wanted any slim chance to figure out more about these two strange young ones with Shade. He certainly could not approach Althahk or Vreuvillä; doing so would eventually be heard of by the guild. Perhaps it was time for another surreptitious foray into the lands of the an'Cróan, such a backward people distantly related to his own.

There was a problem with that as well.

Highly placed sages of his suborder had learned to use Chârmun—"Sanctuary"—and its few "children" about the world as portals from one to another. No one would do so lightly; well, all right, he'd sought Chârmun's assistance a bit more than anyone else had. And now, even though he was not highly placed anymore, nothing could take that ability from him.

However . . . outcast, disgraced, and worse, if he was caught doing so, he did not want to know what would happen. Well, he did think banishment was the next possibility, but they would have to catch him first.

There was a legend reaching back to the beginning of the Forgotten History. An ancestor of the Lhoin'na—and the an'Cróan—had been a leader of the allied forces in the Great War.

Sorhkafâré—"the Light upon the Grass"—took a cutting from Chârmun and left with those who would follow him. Some of the first Fay-born, including wolves whose descendants would become the majay-hì, joined him too. He led them across the world to establish a new territory on the eastern continent. There he planted that cutting, which became Roise Chârmune—the "Seed of Sanctuary"—at the heart of what would become those ancestors' burial ground.

Chuillyon knew this legend was true.

With Chârmun's assistance, he had briefly sneaked into that land a few times over many years. It seemed he would have to do so again for more serious snooping about.

Finally resigned, he rose and left the common house, leaving behind the full goblet. Heading through the city and out its northern side, he entered a path that led out into the thickest part of the central forest. He knew the way so well that he did not have to watch his steps. But as he drew closer to Chârmun's clearing, he slowed to approach with care and peeked carefully around each turn in the path. He listened to the forest as well before sneaking onward.

The last thing he needed was to be caught here, and not just by members of his former caste or the Shé'ith. As he spotted Chârmun's faint glimmer through the forest, he heard voices behind him along the path.

"Are we nearly there?" a deep, annoyed voice demanded in Numanese.

Chuillyon froze and looked about for any place to hide.

"Yes, nearly," answered another. "Chap, you should lead. I have already failed to find where we must go."

Chuillyon knew that voice and ducked off the path. Momentarily tangled in leafy, damp vines, he thrashed into the dense undergrowth, hoping no one heard. There he crouched behind a dank, moss-coated oak.

An instant later, Osha pushed through along the path.

Chuillyon was quickly distracted by someone else.

A red-haired male Rughìr, or dwarf, followed closely behind the young an'Cróan.

Chuillyon recognized the dwarf, though a name escaped him. He had seen the same one in Wynn's company on her visit to his land, just before he had tracked her all the way to lost Bäalâle Seatt. And last down the path came a tall, mature, silver-gray majay-hì.

This was rather disconcerting, aside from Wynn's own black companion. Just how many Fay-born had taken to wandering the world with outsiders?

Once the trio passed by and were a little ways down the path, Chuillyon slipped out of the brush more carefully than he had slipped in. It was not hard to follow them, considering the grumbling of the dwarf, who constantly swatted aside branches and vines that got in the way of his wide body.

What business did these three have so close to the presence of Chârmun?

Chuillyon crept after them.

*   *   *

Wayfarer sat with her legs folded to one side upon the mulchy ground. With Shade beside her, she looked up through a break in the forest's canopy at a clear, starlit sky. And here in this place, there were always majay-hì within sight.

She had grown more accustomed to them via Shade's guardianship and comfort. Sometimes they still reminded her of their kind in her lost homeland who had spied upon her and had likely done so for years before she was aware of them. She no longer feared that.

Wayfarer had never seen—dreamed—of anything like this place.

Strange bulging lanterns of opaque amber glass hung in the lower branches of maples, oaks, and startlingly immense firs. If one looked closely into the trees' thick foliage, tiny trinkets and other odd items could be seen bound to their limbs by raw threads of shéot'a, something the Lhoin'na used to make shimmer cloth. All of those trees loosely framed a broad gully with gently sloping sides that stretched ahead.

Decades of leaf fall had hampered much undergrowth, leaving the way clear for the most part. Yet, ivy still climbed over exposed boulders and around and up evergreens. Bushy ferns grew here and there, breaking through the mulch that now crackled under loping, scurrying paws.

A pack of five adult majay-hì, along with four pups, engaged in their own form of communication all around her. Of course, the young ones were less interested in "talking" and more interested in who could stay the longest atop their rolling, running pile of little bodies. All dashed about past one another in rubbing heads, muzzles, or even shoulders . . . for they spoke with their own memories.

It was a language like no other.

Wayfarer had been learning it . . . hearing it . . . seeing it in her own mind. It now took only the barest touch of fingertips in fur.

Should she wish, Wayfarer could have reached out and touched them as they ran past. Flashes of their memories would be shared with her. If not for Shade guiding her, rather than Vreuvillä, this might have been terror rather than a revelation. But once it sank in, it changed everything.

Vreuvillä had said as much in a strange way. "They will prepare you."

Wayfarer had not known what that meant. Prepare her for what? Then later, she did not care.

She had once believed herself an outsider, reviled and spied upon by the majay-hì of her own lost homeland. When they had come near her, hiding in the bushes and staring, she had thought this indicated their judgment that she did not belong.

How wrong she had been.

Majay-hì here were of all the colors she had known and feared. There were mottled brown, silver gray, near-black ones, and more. But there were none so black as Shade or any white like Shade's mother, the one Wynn had named Lily.

The white majay-hì—Chap's mate and Shade's mother—had set Wayfarer on the path to this place through a terrible journey.

It had taken a while, but Shade occasionally joined the others in their touching memory-talk. Not right now, though. Wayfarer leaned over and rested the side of her face against Shade's neck. Almost instantly, a word rose into her head out of her own memories—in Magiere's voice.

—*Dinner?*—

Wayfarer sighed and pressed her face deeper in Shade's fur. Even for all of the memories shared, she had come to like Shade's "voices" in her head almost more.

"Soon . . . not just yet," she answered, the answer somewhat muffled.

Even Shade was such a complication, though Wayfarer had grown to need her desperately. Shade was "sister" to Wynn, ally of Chane, and even friend to Osha. Perhaps in another time and place Wayfarer might have shunned Shade as she had Osha.

Facing Osha amid all else in this new place while he still thought long-ingly of Wynn was too much. And so, slowly, she had cut herself off from him.

Wayfarer rolled her face out of Shade's neck to gaze down the gulley.

At its nearer end stood a vast fir tree with a trunk nearly as wide as a tower of the keep where Wynn had once lived in Calm Seatt. The hint of a dark opening showed in its bare base, closed off by a hanging of dyed wool in that doorway.

Wayfarer had been unsettled by the "made" structures of a'Ghrài-hlôn'na—after her initial awe had passed. Here, she found comfort within a living tree like those of her own people, even as a temporary home. The wool curtain shifted, maybe from movement inside the tree, and a muffled voice called out.

"Wayfarer?"

"Yes," she called back.

Vreuvillä emerged from the tree dwelling, a circlet of braided raw shéot'a strips binding back her silver-streaked hair. Wayfarer had taken to wearing the same.

She had also cast aside old clothes for ones like the elder Foirfeahkan. She now wore pants and a long-sleeved tunic, as well as high soft boots, and a thong-belted jerkin, both made of darkened hide. There was also a pleated, thick wool skirt of dark forest green split down the front that could be bound around her waist as needed. She rarely wore that, as she did not like how it got in her way.

"Supper is ready," Vreuvillä said, striding closer as some of the pack shifted and circled in around her.

"Is it so late?" Wayfarer asked, sitting upright. "I should have helped." They normally ate well past dusk and into the night, and she always helped with everything.

"I would have called if help was needed," Vreuvillä said bluntly before Wayfarer could apologize.

Such brusque responses—sometimes before a question was even asked—

had become almost normal. At first, Wayfarer had found the Foirfeahkan woman rather sharp. But this was just her way, and she had opened a new world before Wayfarer's eyes.

That new world had not always been comfortable and was often confusing.

Vreuvillä explained that the Foirfeahkan were—had been—a spiritual sect reaching back before what humans called the Forgotten History. And even farther and farther. Vreuvillä did not know how far back they began.

From what Wayfarer understood, the priestess was the last of them.

Their ideology was animistic, another strange word with which Wayfarer had trouble. They believed in the spiritual—ethereal—of this world rather than a theistic focus common to the outside world. They believed—somewhat like the an'Cróan but more—that Spirit itself was of this world forever and not from a separate realm. More confusing at first, the life of Existence had a heart, a center, a "nexus," which was another word that Wayfarer had never heard in any language.

Chârmun—"Sanctuary"—was the center of all.

It was called so because its presence was why the Lhoin'na forest was the last place where the Ancient Enemy's darkest forces could not enter during or since the Great War.

The tree grew in all its mystery and beauty in what others called "First Glade." The true place of that name to the Foirfeahkan was somewhere else nearby. Wayfarer had gone to look upon Chârmun many times, though she had often needed Shade to help find her way through the forest. At first, she had been frightened, and even Shade had been reluctant.

In a hidden, remote place in her own people's forest stood another sacred tree of a similar name—Roise Chârmune, the "Seed of Sanctuary." Its clearing was the last resting place for the ashes of the first an'Cróan ancestors. Only the most honored dead of their people were allowed to have their ashes laid in that place. And most others only visited there once in their lives for a vision by which they took their final name.

Though Vreuvillä revered Chârmun, as the last Foirfeahkan she did not truly worship it. She saw it as sacred in being integral to everything, as were the majay-hì and other Fay-born. Because of this, she could share memories with the majay-hì . . . as could Wayfarer now. "How" was still a puzzle, and, though it was never said, Wayfarer often wondered about Vreuvillä's physical appearance.

The priestess looked in some ways like an an'Cróan or a Lhoin'na and yet neither. This was mostly because of her dark hair—like Wayfarer's—but there was something more.

Was Vreuvillä also of mixed blood?

Was it the same with all past Foirfeahkan?

Vreuvillä never spoke of this, even when asked, though from other things, Wayfarer knew there could be no form of heritage for this calling. All who had become Foirfeahkan did not inherit it; they came to it, as she had now done. In that, her taken name before the ancestors had better meaning.

Sheli'câlhad, "To a Lost Way."

And even that was not the final naming, according to her new teacher. Vreuvillä once mentioned that all Foirfeahkan took a name by their new calling. It was a name of their own choice. Even so, Wayfarer wanted no name but the one she now had, created for her by Magiere, Léshil, and Chap.

At first, she had not known what to expect in coming here, but after initial explanations, Vreuvillä did not spend much time with instruction. Rather, she encouraged Wayfarer to simply exist and feel what was real for herself.

"Commune among the majay-hì," she said, "and with First Glade . . . the true one . . . when the need calls you. These will teach you far more— more quickly—than can I. And after that, there is even more."

At first, and only at night, when even the trees slept, Vreuvillä had taken her to the true First Glade. It was a clearing with a broad circle of slender aspens at the far side. Those trees looked no different from others of their kind, but perhaps they were too pristine for a wild place. Within their circle, the grass was low and clean. And when Vreuvillä breached that circle to stand at its center surrounded by the aspens, her hair suddenly glistened as if she had stepped into a spring dawn.

Silver streaks in her locks turned almost white. Her amber eyes sparked as she raised her face upward. The majay-hì paced softly around the tree ring.

On that first visit and others later, Shade always remained at Wayfarer's side.

The priestess spread her arms low to the sides with palms forward and whispered in a tongue difficult to follow. It sounded like an'Cróan or Lhoin'na but perhaps older. That Vreuvillä heard or felt something answer her was clear, for it was the only time all traces of harshness vanished from her face.

But Wayfarer had neither seen nor heard anything, and Vreuvillä never explained.

Wayfarer had gone to this First Glade several times with only Shade. Though she tried to copy what Vreuvillä had done in clearing all thoughts from her mind, nothing happened. She felt nothing and heard nothing each time; ask as she did, Vreuvillä only answered, "You will receive an answer when they think you are ready."

And when Wayfarer asked, "When who thinks I am ready?"

"That is part of the answer you will receive."

There were too many nonanswers like this.

Days and nights passed much the same, except for "listening" to majay-hì memories in Shade's company. In that, she was almost at peace in forgetting things she had yet to understand. Freedom was hers for the first time among the pack, until Vreuvillä mentioned something else.

Wayfarer pressed about why the Foirfeahkan lived isolated from the world, and the priestess hesitantly whispered . . .

"Jâdh'airt."

Wayfarer frowned. Much as that sounded like a word of her people, it made no sense. Her only guess was something like "an overwhelming desire."

Vreuvillä's jaw clenched, and walking away, she uttered in a low voice, "The true wish."

Again, that was not enough. Other than being just a youthful nothing, it did not seem such a horrible thing. Wayfarer headed after the priestess.

"How is that different from just . . . a wish for something wanted?"

Vreuvillä slowed but did not look back. "Nothing can be created or destroyed in such a way. Only changed . . . exchanged."

Striding on, she had offered nothing more.

Tonight, Wayfarer pressed all such things from her mind. She was glad for the company of Vreuvillä and the pack, and in this moment, she was determined to think only of following the priestess back to the dwelling—and eating dinner together.

The two of them had taken only a few steps when . . .

A leggy, light brown majay-hì ahead to the left whirled from watching over tussling pups. She lunged down into the gulley and stared toward the far end. In less than two breaths, others of the pack stopped and turned.

Wayfarer did so as she heard Shade rumble shortly. Something shook the low branches at the gulley's far end.

A silver-gray majay-hì pushed out through the brush.

"Chap!" Wayfarer shouted, running to him.

There had been a time he was so sacred, she did not dare touch him. Then there was a time when she would but was still in awe of him. And later, even needing him curled up beside her at night, she found the old reverence was still there.

Now she skidded in, fell to her knees, and threw her arms around Chap, nearly knocking him over and sending both of them tumbling. Much as she had come to adore Shade, she had missed the one who nurtured her earliest self-discoveries.

"Oh, Chap!" she cried again, even as he grumbled at her. "You are safe . . . safe!"

—*Yes . . . I missed you too, but enough . . . Wayfarer, enough!*—

She had barely sat back, determined not to cry, when the brush beyond Chap rustled and tree branches parted.

Osha emerged into the gulley's end, and Wayfarer's body clenched.

He stopped just beyond the trees, looked her up and down, and then dropped his gaze.

A part of her still clung to him. Another part found him a distraction for the mix of resentment, betrayal, and longing she still felt toward him. This was why she had stopped going to see him a moon ago.

Wynn had sent him away, but Osha still kept her with him . . . inside.

Chap shoved his head into Wayfarer's shoulder.

—Not now . . . There is much to do—

She should have reveled in the sound of memory-words in her mind from him.

Some of the pack were closing in, a few rumbling softly. None of them knew him, but they knew he was not one of them. She never had a chance to show them.

A wide and stout form with loose red hair thrashed out of the trees behind Osha.

Even at night by the glowing lanterns, Wayfarer recognized him. He was a friend of Chane's who had helped them escape from Calm Seatt. Osha stepped closer behind Chap, watching her again. Even before she realized what all of this meant . . .

—We have . . . the three orbs—

"Where is Chane?" she asked Chap.

"Back in the city, guarding our cargo," Osha answered.

Wayfarer looked up once to see the scowl on his horselike face. And then Vreuvillä appeared, standing over Wayfarer.

"What is the meaning of this overly late visit?" the priestess demanded.

"Forgive us," Osha answered. "It was necessary."

His use of the Lhoin'na dialect had improved.

Wayfarer ignored him and focused on Chap. In recent days, she had worked with Shade on something new. The sharing of memories involved more than mere images, sounds, and touch and smell. There were emotions connected to them.

Wayfarer had shared memory after memory of Chap with Shade, his daughter, showing that daughter how Chap had protected her, befriended her, given her comfort. She hoped this might ease some of Shade's own resentments toward her father.

Now Wayfarer twisted on her knees away from Vreuvillä and looked back. Shade had stepped forward within reach, likely out of habit, for they needed touch to speak her way. She did not approach her father, though at least she was not bristling with hackles raised.

Shade huffed once at her father.

Chap stared back at her, wide-eyed and motionless, perhaps afraid to do anything to ruin even so little acknowledgment.

Wayfarer turned the other way and looked up at Vreuvillä, though she never got out a word.

"Yes, I see it is time," the priestess said, her voice tight as if restraining something. "And you are done learning . . . at least what you are."

Wayfarer rose up and nodded.

"You will come again to finish," Vreuvillä said quietly, "when there is time again."

Wayfarer could only nod, swallow hard, and look around the gulley at its lanterns and all of the majay-hì. This was not her home; that would be somewhere else with Magiere, Leesil, and Chap when all was done. And still . . .

She had known this was coming and did not like it.

Hidden among the trees and dense foliage, Chuillyon absorbed all that he saw and heard. It was almost too much, even for missing pieces that left him frustrated.

After gathering her belongings and saying short good-byes, Wayfarer left with Osha, the dwarf, and the silver-gray majay-hì, and Shade as well.

Yes, I see it is time.

The vexing priestess's words were the crux, but time for what? In a long life in the light of Chârmun, Chuillyon hated the darkness of ignorance most of all. And he was going to do something about that.

CHAPTER TEN

Upon reaching the one city of the Lhoin'na, Chap and the others headed for the stable. After lodging the wagon and horses, they decided to find an inn for the night. Osha mentioned he already had one in mind.

Chap then communicated to Wayfarer that she and Osha should accompany Ore-Locks the following day when he went to purchase supplies.

Standing near the wagon's back, Ore-Locks frowned when Wayfarer related this.

"I do not need the assistance of a boy and a girl in bartering," he argued.

"Chap thinks our presence might make others here more . . . friendly," Wayfarer added.

Ore-Locks scowled but did not argue. "Supplies for a longer journey, even beyond the Sky-Cutter, could take more than a day. I assume we are to help resupply the others we are traveling to join?"

Chane nodded absently, and to Chap it appeared the undead was preoccupied. This time, he wished he *could* dip into that undead's surface thoughts. Still, his mind was busy with other concerns. He had caught some things about the route from the young stonewalker, but not enough for his liking. And facing his daughter also worried him.

Shade lingered near Wayfarer. Whatever had happened between her and Wayfarer in two moons had changed them both.

Chap did not want to risk losing what little acceptance he seemed to have gained from his daughter.

"This time, we will not need to search for the seatt or its entrance," Chane said while fidgeting strangely, "so the journey will not take as long. But Ore-Locks, please do not wear out the patience of the local merchants."

Ore-Locks scoffed. "If they cannot barter adequately, that is not my fault!"

"A little restraint, please," Chane advised. "That is all I ask."

His voice sounded strained, and Chap studied him closely. A light sheen glistened off his pale face. Chap had no intention of asking what was wrong. If Chane were alive, he might have looked ill. Was that even possible for a vampire?

Again, Chap had other pressing thoughts.

Since arriving in this land, he had not stopped thinking about the moment when he, Chane, and Ore-Locks had passed through a large clearing. Even before arriving there, he had seen a glowing building ahead behind the trees, vines, and choking undergrowth.

Though Chap had never seen Chârmun for himself, he had *seen* it in the memory of someone else. Years ago, he had caught the deep memories of Most Aged Father, the ancient and decrepit leader of the Anmaglâhk.

Though it was difficult to believe, Most Aged Father was at least a thousand years old.

Once called Sorhkafâré, he had taken a cutting from Chârmun before leading others all the way to the eastern continent to found the territories of the an'Cróan. While reading the memories of the paranoid madman, Chap had seen an image of First Glade as it had looked a thousand years ago—and Chârmun within that place.

For some time now Chap had contemplated confronting his kin, the Fay, one more time. He had broken with them when they had once attempted to kill Wynn. Due to an error of the same thaumaturgical ritual that allowed Wynn to hear him, she had unwittingly overheard him speaking to his kin. Their outrage and reaction had been swift upon realizing that an outsider was aware of them. He had been forced to defend her in an ugly battle and, in the end, had broken with them.

He needed answers, and his kin before his birth into this world might be the only ones to supply them.

"Do we have enough coin to lodge all of us?" Wayfarer asked quietly. She had not spoken much since leaving the forest.

"We may not need to pay," Osha answered. "The innkeeper knows I train with the Shé'ith."

Hoisting one chest from the wagon, he ushered Wayfarer and Shade toward the stable's open bay doors. Chane and Ore-Locks carried the other two chests as Chap contemplated Osha's claim.

It seemed the Lhoin'na and the an'Cróan had some customs in common. Though anmaglâhk did not earn wages for service, they were given food and shelter. Perhaps Shé'ith were viewed here in the same way. After all, they did function as their people's protectors.

Osha led the way, and after a short walk down immaculately manicured paths off the street, he approached a one-story building constructed of light gray stone, and he set down his chest.

"Please wait here," he said in Numanese before entering alone. Only moments later, he returned to direct everyone around the inn's rear.

"We have three rooms," he said, indicating the closest oak doors in the inn's rear wall.

Chap looked up at Wayfarer.—*I . . . will stay . . . with you*—

Wayfarer might have hesitated and glanced toward Shade, who had already sauntered off to the nearest door. Then she nodded.

The distribution of rooms took no discussion. Chane and Ore-Locks took the third. Osha said he would take the second to himself, but he opened the first door for Wayfarer. Without waiting to see her in, he hauled off his one chest toward his own room.

Wayfarer quickly stepped inside, and Chap followed, as did Shade. This still took him aback, though it should not have, considering how close Shade and Wayfarer appeared to have become. His daughter did not display anything more than acceptance toward him, and he was still afraid of losing even that much of a change.

Something was different. She was different. Still, he had—would—never blame her for any coldness toward him. And it was not the first or thousandth time that he had thought of Lily.

Several years ago, during his time in the an'Cróan lands, he had been accepted as mate by the white majay-hì whom Wynn named Lily. He knew even then that he could not remain with her and would soon leave with Magiere and Leesil and Wynn. But he had also known that at some point, Wynn would be forced to part from them as well.

Chap spent his last night in the an'Cróan forest with Lily, trying to express to her all that must be done. Someone had to be sent to watch over Wynn, for the Fay still feared any mortal knowing of them and perhaps whatever part they had played in all that had happened before or after Magiere's birth. Chap knew they might eventually make another attempt on Wynn's life.

He gave Lily every memory he held.

In faltering with memory-speak, he begged her for something terrible.

One of their children would be condemned to banishment, or at least that was how a child would see it. Only someone akin to himself might stand between Wynn and the Fay. Even just any majay-hì was not enough. And once Chap finished his request, his begging, he lay there with Lily the rest of that night in close silence.

He left her before dawn, her eyes still closed, though she could not have been asleep. Moons later, his children had been born without him, including the one chosen—the one Wynn had later named Shade.

Shade had come to love Wynn, the two now as close as sisters. Something like this appeared to have started between Wayfarer and Shade, though the complications among the three concerning Osha could not be easy on any of them. Regardless, Shade still blamed Chap for forcing her away from home, siblings, and a mother in the absence of a father.

Among other sins, this was another for which Chap could never ask forgiveness.

"Only one bed," Wayfarer said, looking around the tiny room. "Shade, perhaps you could keep Osha company for tonight, so he is not all alone?"

Before Shade could answer, Chap stepped in and spoke to Wayfarer.

—I must . . . go out—

She turned to him with wide green eyes. "At night? Why?"

Shade turned and fixed upon him.

Chap wasn't certain what to think of this and remained focused on Wayfarer. And his answer could not be a lie, not to her.

—It is time . . . I speak . . . with . . . my kin . . . at . . . Chârmun—

"The Fay?" Wayfarer whispered. Her breaths quickened. "You will talk with them? Why?"

Before he could answer, two clear words rose in his own thoughts.

—Not . . . Chârmun—

Chap's hackles stiffened in a back step at those sudden words in his mind. This had never happened before. No one other than his kin had ever spoken to him this way, and not in . . . using . . .

Memory-words?

Shade huffed once.

—Chârmun . . . is not . . . true . . . First Glade—

Chap could only stare at his daughter as she stood watching him. How had she done that?

Those six broken-up words had come in Wynn's voice out of his memories. No creature but another Fay-born with memory-speak—like the majay-hì—could have found such memories, and they would have had to touch him to do so. Most did not understand language—and a specific one—to use memory-words instead of memory-speak.

Shade understood both, like himself, though she was far better with memory-speak.

Chap had always thought memory-words would work only with those who actually used spoken language. Obviously Shade had. And he had never considered anyone with such ability to be able to use it with him.

"Chap, what is wrong?"

Wayfarer's question startled him as much as Shade's first two words. For a moment, he did not know how to answer. Did Wayfarer know Shade could do this?

—*No . . . first try . . . with our kind*—

Was this as unsettling for others he spoke to this way as it was for him now? And all the more so with his own daughter. He reached out hesitantly to search for words in Shade's surface thoughts, and there they were, out of her memories.

"Chap, answer me . . . please!"

Startled again, he looked up into Wayfarer's panicked eyes.

—*It is . . . nothing*— . . . —*but . . . where is . . . the true . . . First Glade?*—

Almost instantly, he saw a ring of aspens in Wayfarer's mind. The girl glanced at Shade and then back to Chap. He answered Wayfarer's unspoken question about Shade.

—*Yes . . . she told . . . me*—

Wayfarer appeared troubled now. Perhaps this was something not meant for outsiders. Then he saw more thoughts surfacing in the girl's mind.

Vreuvillä passed from the dense forest into a clearing that held that ring of aspens. She headed straight for it, entered, and in standing at its center, she spread her arms.

More memory-words rose in Chap's mind.

—*They come . . . the Fay . . . come . . . there*—

On impulse, he tried calling up words in Shade's mind.

—*Can you take me . . . to this place?*—

A brief pause passed.

—*Yes*—

He turned instantly to Wayfarer.

—*Shade . . . and I . . . will go*— . . . —*You . . . remain . . . here*— . . . —*Please open . . . the door*—

He would not expose Wayfarer to his kin for anything, no matter that it appeared Vreuvillä somehow communed with his kin for unknown reasons. Chap could not help wondering of what the priestess might be capable and what she had been teaching the girl.

With a troubled expression, Wayfarer opened the door to let them out.

Chap slipped into the night streets, following his daughter.

Inside the small room that Chane shared with Ore-Locks, he set down the chest he carried. His skin felt as if insects crawled all over him. It had begun the moment he had driven their wagon across the grassy plain to enter the forest.

He had been to this land before, and he had not forgotten its effects upon him as an undead, even while wearing the "ring of nothing." No undead could enter lands protected by Chârmun or one of its "children." The forest would sense such an intruder, confuse it with madness and fright, and the majay-hì would come to pull it down and slaughter it.

Chane had known what to expect, but he had forgotten how bad it would become, even with his special protection.

The moment the wagon passed into the trees, he had begun to feel . . . something.

A nervous twitch squirmed through his body. Then a tingling, annoying itch began swarming erratically over his skin. With no breeze, he had still felt a sensation like dust blown over his exposed face and hands.

The prickling grew.

The forest did not fully sense him, but it sought to do so. It examined him and would not stop, because it could not quite determine what he was. This would continue until he once again passed into the outer plain beyond the trees.

The forest's probing raised another, greater concern.

"Are you all right?" Ore-Locks asked.

Chane did not answer. "I have to go back out," he said.

Ore-Locks set down his chest next to Chane's. "Now?"

"There is something I must gather that can only be found here."

"Should I come with you?"

"No, stay, guard the orbs. If you come, we will have to ask Osha or Chap to watch over them, and that would bring more questions. My task is . . . private."

Ore-Locks frowned. "We have already talked about you and your secrets."

"Not secret, but private. There are flowers that only grow here that I used up in making the healing concoction. I want to gather more." He paused and decided not to mention—for the moment—that such could also be used as a poison against the undead.

"Do you still trust me?" he asked.

Ore-Locks crossed his arms. "You know I do. Get on with it, but try not to take too long."

Chane left his personal pack and took only Welstiel's old one as he left.

Chap followed Shade down the same path he had taken that day with Osha and Ore-Locks. Soon enough, and well before spotting the glow of Chârmun ahead, Shade cut into the undergrowth, and the going became much harder while he kept as silent as possible.

Tonight, they could not attract attention from other majay-hì—or Vreuvillä.

By Shade's actions, she clearly knew this, though Chap wondered what she knew about the wild woman's teachings and influence over Wayfarer.

He tried to push aside such worries as they kept on and on through dark, tangled, wild places.

Chap began to lose his sense of time when Shade dove through a wall of foliage. He followed and was soaked by clinging moisture before he stepped out beside her on the edge of a clearing. Across the way stood a circle of aspens amid a soft glow.

Other than that, there was no way to know why this place was kept secret or how it had come to be. He had to trust that Shade knew more than she shared upon realizing what he had intended to do. Now he hesitated in remembering Wayfarer's memory of the priestess standing at the center of the aspens.

He was no . . . whatever she was, but he was Fay reborn in a Fay-descended body.

Chap stalked an arc in approaching the aspens but did not enter. Shade followed behind on his left. He stared about into the darker forest all around.

I am here, come for you! Answer me!

He had done no wrong in not bending to their unspoken fears. They had carved up, torn, and stolen memories at his birth into flesh. They had tried to kill Wynn. He would not cower and grovel before his kin.

A breeze began to build in the forest.

Mulch upon the clearing's floor churned around his paws.

Fallen leaves rose slowly in a column that turned around him and Shade, illuminated by the aspen circle's light. The forest around them appeared to darken even more, and in that dark, branches appeared to writhe in ways the wind could not have caused.

Chap heard his daughter's shuddering growl laced with a whine that did not stop. He waited, listening to the creak of shuddering branches settle into the crackle of leaves. The rustling chatter suddenly echoed and shaped inside his mind.

What now . . . deviant? You failed to keep the sister of the dead safe in igno-rance. So what more do you wish to know . . . and ignore?

This had always been their goal, to keep Magiere from any possibility of fulfilling the reasons for her creation: to serve the Ancient Enemy, to lead the undead hordes, and to walk in all lands, even those enchanted against the undead.

His kin did not acknowledge how much she had fought this in using her birthright against the minions of the Enemy.

Still, Chap was uncertain what final purpose she had been intended to serve. Another war upon the world had to be focused upon a goal other than destruction and death for the sake of it.

And then there was what he had sensed within two orbs so far.

He would not let his kin bait him into justifications. Yes, he had his sins, but not the ones they tried to put upon him.

Tonight, he would ask the questions.

What are the orbs—the anchors? How were they created and how are they used?

Only the wind's hiss and the chatter of branches answered him. He pressed on.

What answers—memories—did you rip away from me when I chose to be born?

Gusts blew through the clearing, and though he heard Shade snarl, he did not move or look away from the surrounding trees. The hiss of leaves grew to a crackle as a chorus of leaf-wings buzzed like a hornet's nest in his head.

His kin spoke.

Where is your charge? Have you fallen so far as to abandon her? And now you corrupt your own misbegotten flesh by straying so far from your path!

Chap snarled as he answered.

Do not speak of corruption to me or of keeping those with me in ignorance and from taking any side in what is coming. Now the Enemy awakens again . . . and again you do nothing, as you likely chose a thousand years ago.

There was a pause and then . . . *Leave the enslaved alone.*

Chap's thoughts blanked. What did that mean?

The wind began to die. Darkness started to yield to the aspen ring's glow. Branches in the forest settled in silence as the torn leaves fluttered to the earth. Everything fell silent.

Chap rushed to the forest's edge. *Come back . . . and face me!*

No answer came. They were gone, and he had achieved nothing—learned nothing. There was only a hint in what might have been a tiny slip.

—*Where . . . to . . . now?*—

At Shade's memory-words, Chap looked to her watching him. All of this had been another feeble attempt by his kin to sway him to obedience. All that was left was to follow the course he had already set for the others. Tomorrow, they would resupply and then head southeast as quickly as possible.

He answered Shade . . .

—*Bäalâle Seatt*—

There was only one thing he had heard that nagged at him—*enslaved*. What did this mean?

Chane slipped out of his room at the inn.

Leaving Ore-Locks behind, he headed for the great tree arch through which they had first entered a'Ghràihlôn'na. Out on that road, he broke into a jog toward the grassy plain beyond the Lhoin'na forest.

That was the only place he had ever encountered the white flowers called *Anamgiah*, the "life shield."

Though he had a nearly full bottle of the healing potion—which he hoped was correctly made—he had used up the other ingredients necessary. However, there were still two possible uses for the white blossoms themselves, one being their own natural property to bolster life itself.

As for the second potential use . . . well, he did not care to think on that just yet, but he might never have reason to come here again, and he could not waste the opportunity to gather more of the petals.

Along the way, he passed many dwellings and buildings out among the trees. The moon was bright above, and lights from dwellings high in the trees marked them as he passed. He saw no one, for everyone would be high above, in their homes, this late at night.

He broke into a run once the last of those passed out of sight, and he finally saw a break in the trees ahead. Then he slowed and turned off into the immense trees, weaving through to the plain's edge far away from the road. There, he stopped short of the tall grass and crouched to listen. He heard no hoofbeats nor smelled anything made of flesh in the low breeze. Tonight, he had no desire to be seen or questioned by a Shé'ith patrol.

There was only the scent of the golden grass shifting gently in the dark—*Anamgiah* had no scent.

Still crouched, he looked in all directions one last time and then crept out beyond the trees.

The sensation of a thousand insects crawling over him vanished, and he half closed his eyes in relief. Holding off the forest's fear-laced prodding as it tried to seek out what he was had been so pervasive that its sudden absence was bliss.

Chane crept forward in a crouch, spreading the grass with his hands, but only the tops. He did not dare touch what he sought with his hands. He did not have to go far, and he flinched when moonlight raised a tiny white glare between the grass stalks.

It was almost too bright to look upon as he spread the stalks even more.

A dome of white flowers sprouted with the tan grass. Tiny pearl-colored petals—shaped like leaves—looked as soft as velvet, as delicate as silk. They appeared to glow, though the stems and leaves below and around them were a dark green that would have looked black to anyone without his night sight.

The last time Chane had come to gather *Anamgiah* blossoms, he had been foolish enough in his ignorance to touch the white petals, even to hold one in his palm. That had almost ended him there and then.

Black lines had spread through his hand from beneath that one tiny flower. They twisted and threaded through his skin where living blood no longer flowed. He felt his skin began to split underneath those marks as they spread up his forearm beneath his shirt's sleeve.

He had begun to grow cold . . . frigid.

Paralyzing, icy pain filled his black-veined hand and quickly followed those worming lines up his arm into the nearer side of his throat and face. He had cried out and then fallen into darkness.

Ore-Locks and Wynn had found him quickly enough, but he remembered little more than agony.

Tonight, he would not make such a mistake again.

He took a pair of well-oiled gloves from Welstiel's pack, put them on, and dug for the tool kit. Opening the kit, he removed the single pair of tweezers it held. Carefully—cautiously—he began harvesting petal after petal and dropped them onto a piece of waxed paper. When he had finished plucking clean seven blossoms, he folded the paper many times and tucked it back into the pack.

Then he stalled, studying the small tool in his right hand.

How much residue from *Anamgiah* might remain on the tweezers and gloves? He could not afford such a mishap again. Using the tweezers, he peeled the cuff with one glove enough to pinch and pull it off, letting it drop. He then did the same with the other glove, but for the tweezers, he dug for a scrap of cloth and wrapped them up in that to store away for later cleaning. Nothing that had touched the petals ever touched his skin.

Just as he was at last satisfied, hoofbeats sounded out in the darkness. Quickly, he slung the pack over one shoulder and backed his way through the tall grass so that he might hide among the trees. Once again, he winced as the sensation of invisible insects crawling over his skin returned.

Dawn was far off, so he had time. He waited for and watched a trio of Shé'ith ride past at a leisurely pace. Only when they were out of sight once again did he head through the trees for the road.

CHAPTER ELEVEN

Magiere walked through the desert foothills—more conflicted than she had ever felt. She couldn't speak of this to anyone, not even Leesil. Not that he wouldn't listen or care. Of course he would. It simply wouldn't do any good. He couldn't change the situation, and neither could she.

Scouting now seemed futile.

But even if they found the Enemy's hiding place, her hands were tied until they had all five orbs. So they—she—kept searching for any signs of an undead or other servants of the Enemy that might lead them . . . somewhere other than more wandering.

Tonight, the scouting team was larger than normal. Those left behind at camp had become more restless of late. So they'd found a site between foothills with a solid overhang and a deep rear to leave Wynn on her own for a while—at her suggestion. There was little chance she'd be spotted if she kept any light source dim, and she had her sun-crystal staff in case of emergency, though that was good only against the undead.

Magiere now followed Brot'an and Ghassan a short distance ahead, and Leesil strode along beside her. His tan complexion had grown even darker, and she couldn't remember the last time she'd seen him without that muslin cloth tied around his head and draped down his back.

In a sidelong glance, he caught her watching him.

"What?" he asked.

"You're starting to look like a Suman."

"What does that mean?"

Magiere shook her head. "Nothing. Forget it."

Before he could press her further, she spotted Brot'an stopped up ahead. He stood motionless, as if not even breathing. Ghassan had halted as well. Magiere hurried on with Leesil.

An instant later, a familiar hunger built inside her.

Moonlight grew brighter in her eyes. She almost expected Chap to break out in an eerie howl, but he wasn't here. Thinking became difficult as hunger flooded through her and she heard Leesil's steps slow. When she glanced over, she found him staring at her.

Even in just the moonlight, he must have seen her irises had gone black.

Without a word, he hooked the leather string around his neck with one finger and jerked out the topaz amulet. It was glowing. At the extra light, Brot'an glanced back.

The first scream tore the silence of the night.

Magiere's muscles tensed as she was about to charge toward the sound.

Ghassan held one hand up to stop her.

"Wait," Leesil whispered.

She didn't know how long she could wait, but then Brot'an and Ghassan both broke into a jog onward. Another scream pierced Magiere's ears. Her jaws ached as her teeth began to elongate. Leesil grabbed her wrist, and that was all that kept her from bolting past Ghassan and Brot'an as they followed.

Brot'an ran upslope and dropped to his stomach near the crest. Ghassan dropped beside him, and Leesil had to pull Magiere down.

"We cannot interfere," Brot'an whispered. "We must let this finish and follow them."

Magiere choked back a hiss when she saw the slaughter taking place at the base of the downslope. Her night sight exposed five figures with near-white skin and filthy hair setting upon a small group of Suman nomads. Throats were ripped under yellowed fangs. Children were pinned to the hillside's stony exposures. The noise grew as two men with long knives tried to fight back, and both went down quickly. One was torn open at the throat as the other went down, and his scream was cut short in a choke.

Magiere lost all thoughts of anything else. She sprang to her feet, but Leesil grabbed the back of her belt. She barely heard him skid on stone and packed earth as she pulled her falchion and white metal dagger.

Khalidah watched in alarm as Magiere charged, breaking Leesil's grip on her belt and sending him skidding and tumbling after her. Brot'an was up in an instant. Leesil rolled to his feet and pulled a winged blade as he ran on. Khalidah fixed on the back of Magiere's head as sigils and signs filled his sight.

If the dhampir and her consort, along with that master assassin, did not kill all targets before any could flee . . . there would be a trail to follow. Even if one of Magiere's companions died in this rash assault, in her current state she might still rush after a fleeing quarry—and she could keep up.

That quarry might lead her straight to Beloved, and all of Khalidah's delays to gain the orbs would come to nothing. Worse, if she were somehow crippled or even killed, would others continue or turn away?

Khalidah arose as more lines of light spread around his view of Magiere.

Rage consumed Magiere as she ran. Her mind was filled only with thoughts of tearing, hacking, and rending the undead. Her speed picked up in charging downslope, and then her legs shook and buckled for no reason.

She stumbled and then toppled as the baked ground and stones vanished before her eyes, as if her night sight had suddenly failed.

*   *   *

Ghassan fought wildly to regain control of his body as he watched Magiere stumble several times and then fall. Leesil dropped beside her and grabbed her shoulders. Brot'an ducked around them both, watching below for any attention that turned their way.

The screaming faded, the last one cut short to silence.

Ghassan's legs began to move as Khalidah took his body to join the others.

"What happened?" Khalidah asked quietly.

"I don't know," Leesil answered, sounding panicked. He had dropped his weapon and pulled Magiere up against his chest. "Magiere?"

Her eyes fluttered open, and her irises had contracted to their normal state. She sucked in a loud breath before even seeing her husband.

"What happened?" he asked her.

Magiere blinked several times, looked all around, and ran her hands over her face.

"Perhaps fatigue or disorientation made her lose her footing," Khalidah suggested, glancing below to see nothing but the mute silhouettes of corpses. "It is too late to do anything. The undead are gone, and we should leave here. Attempting to track them now could only lead us into an ambush. We will wait to pick up the trail at dawn, when most of their kind go dormant."

Ghassan railed in frustration and impotence. The specter's concern would sound so rational to the others.

Leesil reached for his fallen blade and drew Magiere up as he rose. "Yes, back to camp . . . for now."

There was nothing Ghassan could do but turn his anger upon Khalidah.

I will see you scattered into nothing.

He heard nothing in reply, not even a snicker in the dark.

*   *   *

It took only a day for Osha—along with Ore-Locks and Wayfarer—to purchase necessary supplies. Not long after nightfall, he climbed into the remaining space in the wagon's back with Wayfarer, Shade, and Chap. Ore-Locks climbed up onto the front bench. Chane followed him and took up the reins.

"Everyone present?" the vampire rasped.

Chap huffed once to answer, and Chane clicked the reins.

The wagon rolled out of the stable and onto the street. Osha leaned back against a chest to face the wagon's rear. The others with him here in the back were packed in tight among the three chests, the supplies, and all the other gear.

This was all happening too fast.

Only one night earlier, he had walked into the city with Siôrs while wondering how he would spend his time outside of training. Now he was heading off to find an entrance to a fallen dwarven stronghold.

He had not even had a chance to say good-bye to Siôrs and the others or even pay his due respects to Commander Althahk.

Only one thing brought him comfort.

Wayfarer sat nearby, though she did not lean in upon him as she once had. Shade lay close to her, the majay-hì's head across her thighs. Chap lay farthest back near the wagon's rear, his head upon his paws. Wayfarer did not appear daunted by the prospect of another journey through strange places.

This was not the only change he noticed.

In her, Osha now saw . . . confidence . . . though perhaps it was still tangled in doubts. He understood both personally.

As the wagon neared a southern exit from the city and turned onto a road that still ran through the forest, he studied her whenever he thought she would not notice. She even looked different, though he could not decide if that braided circlet of raw shéot'a strips and soft rawhide clothing were to his liking. He certainly liked the look of her, but at the same time the new attire made her someone he no longer knew.

"Are you sad to leave?" he asked quietly in their tongue, so Chane or Ore-Locks would not overhear or understand.

She cocked her head slightly, watching him. "Not exactly."

Again, she did not sound like Wayfarer—and certainly not Leanâlhâm of older days. For one, she answered his question directly and did not stare at the wagon bed. He had never heard her speak in such a forthright manner.

And likely that confusion showed on his own face, and so he glanced away.

"I have not learned enough . . . I am not ready to leave," she added. "But I do miss Magiere and Leesil, and it is also good to have you again."

In a flash of hope, Osha sought to meet her eyes, but found her looking at Chap. The elder majay-hì huffed at her with one switch of his tail.

Osha hung his head.

Strangely disappointed, though he knew not why, he felt the truth of her words.

He did not feel "ready" in what he had learned either, as he had uncovered no connection between himself, the sword, and the Shé'ith, and no reason why fate would link him to them. Was he sad to leave? He could not be sure. Perhaps had he found a new way to live? Perhaps he would miss Siôrs and the others and even En'wi'rên, though he still had bruises from her instruction. But as to all of this and how it had come to him . . .

It was still because of that sword forced upon him. Could he allow his path to be decided by anything connected to that blade? Finally, he lifted his head to watch the city's southern gate of massive trees grow smaller and smaller.

As he leaned farther back to find a more comfortable position, he discovered Chap watching him intently.

Osha looked away.

*　　*　　*

Chuillyon hid in the darker night shadows outside the stable and watched as the wagon rolled away. The dwarf sat up on the bench with the undead while the young would-be Shé'ith, the girl, and both majay-hì were piled in among several chests and sacks of supplies.

What had brought this unlikely group together and brought them here? And why?

He had to know.

He could give them a head start and purchase a horse to follow at a safe distance. This might yield their final destination, at least. But at a distance, he might learn nothing of them or their goals or how such a strange collection of people had drawn together in the first place.

He could go to Chârmun and travel again to Calm Seatt, for though unknown to most, a child of Chârmun grew in the courtyard of its third and now royal castle. From there, he could make a reasonably quick visit to an old friend.

Cinder-Shard might have a few pieces to this strange puzzle.

But Chuillyon had dealt with Ore-Locks and Chane Andraso before. They had even stayed at the Lhoin'na guild branch once—along with Wynn Hygeorht and the charcoal majay-hì. Both the undead and the young stone-walker were tight-lipped and functioned on their own agendas. A trip to Cinder-Shard might prove a waste of valuable time. He might know exactly what Ore-Locks was doing here . . . and he might not.

Also, in the end, it was the two younger foreigners who bothered Chuillyon the most. Those two were more likely the crux of this odd puzzle.

One had been welcomed by the Shé'ith without any of the traditional petitions and preliminary testing. The other had been taken in by that annoying, renegade priestess of outdated practice, who had been a thorn under Chuillyon's robe for decades. Vreuvillä despised the Lhoin'na sage's guild and all those associated with it. She viewed them as having used Chârmun to give themselves a place of importance in the world. She sneered at the orders of the sages, at their need for ranks and titles.

Why had Vreuvillä accepted the foreign girl?

Chuillyon sighed in frustration; the answer would not be found in Calm Seatt.

That left only his earlier original notion: to visit the world's far side to snoop upon his people's backward cousins, the an'Cróan. Those two younger ones had to have come from there.

So he headed off again through the city. He knew the way to Chârmun so well that he paid little attention to his path, but once he drew close, the night was dark enough in the thickened forest that he risked pulling out a small cold-lamp crystal.

He should have given it back to the guild when he was stripped of his rank and cast out . . . and he had, actually. That he had an extra one, well, it was not his fault if no one asked about that.

Rubbing it lightly in his hands, he held it loosely in a grip to let only a little of its light escape. If Vreuvillä or her pack were about, he certainly did not need such complications. There had been enough already.

Something stood out in the canopy above him.

Tawny vines as thick as his wrist wove their way through the high canopy, some paralleling his path. They were smooth, perhaps glistening from moisture, but he could see a grain in them like that of polished wood.

As he stepped onward, more vines twisted above him, growing broader and thicker the farther he went. Smaller ones appeared here and there, branching off the larger ones. All were woven into the upper reaches of the trees. Soon, they did not glisten as much as faintly glow, as if catching the radiance of the moon hidden from sight farther above.

He used the soft light of these vines to lead him, for he knew they came from where he now traveled. Branches, trunks, and bearded moss were like black silhouettes between himself and a nearing illumination inside the forest itself.

Chuillyon finally stepped out into a broad clearing and idly slipped the crystal away out of sight. Overhead, the forest still roofed the space, but the clearing was covered in a mossy carpet. And there at its center was his old friend.

Chârmun's massive roots split the turf in mounds, some of which would be almost waist high near its immense trunk. Its great bulk was the size of a small tower, and though completely bare of bark, it was not grayed like dead wood. The soft glow seen in the vines and its branches lit the entire clearing with shimmering light.

It was alive . . . because in some ways it was life itself.

"Oh, so good to see you again, as always," he said softly.

He headed toward the great trunk, as he had done many times before.

"Time for another outing, if you do not mind," he added with a faint smile.

When he was close enough to touch Chârmun, he pulled his plain robe around himself and began to lower his large hood over his eyes. Still pinching the edge of his hood, he froze in place, staring.

Some new growth to replace the old was to be expected, but such so very rarely had leaves—not on Chârmun. And that was what he stared at now: a new small sprout with leaves. He had not seen such in fifty-seven years, and that last one he had planted in a secret place of the courtyard in the Calm Seatt's third and largest castle.

Chuillyon released the pinch of his hood. He dropped his hand at his side with a moan.

"Do you not have enough children?" he asked in exasperation. "And where am I to hide this one?"

Chuillyon looked up into the canopy above as if searching for a sign. Finally lowering his eyes, he shook his head, muttering like a petulant child . . . of some seventy-plus years. Still no sign of an answer came.

"Very well, be that way!"

He knew this meant he was to take no action yet, so he left the new sprout on the branch where it grew.

"At some point, you will let me know—one way or another—where *this* one is supposed to go."

It was not a question, though there was no reply.

"And people say I am devious."

With that, Chuillyon thought of the child of Chârmun half a world away in the land of the an'Cróan. He reached out and placed his fingertips like a feather's touch upon the glimmering tree's trunk.

After settling Magiere in their tent to rest, Leesil stepped out and crouched before his pack left just outside. Ghassan and Brot'an stood whispering near their own tent, but both glanced his way in a pause. He ignored them and peeked back into his own tent where Wynn was tending Magiere by the light of a cold-lamp crystal.

Magiere was not injured or ill, but her strange collapse and disorientation bothered everyone, especially him. Normally, quelling her rage and hunger was a challenge. Whatever had happened to her near that massacre had flushed them from her.

Before leaving the Suman capital, he'd hidden a pouch of spiced tea in his pack. He hadn't touched it as yet, for water was too precious to lose any in boiling. But Magiere liked spiced tea, and he wasn't certain what else to do for her comfort.

Digging deep into the pack, he tried to find the pouch, and his hand brushed something else. About to ignore this object, he took hold to push it aside, and stalled. Then, he drew it out.

The narrow tube slightly wider than his thumb had no seams at all, as if fashioned from a single piece of wood. It was rounded at its closed bottom end, and its top was sealed with an unadorned pewter cap. The whole of it was barely as long as his forearm, and what it held . . .

Back in the Elven Territories on the eastern continent, Magiere had been placed on trial before the council of the an'Cróan clan elders. Most Aged

Father had denounced her as an undead. To speak on her behalf, as an outsider and half-blood at that, Leesil had to prove he was an an'Cróan.

He had to go before their ancestral spirits for "name-taking," a custom observed by all of them in their early years before adulthood. From whatever young elves experienced in that ancient, special burial ground, they took a new name. They never shared the true experience from which that came—well, most didn't. At the center of that clearing stood a tree like no other he'd ever heard of, let alone seen.

Roise Chârmune, as they called it, was barkless though alive. It shimmered tawny all over in the dark. The ancestors accepted him, but instead of showing him a vision from which to choose another name, they'd put a name to him:

Léshiârelaohk—"Sorrow-Tear's Champion."

Among the ghosts he had seen of the an'Cróan's first ancestors—though in that he and Wayfarer seemed the only ones who'd met such—there had been one woman, an elder among those who first journeyed across the world to that land.

Léshiâra—"Sorrow-Tear."

She and all those ghosts had tried to fate him, to curse him, and he'd neither wanted nor accepted it. There were few people in this world, mainly one, whom he would ever "champion." And right then, all he wanted was to make tea for Magiere, but he still remained focused on the tube.

There and then, Leesil sympathized with Osha and his unwanted sword. Perhaps he'd gotten off easier between the two of them. In spite, he gripped the tube's cap and pulled it off, tilted the tube, and its even narrower content slid out into his other hand.

It was the proof he'd once needed to stand before the council on Magiere's behalf. He had taken it from the very hand of a translucent ghost, a warrior and guardian among the ancestors. Tawny, leafless, and barkless, the branch still glistened as if alive, and it glowed faintly . . . like Roise Chârmune.

In the years that had passed, he'd discovered that if left in the tube for too long, the branch grayed to dried, dead wood. Or so it had seemed. Dropping it accidentally in the snow, while he, Magiere, and Chap had gone to the northern wastes to hide two orbs, he'd bumbled upon another discovery.

Even in that frigid land, the branch had taken moisture and come back to life.

Since then, Leesil took care to pour a little water into the tube now and then. He didn't know why; it just seemed the thing to do. Still holding the branch, he used the tube to push the tent's flap slightly aside and peek in.

Magiere was sitting up and scowling, which was a good sign for her. Wynn offered her a dried fig, and after briefly arguing, Magiere finally took it. As he was about to let the tent flap fall, the light of Wynn's crystal washed out over the branch, and Leesil started slightly.

He rose up, studying the slender branch in his hand, lifting it upright before his eyes. What was that little something on the side of it? Barely a protruding nubbin, but was it trying to sprout something?

Long tan fingers touched the branch's far side—or rather they were just suddenly *there*.

Leesil sucked in a sharp breath as he heard another one. Before him, touching the branch's far side, was a very tall figure in a black robe.

"Oh . . . oh, my . . . this is not right," someone whispered within that deep, sagging hood.

Leesil jerked the branch away, dropped the tube, and ripped out a winged blade, snapping the tie of its sheath in half. The robed figure lurched back in another gasp as Leesil heard running feet coming fast. The figure's hood whipped toward the sound.

"Wynn, light!" Leesil shouted as he lunged.

"Wynn?" the hooded one whispered, and then shouted, "No, wait, please, she can—"

The voice cut off as someone else—tall and dark clad—slammed into the robed figure and both flopped across the ground in the dark. Another gasp erupted from the hood as Brot'an came up atop his pinned target with a stiletto poised to strike. Ghassan arrived in that same instant, and then light flooded the camp with the sound of a tent flap swatted aside.

"Magiere, stay there!" Wynn called, and then she was right at Leesil's side.

Brot'an held the robed one pinned with a folded leg across its upper chest. His knee was lodged on the sand with his foreleg pressing near the figure's throat.

"What's happening?" Wynn asked in a hurried voice.

Brot'an wrenched the hood aside.

Leesil was still in shock as to how someone so tall had gotten into the camp—and that close to him—without any of them noticing. He even looked about once before focusing on the intruder's face.

"Where did he come from?" Ghassan demanded.

"I don't know," Leesil answered. "He just . . . was just there!"

Light from Wynn's cold-lamp crystal revealed the shock-flattened, triangular face and wide, *wide* amber eyes of a mature elven male. It was hard to be certain between night shadows and the harsh light, but maybe there were faint creases around his eyes framing a narrow nose a bit long, even for his kind.

"Chuillyon?" Wynn whispered.

Finally blinking, Leesil looked over and then down. Wynn's features had gone as blank and flat in shock as the intruder's.

"You know him?" he barely asked.

"He-hello . . . again," the elder elf choked out. "It is . . . is a . . . bit difficult . . . to talk like this."

"Don't let him up!" Leesil barked at Brot'an, though he still watched Wynn.

The little sage's oval face twisted in fury—and she lunged without warning.

Leesil grabbed her around the waist, which wasn't easy with the branch in one hand and a punching blade in the other. But he wasn't letting go of either or her. And then he flinched.

There had been a few times he'd heard Wynn slip, usually in Elvish. None of that had ever been like the torrent of foulness that came out of her now. He couldn't even follow half of it. But as to what he did catch, well, he had to resort to dropping on his rump just to pull the thrashing sage down.

"Let go of me!" she shouted, and followed this up with another word in Elvish.

Now that last word he did know, though he couldn't pronounce it himself—and he didn't like it shouted at him.

"Wynn, desist, now!" Ghassan snapped.

"What is going on?"

Ghassan's head pivoted as he looked over Leesil's head.

Leesil almost swallowed his tongue on hearing Magiere right behind him.

How was he going to hang on to Wynn *and* keep Magiere out of this? Magiere wouldn't even second-guess acting on Wynn's reaction. A sharp pain took that thought as Wynn punched him in the thigh.

"Stop!" he shouted, dropping his punching blade to get a better grip on her. "Magiere, you back off too! Brot'an, let him up but watch him."

Brot'an shifted into his rear folded leg, releasing pressure, though he kept the stiletto poised.

"Wynn, you know this one?" the master assassin asked.

He remained focused on his target. The elder elf half rolled aside and sat up, forcefully clearing his throat and rubbing it as well.

"Oh, yes, I know him!" Wynn shouted.

"So I take it he's sided with the Enemy," Magiere half hissed, half growled.

When she inched ahead into view, Leesil saw the falchion in her grip. "I said back off!" he warned. "Let Brot'an handle this."

"Wynn?" Ghassan asked.

"Chuillyon is always on his *own side*!" she answered. "And that's why he is a pain in my—"

Leesil clamped his free hand over Wynn's mouth and got an elbow in his side for it.

"Hardly fair, Wynn," the mature elf replied hurtfully.

His amber eyes shifted slightly—and widened a bit—as they looked down to Leesil's other arm wrapped around the front of Wynn. And down a little more.

Chuillyon's face again filled with wonder. He blinked slowly, leaning forward in peering . . .

Leesil whipped the branch around his back, out of sight, and that was when Wynn got loose.

By the next midmorning, Wynn's ire had cooled. No, it was choked off.

She had no proof that Chuillyon had interfered with any of her efforts, but she knew he had just the same. He had a penchant for turning up far too often when it was to his advantage, not hers and not anyone else's. Vreu-villä considered him untrustworthy and self-serving.

Wynn might not know why, but she wholeheartedly agreed.

If Brot'an had not stopped her after she'd broken free of Leesil, she certainly would have punched that interloper right where he sat. She was still thinking about doing so as she paced about the camp.

Chuillyon was now essentially a prisoner, sitting near the dead fire and being closely watched by either Ghassan or Brot'an or both. This gave Wynn only minor satisfaction, for it did not solve the problem of getting rid of him. Magiere and Leesil were both in their own tent, and Leesil had put away the branch.

Wynn could see how that object might interest Chuillyon, but the "why" bothered her more. She kept eyeing him as she paced, and his serene expression gave her no clues.

Brot'an sat outside the other tent, watching, supposedly, though he rarely looked directly at Chuillyon. Then again, there was no place Chuillyon could go, and exactly how had he gotten here?

Ghassan stepped out of the other tent with a cup in hand, which he took to offer to Chuillyon.

"I thank you," Chuillyon said with such gracious politeness that it soured Wynn's stomach.

"Where are your white robes?" she asked.

He had barely started to sip the water and lowered the cup with a shrug.

"I have given all of that up," he answered without looking at her.

Oh, that was unlikely. He was too power hungry to ever leave his guild branch—and his special, hidden suborder—by choice.

Ghassan, still standing nearby, raised a dark eyebrow. "How did you arrive here?"

Chuillyon let out a humming sigh through his nose as he looked out across the open desert. "I am not entirely certain, not that the south is without its . . . charm."

Wynn ground her teeth.

Ghassan would never receive any real answer, only politely dry and somewhat snide humor to fend off more questions. Wynn wished she and Magiere could have a little private "talk" with Chuillyon. That would get some answers or confirm her suspicions.

Chuillyon too often appeared—in too timely a fashion—at destinations without sufficient time to have traveled there. Once she had encountered him at Chârmun after last seeing him in Calm Seatt. That was nearly impossible, considering she had used the fastest route by sea and inland from Soráno. And last night, he had been surprised—no, astonished—and then eagerly curious at the sight of Leesil's branch.

And that had been cut from Roise Chârmune, an ancient "child" of Chârmun.

Could it be so simple?

Wynn had seen amazing impossibilities in a handful of years. A few included Chuillyon, such as his shielding Princess Reine Faunier-Areskynna, a royal of Malourné by marriage, from conjured fire racing toward her.

"I think you have some way to transport yourself," she accused, "though maybe it is limited . . . to certain *marked* places."

Chuillyon straightened, her words taking him by surprise; he calmed and took a sip from his cup. "You have always had an imagination that exceeds your exceptional intellect."

If possible, Wynn grew angrier. "Do you know where Leesil's branch comes from?"

For an instant, she thought he might deny such an interest, and then he blinked.

"Do tell," he replied.

"From Roise Chârmune, the tree of the an'Cróan ancestors."

His gaze shifted with a slower blink as he set down the cup but kept his eyes on the stark landscape.

"I am sure that means nothing to me," he said, "but I am curious. Why are you so far east in the desert?" He smiled, still without looking at her. "The possibilities are rather limited."

Wynn glared at him. It hadn't taken him long to reason out where he now was, though the answer would be obvious to anyone from this half of the world.

"If you cannot enlighten us," Ghassan cut in, startling Wynn, "in any way, perhaps another touch of Leesil's branch will send you back to wherever you came from."

Wynn wished Ghassan had not jumped to that implied truth. There was as much to learn from Chuillyon's evasions as from a straight answer. But yes, however Chuillyon had arrived, it had something to do with Leesil's branch.

Chuillyon smiled broadly. "Do you think you can manage that?"

"Yes," Ghassan answered. "I can."

This bothered Wynn. Suddenly she was not so eager to be rid of Chuillyon. The thought of Chârmun, or its offspring, Roise Chârmune . . . or Leesil's branch . . . brought something else to mind.

What was little known before the Forgotten History was that Chârmun and the land in which it grew was the only place the Enemy's undead minions could not go. If it weren't for Chane's "ring of nothing," he couldn't have even entered there now.

Did Leesil's branch have such properties in a lesser way? If so, how could that be activated? And there was still Chuillyon's method of travel to fathom. If he could pass from Chârmun to the branch, reasonably he could go the other way. And being able to take others with him might be useful if the worst came in the end.

There was much Wynn needed to know.

Chuillyon smiled softly as he turned his head, though not toward Wynn. He eyed Ghassan instead. The two obviously had some things in common.

Both were scholars once highly placed in their respective guild branches, one with arcane skills and the other with almost theurgical abilities in nature. Both had fallen and both had been cast out, though the causes for Chuillyon were not clear. Not yet.

"And what *are* you doing out here?" Chuillyon asked casually. "Perhaps I can be of assistance?"

Brot'an still sat passively cross-legged before the second tent's flap, but now he gazed intently at Chuillyon. Whether he saw a use for the errant once-sage or simply some reason to get rid of an "unknown variable," Wynn wasn't certain. She didn't trust Chuillyon, but she did believe he would want to stop the Enemy from rising as much as any of them.

Ghassan's sudden smile was disturbing. "We came out here to hunt undead. I do not see how you could be much help."

"Oh, I could," Chuillyon answered, "as Wynn can attest, at least concerning one wraith."

Ghassan's smile faded. He looked to Wynn. "He fought Sau'ilahk?"

Reluctantly, Wynn nodded. "Yes."

Exactly how was unknown. Chuillyon's influence was more akin to prayers than spells, but he had halted Sau'ilahk several times.

"What else have you done?" Brot'an asked.

Wynn still liked Brot'an more than others did, but his sudden interest after such a long silence chilled her.

At sunset, Magiere insisted they try to pick up the trail of the undead from the night before. Leesil resisted a little, but Magiere still feared they were too late. The undead traveled harder and faster than the living, especially after feeding.

In truth, she didn't know why she'd collapsed and lost her fury when she'd tried to rush in and stop the slaughter. It shouldn't have happened. She feared it ever happening again, and what if it did? All she could do was prepare to leave camp.

Leesil stood waiting. The look on his face told her he was still uncertain about her going back out. Maybe he doubted her as much she doubted herself.

Brot'an offered to remain behind with Wynn and watch Chuillyon, and Magiere agreed.

At the sound of rustling canvas, she turned to see Ghassan emerge from the other tent. Though he was often hard to read, she'd gotten to know his ways well enough to see he was preoccupied.

"What now?" she asked.

He frowned. "I scryed for Chap and Chane's location. They have left the Lhoin'na lands, heading southward, toward the Slip-Tooth Pass. It will still take many days more before they reach the northside entrance to the tunnel running beneath the mountains into Bäalâle Seatt, but they are en route."

Magiere stiffened. "What does that mean for us?"

He sighed as if the rest were unpleasant. "Within two days—and nights— we must turn west if we are to meet them within a day or two of their exiting the southern side of the Sky-Cutter Range. They will never find us out here on their own, and they have three more chests—orbs—with no beasts of burden they can bring through."

Magiere had known this was coming but wasn't ready. They'd learned next to nothing so far. The Enemy was rising, calling its own to the east, but all that was little more than what her gut had told her. She'd hoped to learn the Enemy's actual hiding place before meeting up with Chap.

At times it felt like only Wynn was on her side. Brot'an didn't count, since he'd always pushed for the best tactical choice—and he wanted to meet up with Chap and bring all five orbs together. Ghassan was worse, at times eager to push on and at other times not.

Magiere could feel Leesil watching her; he said nothing, and he didn't have to.

"A night or two," she said. "So we keep looking until . . ."

Even she heard the overoptimism in that, but Leesil merely nodded. As he and Ghassan gathered what was needed, Magiere stepped off to the edge of the camp. Wynn looked over, and Magiere had only to cock her head.

The small sage got up and came to join her. Magiere kept her voice low as she eyed Chuillyon, who made an obvious point of ignoring everyone.

"See if you can get anything more out of him," Magiere whispered.

Wynn nodded. "Of course."

With that, Magiere patted Wynn on the shoulder and headed out with Ghassan and Leesil following. She remembered exactly where to go and strode quickly across the packed sand into the foothills under the endless black sky of winking stars.

Tracking would've been easier in daylight, but none of them could last long walking under the fierce sun, especially Leesil. If she got close enough to her quarry, she wouldn't need tracks to follow.

Before she realized, ahead stood the upslope they had climbed last night.

Magiere rounded it on the desert side instead, steeling herself for what she would find. Spotting the first body, she slowed, and Ghassan and Leesil caught up.

Blood had already dried upon flesh, into the sand and torn clothes, and on weapons still in limp hands or lying nearby. Belongings were scattered from ripped and torn tents. Even three camel carcasses were torn up and lay still in the dark. Gruesome, it was exactly what she'd expected, but the littlest corpses—the children—were the worst.

Nothing could prepare anyone for that.

Even a half dozen undead, if there had been that many, didn't *need* to feed this much. And once sated, they'd slaughtered the rest for . . . who knew why. Maybe just the pleasure. It was as if they baited her, though they couldn't have known she was near. It was like what she'd seen from Chane back in her homeland.

No, this was worse.

"Ghassan," she said.

He stepped ahead and she followed. They stopped beside two half-dug graves with several bodies in pieces with arms and legs gnawed to the bone. She hadn't seen any of that last night, but it told her something more.

These people had been attacked more than once, and on separate nights.

Magiere's jaw locked at the sight of a man's severed head with his face partially torn off. He had to have been digging one grave when he was attacked, but vampires didn't kill like that.

It made no sense.

Leesil looked down beside her. "What in seven hells hap—"

"Back up, now!"

Magiere stiffened at Ghassan's command, just before hunger and rage flooded through her. She pulled the falchion without even thinking, spun, looked in every direction, but saw nothing. Her jaws began aching under the change in her teeth.

All she managed to get out was, "What . . . here?"

"Move quickly!" Ghassan ordered.

Leesil now had both winged blades in hand. He turned all ways, looking about as he took one back step.

Magiere heard a faint shifting of sand and grit, but it didn't come from his step. She heard it again, and then the choking stench of carrion welled up around her. It was too strong for even the carnage.

A fierce grip latched onto her left boot.

Sand gave way before she could jab her sword down, and a blast of grit and sand shot up, blinding her. Something grabbed her belt and then her sword hand's wrist as it clawed up and pulled her down in the sand at the same time.

When her sight cleared, she looked down into a gray-white face with a mouth full of distended, yellow, almost needlelike teeth. The creature jerked her downward as the sand seemed to open under her feet. She screamed as jaws closed on her forearm above the falchion.

Magiere felt herself sinking fast. She released the falchion weighing down one arm and struck down into the gray face with her other fist. When its head whipped aside, she groped for the Chein'âs dagger sheathed beneath her hauberk at the small of her back.

When her hand closed on the hilt, she heard Leesil cry out.

At a hiss of sand, Leesil saw something launch out of the sinking ground beneath Magiere's feet. He pushed off to charge for her, but the sand suddenly gave way beneath his own feet. He sank so fast that his legs became mired. Something sharp raked and stabbed into his left thigh, and he cried out.

He hacked down with his right blade . . . and it struck only sand.

A gray-white, bony face jutted out of the sand now past his knees.

Its mouth opened, exposing what looked like teeth but too jaggedly sharp. It eyes were like black pits that swallowed faint moonlight, and where there should have been a nose were collapsed nostrils.

A clawed hand released his thigh—where it had jabbed him—and hooked its fingers higher into the rings of his hauberk. It hissed once before he slammed his punching blade's outer edge down into its face.

Leesil heard Magiere's screech shift into a vicious, grating snarl. That was all that told him she still lived.

"Get free and run to me!" Ghassan shouted, now sounding farther off. "More may come!"

Leesil understood that, though he didn't look for Ghassan. He didn't have time.

With his blade pressed into the creature's face, he writhed and wrenched one leg out of the sand. Once he'd kicked down into its face, he pushed to wrench his other calf free. In a roll, he slashed his other punching blade's tip as that thing crawled out after him.

When he gained his feet to face it down, something latched onto his left ankle.

Khalidah watched from where he had scrambled to a slab of stone rising from the sand.

Magiere rolled, slashed at one burrowing attacker's face with hardened nails, and then followed with the white metal dagger. Smoke rose amid crackling when the blade split gray flesh down a sunken cheek and into the hollow of a collarbone.

The creature's screaming wail took another two blinks to come.

All that Khalidah saw then were two obscured figures flailing amid tossed sand and smoke. No, he saw one more thing, off to the left beyond Leesil.

Another spot in the sand began to sink rapidly.

A third one was rising.

"Leesil, run to me, now!" Khalidah shouted.

He had no intention of letting either Magiere or Leesil fall prey to these things. He still needed them to get to Beloved—especially if so many of its undead were gathering to it.

At more screaming and screeching, Khalidah glanced toward where Magiere had been. Still, all he saw were two shadows flailing at each other.

*   *   *

Magiere slashed at her attacker again, barely able to see its shape in the dark through smoke and cast-up sand. Her hardened nails tore through something soft in its face—an eye socket perhaps. At its scream, hunger welled up and burned in her chest and then her throat and finally her mouth.

She brought the blade across, below her last strike.

The glow of the dagger's hair-thin centerline disappeared for an instant as it cut into something solid. And that thing's snarls and shrieks choked off instantly.

All of its flailing stopped. Its grips on her belt and hauberk faltered.

She struck down with her free hand where instinct told her to, and her palm slapped upon its scalp. Her fingers closed instantly on sand-clotted hairs, and she brought her blade back the other way well beneath her grip.

Just before the crackle and sizzle of flesh, she thought she heard scrambling upon the sand to her left. Then the head of her prey came loose in her grip.

Leesil kicked into the face of the creature scrambling toward him. Its head lashed back, and he rolled back into a crouch. And it still kept coming. He crossed both blades, dropped forward to one knee, and slashed outward high and low as it closed.

One blade's edge sliced across its sunken belly. The other's tip tore through one side of its neck. It lurched back.

When he expected a shriek or gasp, he heard nothing in the dark. He saw its shape crumple upon itself, and he quickly looked for Magiere.

"No, run!" Ghassan shouted again.

Leesil saw something else in the dark scramble across the sand to his right . . . straight toward where he'd last seen Magiere. From the corner of his eye, he saw his own opponent hunch . . . and spring.

*　　*　　*

Khalidah watched Leesil stall, and grew furious. And for what was now needed, he could not expend energies on widening his sight to see more clearly in the dark. Thankfully, Ghassan would not dare interfere for what had to be done now.

He dug into his robe, pulled out a sage's crystal, and after swiping it once across his robe, he cast the crystal toward Leesil. Sudden light tumbling through the air distracted the wounded creature scrambling after the half-blood.

Leesil was startled by light and looked back.

In that off-balance instant, Khalidah focused with his will and used his thoughts to wrench the half-blood. Leesil arched backward, landing on his back, and Khalidah quickly wrenched him again. Leesil slid, flipped, and tumbled wide-eyed to the edge of the stone slab.

Khalidah snatched the collar of Leesil's hauberk, and by both will and physical effort, pulled the half-blood onto the stone.

"Do you have a crystal?" Khalidah demanded.

Leesil barely gained his feet. "What . . . what did you—?"

"Answer me, now!"

Light beyond the slab vanished.

Khalidah's head swiveled as he looked into the dark. His crystal was gone, and so was the creature that had come after Leesil. That was expected once that thing understood the light could not affect it.

There were still two more out there in the dark—at least two. When he glanced aside, Leesil at least had a crystal out, and Khalidah did not question where it had come from.

"Light it," he commanded, "and toss it toward Magiere. We must get her here on the stone instead of the sand."

That second crystal would not last as long on the sand as his before being pulled down as well. He heard the half-blood swipe the crystal on his thigh.

Light brightened the darkness an instant before the crystal shot out through the air. It landed some thirty paces out, and he spotted a dark-clad figure picking itself up and clutching a dangling object in one hand.

It was Magiere, and the object in her free hand appeared to be a head.

That left only one of the creatures unaccounted for—unless there were more hiding underground.

"What are those things?" Leesil asked.

"Watch the sand around this stone," Khalidah ordered, and then called to Magiere. "Run to us! Quickly!"

"Magiere, come on," Leesil called to her. "Get over here."

Finally she came, and Khalidah got a better look at what she still held. The remaining hair on the severed head meant it was a younger one, or rather that it had been infected and turned less than a handful of years ago.

Magiere's eyes were still fully black, and between her parted lips showed teeth like those of a predator. For an instant, it brought back that terror-filled night of agony when she had torn apart his last host, a'Yamin. He could not help looking down at the white metal dagger in her other hand, and he remembered as well that burned blade cutting him apart.

How fitting it would be if he used that blade on her in the end.

"Back to back," he ordered harshly, and looked away to where Leesil's crystal had fallen. "Watch in all directions. They cannot come up through stone, so they will have to show themselves first."

That the second crystal had not been pulled down caused both relief and frustration. Either the last one had fled—if there were only three—or it knew better than to betray its position, now that its prey was aware of it.

Khalidah would have preferred to take one whole. Perhaps in its hunger-maddened thoughts would have been some memory or notion of exactly where it was being summoned. Even so, by this point in their travels, he had his own notion.

"You know about these things?" Leesil whispered from behind on Khalidah's left.

Khalidah hesitated. How much should he say, considering any answer would bring more questions?

"Yes, I have read of them." He had done more than that. "Old folktales, still told among desert tribes about the eastern provinces before the empire, called them 'ghul.'"

Khalidah heard a low grating hiss from Magiere who was behind on his right. She had not known of them. That was obvious. They had been used to clear outer sentries when forces first approached to siege the ancient Bäalâle Seatt. He had been the one to lead that siege.

"What are they?" Leesil asked.

"Undead, of course, by what they did here, likely coming in the following night after whatever attacked these nomads first."

"Why didn't they wait to get the bodies after burial?"

Khalidah scoffed. "Because they eat the living, not the dead. Once life leaves a victim's flesh, there is no life left to feed them. But they are solitary. I have never read of more than one attacking at a time."

The last part was true, though conjurers under his command had enslaved them in numbers before assaulting the seatt. But any one of his conjurers had been able to control only one ghul. There had been at least three here tonight, possibly working together.

"What about the victims?" Leesil pressed. "Will they . . . get up when the next night comes?"

Khalidah hesitated. Some tales were close to the truth that he knew. They claimed any victim who did not die was possessed by feral demonic spirits with no intellect. And slowly they changed as hunger drove them mad.

Again, close to the truth, but not quite.

"No," he finally answered. "The process—from what I have read—is not the same as for . . . well, there is no word in my language to match your 'vampire.'"

Khalidah said no more, though he listened now that Leesil was silent. Between Magiere's labored breaths, he heard not a grain of sand shift. In a calm night without a breeze, that still did not mean the ghul had moved on. They could not travel at any worthwhile pace underground and never truly did so. To avoid them as with other undead meant waiting for daylight.

When he had said as much and sat down to keep his vigil, Leesil sighed harshly in doing the same. This at least served an additional purpose now that it seemed no true path to Beloved would be found.

None was needed as Khalidah raised his eyes to the starlit, eastern horizon.

It had been a thousand years since he had last come this far, back when he still had his own flesh, but of late, landmarks had been coming back to him. In the dark, clear night to the east, something blotted out the lowest stars for as far south as he could see, just as the so-called Sky-Cutter Range did to the north beyond these foothills.

Another range of mountains marked the continent's far edge, and where the two ranges met a line of peaks. The sight was familiar. Khalidah had wanted to be more certain, to see so himself before turning back for the other three orbs.

Now he was.

But there was a greater concern.

Neither a pack of vampires nor a trio of ghul would have been arranged by Sau'ilahk and Ubâd as bait. How many other of Beloved's servants— undead or not—were headed east?

One dhampir and her followers might not be enough for what was waiting.

It was time to turn back and prepare.

The dreamer fell through darkness, and without impact suddenly stood upon a black desert under a bloodred sky. Dunes began to roll on all sides, quickly sharpened in clarity, and became immense coils covered in glinting black scales. Those coils turned and writhed on all sides.

"Where are you?" the dreamer called. "Show yourself!"

I have always been here . . . waiting.

The desert vanished.

The dreamer stood upon a chasm's lip. Over the edge, the sides did not fall straight down. The chasm walls were twisted as if torn open ages ago by something immense ripping wide the bowels of the earth. Looking upward, the dreamer saw the same, as if the great gash rose into an immense peak above.

Across to the chasm's other side was another wound in the mountain's stone. It was too dark to know whether that was a mere pocket, a cavern, or just a fracture leading to either deeper beyond the stone wall. There was no bridge to that other side.

Some part of the shadows over there appeared to move, and stone cracked and crumbled under some immense weight.

Come to me, child . . . daughter . . . sister of the dead. Come finish what I started with your birth. And let it all end!

Magiere choked, opened her eyes wide, and stiffened upright where she sat on the stone slab. She didn't even know she had drifted off, and she shouldn't have. She began shaking when she realized all fury and fire had vanished. And the sky was too light.

She spun where she sat, leaning to look eastward. Dawn had just broken over another line of distant peaks running southward. She looked up to the left, wondering how the mountains could have moved, but there above the foothills was the jagged wall of the Sky-Cutter Range. And when she lowered her eyes . . .

Leesil was staring at her over his shoulder.

"What?" he whispered. "What's wrong?"

Magiere peered again at those peaks. Once before, in the beginning, she had heard a hissing voice like windblown sand. It had come to her, dragging her on, in the search for the first orb in the Pock Peaks.

And as then, now all she wanted was to go east.

"It is time to return," Ghassan said, rising to his feet. "Any ghul still nearby will not come out while the sun is up. And we need to head west to meet the others."

Magiere was still staring at those peaks when someone roughly grabbed the collar of her hauberk. She flinched before looking into Leesil's bright amber eyes.

And those eyes narrowed.

He knew, and still all she wanted was to go . . . east.

"No!" he whispered at her. "No, not yet."

CHAPTER TWELVE

Although Chap had a notion of the distance from a'Ghràihlôn'na to the north side of the Sky-Cutter Range, he had not seen a map of the region in quite some time. The distance proved farther than he expected. Once the wagon turned off the eastbound road and entered the Slip-Tooth Pass over bare land, he could hardly make out the high range in the distance.

And the wagon rolled on.

They traveled mostly by night for Chane's sake, though now and then some favored hurrying through part of the days as well. During those times, Chane was forced to lie in his dormant state in the wagon's bed under a canvas.

Along the way, the land around them grew more desolate.

They passed through the foothills, and finally one morning, as the sun rose and Chane fell dormant within a tent, Chap made his way up the tallest hillock and then saw that the mountains were nearly upon them.

"Not far now," a deep voice said.

Chap looked back to find that Ore-Locks had followed him, but he returned to eyeing the mountains that appeared to stretch to both horizons. It seemed unbelievable—and daunting—that they would pass beneath those to emerge above the vast Suman desert.

"Wayfarer has a pot of herbed lentils on," Ore-Locks said, and after a pause, he added, "When we last came through, we spent so much time searching for an entrance, we nearly ran out of food."

Again, Chap craned his neck to study the errant stonewalker.

What was the point to that last comment? Was Ore-Locks reminding Chap that he had a history with Shade and Chane, or perhaps that those two natural enemies had such as well?

He and Ore-Locks had never been talkative, but now that Wayfarer was with him again, he spoke mostly with her . . . in their ways.

Chap turned, trotted past Ore-Locks, and headed down toward camp. Over the long days and nights since leaving the Lhoin'na's one city, he had not ceased to think on Wayfarer and Osha, wondering about their futures, as well his daughter's. Clearly, both Wayfarer and Osha felt their time in the eastern elven lands had been cut short, one perhaps silently frustrated and the other perhaps slightly relieved.

While Chap could not explain why, he felt a nagging doubt. Had it been the right thing to pull Wayfarer and Osha from their time with the Lhoin'na? For those two, *something* seemed unfinished. He did not know *what*, but he could not shake this feeling, and it grew stronger instead of fading. He kept such thoughts to himself, uncertain if he should act upon them. Wynn had been promised that Shade would return with Chap and Chane. Magiere had been promised that Wayfarer would return as well. How could such promises be broken?

After a light meal, everyone rested for the remainder of the day. They packed up as dusk arrived so they would be ready once Chane rose.

Soon enough, Chane was at the reins, and the wagon rolled onward. Halfway through the night, they reached the end of the Slip-Tooth Pass. It was not gradual. They arrived almost at the very base of a mountain, and the wagon could go no farther.

"Start unpacking," Chane ordered, dropping from the wagon's bench. "We will have to carry what we need in several trips. But there is only one pump cart available inside the entrance to the pass, and we'll have to pack it carefully."

Uncertain what the last part of this meant, Chap jumped down from the wagon's bed and looked around, at a loss. He saw nothing that resembled an entrance of any kind. Shade came up beside him, and he started in surprise when she touched her nose to his shoulder. He had no time for shock at this physical contact from her when he saw what she shared.

Image after image flooded through his mind, of Wayfarer in the Lhoin'na forest with the majay-hì and Vreuvillä and then Osha with the Shé'ith trainees. The images ended with three memory-words in Wynn's voice.

—*Something . . . not . . . finished*—

Chap closed his eyes, realizing Shade had been struggling with the same worries as he had himself.

New images rose up from her, along with a feeling of sorrow and fear.

This time, Chap saw image after image of Shade with Wynn, of Wynn petting Shade and mouthing the word "sister." These were followed by memories of Shade walking beside Wayfarer in the depths of the Lhoin'na forest.

Chap understood.

Shade—as well as Wayfarer and Osha—should not go on. They should never have left in the first place and needed to return and finish what had been started for both of the young ones, for Osha to learn his link to the Shé'ith and for Wayfarer to understand her connection to the ways of the Foirfeahkan. Both would probably resist; Shade herself already suffered for knowing she had to return as well rather than rejoin Wynn.

Chap could think of only one reason why Shade had waited this long; she had expected him, her father, to realize all of this and act upon it. He should have before now, but like her, he had resisted. Now that they had reached the mountains, neither of them could put off what had to be done.

Promises would have to be broken.

Osha would be the most difficult to convince, so Chap decided to start with Wayfarer. He went to her as she struggled to pull a spare folded canvas out of the wagon's back.

—*Put that down . . . and listen*—

She dropped to one knee before him. "What is it?"

As gently as he could, he called up memory-words in her to explain what had to be. Their time among the Lhoin'na was not yet finished. As little as he understood why, he put his faith in his daughter's judgment as well as his own intuition in the matter. He had no idea what reaction to expect.

Wayfarer touched his face with a nod and lifted her head to call out. "Osha . . . please come."

The tall young elf stalled and handed off a trunk to Chane. When he came near, he frowned, eyeing Chap first and then Wayfarer with growing suspicion.

"Do you need help with that canvas?" he asked her.

Wayfarer shook her head and took a deep breath. "Chap believes that we—you and I and Shade—must now turn back to the Lhoin'na."

Osha's features flattened in shock. At a guess in the dark, he might have paled. Chane dropped a trunk, and even Ore-Locks drew near.

"What?" Chane rasped and glared at Shade. "I promised Wynn to bring you back." He then turned on Osha. "You are all coming with us. That was the arrangement!"

Chap choked down an instinctive snarl. He would not demand the talking hide to argue with the vampire again. He was in charge here, and Chane was going to learn that for the last time.

Before he could take a step, Shade cut in front of him. She went straight to Chane and huffed softly twice. Once again, Chap was disturbed by how deeply his daughter was connected to that undead.

Chane's brow still wrinkled in anger at Shade, but before he could speak again . . .

"She does not want to go," Wayfarer said, looking to both Shade and Chane. "Chap does not wish us to leave either, but he believes there is more for us among the Lhoin'na. It may even have to do with what must be done . . . for where you are going and why."

Chap studied Wayfarer. She seemed so different. How much more had changed in her?

Osha was less than convinced and, after a voiceless hiss sounding too much like Chane, he stormed off. Wayfarer closed her eyes, dropped her head, and swallowed hard.

"I will talk to him," she whispered.

The girl rose and went off after Osha, and Shade followed her.

Chap, left alone, looked up into Chane's seething expression.

"And it took you all this time to figure this out?" Chane demanded. "I do not believe that."

Chap could not restrain a snarl this time, but instead of acting, he looked at Ore-Locks.

—May I . . . speak . . . through you?—

Ore-Locks nodded his consent and turned to Chane, repeating what Chap said in memory-words.

"He did not know whether to counsel us or not," Ore-Locks told Chane. "Like you, he labored under a promise, unwilling to break it but feeling the need to do so. It was Shade who tipped the balance . . . and made the decision for him."

At that, Chane blinked in doubt as he looked off after Wayfarer and Shade. Ore-Locks stepped closer to Chane, and it was clear he now spoke for himself.

"You, I, and Chap can travel faster on our own," he said quietly, "but even after we supply the young ones for a return trip, we will have more than we planned to carry on our own. It is time to get started . . . without any more squabbling!"

With his jaw clenched, Chane looked to Chap one last time. Then he turned away to continue emptying the wagon. Ore-Locks heaved in a deep breath and then exhaled as he too went back to unloading the wagon.

With that, it was decided.

Some things were reloaded into the wagon. Once supplies were sorted out, the younger trio had what they would need to return. The chests with the orbs, the heavy canvas, sacks of food, and flasks of water remained piled on the ground.

Chap had never liked partings that took place in the darkness.

But he watched as his daughter and Wayfarer climbed into the wagon's back. Taking the bench, Osha held the reins and said nothing to anyone. Wayfarer looked down at Chap.

"I will see you again," she almost whispered in a weak voice. Though she tried to smile, the effort was obvious.

Osha flicked the reins, turned the wagon north, and never looked back. In some ways, he had been trapped into this choice. It was clear that he wished to return to Wynn, but he would never leave Wayfarer—and Shade— alone in a foreign land.

It did not take long for the wagon to vanish into the darkness, and once again, Chap found himself alone with a vampire and a dwarven guardian of the honored dead. Chane looked tense and bleak all at once as they turned to preparing their supplies to be hauled into the mountain. Ore-Locks appeared only too willing to assist in moving onward, but they now faced reorganizing supplies for transport.

First, Chane removed the spare clothing from his pack and filled it with apples and onions. In the end, they stuffed as much of the food supplies as they could into any extra space inside the orb chests. While the thought of this bothered Chap, he refrained from protest. They had to reduce the bulk if not the weight of all they had to carry.

Still, even with such condensing, there was much for two people to move in one trip.

Ore-Locks and Chane headed off—heavily burdened—for the first trip.

Chap stood watch over what remained behind, and he waited for quite a while. Finally, the two men returned, and they managed to carry what was left by tying sacks to each other's shoulders and slinging flasks of water on top. One chest had already been transported, and two remained. Chap was alarmed that they had left an orb unguarded, and he would not have made such a choice. One of them should have remained behind and the other should have made several trips. However . . . Chane had always been overly cautious in this regard, so somehow, he must have felt the orb was safe.

Moreover, there was nothing to be done now, and Chap expressing his anger would only delay them further.

Each of the men hefted a chest, and only then did Chap follow Ore-Locks and Chane up the rocky slope along a winding path and into the dark of the mountain.

A short ways up, Chane said, "Wait."

Setting his chest down briefly, he took out his cold crystal and ignited it, holding it with two fingers of his left hand as he managed to lift the chest again. By the filtered light, Chap saw something glinting beneath his feet, and he looked down. Illuminated fragments of flat rock, which appeared to have been cut from stone, had somehow been pressed into the steep slope.

Stretching ahead, there were many more.

Chap followed as Chane and Ore-Locks climbed those ancient steps. Soon the fragments became slightly larger, and Chap noticed they formed two straight lines with open ground in between.

"It was laid down long ago by my people's ancestors," Ore-Locks said quietly.

The path began to curve and snake. They weaved their way through wind-bent trees, jagged outcrops, and rougher terrain, but the path always continued. Finally, like the Slip-Tooth Pass below, the path of rock fragments simply ended at the crumbled side of a cliff covered in heavy brush.

Chap looked to Ore-Locks.

—*Where is . . . the entrance?*—

Ore-Locks glanced back, extended a thick finger in his grip on the chest he carried, and pointed toward the brush. He crouched, set down the chest, pulled some of the brush aside, and sidestepped through while pulling the chest along. In the dark, he appeared to pass into the cliffside itself.

Was this another trick of the stonewalkers?

Chane dropped to his knees, crawling as he pushed his chest along in front of himself. Halfway into the brush, he paused to look at Chap.

"Come," he said.

Then Chane pushed through and vanished as the brush snapped back into place.

Chap finally followed but did not see the narrow, downward hole until he had wrestled himself halfway in. By the light of a cold-lamp crystal held by Chane, at first all that Chap could see was the undead's backside.

A strange gust of stale air blew over him as they emerged in a more-open area.

Chane held up the crystal. Ore-Locks stood farther in, and the crystal's light exposed a stone archway directly above them. They were in a tunnel.

The ceiling was so low, Chane was not able to straighten up, and he remained buckled over as he lifted his chest.

"Go on," he told Ore-Locks, and the dwarf led the way.

Chap began to wonder how much farther they would go, when finally, Chane emerged into a large open area. Chap followed as Chane glanced back.

"This was once like the market cavern outside the Cheku'ûn tram station," he said.

Chap made out large, dead crystals anchored high on the walls. He remembered the station that he and Chane had visited at Dhredze Seatt. Glowing orange crystals above had offered warmth and light amid booths and tents and the scent of roasting sausages. He could barely picture such in this long-dead place.

A large archway dominated the chamber's far side, and there stood Ore-Locks, waiting. It took longer than Chap expected for him and Chane to cross that immense space.

Ore-Locks led onward again. In the next cavern, Chap found himself before an enormous platform at the chamber's center. In the back wall was a large tunnel with three lanes of tracks leading into it.

What troubled him most were the long-dead trams with their lengths of cars stretched out behind them at all the docks. Whatever happened here ages ago, those trams had arrived here and never returned to their origin. And if such were needed to reach the ancient seatt . . .

"Over here," Ore-Locks called before Chap could wonder if any of the trams still worked.

The dwarf led them down the tracks and into the tunnel to find a good-sized cart made of solid metal. Its platform was thick with a high-sided iron storage box on the back end. Perhaps the cart had once been used to service the tunnel and tracks. More notable, it was already loaded with supplies, enough to crowd the cart's two-man pump.

Padding closer, Chap spotted a cylindrical dead crystal the size of his own torso secured at the back of the metal box. It was tied on in a series of loops with a thin rope. Without hesitation, Ore-Locks set down his burdens and hurried over. He untied the crystal and walked around to the cart's front. Chap followed and saw a simpler iron box on the cart's other end, and there was Ore-Locks relashing the dead crystal.

Puzzled, Chap could not keep silent.

—*Why . . . the dead . . . crystal*—

Ore-Locks no longer flinched and only frowned at the words popping up in his head.

"They still absorb and amplify light," he answered. "Something we discovered on our last visit. Chane?"

Chane had stowed his chest in the pump cart and stepped forward to hand Ore-Locks a cold-lamp crystal.

"Step back," Ore-Locks said, and even he looked away.

He swiped Chane's crystal furiously on his pant leg until it was almost too bright to look upon. And he touched it to the larger dead one on the cart's front.

Chap yipped, shut his eyes, and back-peddled as light exploded from the cart's front, illuminating the tunnel ahead for a long distance. Chane shielded his eyes as well and glanced down.

"My crystal would not provide enough light to travel safely at high speed, and we will be moving swiftly with Ore-Locks or me at the pump. Prepare yourself."

Chap grew sick to his stomach as he eyed the cart.

Nights—and days—slipped away, and in the permanent darkness below the range, Chane could only count them by when he fell dormant.

Now, as he once again took his shift at the pump, he listened to the creaking and clattering of the cart.

The pump cart was filled with gear and supplies, stowed or lashed. Chap barely had room to curl up behind Chane's feet. Ore-Locks knelt at the front of the cart, peering ahead, perhaps looking for anything that might obstruct the tracks.

"Try to sleep," Chane said to him.

"Soon," Ore-Locks answered, without looking back.

Chane pumped by night, and Ore-Locks by day. And while the living did not need to sleep a whole night, Chane had no choice but to sleep for the whole day, even here beneath the earth.

There were brief times when Chap grew too sick to ride and took to loping along beside the cart.

That was frustrating to Chane and Ore-Locks, who had to slow down in order not to leave Chap behind. However, Chane understood Chap's need, though did not comment on it.

The same journey the last time—the first time—had been hard on Shade as well. The majay-hì were not suited to living without sunlight and fresh air for so many days in a row, unlike an undead and a dwarf. The only thing

Chane could do was to press onward as hard as he could while awake and when Chap could tolerate the ride.

They stopped for brief periods so Ore-Locks and Chap could eat or to gather water from trickling cracks in the tunnel wall. In this way, they reserved the water in their stowed flasks.

After a while, the monotony of stone walls racing by began to take its toll, even upon Chane. He missed the moon, stars, and open sky. Only Ore-Locks seemed unaffected and able to recognize—remember—familiar points in the tunnel that Chane did not.

Tonight, Ore-Locks suddenly rose and raised a hand, still watching ahead. "Ease off. We are approaching the cave-in."

Chane released the pump and grabbed the brake lever, prepared to apply pressure. And when Ore-Locks began lowering his hand, Chane did so—and more each time the dwarf's hand lowered yet again. Until the cart finally squealed to a halt. Chane found himself staring ahead at something he had almost forgotten.

Another empty cart sat on the tracks ahead. On their first visit, when they had come back out of the seatt, they had found a second pump cart as if someone had followed them. Chane had never learned who. As a result, they had taken that cart—as it was positioned on the track behind their own—to make their way out of the range and Bäalâle Seatt.

In fact, it was the cart in which they now traveled.

Now, beyond the other abandoned cart, was a mass of rubble and stones blocking the tunnel from floor to ceiling. At its top near the tunnel's ceiling was a small hole that he and Ore-Locks had dug to pull Wynn and Shade through.

The thought of Wynn and Shade filled Chane with sudden loneliness.

Chap hopped down and hobbled past the first cart to nose about the rubble. Then he looked back.

"The hole up top runs all the way through," Chane said.

Even his rasp carried loudly under the mountain's silence. He and Ore-Locks set to unloading the cart, and that reminded all of them that there was more than they could carry in one trip. Bäalâle was still a good walk away.

"If you wish," Ore-Locks said, setting the final chest before the cave-in, "I can take you straight through the rubble myself."

Chane balked at the thought of being pulled straight through stone again. "I think not."

Shrugging, Ore-Locks hefted one of the chests. "Suit yourself. You and Chap get started yourselves. I will bring everything else through, as it would take too long to do so through the hole . . . and the chests would not likely fit."

Chap growled, stepping in on Ore-Locks.

Ore-Locks rolled his eyes. "He is talking in my head again. He does not like leaving any of the chests unguarded on one side or the other."

Chane could not disagree. "I will go through first," he told Chap. "You will come through last. One or both of us will be on guard as Ore-Locks moves the chests and other supplies. Is that acceptable?"

Chap was silent for an instant and then huffed once.

As the youngest of the stonewalkers, Ore-Locks did not yet have the ability to take the living with him through stone and earth. He could take the dead—the undead—or anything else nonliving. And this gave Chane a notion for the rest of the journey through the seatt, though Ore-Locks might not care for it, and Chap certainly would not.

Without hesitation, Ore-Locks hefted the first chest and stepped forward, walking to . . . into the packed rubble. While carrying his heavy burden, he turned sideways so that his shoulder touched stone first. The color of dirt and stone flowed into his shoulder, down his arm and side, and up his neck until it flowed into the chest as well as he passed out of sight.

Chap gave a slight shiver as he watched this, and then Chane began to climb. He left everything behind except for Welstiel's pack. It did not take him long to scramble up to the hole. There, he pushed the pack in front of himself as he crawled in. Making his way through the narrow opening was slow going, and he thought it a good thing he had gone first, as he had to reach over or above his pack several times and dig with his hands. This would leave Chap with a somewhat smoother route.

Finally, as he emerged out the other side, he found Ore-Locks waiting, the chest at his feet.

"Go," Chane said as his body slid downward over the rubble.

Once again, Ore-Locks passed into the packed dirt and stone. Chane was still brushing himself off and reslinging his packs when the dwarf came back through carrying the chest with the orb of Water, several sacks of food, and a large flask of water. This continued until everything had been moved through the packed rubble.

Looking up, Chane listened.

Chap's more flexible body must have made his pass easier than Chane's, and only moments passed before his gray head poked out the top of the hole and he scrambled down.

Then came the next suggestion.

"We are close," Chane began, "but far enough that we will use too much effort if not time in moving everything in multiple trips." He looked to Ore-Locks, knowing Chap would argue again. "Could you find the seatt from here . . . through?"

Ore-Locks peered up the tunnel, though without the cart's massive crystal, the light of Chane's smaller one did not reach far.

"Perhaps," Ore-Locks finally answered. "And yes, if so, it would be quicker in moving all this. At least to the exit."

And then, of course, Chap began to rumble.

"I will be walking with *you*," Chane answered back.

"Wait," Ore-Locks cut in, "that means more trips for me."

Chane said nothing, for there was nothing more to say.

Ore-Locks scowled. "Very well. But carry what you can and move on."

Chane hoisted his packs, one chest, and whatever he could manage. Of course there was nothing that Chap could carry.

*   *   *

Chap struggled not to flinch when they began coming upon the remains of thick bones along the way. Large dead crystals in the walls grew closer and closer to one another as skeletal remains grew more numerous, until he saw one dwarf piled on top of another. In places, piles of rubble partially filled the tunnel, half burying the long dead.

There were times that he wondered if they had all died trying to escape. Or had some of those within Bäalâle turned on one another before the end? Then the air slowly changed. Perhaps it shifted slightly, and the echoes of their footfalls did not carry within the tunnel in quite the same way. He was not surprised when they emerged into what must have been the tram station at the tunnel's far end. Of course, there were no trams here; they had all been abandoned centuries ago at the range's northern side.

Chap and Chane briefly looked upon the empty, dust-coated stone platforms before seeking an exit. Rather than the multiple tunnels leading from the stations at Dhredze Seatt, here only one huge archway led into a tunnel straight ahead. Upon stepping through the arch, he was unprepared for the sight that awaited him and nearly ignored the waiting pile of supplies that Ore-Locks had already transported. Once again, an orb had been left unguarded for a short while, but there seemed little way to avoid this while attempting to transport everything.

And . . . this place appeared utterly deserted.

The word "vast" did not begin to describe the massive sculpted cavern. It could have held a sizable village, perhaps a whole town. Padding slowly forward past the piled supplies, Chap looked around in awe, both with fear and wonder.

At this depth, he was standing in an architectural impossibility. Enormous crumbling columns some fifteen or more yards in diameter held the remnants of curving stairwells on their exteriors. Walkways ran around the walls at multiple levels. Broken landings at certain points showed where causeways had once spanned between the columns. Only three of eight columns were still fully erect, reaching to the high ceiling more than fifty yards above. And that dome had massive cracks in it, judging by what little light from Chane's cold-lamp crystal could reach the heights.

Chap stepped farther in past the rubble of a great stairway. Perhaps it had led to levels above connected to the tiers of walkways. And he looked across the floor . . .

The bodies appeared more preserved in here. Skeletal remains of thick bones were half covered in remnants of decaying armor with corroded blades exposed through rotted sheaths. One still wore an ax on his back, and a tarnished thôrhk lay among the shattered bones of his neck. Another skeleton, perhaps a female, lay a few paces ahead. Her bones still bore a ring with a dark stone and a necklace of metal loops.

Chap was nearly overwhelmed by the loss and sorrow that filled this silent place. The scale of death was too much to absorb. From what Wynn had told him, Bäalâle had been infiltrated by one or more of the triad of the Sâ'yminfiäl—the "Masters of Frenzy." Those sorcerers had driven the seatt into madness as they used the orb of Earth to burrow in beneath this place.

At a heavy footfall behind, Chap whirled with all hackles stiffening, but it was only Ore-Locks with the last of their supplies. The young stonewalker said nothing as he looked about.

Chap could see Ore-Locks was equally affected, though this was not the first time for him.

Familiarity would never take away the implied horror and madness within this silent place.

"We need to pass through here and out the other side," Chane said.

Ore-Locks did not move, did not appear to hear, and looked left for one of the great openings into this central place.

"Do you think *they* will come . . . again?" he whispered.

Chap tensed, fully wary, but without understanding, he looked up.

Chane watched Ore-Locks. "Who?"

"Gí'uyllæ . . . *the all-eaters.*"

Chap knew that word from Wynn. In the bowels of this place were immense winged reptiles that ate anything, including stone, and spat fire. And they were called by other names in other cultures, such as "weürms," "thuvanan," "ta'nêni" . . . "dragons."

"I do not think so, even if they are aware of us," Chane answered with less certainty than Chap preferred. "They gave the orb of Earth into your safekeeping, and they know you as the blood defendant of the one who stood with their ancestor in the fall of this place."

Chap hoped Chane was right.

With a shaky breath, Ore-Locks turned to the pile of supplies and chests. "How far to the exit?"

"Not far by what il'Sänke told me," Chane answered, pointing across the way to one tunnel. "When he entered from that side, he spent days searching caved-in paths and dead ends to find a way in, but he explained clearly how we can use that tunnel to get out."

"So that passage leads directly to an exit?"

"Not quite," Chane answered. "Chap and I will have a good deal of rubble to cross on one side of the passage, and the exit comes out beneath a boulder. As to the supplies and chests, you will have to again bring most of them through stone."

Ore-Locks nodded, and his gaze wandered for three breaths before he answered. "And what do we do once we are out?"

This much Chap already knew.

"We wait," Chane said, "and we watch. We would never find the others on our own, so Wynn and I . . . and Chap arranged a signal. We will be able to see it at a great distance at night."

Ore-Locks did not reply at first. He looked about, up and around, his expression turning more grim by the moment.

"Then let us leave this place quickly," he said.

Chap could not agree more as he huffed once.

*　　*　　*

Wynn was exhausted as she pressed westward with her companions along the desert edge of the foothills. The previous night, Ghassan informed her that Chane and Chap were closer, though he was uncertain how close they were to Bäalâle.

How many days and nights had they been doing this?

Putting aside hunting for undead to trek westward was not the relief she'd expected. Hopefully, Chane, Chap, and the others would make it out of Bäalâle by the time she got close.

There was so much they needed to discuss.

She put one foot before the other, pushing forward.

There was also a great need for the supplies Chane and Chap had agreed to bring.

She was tired of figs and smoke-dried meats. No matter how much Ghassan spiced and recooked them in sparse water, they were . . . horrible. At that thought, she looked at him out in the lead.

"Are we closer?" she asked.

With a frustrated sigh, he answered, "Always."

Wynn looked back beyond Chuillyon, forced to lead the camels, and beyond Brot'an watching over their "prisoner." Leesil and Magiere followed last, though there was a time Magiere would have been first going anywhere.

Magiere looked back, walking sideways to do so. Wynn waited for Leesil to grab Magiere's arm and pull her around again . . . and again.

Wynn worried what might happen with Magiere once they all returned eastward.

After the night of the ghul, Magiere had changed. She listened, was coherent, and no longer grew angry at not tracking undead. She had also reverted to a state Wynn had not seen in years.

Magiere was too much like she'd been when they had left the an'Cróan lands in search of the first orb. She was having dreams again . . . hearing that voice again. The dreams had become less frequent the farther west they traveled, but this thought brought no relief either.

Wynn was sickened with fright every nightfall, especially when she didn't see an answering "light" out in the dark. This time, the sun hadn't even dipped fully below the western horizon when she stopped.

"Ghassan, get out your looking glass."

He turned in a sharp stop, lifted the front of his hood, and stared at her.

"It is not even dusk yet," he argued. "They will not see a sage crystal in—"

"Then I'll use the staff!"

"No!" Ghassan returned. "Even if they see, it is too bright and might—"

"We are far enough that anyone—*anything*—heading east will not see it."

At the snuffling of camels, and their smell, Wynn half turned to find Chuillyon watching her. Brot'an closed in.

"Don't start," she warned before he could say anything. "I'm doing this, and I'll do it again after full dark, if need be."

Brot'an looked ahead and merely nodded once.

"Leesil," Wynn called, "get up here."

He already had his cloak stripped off when he approached, and Wynn tugged the sheath off her staff to expose the long sun crystal atop it.

"Everyone look away," Wynn warned. "I am the only one with glasses. Leesil, grip the staff above my hands so you have a reference point . . . without looking."

Sighing, Leesil did so with his free hand. Wynn didn't check if the others were ready as she focused. Ghassan stepped back past her in assembling his leather and lenses into the looking glass. As dusk deepened, Leesil whipped his cloak up over the sun crystal.

Wynn no longer even needed to speak the phrases aloud; she needed only to think them, and she held the dark glasses up over her eyes.

. . . *Mênajil il'Nûr'u mên'Hkâ'ät.*

As those final words flashed through her mind, the sharp and sudden light cleared the pure blackness from her glasses, even with the crystal shrouded by Leesil's cloak.

"Now," she commanded.

Three times, Leesil whipped his cloak off and then back over the sun crystal, and then Wynn let the crystal go out. She dropped the glasses to let them dangle on their cord around her neck.

"Anything?" she asked, looking back to Ghassan.

After a long pause, he answered, "No."

Wynn turned on Leesil. "Again," she ordered.

And again she lit the staff, and again he flashed it three times.

Wynn didn't ask again as she watched Ghassan stare ahead through the looking glass. She wasn't even aware of counting tense breaths until she hit seven. Closing her eyes and slumping, she didn't look at Leesil and halfheartedly mumbled, "Again."

"Wait," Ghassan said.

Wynn looked up.

Ghassan stood perfectly still for two more breaths and then lowered the looking glass to point ahead.

"There! Watch for it!"

Wynn did so . . . and she saw the faint triple wink of a light ahead. Her breath stopped completely.

"Let's go now," Leesil said.

Wynn grabbed his arm. There was more need to be certain.

"What are you waiting for?" Leesil asked.

With the sun not yet set, Chane would still be dormant. That meant Ore-Locks, or at best Chap, had somehow used a cold-lamp crystal to signal. There was one more step that she and Chap had agreed upon for safety, in case the worst had happened.

The Enemy's forces could be on the move elsewhere. Wynn had to be certain those other three orbs were in the right hands before she brought two more within reach.

"How many flashes?" she asked Ghassan. "How many . . . the first time?"

He frowned in puzzlement at her. "Five. Why?"

"We veer into the desert and wait for full night," she said. "Then I signal again."

"What?" Leesil said. "What's this about, Wynn?"

This was all that she told any of them, and she ignored all questions. Her next signal was to be one more than the count received. The next response would be one more added to that. And even Chane would not know this until Chap instructed him.

Only in this way would Wynn know—and Chap know—for certain who was coming and who was waiting.

Later that night, even after the proper signals had been exchanged, Chap crouched upon a rock outcrop in full view of the desert below. He had instructed Ore-Locks and Chane to remain out of sight up here until he acted. They had hidden the supplies and three orbs higher above.

Then Chap saw Wynn leading the way upward before she spotted him.

He huffed once but never looked back for Chane and Ore-Locks.

He lunged off the outcrop, racing downward. Wynn spotted him quickly enough and broke into a run herself. She ignored calls from Leesil and Ghassan to wait, and they collided as she fell to her knees, dropped her staff, and wrapped her arms around Chap's neck.

"Oh, thank goodness." She sighed, pressing her face against him.

—I missed you too—

It was a relief to speak with her in their way rather than to dig for memory-words.

At quick footfalls behind, Chap twisted his head and saw Chane leading the way downward with Ore-Locks following. Wynn rose up, rushed to Chane, but stalled. She might have intended to throw herself at him but instead grabbed his right hand in both of hers. The others from below caught up, but Chap was still watching Wynn . . . with Chane.

They both looked dusty and travel worn, but she just gazed up into his face in relief.

Chap did his best to swallow down any disapproval.

"You are here and safe," Chane whispered, clamping his other hand over the top of hers.

Wynn nodded with a heavy breath and half turned to Ore-Locks. Then she looked beyond him and upslope.

Chap steeled himself for the worst that would come.

"Shade!" Wynn called. Her puzzled gaze moved back to Chane. "Where is she . . . and Wayfarer and Osha?"

Chane was silent. Ore-Locks did not move at all.

"Yes, where's Wayfarer?"

At that sharp demand, Chap's head twisted around to see Magiere closing on him. Leesil was not far behind her.

"Chap?"

He twisted the other way to find Wynn closer now with a dimly lit cold-lamp crystal in her hand. He was trapped between the two women. Not unexpected—and not the way he wanted to explain—but he started of course with Wynn.

—*Wayfarer is well and safe and still among the Lhoin'na. This was her choice, and Shade remained as well to watch over them*—

At Chap's words, Wynn's face paled. Magiere strode up past Ore-Locks while looking about. In his distraction, worry, and concern, Chap did not hear until too late . . .

"What did you do now?"

He whipped around and looked up into Leesil's angry eyes.

Then Brot'an and Ghassan closed in and—Chap was suddenly stunned at the sight of a tall, mature elf he had never seen before. Who was this obvious Lhoin'na, and how had he come to be among the others? A torrent of questions overran Chap's shock and suspicion, but one sharp demand cut off everything else.

"I'm waiting!" Leesil demanded.

"It is not his fault."

Chap turned at those rasped words and almost snarled at Chane for silence. He thought better of that in the last instant. No one here but Wynn fully trusted anything Chane had to say, and she already knew this was not entirely Chap's doing. Most of the others quieted down the instant Chane went on.

"I tried to make Shade come." Chane stalled with a glance at Wynn. "She told Chap that Osha and Wayfarer were not done with . . . whatever they went for among the Lhoin'na. Wayfarer insisted that all of you would . . . should . . . understand."

A dangerous moment came when Magiere stepped toward Chane. Wynn grabbed Magiere's arm, but that was all.

"I am here, as is Chap," Chane added, and looked down only at Wynn. "Shade will keep Wayfarer—and Osha—safe, as was intended by sending them away for whatever true or half-true reasons. When we can, we *will* go to find Shade."

Wynn slumped and closed her eyes.

"You have the other orbs?" a clear voice asked.

Chap did not have to look as Ghassan stepped close and looked down as if expecting Chap to somehow answer. He would have preferred to say nothing, especially to this one, but he glanced back at Ore-Locks and huffed once.

"Hidden above," Ore-Locks answered, "along with the extra supplies we brought."

Again, Chap studied the tall elf, who had remained silently watchful the whole time. Not long after, they set up camp, and everyone took to sorting out supplies. It troubled Chap that there was one person present whom he did not know. He did not relish the thought of killing any more than necessary, but for what was coming, he would do so if not satisfied, as he watched the unknown interloper sitting there across the low flames and silently listening to everything.

There was much for everyone to relate to one another, and they had all been apart for so long. Magiere shared what had been learned of undead migrating eastward, including at least one kind they had never encountered before. Ghassan claimed that they had a good notion of the Enemy's general location, though he did not elaborate.

Chap had little faith in the fallen domin's word, especially since he could not dip the man's memories, surface or otherwise. But none of the others, including Magiere, said anything to counter Ghassan's claim. As Chap absorbed this, Leesil asked Ore-Locks a few questions about the journey. When the dwarf began to answer, Chap quietly slipped off from the circle around the small fire.

As much as the others relished some of the fresher foods brought, especially the apples, one member was missing from the circle around the small fire. Wynn sat off on her own, and he circled around her. After what she'd heard about Shade, he waited before sidling in next to her.

—*Who is the Lhoin'na?*—

She barely turned her head. "Chuillyon. Another fallen sage, like Ghassan . . . but different."

—*How did he come here?*—

Wynn turned away.

Chap needed answers, but he was uncertain whether to press for them yet.

"I know Shade is safer with Osha and Wayfarer," Wynn said quietly, "and sending her with them was my idea. Maybe that's better, considering what we are going to do . . . where we're going next, but I feel so incomplete without Shade."

Chap could not think of anything to say to this. How many years had passed since he had been taken as a pup to a desperate half-breed boy trapped in a dark and bloody world? And he knew he would never again want to be separated from Leesil and Magiere, but hard choices were coming. Some were here already.

When he had first begged Lily to send one of their children across the world to Wynn, it had been an ugly thing to do. And worse for leaving a mate he still believed he might never see again. How it would change other things and affect other people was something he had not thought of then.

—*Shade must do what I cannot. I had to return to be with the others . . . with you*—

Wynn hung her head and closed her eyes.

Chap desperately needed answers to what had changed since he had left, but he stayed silent in waiting. Without even looking, Wynn slung her arm around his neck and buried her face in it. He envied her in one way.

Wynn might always be closer to his estranged daughter than he could ever hope to be. And now that cost her as well.

—*I am sorry*—

"No . . . no," she whispered. "I'm sorry. It's just hard."

He kept still until she sat up and looked at him.

—*And what about Chuillyon?*—

Wynn glanced once toward those nearer the fire, and at the tall elf.

"I believe he somehow uses Chârmun to move between it and its . . . children. Leesil was holding his branch from Roise Chârmune some nights ago, and Chuillyon just appeared."

Chap's ears stiffened upright at even the possibility.

—*Has he confirmed this?*—

"Some—not all—perhaps only enough to make us trust him. I'm half guessing the rest. The last time I was in the Lhoin'na lands and first saw Chârmun . . . *he* was suddenly there. There was no way he could've gotten into that clearing without being spotted."

—*Can he be trusted?*—

Wynn snorted. "No! But I think he'd do anything to stop the Enemy from returning. That puts him on our side for now."

And they turned to more details from Wynn's past. Chap learned of how Chuillyon had more than once foiled an undead wraith's conjury, though most of what he had done was only defensive. That left one other piece to puzzle for another notion developing in Chap's thoughts.

—*Where is Leesil's branch?*—

"In his pack."

Chap fell silent while turning over everything that Wynn had related. Some of the others near the fire occasionally glanced their way, for he and Wynn had been off on their own for a while. And when Magiere stared too long . . .

Wynn smiled. "Sorry. We're just catching up."

Chane then rose and faced her, though he looked right at Chap. "Now that the orbs are gathered and the likely place of the Enemy has been found, what is next?"

Ghassan's irises appeared nearly black in the dark as he answered, "We head east again."

CHAPTER THIRTEEN

Leesil felt anxious and trapped. All along the journey west to rejoin Chap and Chane, the farther they'd gone, Magiere's dreams had continued to lessen in frequency, until they stopped altogether. This should've come as a relief.

It hadn't.

Back when Magiere had first led him, Chap, and Wynn into the Pock Peaks after the first orb, she'd often awoken in the nights and cried out. That was how everything had started, and here in this foreign land, when they'd turned back along the range, she hadn't made a sound. Not after that night on the stone slab spent waiting out the ghul.

After that, on the trek toward Bäalâle, Leesil wouldn't even have noticed the change if he hadn't awoken one night for no reason. He'd found Magiere sitting up in the night and silently staring back the way they had come. She hadn't even known he'd awoken until he touched her arm. She'd jumped slightly and stiffened as if he'd awoken her.

The farther westward they traveled, the more withdrawn she'd grown.

And then, they'd finally met up with Chap, Chane, and Ore-Locks and turned back eastward once again. All along the way, Magiere had remained quiet and withdrawn. He couldn't bring himself to ask her what was wrong, partly because he feared the answer.

Now, far to the east again, Leesil crouched on a stone knoll, their camp hidden off behind him in the foothills. Out in the dark stood one peak in the crook of the range's turn along the eastern coast. The only way they even knew it was *the* peak was because of the fires.

Bright spots below his vantage point were scattered at the mountain's base, into its lowest foothills, and out into the open, parched plain. Even the undead valued fire, but so many flicking spots of light told him that a horde had gathered.

—*How . . . many?*—

Leesil didn't start at Chap's broken memory-words in his head. He rose to his feet as the dog came up beside him.

"At least a hundred, maybe more," he whispered. "Not a full army but enough."

They both knew there were too many below to sneak past while carrying five orbs into the mountain, however and wherever they might find an entrance.

Chap peered down over the high knoll, and Leesil wasn't sure what to say.

How many times had the two of them stood like this, trying to find a strategy to succeed and get out? This time they didn't see a way in, let alone an escape.

—*Magiere . . . cannot go . . . near . . . the Enemy . . . her maker*—

That wouldn't make things any easier, and telling her would be even worse.

"So, what next?"

—*The only possibility . . . is to split into . . . two groups*— . . . —*One . . . to infiltrate . . . the peak . . . the other . . . to draw . . . the horde*— . . . —*Magiere must . . . lead . . . the second . . . not . . . the first*—

Leesil wasn't quite ready to agree, but he hadn't thought of any other options that might work. Anyone who drew the horde's attention stood little chance of survival, even with Magiere. Then again, the first group would be walking into . . . what?

"We don't even know how to use the orbs, except to blindly open them all at once. You saw what the orb of Water did in the cavern beneath that six-towered castle."

Chap didn't reply.

They'd both been there when Magiere used her thôrhk—her orb key— to open the orb of Water where it waited for a thousand years. Instantly, it began swallowing all freestanding moisture. If they'd let it finish with that, would it have done the same to anything living?

—*The orbs . . . are a . . . last . . . resort . . . if you find . . . the Enemy . . . fully awake*—

Leesil scoffed. "I heard you . . . every other time you said it."

They had no idea what they would find, what the Enemy really was, or if they could kill it. They only hoped they'd never have to use the orbs. Chap didn't counter his spiteful reply, and this worried Leesil all the more.

"If we have to, do you have any notions about using the orbs?"

Chap turned away.

—*Perhaps*—

Chap returned to camp, taking note of who was in plain sight. They had no fire and used dimly lit cold-lamp crystals only as needed. One tent flap was flipped fully open, and he saw Chuillyon sitting cross-legged within, his eyes closed. Chane sat talking with Ore-Locks on the camp's other side. Ghassan stood silent, head bowed, near the desert side of camp, apparently lost in thought. Magiere sat beside Brot'an. Both were tending and sharpening their weapons in silence. Wynn was nowhere to be seen, so she had to be in the second of now three tents.

Magiere glanced up and spotted him. "Where's Leesil?"

—*He is coming . . . soon*—

Chap went to the tent he shared with Leesil, Magiere, and Wynn. Shoving through the entrance flap, he found the young sage kneeling between two familiar chests—those for the orbs of Spirit and Air.

Was she sitting vigil? At least she was alone, and she would not question what he asked of her. Wynn trusted him, at least in all greater matters. Upon hearing him, she turned on her knees, and he steeled himself.

—*I need you to open the chest for the orb of Spirit*—

She blinked. "Why?"

—*I need to know more, as much as I can, about the orbs, should they have to be used*—

Wynn still studied him, as if measuring his words. Then she opened the left chest, reached in, and pulled back the cloth as he approached.

He remembered all too clearly that when Magiere had opened the orb of Water, he, she, and Leesil had each sensed or seen something different.

He had felt the presence of a Fay, a singular one.

Magiere had sensed an overwhelming undead.

Leesil had seen the head of a great serpent . . . or dragon.

"What are you going to do?" Wynn whispered.

Chap believed one of his kin was inside this orb and perhaps each one of them. Of the Enemy's minions they had encountered, most had been especially obsessed with the orb of Spirit. So it was the logical orb to try.

Lifting a forepaw, he reached over the chest's side and never hesitated as he touched the object's strange smooth but faintly rough surface.

The tent, the chest, and Wynn vanished.

A world—and his life—rushed by, all tangled and obscured in a mist like gray clouds trying to envelop him. In flickers of what he could make out, he thought he saw his own life played out in glimpses, but always moving backward . . . always growing darker . . . until he saw nothing.

A hiss grew in the dark over a scratching on stone so loud and harsh that he then heard crackling, as if the stone broke. A reddish light grew somewhere ahead. For a moment he thought it was flame, though its shape changed to the maw and then the eyes—and then both—of some immense reptile without limbs. But it was not a snake, not even a serpent, judging by those armored scales on its coils.

Was it like what Leesil had claimed to see when Magiere opened the first orb?

Chap could not remember this placeless, timeless moment. As before in the white mist, this time in the black mist, like broken clouds of swirling soot, he saw something . . .

Bodies in strange clothing or armor gathered like ghosts. Their faces and limbs and any other exposed flesh were pale as death. A whisper carried in more than one voice, over and over.

. . . Beloved . . .

Hovering in flickering glimpses behind each figure was the red-haloed shape of that black-scaled dragon. He recognized two of the pale faces.

The first had almond-shaped eyes in a narrow face draped with tangles of silken black hair. Though her irises had been crystalline then, in this vision they were so dark, they might be chocolate, nearly black.

Li'kän had been the mad and near-mute guardian of the first orb, and Chap recognized the other.

Likewise, Qahhar, with his thick eyebrows and shiny, dark locks, looked as Suman as Ghassan. But he was as pale as all the others—thirteen in all.

These were the Children from the poem scroll Chane had brought to Wynn, but Chap never had a chance to see the other faces clearly. They crumpled into the black mists as if dying upon the whisper of . . . *Beloved.*

He saw again the fiery maw and eyes of the dragon, suddenly smothered to nothing.

In their place came flickers of his own life, his own existence, but again moving backward in time.

Magiere and Leesil discovering the secret that he was Fay.

Living on the road with Leesil after the young half-breed fled the Warlands.

Eillean, Leesil's grandmother, bringing him as a pup to Cuir'en'neina, Leesil's mother.

Being born and then . . . nothing . . . but more whispers that he now felt more than heard.

Nothing . . . no more . . . nothing . . .

Let there be something . . . some . . . thing . . . for us . . .

He felt himself without body, without mind, without anything but thoughts. The overlapping chorus of whispers was so mournful, like ancient, timeless children mourning in the dark.

A chorus of voices whispered in Chap's spirit, like when he had viciously turned on his own kin when last communing with them. Now it was as if he had gone back even further to that time without time when he had existed as one with them.

I—we—must exist.

He felt them—himself, both, one—though no longer with flesh or presence. He felt five pieces of them—of himself—being torn out, though they went willingly for the sake of all . . . of the one.

We will make our existence.

Then there were the many within the one.

He remembered the beginning of Earth, Water, Air, Fire, and Spirit—the first of any *thing.* Five parts of the Fay—of him and all that was One— sacrificed themselves in separateness. This ended the Fay's nonbeing amid an endless, timeless nothing. There was a *place* and a *time* for it—they—to *be.*

Upheaval quickly followed. He could not remember its cause, what it was, where it started . . . who was its source. Then he was alone, barely aware of his *self.*

Nothing more came to him, and what followed began with a mournful loneliness in isolation. No, that was not from him but from some other, though he felt it now. Was that from all of them or from only another *one*?

It built quickly, making him frantic, then panicked, and finally it became a desperate fury to escape at any cost . . . from what?

He thought he heard distant screaming.

And that *one* of fright and fury died, he could feel it—but it was still there, aware even after its own death. That face of the dragon shaped in fire winked away, but he could still hear its hiss . . . and the sound of scraping scales on immense coils exploded in another scream.

"Chap . . . please . . . *breathe*!"

He knew this voice, or he should. Not the fiery one that had died and not died. It was another being, but he could not find the name for it.

"Wake up, Chap, please!"

Was someone speaking to him? Was that his name?

"Don't you leave me, don't you dare . . . Magiere, get in here!"

He should know a name for that voice. Then came something else that he *heard*: a rustle, perhaps canvas, and rapid vibrations against his side, his body. Did he have a flesh and form? Footfalls brought another voice.

"Wynn, what's wrong?"

"Magiere, he won't move, won't breathe. His eyes are open but . . . he isn't breathing."

A hard touch on him pressed and shook him. He had a body, but it was only a shell. He could not move it or escape from it.

"Chap, answer me—*now*," snarled the second voice. "Wynn, what happened?"

"He touched an orb, only for an instant, and . . . and then he dropped."

"Move aside," a third, deeper voice ordered.

"Brot'an, there's no . . . What are you doing? Why'd you bring *him*?"

"Move now," that third voice repeated, cold and sharp. "Wynn, back away."

Chap—if that was his own name—felt someone touch him again, perhaps on a shoulder. The following whisper was so close that it blocked all other sounds.

"Time to come back, old guardian. You are not done yet, as a guess."

Warmth spread from the touch.

A light grew in the complete darkness until a soft glimmer took shape. He vaguely knew the form from somewhere as its glow coalesced into squiggly lines, which became branches, all of which sprouted from a thickening trunk. It was tawny and warm to the sight, and he had seen it somewhere before.

"A bit longer," that last, fourth voice added, tainted with puzzling humor. "At least, from what Chârmun tells me."

He knew that name was for what he saw in the dark. His panicked fury fled from its light. Other shapes began to form in his darkness and as a tree slowly faded from sight. With them came smells thickened inside a dim tent. The only true light now was a cold-lamp crystal lying near his head, between him . . . and Wynn.

She collapsed atop him, sobbing in relief.

Chap rolled his head enough to see the others.

Near where Wynn had knelt, Magiere's eyes half closed as she sagged in a heavy breath. And the one still touching him, Chuillyon, looked down upon him with a wry smile. Behind him, Brot'an was on one knee, ever watchful.

Thankfully, the chest with the orb of Spirit was closed. Wynn must have had the presence of mind to close it.

Ghassan stood in the tent's opening as if he had just arrived . . . with Chane and Ore-Locks still outside but looking in. Leesil was nowhere to be seen.

Why did Leesil's absence suddenly terrify Chap?

Worse, he remembered that darker moment when panic had been eaten by fury. Had either of those emotions been his, or had he merely felt them from that other, the one who had died and not died? But who and why?

Chap remembered the last words of his kin. Those had to have some meaning for what he had seen—lived—in touching whatever lay within the anchor of Spirit, but he still could not find the full meaning of . . .

Leave the enslaved alone.

And why had he seen a dragon . . . the dark and fire-shrouded face of that great weürm?

*　　*　　*

Kneeling before Chap, Wynn grasped his face with both hands. "Talk to me."

He looked up into her brown eyes and then struggled to look around at the others present. For just an instant, she thought he paused in staring at Chuillyon, which confused and then worried her even more.

—You must help me—

"Of course," she answered. "We will get you on my bedroll, and Magiere can find some water for—"

—No . . . help me with Chuillyon—

Wynn stiffened. There was nothing she could think of that was worth involving that trickster, unless he was the only way to escape if everything went wrong.

—It involves his assumed ability to travel between Chârmun and its children . . . its separated parts—

"What?" she asked in obvious alarm.

"What did he say?" Magiere demanded, crouching close.

Wynn stiffened, suddenly wary of answering in the presence of some of the others.

—We will need Leesil's branch. If we hope to win this battle, you will do as I instruct. First, remove Ghassan and Brot'an, and then find Leesil—

Chap sounded desperate as well as urgent. She didn't like the guesses that came to mind without a full explanation. As always, she had to trust him again.

"Everyone, give us some privacy, please," she said. But as Chuillyon nodded and rose to follow Brot'an and Ghassan, she told him, "Not you . . . You stay."

Chuillyon stalled, raising one eyebrow in puzzled fascination.

Oh, she so hated it when he did that!

Wynn turned to Magiere in a low whisper. "Go find Leesil, quickly."

*　　*　　*

Not long after, Khalidah stood near the edge of camp, weighing his options. Ore-Locks and Chane once again sat together, speaking in low voices, but occasionally Chane glanced over at the center tent in what might be concern.

Khalidah too wondered what was happening inside that tent. He had no idea what had caused the majay-hì to fall, and this concerned him slightly, but he had come upon the scene too late and no one had offered an explanation. He had not wished to risk scrutiny by pressing Wynn or Magiere. Anyway, the majay-hì appeared to have recovered with the help of the enigmatic elf.

Within moments of Khalidah and Brot'an having been sent from the tent, Leesil had come back into camp, and Magiere had drawn him inside. Their voices were too low to hear. It was tempting to use sorcery to listen in, but Brot'an was still out here . . . and watching.

Well, if Wynn wished to plot and plan in secret, let her. It helped keep the attention off him, and he had his own plans.

Deciding upon a current course of action, he turned to Brot'an. "I may as well be useful," he said. "We passed an area that might be a good hiding place for a well. I will take a look."

Brot'an watched him with no expression. "Should I accompany you?"

Khalidah raised one hand. "No, that is not necessary. You might be needed here, and I can hide more quickly alone if I encounter something."

Without waiting for an answer, he slipped out of camp, heading west. While he had been away on the long trek to meet Chane and Chap—and the three remaining orbs—Sau'ilahk and Ubâd had remained here. No, it was not a mistake, happenstance, or even the scouting of Brot'an and Leesil that had led to the selection of this spot to camp.

It had all been his subtle doing.

He walked through the foothills in long, steady strides for some time. Upon nearing the other camp, as usual, he encountered the ghost girl first.

Either she or the masked creature who controlled her always sensed his coming. He passed her watchful stare and soon came upon Ubâd's wheeled litter with his lashed, preserved corpse on top. His two overmuscled corpse servants likewise were always silently nearby.

Sau'ilahk crouched beside a glowing oil lamp.

He rose at the sight of Khalidah. Even out here after so many nights, his pale, handsome face appeared clean and flawless, as did his blue-black hair. He had always been vain.

"You have all five orbs in your possession?" Sau'ilahk asked without greeting.

Khalidah kept his tone measured, though his answer brought him relief and joy. "Yes."

Sau'ilahk scowled, less than pleased. "Then you should have contacted me via the medallion long before now!"

"Yes, you should have," echoed the ghost girl for Ubâd. "We have been waiting in ignorance while the horde grows."

Khalidah barely glanced at the corpse on the litter. The three of them might be in league, but he had no intention of telling them anything more than was necessary—when necessary. Certainly they had done no more for him. And of late, he had begun to question Ubâd's inclusion in this triad of betrayers.

The puppet master of ghosts or corpses seemed of little use for what would now come. Ubâd, as a necromancer, might have had value in the imperial capital, but in facing the horde or manipulating those who would enter Beloved's mountain, such skills would be of little help. Well, perhaps they might.

Without full certainty, Khalidah put this aside until it could be tested.

"All that matters is that we have the orbs," he said, "and the dhampir and those with her now plan to infiltrate the peak and locate Beloved."

Sau'ilahk's eyes narrowed. "Then why do we not take all of them unaware, kill them, and take the orbs?"

Khalidah shook his head. "To use the orbs against Beloved, it is better to let some of them carry the chests inside the mountain. That is what Beloved wants—Magiere with the orbs—so we wait to play our own hand until necessary. It is doubtful any forces below would recognize any authority in us if we try approaching without her."

"Yes, but anyone else—including you—among the dhampir's group faces that same risk if they are seen," the ghost girl countered.

Khalidah refrained from smiling; these two were so deluded in their hunger for vengeance.

"Depending on the final plan by the dhampir and the others, we can attain our goal if the two of you use your own methods to help distract the horde. Remain in the shadows, but pull their attention and allow me to slip past with a small team and take the orbs into the peak."

Sau'ilahk fixed on him intensely. "You will enter while we remain outside? I think not."

Again, lack of trust reared its head.

"I have infiltrated the dhampir's group," Khalidah replied with quiet scorn. "And was it you who employed a single anchor to bring down Bäalâle Seatt?" He looked from Sau'ilahk to Ubâd, ignoring the ghost girl. "Of the three of us, who could manage all five anchors to fulfill our goal?"

Neither of them answered.

"If we are to succeed," he went on, "you will distract the horde and leave the rest to me."

Sau'ilahk watched him silently without blinking. As to Ubâd, who knew what he would have done if he were not just a corpse.

Neither of them had grounds to argue further, though Khalidah knew he had pushed them to their limits. He was the only choice to enter the peak, though his cohorts both knew this left him in control of all five orbs. And though they were both now a threat, this was the arrangement he had planned from the start.

*   *   *

Chuillyon reappeared beside Chârmun, still partially surprised over why if not how. It could not be luck.

He had blundered into a group that had unearthed all five anchors of creation, brought them together, and was now determined to use such to destroy the Ancient Enemy . . . who was awakening and calling its servants to itself.

Such things did not happen by chance, and neither did his dropping unwittingly among them.

He frowned deeply as he looked up into the glimmering branches above.

"You could have told me first," he grumbled. "And others think I am devious!"

Tonight, Chap and Wynn had kept him inside their tent and made a shocking request—no, demand. At first, he had been speechless, convinced it was impossible to fulfill. Wynn was certainly less polite than ever before. He realized he could not refuse to try, at least not to their faces, though he had every intention of applying all his powers of persuasion.

At his agreement, Wynn had held up the branch, which she had requested from the half-blood. And with a touch upon it, Chuillyon had returned home. Now he could not fail in what he promised.

Looking up, he again saw the small new sprout with one leaf growing from a low branch of the Chârmun.

"You could have told me what you had in mind," he chided, "instead of letting me blunder into it. It appears that again, I am not the only one prone to pranks."

He dug about inside his robe, pulled out a small knife, and unsheathed it. About to reach for the tiny branch, he froze.

Chuillyon looked warily about the clearing and listened as well. Being caught by Vreuvillä or one of her pack would be a worse twist than using

Chârmun for a trip. And soon enough, he would have to face that savage priestess to accomplish all that was needed. When certain neither was nearby, he set the blade to the base of that tiny sprout . . . and hesitated.

"I would beg forgiveness, but obviously this is what you intended."

He cut the tiny leafed branch—barely more than a twig—in one clean slice.

Cradling it in one hand, he lingered, and smiled. It was so much like another tiny precious child he had cared for long ago. That one he had personally given a new home in a hidden alcove of the courtyard at the third and greatest castle of Calm Seatt.

And then he grew sad and worried. This one would not see that kind of peace.

"I swear I will do my all for this one," he whispered to Chârmun, as if speaking to a mother or father or both.

He tucked the little sprout of branch into an inner pocket of his robe and looked to Chârmun again.

"Bless me, please, for I will need it."

Then he slipped away into the forest.

Wynn emerged from the tent, followed by Chap first, and then Magiere and Leesil. Ghassan was nowhere in sight, but Brot'an, Ore-Locks, and Chane all turned her way. Brot'an immediately walked over, pulled the tent's flap, and peered inside.

Wynn looked down to Chap, gently placing a hand on his back. "How are you doing?"

—*Better, physically; as for otherwise, it does not matter anymore*—

It mattered to her, though, for whatever Chap had been through when he collapsed, she didn't know what else she could do for him. What mattered most was that she had not lost him.

"Where is Chuillyon?" Brot'an asked. "There is no one in the tent."

Wynn braced herself before turning to face him. "We sent him to check on Wayfarer and Osha and Shade, through Leesil's branch."

It was not a lie, not exactly. Chap had demanded that the rest be kept secret. There had been no point in arguing with him.

Brot'an rarely betrayed emotion at all, but his eyes narrowed, buckling those four scars that skipped over his right eye.

"Chuillyon will return soon," Wynn assured. "Magiere was worried about Wayfarer when she didn't come with Chap. Chuillyon is the only one who can . . . look in on the girl."

Magiere and Leesil neared. Though they'd been inside the tent and had been involved and informed regarding Chuillyon's part in the plan, even they did not know everything.

"If you have concerns," Wynn added to Brot'an, "take them up with Magiere."

The master assassin's jaw might have clenched slightly. It was hard to tell. He would know that he was being kept in the dark about something. At present, there was nothing he could do about it. Chuillyon was already gone, and all Wynn—or anyone—could do was wait.

If only it could have depended on anyone but Chuillyon!

CHAPTER FOURTEEN

The following evening, past dusk, Wynn noticed the others gathering in between the tents, and she knew it was time. The full creation of a plan was about to be discussed openly. Though she suspected some of them had been ready to begin earlier that day, everyone waited for Chane to rise.

Whether they accepted him or not, hated him or not, they all knew he would be needed for what was to come. And he and Chap had traveled up an entire continent to retrieve the missing three orbs. Chane had earned his place here as much as any of them.

Magiere and Leesil settled next to each other with Chap to Leesil's left. Brot'an crouched on Magiere's other side. Chane and Ore-Locks stood slightly aside and both looked to Wynn, so she went to join them. A moment later Ghassan emerged from a tent.

He had been angry last night upon returning to find Chuillyon gone and, for some reason, he blamed her exclusively. She'd kept Leesil's branch and also kept quiet about its use at Chap's insistence.

Ghassan glanced around and raised one dark brow at her. "Has your elf returned?"

"He isn't mine," she corrected. "And no, he hasn't. But everyone else is ready, so we should begin without him."

As she, Chane, and Ore-Locks stepped closer into a circle with the others, Ghassan wouldn't let up.

"Then we start with the truth, right now," he insisted. "Why did you send Chuillyon back home? And you can skip any more nonsense about him checking on Wayfarer."

His tone bordered on threatening.

Magiere fixed on him, her expression darkening, and Chap rumbled low in warning. Perhaps one or both were about to intervene, but Wynn needed no such protection.

"Chap feels some things should be on a need-to-know basis," she countered, "and I agree whether you like it or not. This is not a matter of trust but for the protection of everyone should any one of us be captured instead of killed. We cannot be forced to tell what we don't know."

At that, Brot'an frowned but didn't argue. He might agree with Chap in principle, but he would also see that if she were taken, it would not matter what the others didn't know. And Brot'an was right about that.

Very little could be done to Chap to get anything from him. Not so for her. But Chap had been as careful as possible. Last night, he had merely asked Leesil and Magiere to trust him in sending Chuillyon back. He had not shared his plan even with them. However, he had told Wynn most of it, or so she believed.

Leesil glanced nervously at Magiere, and Wynn knew there were several reasons why.

"Can we get on with this?" he asked.

Ghassan studied him coldly. "By all means."

Leesil opened his mouth, closed it, and took a deep breath before he began. "Chap believes the only way we might succeed is to break into two teams. One team to distract and draw off the forces below while the other team finds a way into the mountain . . . with the orbs."

Magiere straightened upright, turning on him where he sat. "What?"

Leesil ignored her. "The first group must do anything to keep as many of the Enemy's forces from seeing and following those infiltrating the peak. Without that, we fail before we even start."

Ore-Locks and Chane had been silent so far, but Chane asked quietly, "How do we decide who goes with which group?"

Chap's head swiveled, and Wynn found his sky blue eyes locked on her.

—*Help Leesil*—

"By ability or usefulness," she answered. "Five heavy orbs have to be carried in, and that means Chane, Ore-Locks, and Brot'an, with Leesil leading."

The skin over Magiere's cheekbones drew back. Before she could fire off an argument, Ghassan spoke up.

"I may not be as strong as they are, but I have skills they do not, such as shielding infiltrators from nearby detection for short periods or moving an orb by means other than strength . . . and there are five orbs."

"Your inclusion had already been decided," Wynn said to him, "if you had let Leesil finish. There are other things for which you will also be needed."

Wynn tried not to look around at everyone present, for she knew that by the end of tomorrow night, she might never see some of them again.

Watching Magiere grow angrier by the moment, Chap readied himself to stop her before a verbal onslaught started. He was too late.

"I am going for the Enemy!" she stated, rising to her feet. "No one else before me!"

Chap also rose as he snarled.

—*Success . . . is all . . . that matters*— . . . —*There is more . . . to be . . . said . . . in private*— . . . —*Sit down . . . now*—

While he called up those words out of Magiere's memories, Leesil had lurched to his feet and stepped in on Magiere.

"Sit down," he ordered as well, "and hear the rest of this out."

Magiere blinked, still breathing hard, and Chap waited and watched. Leesil seldom spoke harshly to her or gave her orders. That he had done so as well left her hesitant.

"Please, Magiere," Wynn added.

Magiere did not sit but stepped back, remaining silent, and Wynn continued as Chap had instructed her.

"The optimal time would be daylight, dawn," Wynn continued, "when the undead fall dormant. But it is unlikely that all of those below are undead. Worse, it would be that much harder for the second group to sneak in, so we have to do this at night." She paused. "And Chane won't be able to help until then . . . and we need him."

Chane glowered at her, now as openly suspicious as Magiere had been before her outburst. His eyes turned nearly clear.

"And where will you be?" he asked Wynn, as if he didn't know already.

"With Chuillyon, when he returns," Wynn responded.

Chane's brow furrowed as he shook his head, and Brot'an spoke for the first time.

"The vampire is the only one making sense. How are Wynn and Chuillyon to distract the horde, even assuming Chap and Magiere will join them?"

Chap wished there were a way to keep Brot'an even more in the dark.

Wynn was far less confident than she sounded. She'd known how difficult Chane would be once he realized he would not be with her. Chap looked up at her.

—*Tell them it is possible to distract the horde because Magiere will be with you*—

Wynn related this aloud, and Magiere turned on Chap.

"What do you mean?"

As Chap continued speaking into Wynn's head, she explained to the others.

"If the infiltration team is spotted, Magiere may be able to hold the undead forces through her dhampir nature—either in controlling some, as was once hinted at long ago, or in simply being seen as a prime threat to them . . . or both. I'll have the sun crystal ready, if needed, to keep them at bay."

Magiere shook her head. "What do you mean . . . controlling some of them?"

Wynn didn't like that part herself. "Chap will explain more in private."

Chane hissed, and even Ore-Locks scowled, though he knew less about the others than anyone.

"Chap believes we have a good chance," Wynn went on. "One group *can* distract the forces long enough for the other to find an entrance into the mountain."

"How and where?" Ore-Locks demanded, speaking for the first time.

—*Enough! Move on!*—

Wynn winced at Chap's sharpness in her head. She was growing tired of his harsh insistence while simultaneously dealing with the others on all sides.

Looking to Magiere, she said, "He wants to speak with you and me alone."

"We have not finished here," Ghassan challenged, eyeing Chap. "We have barely started, and why is *he* in charge?"

Chap turned away, padding out of camp, and without a moment's hesitation, Magiere strode after him.

Wynn couldn't guess which one would do the talking—shouting—first. And they were both leaving so fast that she had no time to speak with or even glance toward Chane before hurrying after them.

Magiere closed on Chap as he rounded a craggy knoll. He stopped near several large boulders and sat without turning or looking back. Wynn arrived and scurried past Magiere toward Chap.

"You could have handled that better!" Wynn scolded Chap. Then she straightened suddenly, eyes widening. "Oh, really? Well, I am tired of being your surrogate mouth *and* the first target for the others . . . because of you!"

"You won't be my target," Magiere growled as she rounded them to face Chap. "I'm going inside the peak, you understand!"

She wasn't letting anything—anyone—tell her otherwise.

—You cannot—

Magiere's anger started to burn up her throat.

—Remember . . . what I told you . . . through Wynn . . . on the night in the an'Cróan . . . forest . . . after . . . your trial—

Startled, Magiere hesitated. "What does that have to do with anything?"

—Sit down— . . . —I will speak . . . through Wynn . . . to recount— . . . — You will . . . listen . . . to her—

Magiere didn't need the sage to recount. She'd never forget that night, and she didn't need reminding. Before she could tell this to Chap, he locked gazes with Wynn. After a moment's hesitation, the sage began.

"No undead existed before the war at the end of the Forgotten History, not that we know of. No undead rose but from humans. No undead walks into elven lands . . . except you." Wynn paused and stared without blinking as Magiere thought of one exception . . .

"Yes, Chane can enter elven lands," Wynn confirmed, "but only because of the ring he stole from your half brother, Welstiel."

Though she went on, Magiere already knew the rest.

In the dank forests of Pudúrlatsat, on the eastern continent, Chap had fallen prey to a phantasm cast by Vordana, an undead sorcerer. Magiere, herself—and Leesil—had suffered the same. Though they'd all experienced some portent of the future, each had seen it differently, based on their own worst fears. That, and perhaps something more hidden in each of them.

Chap's had been the worst, and right now Magiere wished he'd never told her.

He had seen her leading an army—a horde—with ranks of creatures driven to slaughter. She'd stood at the head of those forces in black-scaled armor, fully feral with her dhampir nature unleashed. Among the horde were the shadowed and gleaming-eyed figures, as in some of Magiere's own delusions and nightmares.

The undead followed her into a thriving forest.

Everything withered and died in her wake under their hunger.

Wynn went on.

Magiere had been imbued—infected, cursed—at birth with the nature of a Noble Dead. And yet, unlike them, she was alive. She had been created inside her mother's womb by a ritual that used the blood of five sacrifices from the original races of the world . . . the Úirishg.

The Ancient Enemy had arranged all of it, and by that and the life within her, Magiere could go anywhere she wished.

The undead could not, especially into those lands protected by Chârmun or its offspring—unless they followed her. And since that night in Pudúrlatsat, that had been Chap's reasoning for why she had been made.

Magiere didn't like it but couldn't argue about it.

"And then there's something not about you," Wynn said. "Remember that Leesil was given a name by one of the an'Cróan's spiritual ancestors called Léshiâra—'Sorrow-Tear.' She named him Léshiârelaohk—'Sorrow-Tear's Champion.'"

Magiere back-stepped once, trying to draw a breath.

"In that, he was also *created* . . . or re-created," Wynn added, "for a purpose, like you."

Nothing Wynn said was anything Magiere didn't already know. To think of Leesil as the *other* side for what Chap saw as her purpose was too twisted, too cruel.

"Don't you see?" Wynn asked quietly. "Leesil has to be the one—and not you—if we believe anything about what we've encountered since we met. He has to go for the Enemy while you have to lead the horde away . . . somehow . . . from him."

Magiere didn't know if Wynn now spoke for Chap or herself or both.

"That is Leesil's only chance to fulfill his fate and for you to escape yours," Wynn added, "even if any living forces below turn another way and do not follow the undead after you."

In another back step, Magiere's heel struck a boulder. She dropped down onto that stone and sat looking from Wynn to Chap.

"You told him already, didn't you?" she accused, fixing on Chap. "You already got to Leesil."

Chap crept in to sit before her.

"We had to," Wynn answered. "If we revealed too much too soon, you would have gone to him first. And he would have gone anywhere with you. It cannot happen that way."

As the truth sank in, Magiere went numb. Wynn came to crouch beside her, but she couldn't look at either of them anymore.

"I will be with you, and so will Chap," Wynn said. "Together, we will make certain Leesil and the others have a chance."

In Magiere's own phantasm on that long-lost night in the forest, she had turned on Leesil with the horde and killed him. She'd thought that if she kept clear of the undead here and now, she could wipe away that nightmare and keep Leesil safe.

But even now they'd been doomed to different sides.

"I need to talk to Leesil," Magiere said. She left without looking back.

Leesil sat in one tent, trying to shut out the sounds of the voices outside. When Magiere, Chap, and Wynn had left, he'd had to cut off anyone else from following. Ghassan had been the worst, and for an instant, Leesil had wondered what the fallen domin might do. When Ghassan slightly turned away, Leesil had done the same by retreating to the tent.

He already knew what Wynn and Chap were doing.

They'd spoken to him before tonight. It all made sense, and still he had instinctively argued. No matter that he couldn't get around them and why things had to be this way.

Magiere could never go near the Enemy, for that was what it appeared to want.

The tent's flap was pulled outward, and Leesil tensed all over. Whether it was Magiere coming at him, now that she knew, or Ghassan with more arguments, Leesil was in no mood for either.

To his surprise, neither of them crouched in the opening.

Instead, Chane peered in. "May I enter for a moment?"

Leesil didn't know what to say. Chane was the last one he'd expected.

"What do you want?" Leesil asked.

Chane dropped to his right knee and pivoted in to close the flap. He then turned about and hesitated. Did he actually take a deep breath and let it out slowly?

"We all know the Enemy can reach for and call its own anywhere," Chane said quietly. "It can control them, though with differing influence. You saw as much with two of its Children that you faced. And I—and Wynn—saw hints of the same with Sau'ilahk, the wraith."

Leesil didn't respond, though he already suspected where Chane was going with this. It was something that had terrified him for too long.

"What if the Enemy seizes control of Magiere?" Chane asked.

Leesil's first instinct was to snarl denial, but he couldn't. This time, there was no doubt that Chane took a labored breath and let it out before raising a hand, its back side toward Leesil, and spreading his fingers.

"This could protect Magiere . . . while out there facing the horde," Chane said.

Leesil's confusion passed in a blink, for on the middle finger of the undead's hand was a brass ring. Once or twice, he'd heard it called the "ring of nothing."

What was Chane really up to?

"We both have a woman we wish to protect," Chane continued, "but neither of us can do so in what is coming. This ring might keep Magiere from being used, though that has another risk."

It didn't take long for Leesil to work that out. If that ring hid Chane's undead nature and also hid him from the Enemy, would it affect Magiere's chance at controlling or at least calling out the undead? Would it hide too much of her nature?

Of course this wasn't really about Magiere but about Wynn. If Magiere couldn't influence the undead among the horde, both Magiere and Wynn stood even less chance of surviving.

"You see the catch," Chane said, "so I came to you before her. This is not just my decision, though I would have preferred it so."

Leesil eyed Chane and then the ring. There was even more to it. If Magiere failed to draw off even part of the forces below, there would be little chance of gaining the mountain without being seen. And as important . . .

"Yes, I would be detectable without the ring," Chane finished in response to Leesil's thought.

He was weary of choices like this, and it was so strange that this monster even asked. Then again, was there a difference for how much blood Chane had spilled in his youth versus what Leesil had spilled? Yes, for he hadn't killed for pleasure. Still, strangely, Chane had asked only him.

"No," Leesil finally answered.

Chane's eyes widened slightly.

"Magiere's not the only one who might be controlled," Leesil added. That was the true catch for when—if—they got close to the Enemy. For that, it wouldn't matter if Magiere succumbed or not. They would be ruined if Chane and not Magiere fell under the Enemy's influence.

Chane lowered his eyes and nodded. Pivoting on that one knee, he pulled aside the tent's flap.

"Chane," Leesil whispered.

And Chane froze, turning his head but not fully looking back.

"If something does happen to us in there," Leesil began, "and you're the only one who can't be influenced . . ."

Chane turned more and looked directly at Leesil. Nothing more needed to be said, and Chane nodded once. He was gone faster than he'd entered, leaving Leesil alone with his doubts and fears.

He knew Magiere would be coming to him soon.

"I don't like lying to our friends," Wynn whispered after Magiere was gone.

Chap looked up.

—*We have not*—

"Don't," Wynn cut in. "I do not need lies to comfort me."

—*We simply told each only what they need to know. Some things cannot be shared with the others, for the safety of all*—

Wynn got up and headed off. "That's a lie as well. And how much have you not told me?"

Chap followed at her side but didn't answer.

When they returned to camp, neither Magiere nor Leesil was in sight. Wynn looked to one tent and knew they were both in there. She couldn't imagine what they might say to each other, but more than likely Magiere was going at Leesil for his part in what she hadn't been told until too late.

Chap stared off between the tents at the chests now covered by a tarp. And when Wynn looked away, she caught Chane watching her.

He stood as if he were in quiet talk with Ore-Locks, though the young stonewalker appeared to be doing all of the talking. At a sharp word from Ore-Locks, perhaps for being ignored, Chane started slightly.

As to Ghassan and Brot'an, both were off to either side on their own, one pacing and the other settled cross-legged on the ground as if this were any other night.

Wynn looked down and found Chap still studying the tarped chests—the orbs. She had no idea what he was thinking, and she knew he'd never tell even if she asked.

"I'm going for a rest in another tent. Call me when Magiere finishes with Leesil . . . or the other way. And then we will all finish any more talking and planning."

She headed off for Chane and Ore-Locks's tent to be alone, wondering if she even had the strength for more planning after facing down Magiere. Then she heard footsteps come closer outside the tent.

"Wynn?"

She closed her eyes. She wasn't up to a fight with Chane either.

"What is it?" she asked tiredly.

Without invitation, he entered, crawling in to sit beside her. She didn't look over until she heard him fiddling with a pack. It was the second one, the one he never let anyone touch. Whatever he was checking for, he didn't pull it out.

"Please don't start," she said.

"What did you and Chap say to Magiere?"

"We convinced her that she can hold back the horde."

"Can she?"

Wynn didn't have an answer for that.

"And you still wish me to go with the team infiltrating the peak?" he asked.

Wynn's thoughts turned back to the first time she'd ever seen him at the guild's annex in Bela, now on the other side of the world. She hadn't known then what he was and had seen only a handsome, somewhat dour young nobleman hungry for scholarly pursuits. Had she started to fall in love with him even then? Or had it been just a naive infatuation with his attention in a faraway land?

"I know you would die for me," she whispered, "but your dying, again, won't help anything, not even me. So you know the answer, after all the time we've been together. We cannot fail now, or nothing else comes after . . . for any of us."

Chane remained silent.

Wynn had a strange feeling his question was only half earnest. Yes, he wanted to stay at her side, but somehow he must have known the answer before he'd asked.

"Leesil needs your strength," she added, "and Magiere needs my skills and my staff." She hung her head, exhausted and drained and desperate.

Chane still said nothing.

"I love you," she whispered.

When she finally raised her head again, he was staring at her without blinking. Then he suddenly twisted away, jerked open that same pack, and wrenched something out.

In his hand was a widemouthed bottle with a wax-sealed stopper.

Wynn could smell something familiar, and before she could ask . . .

"This is a healing elixir," he said. "I made it from the white *Anamgiah* petals. Take it with you for whatever you need, for . . . anyone whose life is in immediate danger." He hesitated. "But do not try it with Magiere. Because of her nature, the part like me, it would be harmful."

Wynn shook her head in puzzlement and looked up at Chane. Those going with him might need this as much as she or those with her did.

"If I cannot protect you myself," he whispered, "then I will do so in any other way possible."

Not knowing what to say, she reached out for the bottle. Instead, she wrapped her small hand across his larger one holding the vessel. And after a moment . . .

"We need to go out and finish planning."

The following midafternoon, Chuillyon planned a brief trip back to the desert. He had traveled with Wynn's group long enough to know that they would sleep during the day's worst heat. Still, he had no idea where he might arrive and was relieved to reappear inside a tent.

Magiere, Leesil, Chap, and Wynn were all sound asleep at his feet where he crouched with his hand touching the branch of Roise Chârmune. Wynn had earlier agreed to leave the branch out all day and into the night, just in case.

Chuillyon gently touched her shoulder. Her eyes fluttered sleepily and then widened at the sight of him. He quickly put one finger over his lips and then pointed to the tent flap. Slow and silent, they both crawled out of the tent, leaving the others asleep.

"Is everything arranged as Chap instructed?" Wynn whispered in a half panic.

He smiled and nodded once. "Either I have not lost my persuasive way, or mention of your name holds more sway than I realized."

She did not smile back. "So it's all set?"

"Almost." Reaching into his robe's pocket, he drew out the new sprout cut from Chârmun. "This is a little something extra."

"That's . . . is that . . . ?"

"Oh, stop stammering. I will go into the hills between the range and peak and hide it somewhere. From there I can use it to return home—and then back later. But you will not see me again until you and yours act. The timing of this is the real reason I came to you."

Her eyes were still on the sprout as she answered, "Tonight at dusk."

Chuillyon stalled in a frown; that was sooner than expected.

"All will be ready," he replied. "And Leesil has agreed to lead those heading for the peak?"

"Yes."

He leaned down closer to Wynn. "Tell him to keep the branch on him at all times, no matter what else happens. Only in that will I be able to reach him and the others, should escape or assistance be needed."

Wynn nodded, though the notion brought no relief to her expression.

Chuillyon smiled wryly one last time, and turning away, he added, "Until tonight, young Wynn."

That evening, Wynn helped with final preparations. After the orbs in their chests were rigged on tent poles, so that two at least could be carried efficiently by pairs of those going with Leesil, Wynn distributed the orb keys—or thôrhks. Though there were five orbs, only three keys had been recovered whole.

Wynn gave one each to Ore-Locks, Ghassan, and Chane. Each man hung the thôrhk around his neck. Brot'an received none and did not argue or appear to expect one. Chane had hidden both his packs and his cloak, though who knew if he had stashed anything from those somewhere on himself. He wore only a dark shirt, pants, boots, both his swords, and a coil of rope over one shoulder. Ore-Locks had stripped down to pants, boots, and shirt as well, but he wore his stonewalker daggers in his belt and the sword with a width nearly twice that of Chane's longer one. Ghassan appeared much the same as always, though he too wore a coil of rope.

And there was yet one more orb key unlike all the others.

Leesil was to be given Magiere's more singular one.

Back on the eastern continent, Magiere and Leesil had been taken down to the fiery home of the Chein'âs before even finding the first orb. That subterranean race that lived in a realm of Fire made all the weapons and tools for the Anmaglâhk. They gifted Magiere a dagger of white metal and a thôrhk to match, the only other thôrhk in the world that would open an orb.

Magiere now stood before her husband, wearing her studded leather hauberk. With her falchion belted on her hip, the white metal dagger was once again strapped inverted beneath the back flap of her hauberk. She had pulled her hair into a single thong-lashed tail.

Carefully, she fit her thôrhk around Leesil's neck.

"Bring it back to me," she said.

He nodded. He wore his ringed hauberk. His muslin cloth was gone, and his hair was pulled back at the nape of his neck. He had a long rope in a coil loosely over one shoulder and across his chest. Both winged blades were strapped to his thighs, and Wynn knew he had at least one white metal stiletto up his left sleeve.

Finally, Leesil took the last step that he had prepared for himself and those with him. Soot from the dead campfire had been mixed with a bit of oil and water. This he smeared over his face and neck, having all others going with him do the same, especially Chane with his extra-pale skin.

When Leesil rose again, Wynn stepped toward him with the branch from Roise Chârmune. She didn't even ask and grabbed his right wrist, placing the branch on his forearm and lashing it there with bits of leather thongs.

"What are you doing?" he asked.

"This way you will not lose it and always have it ready."

He scowled at her. "So what are you not telling me this time?"

"Just keep it there." She dipped some muck by the dead fire to spread over the branch.

Leesil sighed, probably tired of so many secrets, but what he did not know could not be taken from him. That branch might be the last way to get to him and the others . . . if anyone else was left alive and the worst came about.

More than likely, such an option might not matter by then.

Chap came up beside her.

Earlier, she had let him know about Chuillyon's brief return and about the new sprout from Chârmun to be hidden somewhere between the foothills and the peak. This was the only way he would have let Leesil keep the branch.

—*All else is ready?*—

"Yes," she answered, hoping she was right.

Leesil and Chane hefted the first two chests on two poles, Ghassan and Brot'an the next pair, and Ore-Locks picked up the final chest.

Ghassan looked to Wynn. "We depend on the rest of you to distract the horde."

Though she nodded, she looked to Chane and found him watching her. They said nothing, for any words at all might be too much like their last.

Going to Leesil, who gripped two pole ends, Magiere grabbed his neck and pressed her forehead to his. When she let go, that was all, and Leesil led the others out into the growing darkness.

—And now we hurry—

After giving this command, Chap stalked off another way. Wynn gripped her staff and followed with Magiere at her side, both of them watching the sparking of campfires below at the peak's base . . . where the undead were already rising.

CHAPTER FIFTEEN

Magiere followed Wynn and Chap down through the foothills toward where the Sky-Cutter Range met the mountains running along the eastern coast. She tried not to let herself think or feel anything. The three of them made certain to remain unseen. Down near the base, they were not on sand but rough, hard-baked earth, and there they split up.

Wynn headed off slightly south and east into the southward range's foothills. She needed to find a vantage point that would allow her quick access into the open should Magiere lead or drive the undead toward the sun-crystal staff. She already had specially made dark-lensed glasses dangling freely around her neck.

Chap went north in case any stragglers from the horde went that way or swerved back toward the peak to threaten exposing Leesil and those with him. As the dog faded away in the deepening darkness, and Magiere could no longer see him, she had a feeling he would not go far.

And there she stood, all alone.

Her right hand dropped to the hilt of her falchion, as if needing reassurance it was there. Unlike most weapons, its blade could inflict pain and wounds on the undead. Besides her Chein'âs dagger, it was the only weapon she'd ever seen leave scars on any undead who survived its strike.

She looked toward the peak that Leesil and the others crept toward, even now. The campfires out in the open and partly up the slopes were easier to see. There was even a hint of vegetation low on the craggy rise, if firelight was enough to show such.

Magiere slipped toward the lowest campfires on the baked plain, and residual heat from the day still rose around her. She slowed when she began hearing grunts, hisses, and guttural words she didn't understand, and she veered more eastward toward broken ground and any stone outcrops.

Hunger rose inside her; it burned up her throat from her gut.

Points of firelight brightened in her widening sight as her irises blackened and expanded.

She looked again toward the upslope of the peak, but there was no real hope of spotting Leesil's group in the dark. Creeping up behind a rock formation, she peered around it for her first clear glimpse of the horde.

Leesil had been right. There were a hundred or more at a guess. As her jaws began aching and her nails began to harden, she fought to keep her wits.

Among the Enemy's gathered servants, she saw many faces pale and glistening by firelight. Those—the vampires—stood mainly erect in their tatters of clothing, mostly the long robes of desert dwellers, likely scavenged off their prey along the way.

There were other creatures in the dark. Some with gray-white skin had to be ghul, though there were not many.

She spotted another type of hulking beast. They walked on twos and fours in mismatched armor and carried scavenged weapons from swords to crude clubs to other things she couldn't make out. She knew them from when she'd traveled north in the frozen wastes to hide two orbs. They were the goblins.

There were more goblins than vampires within sight, and that wasn't good, for she wouldn't be able to influence them—as they were not undead. Each looked like a twisted cross between a huge, overfurred ape and a dog with a short, broad muzzle below sickly yellow eyes. Longer bristles sprouted around their heads and in tufts on peaked ears.

They moved in small packs, clambering about, and then made teasing feints at the vampires, who snarled or lunged one step to drive them off. Any ghul nearby vanished or scuttled off, likely looking for softer ground in which to burrow.

There were other creatures she didn't recognize, including some who appeared almost normal but stood staring in one direction, never blinking. Looking at one, she saw its skin looked nearly as pale as that of a vampire. But upon closer study, the skin was somehow sickly and shriveled on its face, exposing the contours of bone beneath.

Rage and hunger grew in Magiere, and she had to close her eyes to hang on to awareness and conscious thought. She had become a victim of fate, as had Leesil, though both of them had denied and evaded it for so long. Now it was he, and not she, who would face the Enemy.

She had to draw the horde away from him somehow.

Even Chap hadn't known exactly how she was to do this. There was only what he'd speculated.

—The Enemy can . . . find . . . call . . . its servants— . . . —The undead . . . we know . . . for certain— . . . —You can track . . . those . . . with hunger— . . . —Start . . . there—

Magiere stopped struggling to hold down her rage and hunger. She let it rise up until the light from the campfires burned her eyes and her jaws would barely close against her elongated teeth. Pulling her falchion while she still had the wits to do so, she rushed into the open.

Someone else was waiting . . . somewhere. She had to draw them . . . to that one.

It was so hard to think, to remember, that Magiere fought to choke down the first shout until she could.

Wynn . . . it was Wynn who was waiting . . . ready.

Magiere let go with a snarling, enraged cry from the back of her throat.

All motion in the camp stopped, and all she heard was the distant crackle of the campfires. So many eyes—some sparking from the light of the flames—turned her way.

Leesil and the others skirted the peak's base at the southern side.

In creeping wide to the desert fringe, they had often crouched low, dropping the chests and drawing weapons at any sudden sound. Only when nothing came at them out of the dark or when Ghassan assured them that he sensed nothing nearby had they moved on.

Now, a short way up the peak's southern side, Leesil glanced over the edge of the deep stone gash in which they hid.

It appeared they had a fairly clear path upward. None of them knew what lay up there or where they might find an entrance . . . if the Enemy was truly inside the mountain.

Leesil dropped back down into hiding. Ghassan knelt beside him with eyes closed in concentration. Chane and Ore-Locks watched the domin as well. Only Brot'an appeared unconcerned, though with his face darkened by soot, it was hard to tell.

"Well?" Leesil whispered to the domin.

He wasn't certain in the crevice's deeper darkness, but perhaps Ghassan frowned before opening his eyes.

"I do not sense any sentient presence nearby," Ghassan answered.

The domin's abilities had often troubled Leesil but not now, and he signaled the others by gestures to make ready. The bulk of the horde's encampment below suggested any entrance into the mountain would be straight up from it, and by this time, somewhere near the horde, Magiere should be in place.

Though they hadn't needed her help to get this far, the rest was something else. They would need as much distraction as possible once they spotted the entrance. There was also the possibility of guards above.

"Watch for movement," Leesil whispered, "for the sound of anyone or anything above. That could lead us to an entrance, but we can't get caught out in the open."

Looking around, he saw no movement at all. Bent, low shrubs and rock outcrops helped to hide them but also obscured his view.

"All of you remain with the orbs while I scout," Brot'an said, and then pointed at Ore-Locks. "If you hear three clicks in the dark, can you come through stone to the same spot where I am?"

Though Leesil always hesitated at taking Brot'an's advice, considering the master assassin always had a hidden goal, he couldn't think of a better option in the moment.

"Yes, I can find you," Ore-Locks whispered, "so long as you remain where you are."

"Good, but be quick," Brot'an acknowledged. "We may need to clear the way."

Only then did the old assassin look to Leesil, and Leesil nodded his agreement.

Brot'an spun and silently climbed out of the crevice's upper end. More disturbing was not even hearing him after a single breath.

It wasn't long before the waiting made Leesil begin to fidget and then to think too much. The latter was never good once a mission like this was in process.

"We take much on faith," Chane suddenly whispered. "First, that the Enemy is above because the horde is below. Second, that it is inside the peak. Third, that there is an entrance . . . within reach of the horde."

Leesil bit down against snapping back. The last thing he needed was anyone else, especially Chane, echoing his own worries.

"The Enemy is inside," Ghassan stated.

"And how do you know this?" Chane challenged.

Ghassan didn't answer at first. "I know."

That certainty didn't relieve Leesil at all.

At a sudden roaring cry echoing up through the dark, Leesil clenched all over. He wanted to rise and peer out of the crevices, but he didn't. He wouldn't be able to see anything, but he *knew*.

Down below, Magiere had shown herself.

Chap had watched in secret as Magiere worked from one hiding spot to the next.

He watched even as she had stepped into the open.

Magiere—by threat, challenge, or somehow calling the undead—had to lead them away into the reach of Wynn's staff. Until then Chap could not even risk helping either of them.

His task was to deal with anything that might get away from Magiere or Wynn's crystal and turn or flee toward the peak. He had to help protect Leesil's group. He could only hope any living forces would follow once the undead ones took off after Magiere. But there were so many.

Magiere's savage cry had nearly made Chap sicken with fear. Then the night grew too quiet as the sound faded, and Chap's thoughts raced over the worst that might come.

If the Enemy could speak to Magiere in her sleep, it could call to its own followers for help if threatened. Or it might call to her.

There was nothing he could do but hope it did neither, at least until too late. Everyone had known though never spoken of this. And because of it, they knew that not all—if any—might live through this night.

Chap hated uncertainty and, as of yet, he had no idea what Leesil would face. They had only one chance to reach the Enemy.

Then he heard something behind him and spun about, silent but with his hackles stiffened.

Out of the dark came a tall, slender form in a long dark robe with a full hood pulled up and forward. Chap immediately snarled and made to lunge.

"Wait, please!"

At both the whisper and the figure's raised hands, he hesitated. One hand quickly reached and pulled the hood partially back.

Chap froze at the sight of Chuillyon's large amber eyes barely catching the moonlight. And then came the other cries, howls, and guttural shouts behind him. As he spun back, he knew the battle had begun.

When he glanced back the other way again, Chuillyon was gone.

Indecision froze Chap, for too much might have already gone wrong. He charged out and downward to the side of a rock outcrop and skidded to a stop in shock. Rage and hunger nearly tore a howl from him.

Magiere still stood in the open, but dozens of the horde had begun turning on one another. Through the darkness, he barely saw vampires and ghul assaulting goblin packs, who in turn became frenzied with rage. The undead members of the horde were attacking the living members.

And when Chap looked again, Magiere was gone.

He lunged and leaped to the outcrop's top in searching for her, but if she had charged into the horde, the fighting was too wild and intense to spot her in the dark. His own rage and hunger grew stronger.

He dove off the outcrop to charge in to find Magiere.

Then . . . a chorus of howls broke over the chaos and screams, and when he halted, he heard it—them—more clearly upslope behind him. He looked back.

Majay-hì of all tints and tones poured out of the dark. They charged straight at him with teeth bared—and rushed around and past him. He never had a chance to turn, for another pack raced out of the dark from upslope.

Two upright forms ran with several majay-hì coming much slower to stay around them. Wayfarer sprinted behind a huge mottled brown male. Beside the girl came a four-legged black shadow with eyes that sparked—Shade.

On the second pack's far side ran a wild-looking woman who had drawn a long, curved dagger that was almost a short sword.

Chap recognized the priestess called Vreuvillä from when he had gone for Wayfarer in the Lhoin'na lands.

Chuillyon had succeeded in at least one of his secret tasks.

He must have come through via the sprout from Chârmun to check the timing before going back and then sending the majay-hì packs through the same way. How he had managed to get so many through was not a puzzle for now but later—if there was a later.

Chap held his ground and looked toward the battle. As unnatural enemies of the undead, majay-hì leaped without fear into their targets, driving them down, tearing and rending, and the wave of the second pack raced in around him.

This was not how it should have happened; Magiere should have led the undead away already.

Perhaps she could not. Perhaps her own hunting rage had simply inflamed their own. And if even most of them went down while fighting the living— or succumbed to the majay-hì packs—there would still be a mass of living opponents.

Wayfarer slowed and almost stalled, looking his way, and Shade wheeled around him.

Chap saw something in Wayfarer that suddenly frightened him. She no longer showed any of the fear he had so often seen in her. She turned with Shade and ran onward on the tail of the second pack—and he wanted to go after her and his daughter.

Yet, there was only one thing he could do.

Chap spun and raced off where Wynn hid.

The sun crystal, if ignited close enough, might take most of the undead by surprise. And it might also stun the living enough for him to find and get to Magiere, if she still lived. It was the only way to regain control, even briefly.

A shimmering, small form appeared ahead in his way, and Chap stumbled, slowing until he saw what it was: a transparent girl in a tattered nightgown, bloodied at the throat. He had seen her once before in the dank forests of eastern Droevinka—one of Ubâd's enslaved ghosts.

"Majay-hì!" the ghost girl shrieked at him.

There was too much hate in the voice for one who had died so young. Could this utterance have been instigated by Ubâd himself? That seemed impossible.

Chap had killed the necromancer himself and ripped the old man's throat to the spine. Before he could even look, two large, heavily muscled men—with dead eyes—stepped out from behind a rock formation. There was something between them, and one of them tilted it.

The wheel cart's bed rocked forward until its lead end clunked against stone, and lashed to it was a black-robed form held erect by bonds. His hands, folded and bound over his chest, were bare, exposing bony fingers. Where his face should have been was an eyeless mask of aged leather that Chap remembered, and that ended above a bony jaw supporting a withered mouth.

Ubâd's neck was now wrapped or strapped with something that held his head erect.

Chap snarled, and something like hunger but not filled his gut. The decrepit ghost master had somehow used his own skills upon himself, as he had done with the girl and his corpse guards.

"Kill him," the ghost girl ordered. "Take his head off!"

Both dead men beside the litter drew curved blades and rushed forward. One passed straight through the girl.

Wynn was waiting somewhere beyond them, and Chap could still hear the battle below in the dark. The first corpse guard swung a blade at his head.

Chap ducked aside and leaped. As the man straightened to right himself, Chap's front paws struck his target. The guard toppled, hit the rocky ground on his back, and Chap's following weight came down to crush a weak rush of fetid air out of the walking corpse. With no time to finish with the first, Chap bolted for the second man—but there was the ghost girl in his way.

"Die . . . dog!" she screeched an instant before impact.

Icy cold trapped the air in Chap's lungs. Everything whitened before his eyes like a flash of light. When his sight cleared amid a stumble, the other corpse attendant had retreated to the litter cart, sword in hand. And the dark around Ubâd's body began to waver like the heat of the desert under a noon sun.

A translucent soldier appeared as if walking out of a rippling lake. His hauberk and abdomen were slashed open, exposing organs to spill out. At another waver of color forming in the dark, Chap quickly glanced toward the litter cart's other side.

A short, bony, tattered young woman appeared. The rough line of bruising around her throat showed where she had been strangled. She opened her mouth and exposed her missing tongue. Whispering voices began to grow all around.

Chap flinched away from another ghost suddenly off to his left. A shirtless, scarecrow-thin peasant boy faded in and out. Starvation had left the specter of his ribs and swollen paunch clear to see.

And the second of the corpse guards charged in an amble.

Chap dodged right at the downward hack of a sword, and then the starved boy flew at him . . . through him. Chap's jaws locked open, but he could not breathe. Cold seemed to rise out of his bones and into his flesh.

"Can you feel your death," the ghost girl spat, "even before you die?"

The corpse guard swung at him again.

Chap stumbled sideways, now gasping for air as if it were winter. His fright grew.

Below in the battle, he had only seen lower servants of the Enemy. With Ubâd here, what other more powerful servants might have come?

Another—and another—ghost manifested in the dark.

Chap could not survive this alone. Panic took hold, and all he could think of was something that had only worked once long ago.

On a frigid night in the Pock Peaks, in their search for the first orb, Wynn had been lost in the wild amid a blizzard. He had gone out alone to search for her, failed, and in desperation . . .

—*Come . . . find me . . . and bring light!*—

If only again she could hear him now.

CHAPTER SIXTEEN

Chane was crouched near Leesil and Ghassan when he heard the clicks in the dark. Ore-Locks rose and, without a word, ran into the crevice's stone wall. Somewhere above, Brot'an had found something and signaled for Ore-Locks to come.

Then a wild-sounding cry carried up from below.

"What is that?" Chane rasped.

Leesil had already half risen, as if to peek out of the crevice, but he stopped. The cry lingered but was quickly tangled in sounds of clangs of metal and guttural shouts. Chane rose to look downward. Some campfires appeared scattered by the number of tiny orange glimmers that flickered quickly from many forms rushing about amid screams, snarls, shouts, and more.

Somehow a battle had erupted in the camp, and Wynn was below somewhere with nothing but her staff.

"Magiere and Chap are with her," Leesil said quietly. "She'll be all right."

Chane had no patience for reassuring lies. How had he let himself be talked into this? As he began to glance upslope, a chorus of high-pitched howls exploded in the dark. He twisted back to look down again as he heard more and more of those eerie sounds.

"Majay-hì?" Leesil whispered, rising sharply to follow Chane's gaze.

Chane turned to Ghassan. "Do you know anything about this?"

The domin shook his head. "No."

The sound of a soft footfall on stone reached Chane's ears, and he reached for a sword.

Brot'an stood in the crevice's top. An instant later, Ore-Locks stepped out of the crevice wall's stone, appearing less than relieved. Chane did not have a chance to ask anything.

"I found a possible entrance," Brot'an whispered, "beneath an overhang. But I only suspect so because of the guards present. At a flash of something in the dark, I crawled closer after signaling for Ore-Locks. The entrance is guarded by . . . things I have never seen before. I could not count their numbers but saw outlines of at least two the height of myself. Sounds indicated there may be more nearby, so we both returned."

Chane did not like this. With the exception of Osha, he had never encountered anyone as tall as Brot'an. To face two or more while bearing the chests was not possible. Everyone fell silent, likely contemplating the same thing.

"And," Brot'an added, "given these are guardians of the Enemy, I suspect mere arrows would not dispatch them. My making such an attempt would only give away any element of surprise in our favor."

That was worse, considering what Chane had seen of the assassin's use of the bow hidden beneath his cloak and tunic.

Leesil asked Ore-Locks, "Wynn said you can take Chane with you through stone. Is that true?"

Chane tensed, and Ore-Locks's brow wrinkled.

"Why?" the dwarf asked.

"We can't fight while carrying the chests," Leesil answered. "From here, can you pass through stone and move upward until you reach the passage inside, down a ways from the entrance under the overhang? Can you do it with you and Chane bringing at least two chests at a time?"

Ore-Locks finally nodded.

"Then the rest of us will clear a direct path," Leesil added, looking to

Brot'an. "Or at least keep the guards distracted while the chests are moved. If the opening is that well guarded, it has to be an entrance."

Though this sounded risky, Chane could think of nothing better, and they had already lingered too long.

Leesil pushed past everyone to start climbing out of the crevice's upper end. Brot'an followed, as did Ghassan. And then Chane was alone with his old comrade.

Ore-Locks shook his head. "I have never taken part in anything so haphazard."

Chane agreed but did not reply. Too much was being planned in the moment, and he could not stop thinking of Wynn, wherever she was. Leaning down, he gripped one of the poles strung between two chests. A sharp rise of noise broke from below.

It repeated like rolling thunder. Ore-Locks rushed past the chests and Chane to the crevice's bottom end.

"Horses!" the dwarf whispered.

Chane dropped the pole to join him. He had neither seen nor heard horses in the camp, but it was dark for even his eyes. His astonishment bordered on disbelief.

"Elves!" Ore-Locks said. "Never thought I would be glad of them."

Chane's night sight widened. He saw tall Lhoin'na riders in dark attire, scattering in a wave as they charged across open ground below at the mountain's base. The only way that he knew who they were was by the glint of unsheathed swords and light-colored hair pulled up in tails.

Shé'ith riders.

This must be why Chuillyon had left, likely at Chap's or Wynn's urging and instructions. Checking on Wayfarer, Osha, and Shade had been an excuse, though how the Chuillyon had brought these forces in was a puzzle.

Chane grew furious, for no one had told him. Now a pitched battle raged close to Wynn. One rider caught his attention, for even in the darkness, he could see that one's hair was brighter and his attire differed from that of the others.

"Osha!" Chane rasped.

His maimed voice could not carry over the distance. Even so, shouting would reveal their presence. He grabbed Ore-Locks as he pointed.

"Can you get to that one and turn him our way?" he asked.

"We do not have time! We must get through the mountain while the others distract the guards."

In all his life, Chane had rarely begged for anything. "Please. For Wynn."

Ore-Locks scowled, grumbled with a breathy exhale, and did something Chane had never seen before. He sank like a rock dropped into a pond and vanished under the mountainside.

Chane rushed to the crevice's lower end. He crouched, rigid and tense, waiting to see where the young stonewalker would reappear as he watched Osha's horse charge onward with the Shé'ith.

A distant clank of steel rolled downslope through the night.

Chane spun and looked upward through the dark as his panic rose another notch.

Leesil and the others had already engaged the guards.

Leesil crept after Brot'an, and then both of them flattened against the slope as they neared a place where he finally spotted the craggy overhang above. He heard Ghassan behind him.

Brot'an finally stopped, as did Leesil.

There was no more cover the rest of the way up. If there had been any, it had all been cleared away, likely for a defensible position.

Brot'an's head turned, as if looking back, though Leesil could not see the scarred face within the dark hood. Brot'an curled his fingers to pinch something between the first two, and Leesil heard a stiletto slide out into that hand.

Brot'an went utterly still, his face still unseen in the pit of his hood.

Leesil understood and quietly unlashed his left punching blade. At that, Brot'an's other hand slipped behind his back where he half lay on his side. That hand came back into sight, gripping a white metal, hooked bone knife.

They had to close the last distance at a run.

Leesil carefully levered up on one arm for a better look.

A hulkish form, as tall as Brot'an, dressed only in a waist-wrap, trudged toward the deeper dark below the overhang. It stopped, turned to face down the mountainside, and a nearby pole torch exposed it.

Leesil stared, not understanding what he saw. Ghassan drew a sharp breath behind him.

"Locatha," the domin whispered.

Leesil didn't know what that meant as he continued taking in the sight of the huge guard.

A hairless, scaled head with pure black eyes above its protruding muzzle looked down the mountainside. Whether it could see the battle below, Leesil couldn't tell.

Its shoulders, broader than a man's, were covered in glistening scales larger than the ones on its head. Those plates ran up its thick-based neck. In one hand, it steadied a double-thick spear's shaft, but the blade atop that was the size of a short sword, at least.

"You know of these creatures?" Brot'an whispered without looking back.

Ghassan was slow in answering. "They are hard to kill and possess limited mental function. Both are useful qualities in a guard."

Leesil didn't bother to ask how the domin knew this.

"My skills are of minimal use on such minds," Ghassan went on. "Take out their eyes first, if you can. Their hides are difficult to penetrate."

The last of that was obvious as Leesil clenched his jaw. They hadn't even gained access, and now this? The best option he saw was to keep the guards distracted while Chane and Ore-Locks snuck in the chests. And then what?

"Draw and divert," Brot'an whispered, again without looking back. "Kill after."

And how were they to do the latter? The largest weapons between them were Leesil's punching blades. He wouldn't know until too late if one of those could penetrate an armored hide deeply enough. Just the same, he pulled the other blade, and after one more breath . . .

Leesil sprang up at a run, hoping to take advantage through surprise. He heard Brot'an right behind him as they raced to close the distance before being spotted.

Wynn grew frantic where she crouched, watching the battle below. But no matter what she could make out in the dark, she saw no sign of Magiere.

Had Magiere lost herself completely in facing so many undead? She was supposed to have led them into the reach of the sun crystal's light.

Wynn almost stopped breathing. She watched as racing, screaming, and growling silhouettes down there threw themselves at one another. Now and then, some were briefly exposed by scattered firelight, and what she saw was best forgotten. Then she heard the howling and quickly rose up.

Chuillyon had brought majay-hì packs as planned, along with Vreu-villä . . . and Wayfarer . . . and Shade. Wynn forced herself to stay put. She desperately hoped Chuillyon had also been able to move Osha and the Shé'ith.

—*Come . . . find me . . . and bring light!*—

Wynn whirled around too quickly and almost fell, looking for Chap. He had to be here—somewhere—for him to speak to her like only she could hear in her mind.

But she didn't see him anywhere.

She ran down a ways, looking northward. Had he gone with the packs into the battle?

—*Come now . . . with the staff*—

Again, Wynn looked everywhere and still didn't spot him. How was he doing this? Where was he? Had something changed, gone wrong?

—*Wynn!*—

Panic nearly overwhelmed her, and she looked to the battle again. Magiere was down there somewhere, and possibly Wayfarer and Shade as well with the pack. There was nothing she could do for them except ignite the staff.

It wasn't time for that yet. Such an act might only cause more chaos and reveal her too soon.

Wynn took off, running northward along the base of the foothills. She hoped she could find Chap before something else spotted her.

Chap swerved away from another sword strike by the second animated corpse. He passed halfway through another ghost before realizing too late, and an icy chill shot through his bones.

Everywhere he turned, there were more glimmering, translucent forms having come for him out of the dark. And the first overmuscled corpse guard was rising up again. With both already dead, killing one of them seemed impossible. There were too many spirits as well.

He had to get to Ubâd.

The necromancer controlled all of the dead present, whether dead or undead himself. But there was no clear path to that still and silent robed body erect upon the tilted litter.

Then . . . brilliant, white light exploded from behind Chap. For an instant, he could see nothing as he went white-blind. He heard the ghost girl's screaming wail. The sound faded, as if growing distant, as his eyes adjusted.

Wynn had come! She had ignited her staff.

Chap saw one of the dead men turn toward the light's source.

The spirits all around Chap wavered, some vanishing like vapor in a breeze under the glare. But not that one dead guard and likely not the other.

He had only one choice. To save Wynn, he had to abandon her for the only target that mattered.

Chap lunged around the dead guard in his way, racing for the litter. With each paw-strike upon the parched ground and stone, he called upon the Elements of Existence without time to stop and root himself in them.

From Earth beneath him, Air around him, Water within him, and his heat for Fire, he mingled these with his Spirit. He could only hope this worked. It was not until the last running paw-strike that he felt himself begin to *burn*.

This time, Wynn would not have mantic sight to see the blue-white phosphorescent vapors that rose like flames to flicker across his form.

He leaped.

His forepaws struck Ubâd's chest and bound arms. The litter rocked wildly backward, and Chap nearly tumbled off.

Ubâd would call his servants here to his aid and forget about Wynn.

Chap tore at the dusty robe to get his claws into the necromancer's dead flesh. He did not think of a guard's blade coming down on his back. He forgot any of the spirits fighting to remain outside Wynn's light and come for him. He thought only to feel the elements within him.

Ubâd's corpse began to quiver as if awakening.

The stench of burning flesh rose around Chap, though he saw no smoke.

The necromancer's withered, crossed hands began to wither even more, until the skin appeared to cinch in tight around the bones. Black fluids leaked out around the eyeless mask as the body became still. Even then Chap did not hear how quiet everything had become, except for the distant sounds of the battle.

He raised his head.

Everything was dark again. Not one spirit remained in sight, not even the girl. When he looked back, both dead guards lay on the ground. The nearest was facedown within arm's reach of the litter, a sword still gripped in his outstretched hand.

And there was Wynn three strides to his right.

She turned about with the staff still held at the ready, though the crystal was darkened now, as if she too could not believe all the spirits were gone.

Chap again noticed the sounds of the battle in the distance below the foothills.

Wynn was here, but Magiere was not with her. Wynn had ignited the staff in the night, and its light—and its location—would have been seen everywhere, even by the Enemy's forces.

Chap leaped off the litter and bolted past Wynn.—*Run . . . away from here . . . now!*—

Leesil had barely raised his right winged blade in charging the first locatha in sight. Its short-sword-like blade atop that double-thick spear shaft slammed down on his own weapon.

Impact raised a sharp clang in the night. His knees buckled as Brot'an ran past him.

How could this scaled hulk move so fast?

He lost sight of Brot'an and only heard a racing scrape of metal. As he slashed his blade aside and couldn't get from under the pole-sword, he saw the master assassin duck around the locatha.

It was so big that Brot'an vanished completely.

That thing swiped backward with a clawed or taloned hand at the master assassin—and the hand was big enough to grab a head in its grip. There wasn't a mark on the monster that Leesil could see.

Brot'an's blade had done nothing to it, and Leesil hesitated too long.

When he spotted its tail, everything happened too fast.

Ghassan hadn't said anything about a tail.

The locatha tried to twist with its swipe at Brot'an, and its long tail lashed the same way behind it. The tail never connected with anything.

Brot'an's left arm appeared suddenly and wrapped across the scaled hulk's broad neck.

His cowl-shrouded face rose above the reptilian guard's right shoulder, and his right hand flashed out, across, and then back. Something glinted red-yellow in the torchlight as it tore back the other way above the locatha's extended muzzle.

Brot'an's hooked bone knife ripped through its right, black-orb eye.

Its maw widened in shock as it let go of its sword-spear. The spear's blade slid off Leesil's winged one. Long and sharp teeth in those widened jaws were like those of no serpent or snake he'd ever seen, and its rasping hiss tore at his ears.

Leesil hesitated as he saw another one charge out of the darkness under the overhang. He rammed his right winged blade into its sheath and pulled the stiletto up his left sleeve.

Ghassan had been right, and Brot'an had exposed the only way to kill one of these things.

Leesil had to get close—too close—to do it, and if he died instead, even Chane might not finish what they'd started.

Still staring below, Chane spun at a heavy footfall behind him and reached for his dwarven longsword. He did not need to pull the mottled steel.

Ore-Locks stepped past the chests toward him, glowering. Chane said nothing and turned back, looking everywhere.

Over a roll in the slope below, someone appeared on horseback. When the animal jolted to a stop, the rider dropped and came running with a bow in hand. Before the man crouched upon the crevice's right lip, Chane already knew Ore-Locks had succeeded.

Osha's face was obscured by the dark, but he panted in exertion as he looked down upon Chane.

"What?" he asked. "I must get below!"

Chane wasted no time. "Wynn may be down in that battle."

In alarm, Osha straightened back up and looked below.

"Wait and listen!" Chane rasped.

Osha's head swiveled back.

"She is carrying a bottle I gave her," Chane rushed on. "It contains a potion like no other. Find her, and if she falls, even from the worst of wounds, it might save her . . . or anyone else."

Osha's eyes widened and then narrowed. "Now? You tell me this only now?"

Chane realized he should have said something about the potion itself before, but he had given Wynn the bottle only last night.

A sudden, bright flash rose to the north.

Chane instinctively looked toward it, even as he felt his skin tingle uncomfortably as if it were beginning to burn. Then he had to duck below the crevice's edge, knowing what that light was. Ore-Locks rushed in to peer over the crevice's edge. That light lingered for at least three breaths—and then everything turned to full night once more.

Wynn was still alive, at least for now.

"Enough delay!" Ore-Locks said.

Chane heard Osha running for his horse and sprang up to go after the elf. Ore-Locks grabbed his arm. Chane had to let hunger flush through him to tear out of that grip, and he scrambled up and over the crevice's side.

"Wait!" he rasped.

Osha did not stop.

Chane rushed after to grab him, and Osha spun, whipping back his bow as if to strike with it.

"That liquid has another use!" Chane rasped.

Osha froze.

"It was made with white petals," Chane hurried on, "from flowers that grow only in Lhoin'na lands . . . and your homeland."

Osha slowly lowered the bow as his large amber eyes widened.

Chane knew that Osha had seen such flowers.

"I touched one, once, briefly," Chane said. "I barely rose again after a night and another day. The distilled liquid, such as on an arrow's tip, would have finished me or anything like me. If need be, use it and do not hesitate."

Osha stared blankly at him.

"Do you understand?" Chane demanded.

Osha backed away in unsteady steps. Without a word, he grabbed the saddle and swung up into it. The horse wheeled to charge off without the nudge of heels.

"Are you done?" Ore-Locks asked angrily.

Chane lingered an instant longer.

There were more than just undead down there in that battle. There were other dangers to Wynn—to all of them. By the sound of the battle's prolonged chaos, Magiere had failed to lead off the undead. More than likely, she was as lost to her own hunger as anything else down there.

Chane had known such bloody euphoria.

Nothing anyone could have done then would have brought him out of that state.

"Get moving!" Ore-Locks ordered.

Chane looked toward where that flash had erupted in the dark. He then turned at a run for the crevice and the chests.

Leesil dropped and rolled again. Another long blade atop a thick haft struck close to his head. The clang deafened his left ear as rock chips struck his face. He barely heard Brot'an and the other—half-blinded—locatha still engaged.

Not once had Leesil gotten close enough to thrust a stiletto into the second one's eye. He couldn't get behind it, for its thick and long tail swung around at him every time he tried.

He came to his feet again, and everything got worse.

A third, hulking, scaled form came around the overhang's far side.

This one didn't carry any weapon, but it didn't matter. Leesil was already winded from trying to stay alive long enough to kill something. That was his last thought as the second one swung hard with the butt of its sword-spear.

Leesil dodged, rolled again, and saw . . .

Brot'an somehow got inside the first one's swipe. He rammed a stiletto through its already maimed eye, driving deeper this time, but its clawed hand came down on his right shoulder. The stiletto's hilt ripped out of Brot'an's grip as he went down, and the creature's head whipped up and back.

At this first one's screech and thrashing, the second one looked toward it.

Leesil rushed in, hopped, and planted one foot on the second's dangling spear haft. He was up at its face by the time it turned those black eyes back on him. He heard the third one closing in but didn't dare look away. And he thrust his stiletto as hard as he could into the second locatha's nearest eye, using every ounce of strength to drive the blade into its head.

Something struck his side.

His breath rushed out.

Everything flashed white before his eyes from pain, and he went numb in shock.

He couldn't breathe as the world turned black.

Vertigo and pain took over.

He felt himself slammed sideways into something. The jar brought agony as he tumbled over and over. How many times before instinct came back? He clawed with his free hand at whatever hard surface he'd hit, though it seemed to take so long to stop himself. When he did stop, he fought for air as his sight slowly returned.

Everything was dark except for flickering red light upon stone. Something huge stepped between him and that light. Silhouetted in flashes and flickers, it hissed at him.

He heard—felt through the stone beneath him—heavy footfalls coming.

But all that Leesil could think was . . . *Where is my Magiere?*

Pain, hunger, fury—there was nothing else.

Magiere barely heard the screams. Was the last one hers . . . or from her last prey?

Another white face suddenly appeared before her.

It nearly glowed in her fully widened sight, and those eyes—irises—without color made hunger burn until its pain drove her again. She struck, not knowing with what or how.

As its jaws widened, exposing feral teeth and fangs, a heavy blade cleaved into its face.

Its skull split halfway through.

Blackened fluids welled and splattered across steel.

It went down, slipping from her sight, but there were always more.

Some were not pale, and she lashed out at the bristled head that appeared, its face like an animal's overlying bones barely human. Hardened nails tore into its jaw, grated on bone beneath, and she thought she heard the sounds of screaming.

This meant nothing, and neither did her own pain, for the hunger ate any agony and fed upon it.

White light filled the dark sky as more screaming rose all around.

The sound tore at her ears and into the skull. The light hurt her eyes and skin. Even hunger couldn't eat it away. Fright took its place.

Magiere thought of something . . . something . . . she'd forgotten.

The longer that light hurt her, the more its pain tried to make her remember.

Then it was gone, leaving only darkness for an instant. All around her, there were still shouts, snarls, sounds that could never be human. Compared to what she'd heard only moments ago, it all seemed as quiet as whispers.

The howling and snarls grew louder. Screams, shouts, and worse answered.

Magiere stared about at forms racing and charging and tearing at one another again. Some of them were true animals . . . wolves but not.

And that light was gone, so where was Wynn?

Magiere remembered.

She'd lost herself and rushed into the slaughter that she'd started. Every undead in sight had turned on anything living, as if it felt her own hunger. What had she done? She should've led, lured, or driven them to the light of Wynn's staff.

And that light had come and gone.

Magiere's fragile awareness almost broke when she saw one majay-hì—and another and another—tear through the horde around her. There weren't enough of them. Magiere spun, her body now in agony from every wound she'd taken, but she hacked and tore her way north out of the carnage.

She had to find Wynn and that light.

Wynn gripped her staff with both hands. She stood in the darkness, hidden now near the edge of the battle. Chap was still and silent beside her, likely at equal loss for what to do.

There was no place else they could go.

Running to some other vantage point would have only made it harder to close in when needed. They could only hope they wouldn't be spotted by anything in that chaos before they had to act.

Magiere had to be in there somewhere.

Wynn couldn't tell one thing from another in the dark amid those black silhouettes setting upon one another. She heard the packs of majay-hì, but they were not going to last long against so many.

"Where is she?" Wynn whispered.

Chap didn't answer, but something broke out of the masses in the dark. One form seemed to run toward them, and Wynn snatched the glasses dangling about her neck.

Whether that was Magiere or not, she would have to light her staff again. In spite of that weapon, she couldn't stop the fear.

—*Think only of the staff's light . . . and be ready*—

Chap's words were no comfort.

Wynn saw more night-shadow figures break from the battle and chase after that first one. When that one came even closer, she thought she was prepared. The first glimpse of a pale face, wild black hair and fully black eyes, and a hauberk darkened with stains made her sick and horrified.

Magiere slowed at the sight of Wynn and turned to face what followed her.

Wynn fought the urge to run to Magiere and raised the staff's crystal high.

And still, Chap didn't give the command.

More figures came rushing toward Magiere. All she did was raise up the falchion, gripping it in both hands, and stand there. Filthy hair and feral faces became clear to Wynn's eyes. She heard them now—their snarls, shrieks, or shouts—over the battle's noise as they raced toward that one lone figure standing in their path.

Magiere raised her blade higher.

Wynn pressed the glasses with their dark lenses over her eyes, not wanting to see what would happen, and . . .

—Now—

Chap bolted, putting some distance between himself and the impending light.

The words tore out of her mouth instead of flashing through her thoughts.

"Mên Rúhk el-När . . . mênajil il'Núr'u mên'Hkâ'ät!"

White light erupted from the staff's crystal and burned away the night above and around Wynn.

Light exploded behind Magiere. It felt like fire all over her exposed flesh, and yet it did not affect her otherwise. It did not even slow her down.

The closest one coming at her was a ghul.

It was instantly swallowed in smoke exploding from its own flesh. Amid wails rising to almost human screams, it fell and began thrashing, trying to burrow into the hardened ground. Two pale-faced figures rounded it, and then staggered as flame sprouted to dance over their exposed hands and faces.

The frenzied terror of so many screams, shrieks, and wails smothered all sounds of battle left behind. Those farther back and too far to see scattered.

Magiere's self-control broke again.

She rushed into the smoke, taking off a charred head, and before it hit the ground, she'd already fixed on her next prey.

Leesil braced for the charge of the last locatha—or the only one on its feet that he could see. He rolled and flopped aside as it tried to stomp on him. When he tried to push up to all fours, its immense tail came around at his head, and he had to drop again. His right hand was empty. The stiletto was gone, but he still held a winged blade in his left hand.

That scaled appendage whipped across his hair in passing too close.

There was no chance to look for Brot'an or the second guard that he hoped he'd put down. He shoved off, sliding backward, and rolled over to gain his feet.

Leesil pulled his second punching blade, and that thing was still coming.

At a sudden scraping thud, it buckled forward in a lurched stop . . . and turned.

Leesil saw Chane right behind the third locatha with his longsword drawn and double gripped. He—and hopefully Ore-Locks—must have arrived inside the passage and run toward the fight.

Chane's eyes widened in shock as the huge guard spun on him. Leesil didn't see a mark on its back from Chane's strike, and then he spotted Ghassan stepping out of the darkness from beneath the overhang—as if he had gone inside the entrance.

Leesil had forgotten the domin was even with them, but what was Ghassan doing in there?

Another movement pulled his gaze.

Brot'an pushed up off the ground, the first guard lying still at his feet, its face covered in blackish red blood. The second locatha lay still as well. Leesil's stiletto must have driven in deep enough. And just as Leesil quickly looked back to the last guard . . .

Brot'an stumbled.

Leesil flinched at the sight. For Brot'an never stumbled. Then his gaze met Chane's for an instant. Chane's shock vanished, and he raised his sword in a step to strike again. Leesil knew what Chane was doing. Ore-Locks then charged out of the dark and past Ghassan, his broader blade already drawn.

Their weapons weren't going to put that thing down, but they would keep its attention.

Leesil fixed on the locatha's thick, whipping tail. As Chane lunged just before Ore-Locks closed, Leesil knew the creature was still aware of him behind it. He wasn't in a good way, judging by the pain in his side, but when he heard Chane's blade scrape off the scaled hide, he charged.

Everything depended on Chane—and Ore-Locks—so that thing didn't have a chance to turn around. Leesil waited until Ore-Locks swung the heavy blade. He heard it hit, saw the locatha recoil, and he leaped.

His left foot struck the base of its tail. He pushed up and wrapped his left arm, winged blade and all, around its neck below its jaws. Its large hand instantly clamped on his forearm, and even with the winged blade biting its palm, that grip crushed down. Ignoring the pain, Leesil rammed the point of his other winged blade into the side of its right eye.

He almost lost his hold when its head thrashed back.

He had to lean aside or be hit in the face, and he rammed the blade again, this time into the base of its jaw. He didn't even know if Chane or Ore-Locks was still hacking at it until it began to teeter backward. All he could do was throw himself off it.

His side hurt even more when he slammed down and had to thrash over out of the way before it fell on him. When he rolled over, he saw something he'd never expected.

Ore-Locks dropped on top of that thing, or right beside it, and sank into the rocky surface. And as he did so, he wrapped one arm over its bloodied head and pulled the head down—straight through the stone.

The whole scaled body convulsed, limbs thrashing, and then it lay still.

Leesil just stared, not blinking, until Ore-Locks resurfaced partly, but he didn't come fully out of the ground. By torchlight, he looked utterly strained and weakly reached up with one arm. Leesil tried to scramble toward him.

Chane's sword clattered on stone as he dropped it, grabbed Ore-Locks's arm with both hands, and had to heave to pull the dwarf out atop the stone slope. Ore-Locks half lay there, and Chane snatched up his sword again, raised it, and turned to make certain neither of the other two guards moved at all.

Everything seemed so quiet for so long.

Leesil didn't even hear the distant sounds of battle over his own labored breaths.

Another flash of light below the mountain made everyone turn. Leesil stared down the mountain. The light did not go out this time, but it remained like a beacon in the distance.

"I apologize for not assisting," Ghassan said, breaking the silence.

"Where were you?" Leesil panted out.

"As I said, I could do nothing against these creatures," the domin answered, "so I scouted the path inward for anything else in our way."

Leesil eyed Ghassan, not certain how much he believed in those words. Brot'an was on his feet, seemingly whole and steady again.

"We need light," Leesil said, going to retrieve his fallen stiletto.

Ghassan took a crystal from his pocket. "I will lead the way."

"Not yet," Chane said. "We had only brought two orbs through when we saw what was happening. They are not far inside, but Ore-Locks left them hidden in stone. As soon as he is able, we will bring the others."

Some small part of Leesil was almost relieved at the short delay, and he simply sheathed his weapons and dropped down again. It didn't matter how Brot'an looked or acted; Leesil knew he was injured. And what else waited for them inside the mountain? A few outer guards wouldn't be the only ones, not in this place and not even after a thousand years.

Leesil glanced back toward the entrance, thinking on his wife. There was no way to know the fate of Magiere and those with her.

*　　*　　*

Chap went numb, watching the carnage.

Wynn clutched the still-ignited staff, but Magiere was a good distance away on the edge of the light's reach, and she had lost herself completely. She charged, hacked, or struck at one after another through smoking carcasses until she had nearly reached the battle's fringe once again.

Part of him feared getting near her, the same part that shrank from what might be necessary, more so with every moment. All that stopped him from acting to stop her was the memory of the guide he had left for dead in the wastes.

Could he bear to look into her vacant eyes, staring up at nothing like an empty husk?

Magiere had barely regained herself to seek out Wynn and the crystal's light, as she should have done at first . . . but now?

One thing gave him hope.

There were riders charging through what was left of the horde.

They raced through the chaos in twos and threes. Chuillyon had succeeded in bringing Shé'ith along with the majay-hì packs. At least the chaos that Magiere had caused put those two factions at the advantage, for the moment.

Osha had to be one of those riders, still one of them, or so Chap hoped.

And where were his daughter and Wayfarer?

So long as Wynn was exposed, Chap could not even search for them, let alone rush at Magiere. Wynn was the only one besides Ghassan who could use the staff, so Chap feared leaving her unprotected.

Indecision crushed him—until he saw a black four-footed form run around the fringe of the chaos. Others of its kind were around it.

Chap howled loudly at the sight of Shade. The black form veered off, racing toward him, and Chap sprang forward as he called into Wynn's mind.

—Stay back until I call . . . or until you have to escape—

How many times would necessity force him to leave behind the ones he most wished to protect? Even as he and Shade closed on each other, he could not help looking for Wayfarer, hoping she had not followed the packs into the bloodshed.

Shade closed on him and shot past to wheel around. He slowed only until she caught up at his side. Though she must have wanted to race back to Wynn, he might need her to help stop Magiere.

The only other option for him would leave Magiere as an empty husk—and leave him with one more sin he could not bear.

Now that he knew memory-words would work with Shade, it took only one glance.

—*Come*—

As they closed in, he saw the bodies, mangled, bloodied, and broken, as the living and undead stepped upon them in tearing at one another. One he feared was an elven rider, for it was draped over the still bulk of a butchered horse. Another was clearly a majay-hì torn almost in half. There were more of the goblins than any other, but also humans—either living or not before they went down.

Far more numerous were those still fighting, among them majay-hì of varied hues launching at what had to be undead. They only turned on living enemies when they had to do so.

Two riders pounded and trampled through others toward a huge form Chap had never seen before. It was taller than any an'Cróan or Lhoin'na and was covered in scales.

Chap's focus shifted to Magiere still ahead in the chaos, and again his doubts took hold. In her current state, she was the greatest threat to any undead present. Should he stop her now or wait and let her continue? He veered off toward the east, holding his distance from her, until he was near the fringe of the foothills . . . and too far away from Wynn.

She had to keep that staff lit, and even that would not hold off anything but an undead. He tried to see Magiere more clearly, to get a look at her face, but she charged into another cluster of combatants.

In despair, Chap looked up and down the eastern fringe of the battle. Two forms spun out of the carnage, surrounded in a circle of wheeling and snapping majay-hì. Wayfarer and Vreuvillä backed toward the rise of rocky hills.

A vampire and a ghul on the outskirts of the battle spotted them.

At the sight of this, Chap lost all sense of reason and charged for them.

As Wynn watched Chap run, she clung to the staff with both hands, and her only thought was to keep the crystal ignited. She'd never kept the light burning for so long, and she was exhausted from her efforts in the battle thus far.

Still, in this moment, she had one task and one task only.

To keep light flowing outward into the night.

CHAPTER SEVENTEEN

Wayfarer shuddered as she backed away from the battle behind Vreuvillä. She was sick with fear at what she had seen—and where was Shade? They had lost each other in circling around the battle's eastern side as the remainder of one pack dove in and out. Where was Osha?

Yet even all of this worry and confusion could not wipe away one previous, horrifying sight.

A sharp light had risen suddenly to the north, and so she had known Wynn was out there. But by that light, the warrior woman she had come to care for and respect so much was barely recognizable.

Magiere's fully black eyes, like those of some other creatures out here, terrified Wayfarer. She had wanted to run both to and away from the sight, but Vreuvillä had insisted, "Stay close to me."

The sound of tumbling stones now behind her did not wipe away that vivid memory until she heard them a second time.

Wayfarer twisted around in fright as Chuillyon half slid, half hopped the last steps off the rock slope of a foothill. He slowed and stared out beyond her.

It was the first time she had ever seen him without a half-amused expression on his long face. She thought he might start to weep in looking to the battle behind her. Vreuvillä fixed Chuillyon with a cold glare.

There was no liking between them and never would be from what little Wayfarer had learned.

Chuillyon's gaze still focused somewhere out beyond the priestess.

Then Vreuvillä spun toward the battle, dropped to a half crouch between two majay-hì, and spread her arms with her long curved blade ready.

When Wayfarer turned, someone grabbed her from behind. Another of the pack rushed in front of her on guard. She heard Chuillyon whispering some chant as his arms closed around her. Two *things* rushed at them over the open ground from the battle's edge.

One had a face as white as a corpse. Human-looking, its irises sparked like colorless crystals in the distant light of Wynn's staff. Flapping shreds of clothes were stained red and black in spatters and smears.

The second one was naked with nearly colorless flesh, even to the slits where there should have been nostrils. All over it, bones showed beneath shriveled, shrunken skin, and it began to outdistance the other one.

A handful of majay-hì rushed for the first attacker . . . just before a huge silver-gray dog came out of nowhere and slammed into the naked monster.

Wayfarer could not help a gasp, cringing back against Chuillyon, as that gray majay-hì tumbled with the creature and came up atop it. It began savagely shredding flesh with it teeth and claws. Amid the growls came that thing's screams. She lost sight of it for an instant, looking to three of the pack that set upon the pale one in shredded clothes. But for the first . . .

She knew who it was.

Wayfarer had seen few majay-hì as large as that one except for Chap.

A pure black majay-hì suddenly charged in to help the gray one, but its prey had already fallen limp and silent.

Chap lifted his head and trotted toward Wayfarer, his muzzle stained with black fluids, but it was Shade who reached her first, brushing her hand without passing any memories. The pale target of the other three majay-hì somehow broke free and scrambled back toward the chaos.

Wayfarer pulled from Chuillyon's hold and dropped to her knees to grab Shade first, but she then threw one arm around Chap's neck, ignoring the stains that his head smeared upon her shoulder.

He had wanted the majay-hì and the Shé'ith to come here this night. She and Osha had helped make that happen, though Vreuvillä had been reluctant to deal with Chuillyon. None of them could have known Magiere would not gain control over the undead among the horde, or lose control over herself.

"What do we do?" she whispered.

Before Chap could answer, Vreuvillä brushed her free hand over a majay-hì's head. That one wheeled to bump shoulders with another, which in turn did the same, and onward. Whatever message the priestess gave to the first spread quickly as half those nearby dispersed, running off in both directions parallel to the battle's edge.

Wayfarer quickly touched a passing mottled one before it rushed northward. She caught the message passed through the pack via memory-speak.

Chap asked her a question.

—*What . . . is happening?*—

She was too focused on turning flickering images, smells, and sounds into needed words. And when she did, she hesitated.

"They are to find all of their kind," she answered, "and pull back to any fringe and out of reach."

Chap's eyes widened in his stained face. The instant he looked to the priestess, Shade spun as well and snarled, but Vreuvillä had already rushed Chuillyon.

"Heretic!" she accused. "I will cut you for every one of *us* lost because of your deceits—and leave you to bleed out like them!"

Wayfarer rose, fearful of what might happen. Vreuvillä saw herself as one with the packs, and even Wayfarer had come to feel this in some ways, but she had no chance to intervene.

"I could not have known," Chuillyon answered, and looked out again toward the battle. "Not that, not this."

—*She is . . . correct . . . for now*—

Wayfarer's eyes dropped to Chap.

—*Magiere . . . may attack . . . anyone . . . now*—

"What is he saying?" Vreuvillä asked, her voice filled with fury.

Wayfarer flinched.

"He says you are right. Keep the packs out of the battle for now." And then, at more of Chap's memory-words, "Let the undead turn on others in the horde, such as the goblins, and decrease their numbers."

Wayfarer did not mention Chap's concern about Magiere. In her current state, Magiere might slaughter anything that got in the way of her going after the next undead in her sight.

"Where is that light coming from?" Vreuvillä demanded.

"It must be Wynn Hygeorht," Chuillyon answered. "And her staff, with a unique crystal."

"How long can she keep it ignited?"

When no one answered, Wayfarer's fright increased.

Vreuvillä's savage and mournful eyes only looked upon the battle. "You must go! I will stay with our own . . . for changes that may come."

Wayfarer nearly stopped breathing. "What am I to do?" she exhaled.

"Wish for the light."

—*What . . . does this . . . mean?*—

Wayfarer could not answer Chap. She had never done what Vreuvillä now asked—a true wish, as some would think of it who did not understand. What if she could not? What if she failed, and Wynn could not hold that light any longer? What if Wayfarer herself could not maintain that "wish" for long enough?

And what if she succeeded at what price?

—You . . . must . . . try—

Wayfarer found Chap watching her. Had he caught what she feared surfacing in her thoughts? Before she asked, his head swung aside, and he huffed at his daughter. Shade circled in, wriggling her head under Wayfarer's left hand.

—Follow—

Shade took off northward, but Wayfarer still stalled as Chap headed for the battle.

"Where are you going?"

He halted, and his stained face swung toward her.

—To stop . . . Magiere—

In panic, Wayfarer shouted to Vreuvillä, "Help him!"

Wayfarer had to turn away and run at Shade's bark. She followed as Shade veered closer to the foothills and away from the battle's edge. The noise of bloodshed grew less overwhelming, mostly because of her panting breaths at trying to keep up with a majay-hì.

She did not hear the hoofbeats until they were almost at her back.

Wayfarer veered left, screaming, "Shade!"

When she spun to face whatever threat, nothing more would come out.

Osha quickly reined in his horse, or perhaps it pulled up on its own to a stuttering stop. He looked down at her and then back along the edge of the foothills. He suddenly thrust his hand out and down at her.

She knew he had not abandoned the other Shé'ith for her.

There was no time to feel anything even though he had come for Wynn.

Wayfarer took his hand, but she had to jump and wriggle to get up behind him.

"Go," she shouted around his side, and Shade wheeled and bolted off again.

Osha's mount lunged, and Wayfarer threw her arms around his waist. The farther they raced toward the light, the more they left the sounds of rage and agony behind.

Then an agonized scream carried from something ahead.

The light went out.

Sau'ilahk lingered in hiding, clutching the medallion around his neck at a loss. Khalidah had instructed him to help distract some of the horde long enough for Leesil's team to slip past—without knowing they had received any help. So Sau'ilahk and Ubâd had split up, each with several plans to distract the horde, and he waited—and waited—for Khalidah to contact him and tell him when to act.

Even as majay-hì and Shé'ith had come out of the foothills, he still waited for a message from Khalidah.

At the bright light appearing twice in the night, going on and on the second time, he knew Wynn Hygeorht was out there to the north with her staff. At first, he had cringed down behind a boulder in fear that it might affect him as normal sunlight did not.

Nothing had happened to him, and he had risen to squint northward.

Still no word came from Khalidah.

His hatred for the wayward little sage grew into satisfaction, replacing frustration. Soon enough, he had to look away, for he now had eyes that could be damaged.

And this thought brought him a smile.

Blocking out the world, he focused inward. Within his thoughts, he stroked a glowing circle for Spirit upon the ground's heat-baked earth. Within that came the square for Earth, and then a smaller circle for Spirit's physical aspect as Tree. Between all of those lines, he stroked glowing sigils with his intention.

Spirit to the aspect of Tree, Tree to the essence of Spirit, and born of the Earth. His energies bled into a pattern that only he could see, and he began trembling in exertion.

A shaft of blood-black barked wood cracked the earth.

It jutted upward, slowly thickening until that limb bent over, somehow suppler than it appeared. Along its length, six tinier limbs sprouted to rip its body from the ground. A small knot of ocher root tendrils twitched around its base as it faced him.

Sau'ilahk bled even more energy into his creation.

Bark peeled back around the root-knot. Tendrils coiled tighter and tighter into a ball, and that sphere took on an inner light.

It *blinked* at him.

A flexing wooden lid of snarled tendrils clicked over a glowing orb for an eye. The newly created servitor then spun away to skitter off into the night.

"No," Sau'ilahk whispered.

The servitor barely hesitated, and Sau'ilahk reached for the fragment of his own consciousness embedded in his conjured creation. It halted, twitching and fidgeting, until it finally submitted to its creator's will.

"Go to the light," he commanded. "Attack the one who holds it."

The servitor skittered away.

Sau'ilahk's eyes hurt too much when he looked toward that glare. And this thought sparked a cruel inspiration.

"Wait," he said.

The servitor halted.

Sau'ilahk winced and blinked as he looked toward the crystal's light. He did not have to speak and only smiled. The servitor would know his will, and it quickly raced off.

Wynn struggled to maintain focus upon the sun crystal. She had never before held it alight this long. And worse, its glare and the dark lenses shielding her eyes made it difficult to see anything at a distance.

She knew only that whatever undead had not burned and fallen had fled back toward the horde, and Magiere had followed them. They were all too far off beyond the staff's light to see. She longed to know what had become of Magiere and Leesil—and Chane—but the staff and keeping the undead in check were her purpose.

She blinked, growing tired, shaky, and weak.

This close to the crystal and under such strain, even the glasses were not always enough. She did not notice something else until she heard it over the distant sound of fighting. Then it was so close, like a broken branch dragged over hard, rough ground.

Click-click . . . click-click . . .

It was too rhythmic for a tumbling branch with no wind to drive it.

Wynn looked about through the narrow view of the darkened lenses. She had to turn her whole head. When she spotted something, it did look like a branch—branches—but the color was wrong. The bark was reddish in the crystal's harsh light.

A chill took her as the branch sprang at her, growing too large in her narrow view.

She screamed in pain as it struck her face.

Clutching at it, she released one hand's grip on the staff. The living branch clawed her face, trying to get under the glasses at her eyes, as other parts of it clawed toward the back of her head. One of those legs hooked the cord about her neck. She thrashed, still clinging to the staff with her other hand . . . as the glasses were torn off.

Blinding light filled Wynn's view.

When she clamped her eyes shut, all she could see was white as she fell. Her breaths came too fast for her to cry out, and her eyes felt on fire. She could feel tears on her face as she pushed up, only knowing that she had fallen when she braced both hands on the ground—both hands empty.

She'd dropped the staff.

She heard the skittering sound again, but everything was dark. When she looked about, turning her head toward the distant fighting, she couldn't see even the red spark of fires. The skittering grew nearer, as if coming for her again.

And she still couldn't see it.

"Hold," a voice commanded.

Wynn froze, listening. Her breaths came and went quickly, and as she looked up, there was no moon, no stars, only more blackness before her pained eyes.

"How good to see you," taunted the voice. Wynn knew that voice, for it had once belonged to the young duke of Beáumie Keep.

"Though you will never see me . . . even one last time."

Sau'ilahk was here, and Wynn was blind.

Sau'ilahk could not recall such contentment, even unto ancient times, when all had looked upon his beauty with awe as the high priest of Beloved.

Wynn Hygeorht had taken nearly everything from him, and now he had her on her knees.

"Where are your protectors?" he whispered in mock concern as he circled her. "How careless of them, especially your favored vampire." He watched with joy as she twisted in panic toward his voice. "What would pain him more, to find you in pieces . . . or still pretty but lifeless? Or did you think you would be the only one to suffer when I found you again?"

He listened to her racing breaths and watched tears stream from her sightless eyes. He had no control over vengeance against Beloved, but she would be the release for his frustration.

In one rapid step, Sau'ilahk grabbed her by the throat.

Her hands latched onto his wrist, and she clawed at his fingers as she began to choke. That sound was pure joy, and he squeezed his grip slowly tighter and tighter.

No, he would not kill her this way. That she might think so in this moment was only a delicious morsel before feasting on her life.

"Enough!"

Sau'ilahk twisted quickly around at a new voice, dragging Wynn by the neck. He had not heard anyone approach, but five strides away stood a very tall figure in a dark robe and hood. Perhaps it was too tall to be human; that one word had been lightly tainted with a Lhoin'na accent.

"Release her now," the figure ordered.

Its hands rose slowly to brush back the hood, revealing the face of an aging Lhoin'na.

Sau'ilahk knew this one, who had been in the deep realm of the stone-walkers when he had invaded there to follow Wynn to a lost anchor—an orb.

Chuillyon had worn a sage's robe then, though it had been white.

A sharp pain exploded in Sau'ilahk's knee.

When his foot shifted under the impact, and his left leg buckled, he lost his grip on his prey. He glanced down as Wynn scrambled blindly away, not using the hand with which she had punched his knee. Instead, she curled that hand against her chest.

After so many centuries without flesh, physical pain had taken Sau'ilahk by surprise.

It would not happen again.

Chuillyon reached Wynn by the time Sau'ilahk regained focus. The mis-dressed interloper pulled the miscreant sage to her feet.

Sau'ilahk had dealt with Chuillyon before and knew to be wary. Wynn was now secondary, though protecting her would be the elder sage's weakness. Then he heard Chuillyon's whisper.

"Chârmun . . . agh'alhtahk so. A'lhän am leagad chionns'gnajh."

Sau'ilahk quickly looked for and spotted his stick-creature servitor. "Kill!"

The spindly legged thing coiled and leaped, arching straight for Chuillyon's head.

The elf neither flinched nor fled and pulled Wynn close in his arms.

Sau'ilahk's fury chilled, for he had seen this before.

His servitor shattered into loose twigs in midair, coming apart an arm's length from its target, as if it had struck an unseen barrier. The light of its one orb eye was extinguished.

Sau'ilahk felt his connection to his creation sever.

Dull pieces of wooden branches rained down harmlessly to the ground around both sages, neither dressed as they should be. Rage returned, and he charged, closing the distance in an instant.

He did not bother drawing a sword and tore the young sage out of the elder one's arms.

Sau'ilahk latched his right hand around the elder one's throat. That renegade sage might be able to nullify conjury, but his skills would save him from a physical assault.

And again, Chuillyon did not move. Sau'ilahk would not hesitate to feed on the aging sage, as troublesome as Wynn Hygeorht, and then he could finish her at his leisure.

Something struck his right shoulder, and he lost his grip in agony. Stumbling and tripping in a back step, he saw a black-feathered arrow protruding from his shoulder.

The wound began to burn within.

Bow still in hand, and its string still thrumming, Osha reached over his shoulder to his quiver for another arrow as he gripped the horse with his knees. Even with Wayfarer clutching his waist, and Shade charging ahead, he knew his target for what it was.

It was not the young duke.

Chane had claimed he destroyed the duke's body and the foul spirit within it. While Chane might be a dark thing, he was no liar. Somehow, Sau'ilahk had survived in that body seized through the use of an orb.

"Get to Wynn and light the staff," Osha shouted, not looking back to Wayfarer.

His fingers touched the arrows in his quiver. He quickly found one without threaded ridges, pulled it, and drew it in one motion, not even looking to its white metal tip. He squeezed his knees twice, and the horse slowed. As he felt Wayfarer release his waist and slide off, he saw Chuillyon.

How had that one beaten him here? Wayfarer had said she left the elder sage behind with the priestess.

Sau'ilahk then saw him, and quickly gripped the first arrow to rip it out.

Osha released the bow's string.

This time, he did not need to tilt the bow's hidden white metal handle to direct the arrow's flight. It struck below the half-undead's right cheekbone.

Sau'ilahk's head whipped back as he spun off balance. His enraged shriek came late after Osha's own angry hiss that the arrow had not finished him. Shade charged straight at Sau'ilahk and sprang at a full run. An instant later, Wayfarer reached Wynn's side, and Chuillyon rushed out after Shade.

Osha's mount closed on and rounded the two women as he drew and fitted his second-to-last white-metal-tipped arrow.

Shade hit Sau'ilahk in the chest with both forepaws, and he went tumbling over backward. After a rebound, she whirled to go at him again.

"No," Chuillyon shouted. "Hold, Shade."

Osha stalled in shock.

Sau'ilahk rose, his eyes widening, and as if on instinct, he turned and ran.

Osha did not care what became of Sau'ilahk as he swung off his mount. He ran straight to Wynn, sitting on the ground and supported by Wayfarer, and he ignored everything else as he dropped to one knee.

"Are you injured?" he asked.

Almost instantly, Shade pushed in beside him, dropped one of his arrows from her jaws, and pressed her nose into Wynn's neck. Wynn appeared to fumble in an attempt to grip the dog's neck but did not look at anyone. She was staring downward at . . . nothing.

Chuillyon neared to stand above all of them.

"Osha, is that you?" Wynn asked, a tremor in her voice.

"Yes, certainly, I am . . ."

He could not finish. Wynn still looked at no one, not even Shade, though both her hands were clutching the majay-hì's thick fur.

Osha turned cold inside, looking first into Wynn's wandering eyes. In the dark, he could just make out the wet cheeks of her oval olive-toned face.

He looked to Wayfarer. Why was she crying as well? Then he felt sick. Still trying to deny what he saw, he waved a hand only a palm's breadth before Wynn's face.

She did not blink or flinch.

Her glasses lay on the ground not far from the staff, its crystal now dark. Without thinking, Osha grasped Wynn away from Shade and Wayfarer and pulled her into his chest. She felt so small in his arms.

"Help Magiere," Wynn said, clutching the front of his jerkin. "When I last . . . saw her, she had become lost to herself again and ran into the horde."

Osha's chest hurt as if something had broken inside him.

"No more time for grief," Chuillyon said. "Get her up! Wynn, you must light the staff again and keep it lit."

Osha was about to lash out at Chuillyon when Wayfarer grabbed his arm with both hands. He glared between them both. How could they be so cold, so heartless? But some of Wynn's warning slipped through.

Magiere was now a danger to them all, one way or another. He remembered why Chane had sent him and ran his hand all over Wynn, searching her clothing.

"Where is it?" he demanded. "Where is the bottle Chane gave you? You must drink it quickly to heal your eyes."

Wynn went still in his arms. "No."

Osha froze. "You must drink it!"

"No."

Chuillyon spun away and in three steps picked up the staff—and the glasses. What good would the latter do anymore?

"Get her up, now!" he commanded, closing on them again.

"I—I can't," Wynn gasped out, dropping her head against Osha's chest. "I'm too weak."

"The potion will heal you," Osha insisted. "Perhaps give you strength again."

"No!" Wynn cried, pushing away from him. "This isn't a wound of flesh, blood, or bone. It may not be a wound that can be healed, and I won't waste the potion on myself."

"It is the only way," he insisted.

"Use it to stop Magiere," she pressed.

To stop Magiere? What was she saying?

Everyone fell silent in confusion, and before Osha could ask, Wynn began digging into her short-robe.

"Please, Osha," she begged. "We did this to her, or Chap and I did. Magiere must be stopped, any way that we can."

Still he hesitated, though he then remembered Chane's words.

The liquid is also a poison to the undead.

Wynn finally withdrew a small bottle from her short-robe. Did she know what else that fluid might do?

"Please!" Wynn insisted, blindly holding out the bottle. "Dip your arrows in this. Stop her any way you have to."

"I can help Wynn here," Wayfarer whispered, and looked up to Chuillyon. "Perhaps . . . to keep the staff lit."

Osha's bow lay on the ground beside him. He glanced at it and back to Wynn.

How could she of anyone ask him to kill again? Even if he took great care, if that fluid killed whatever undead nature lay within Magiere, would it not kill her as well? Was that nature not part of the way she had been born—what she was?

And what if the potion did not stop Magiere?

"You have to do this," Wynn said. "No one else—perhaps not even Chap—might survive getting too close to her. You have to use your bow."

Looking around at all of them, Osha stalled in meeting Wayfarer's intense eyes. There was no one else who could do this—and he took the bottle from Wynn. Hefting his bow, he silently turned away.

"If you fail," he said, walking away, "take the horse and flee."

Only Shade tried to follow him.

"No," he said without looking back.

Their task now was to reignite the staff, and his might be to kill a friend.

Osha ran toward the battle.

Wayfarer watched the one man she both loved and blamed run off in the dark. Osha had not come for her but for Wynn. How many times would she be only an afterthought to him?

There was no more time for selfish thoughts as she looked to the young woman still sitting beside her.

"Is he gone?" Wynn asked.

"Enough!" Chuillyon interrupted, and leaned out the staff, its crystal nearly over Wynn's head. "Both of you, up."

Wayfarer took hold of Wynn's arm, helped her rise, and guided her hands to take the staff.

"Take these," Chuillyon added.

Wayfarer stared at the glasses, their lenses darker than the night. The tall Lhoin'na had thrust them at her and not Wynn.

"You will need them," he added, "if you can help her."

With one glance at Wynn, Chuillyon turned away, walking slowly toward the distant battle.

"I will do what I can to stop anything coming for you," he added, and then paused to glance back at Shade. "Perhaps you should come as well?"

Shade stood by Wynn's side.

"Go on," she whispered, pushing blindly on the dog.

Wayfarer saw Shade look to her, though not a word rose in her thoughts.

There was nothing worthwhile to say for a majay-hì now caught between two women over a man who wanted only one of them. Shade turned away to follow Chuillyon.

Everything now depended on Wynn's finding the strength to ignite the crystal again and keep it lit. And that depended on Wayfarer doing something she had never done before.

Wynn reached out her nearer hand, fumbling toward Wayfarer. Wayfarer grabbed that hand, and Wynn guided it to a grip on the staff just above her own.

"Put the glasses on," Wynn said weakly, turning her head but not her eyes. "And look away. Even so, you will know if the crystal lights up . . . by whatever you are going to do."

Wayfarer grew sick with panic as Wynn double-gripped the staff below her own hand. And as Wynn began to whisper, too many "ifs" swarmed Wayfarer.

What if the staff would not light? What if Wynn could not keep it lit? What if she did but then faltered and Wayfarer could not keep it lit? And still worse . . .

What if she could?

Wayfarer put on Wynn's glasses as Vreuvillä's warning hammered in her thoughts.

Nothing can be created or destroyed in such a way. Only changed . . . exchanged.

Wayfarer gripped Wynn's shoulder with her other hand as she looked away. And all she could do was what she had been taught. She looked—felt—for the Elements in all things, the Fay that was . . . were in all things.

From the heat—the Fire—in her own flesh. From the breath—the Air—she took in rapid pants. From the blood—the Water—that flowed through her. From bone and sinew—the Earth—of her own body.

From the Spirit that she was.

Answer my need . . . my wish . . . ay jâdh'airt.

The night lit up, even as Wayfarer continued looking down.

She flinched and stopped breathing but rapidly refocused so as not to lose what she had asked for. That light was so bright, she could see the cracks in the hardened earth—brighter than at any other time she had seen Wynn light the staff.

Relief almost made her look to the crystal, but she stopped herself. Relief almost kept her from thinking.

Only changed . . . exchanged.

Somewhere in the world, the light of the sun was diminished, for that came to the staff so long as she wished it here.

CHAPTER EIGHTEEN

Leesil followed Ghassan down the passage into the mountain by the light of the sage's cold-lamp crystal. Ghassan gripped the crystal while carrying a single chest, so its illumination wobbled on the passage walls with every labored step. Leesil struggled to haul two chests strung on poles with Brot'an behind him. Chane and Ore-Locks bore the final two chests. Leesil began growing concerned as Ghassan continued glancing into the side tunnels.

Those other passages were obviously dug out long ago. Though the domin paused a few times, he never appeared lost or in doubt. He walked like someone recalling the right route without even thinking. Ghassan had claimed he'd explored places like this in his youth, but it was highly unlikely he had explored this one.

Leesil pulled up short, dropped his ends of the poles before Brot'an halted behind him, and grasped Ghassan's sleeve.

"What are you looking for?" he demanded.

Ghassan turned, the chest still in his hands. "Pardon?"

"You seem to be looking for something, but if you haven't been here before . . ."

A flicker of surprise on the domin's face was followed by something else, but Leesil couldn't tell what.

"Of course I have not," Ghassan answered sharply. "I am seeking, even guessing at, the best downward path to wherever the Enemy might have sought refuge."

Leesil had little option but to accept this explanation, though it still bothered him. Simply studying the mouth of a passage wouldn't reveal where it led. Glancing back, he assessed the others.

Chane had a crystal as well, though it was not glowing right now. Even as an undead, he looked almost as worn as the rest. Whatever Ore-Locks had done to pull down that last locatha had taken something out of him. And no matter what Brot'an said or didn't say, he was wounded. Leesil's side still ached, and the ache turned to outright pain when he crouched to lift the poles and chests again.

"Get on with it," he said.

Ghassan did so as Leesil adjusted the poles' front ends. Then the domin stalled again, but this time stood staring ahead.

"What is it?" Leesil asked.

"A cavern," Ghassan whispered, seemingly more to himself than in answer. He moved on. Not far ahead, his crystal's light exposed a broad widening of the path.

Four pale white men stood in the way, each with a sword sheathed on his hip.

Leesil knew a vampire when he saw one.

Having been so burdened and tired, he'd forgotten to pull out the amulet that would've glowed to warn him before now. He dropped the poles in the same instant as Brot'an and heard the same for Chane and Ore-Locks. The impact of multiple chests echoed along the tunnel.

Leesil gripped the handle of one winged blade and drew the weapon from its sheath.

"Wait!" Ghassan hissed under his breath.

The four blocking the way wore matching black clothing—simple pants and shirts. All of them had hair down to their shoulders not quite as black as their attire. None had drawn a weapon. The tallest one stepped forward. He looked first at Ghassan and then the chests. Puzzlement flooded his features.

"Where is Beloved's child?" he asked, almost as voicelessly as Chane.

Leesil tensed.

"Child?" Ghassan asked dryly.

Leesil already knew whom that meant: Beloved's child, Magiere.

The Ancient Enemy had plagued his wife's dreams, tried to lure her in, and now this. Chap had been right never to allow her into the mountain. The undead quartet seemed to have expected her. Worse, they didn't look one bit surprised by anyone else who'd come.

The tall one's gaze dropped again to the chests. "We will take the anchors. You will go and bring the child."

As Leesil took two steps forward, Ghassan set down his chest and straightened.

"Really?" Ghassan answered barely above a whisper.

Doubt made Leesil glance toward the domin.

Ghassan blinked slowly, maybe lazily. Did his lips move in a soundless whisper? He then blinked rapidly and appeared to relax.

The tall vampire leader's features went slack, and his eyelids drooped. Neither he nor the others moved at all.

"Take their heads off in one strike," Ghassan ordered. "Preferably at the same time, so as not to arouse the others as one drops."

Leesil hesitated and looked back to Brot'an.

Brot'an only watched the four intently and did not move. Neither did Chane or Ore-Locks, though Chane wore an angry frown as if he did not care for how easily this had been done.

Neither did Leesil. Though he knew Ghassan was a skilled sorcerer, some-how what had been done exceeded anything he had seen the domin do before. It was unsettling, and he turned his suspicion on the domin.

Ghassan's eyes narrowed slightly. "Since when have any of you been squeamish at the thought of—"

He broke off, quickly glancing back to his targets.

The one on the rear left shook his head slightly.

The tall leader blinked. His face wrinkled in a silent snarl as he jerked his sword from its sheath.

Leesil saw no choice and rushed in, catching the undead's sword with his winged blade. The clang of steel pierced his ears—and head—as he shoved with all of his weight to drive back his opponent. He only managed one step, and then Chane was beside him.

Chane rammed the shorter of his two swords through the leader's rib cage and jerked it back out.

Ore-Locks thundered past at another undead closing in a rush.

Leesil knew any vampire would be stronger than he was, much harder to kill, and the longer this went on, the worse the odds would become.

"Get another one!" he shouted at Chane.

As Chane rushed on, Leesil gripped the back of his one drawn blade with his other hand. He thrust the blade's broad point into the leader's other side, levered as it sank in, and heard the muffled crack of ribs. Before his target overcame pain and shock, he shouldered the undead into a retreat, which freed his blade. He slashed the weapon toward his opponent's throat.

It tore through the side of the vampire's neck.

Black fluids splattered over Leesil's arm and onto his face.

Chane went for the next nearest target in the passage's wider section. Four undeads would think they had an advantage over the living. While those with Chane were worn or wounded or both, it was not this worry that set off the beast inside him. It shrieked in alarm, and his own sense of reason warned him about what was wrong.

These guardians had been expecting them . . . and Magiere.

As he closed, his new opponent snarled at him, exposing elongated teeth.

The vampire would not have seen him clearly in the dark tunnel, even with Ghassan's crystal glowing. And while he wore his "ring of nothing," these four could not sense him for what he was.

Chane let his hunger rise and answered in kind, exposing his own teeth.

His opponent's eyes widened in hesitation, and Chane rushed inside its guard, striking with a fist first. Its head whipped rightward with the crack of impact. He followed with his blade.

Steel sank through shirt and flesh, grating along ribs, and shock rather than death stunned the vampire. Chane wrenched out the sword, blackened with its fluids, and struck, aiming for his opponent's neck. His blade had barely broken through the vertebrae when the vampire's head began to topple off.

Chane spun before the head hit the tunnel's floor. He looked quickly among his companions for who was in the worst position.

Ghassan had his back to the tunnel's left wall, and Leesil had already put down the first, tallest one. Another body could be seen beyond Brot'an, whose right hand and hooked knife were both coated in black fluids.

The last one lay in black-spattered parts at Ore-Locks's feet. Its upper half still squirmed, but this ended as Ore-Locks's double-wide sword clanged down through its neck.

For an instant, all of them stood looking from one body to the next. Only the sound of their labored breaths filled the silence. It had all been too easy, and this made Chane suspicious.

"Get the orbs," Leesil finally commanded, sheathing his winged blade and glancing warily at Ghassan.

Chane also glanced at the domin, not knowing what to think.

Leesil said nothing more as he lifted the front ends of the poles for two chests.

Four vampires had expected their arrival, possibly that of the orbs, and of Magiere as well, as if addressing mere couriers or attendants. Did the Ancient Enemy know they would come?

Still, they could only go onward. Chane hurried to join Ore-Locks as

Brot'an grabbed the rear end of the poles behind Leesil. But Chane continued to study Ghassan as the domin lifted his chest and stepped into the lead. It was not long before they stopped again.

"Valhachkasej'â!" Leesil hissed.

Chane stared ahead, at a loss. Though they had stepped into a great cavern, they could go no farther. They stood before the lip of a broad and wide chasm. All of them set down their chests again, and Chane reached the edge just after Leesil.

The chasm was so deep that Ghassan's light did not reach the bottom. The same was true for the heights above, as if this gash within the mountain rose upward as well. It did not go straight down for what they could see. Its sides were twisted and jagged, as if it had been torn open ages ago by something immense ripping wide the insides of the peak. As Chane looked to the far side, he barely made out the black outline of another wound in the mountain's stone.

There was no bridge to that other side.

He turned to Leesil. "Now what?"

Sau'ilahk ran into the battle—or what was left of it—to escape any pursuit or those arrows that had burned like acid upon penetrating his flesh. Along the way, bodies half charred or utterly blackened littered the plain. Soon, the sounds of the battle surrounded him.

Now there were more bodies scattered in red or black pools and stains, either whole or torn apart.

He slowed to a halt and looked behind him.

There was no sign of pursuit, on foot or horseback. Turning back to the battle, he second-guessed his choice to hide in this chaos or lure into it any who came after him. Then he heard the sounds of howling and cast about for its source.

Two forms on all fours raced along the battle's westward edge toward him.

He knew those were majay-hì. Whether they knew what he was or not, they would when they neared. There was not enough time to conjure any-thing to defend himself, and he would need his reserves for something else.

He pulled his sword, though he had little skill with it, and fled farther into the battle. He went only far enough to be out of sight and then swerved eastward. Whatever might have been on the arrowheads that struck him still burned within the wounds in his shoulder and face. After centuries of lost beauty, damage to his appearance simply added salt to his wounds.

He wove through combatants tearing at one another, from goblins still much like those of his living days to at least one locatha set upon but unvan-quished by three Shé'ith. One majay-hì in the fray spotted him; it was turned aside by a half-charred, half-naked vampire with manic, feral features. Among all of this were ghul tearing and biting at anything living, and other things he did not recognize.

Only twice did he have to strike awkwardly at something as he raced to the battle's eastward fringe. There he paused, looking both ways, caught amid indecision.

Sau'ilahk saw majay-hì ranging north and south along the fifty yards of open space to the edge of the craggy foothills. He did not know what was happening with Khalidah and Beloved, and everything here had gone wrong. In this chaos, Beloved would soon have little or no army, but while that remained, the battle was the only place he could hide.

Wynn and her companions had once again lost the element of surprise, but what if Khalidah failed in that as well? Grabbing the medallion around his neck, Sau'ilahk focused his thoughts.

Khalidah! Answer me!

Again, no reply.

Rage and frustration overwhelmed him. The dhampir—the "child"—had to be in here somewhere amid the slaughter. Why else would every other witless, undead tool of Beloved not flee for its own survival? It had to be she who had sparked this frenzy.

And if he could not strike directly at Beloved . . .

At the fringe of the carnage, Sau'ilahk began desperately conjuring another servitor—and another and another.

Leesil gazed across the chasm, at a loss. The presence of those last four vampires told him they were on the right track, but what did that matter?

"Now what?" Chane asked in his irritating rasp.

Panicked frustration overwhelmed Leesil. They couldn't give up.

Then he thought of what he'd seen Ore-Locks do. He looked left and right below the chasm's lip, but Ghassan's light didn't reach far enough.

The domin's expression flickered before he turned right and walked along the chasm's edge.

"There," he said, pointing off level into the chasm's darkness.

Leesil hurried over, hearing Chane behind him. He couldn't see anything at first.

"There is a glint there," Chane said, pointing.

Leesil saw it, perhaps caused by the crystal's light reflected off some ore vein. There was a wall in that beyond a stone's throw, so he hoped, but there was no ledge by which to reach it.

"I can attempt to float us across the chasm, one by one," Ghassan suggested. "It will take time. And the more exertion, the greater the risk of losing someone, as well as an orb."

Leesil peeked over the chasm's edge into the pitch-black below. Half turning, he found Ore-Locks right beside Chane, though Brot'an remained guarding the chests.

"I'm not some bat to go flitting about!" the dwarf growled, and then peered off into rightward darkness. "If there is a true wall back there, I can go through stone to the other side, but only Chane can go with me that way. As to the rest of us . . ."

Ore-Locks shrugged, and Leesil didn't care for Ghassan's notion. He had another idea.

"Everyone take off any rope you're carrying," he said. "Brot'an, get your bow assembled."

"You have something else in mind," Chane said. It wasn't a question.

Leesil nodded. "You and Ore-Locks try to get to the other side with two chests. Once there, Brot'an can attempt to shoot the rope across. If it doesn't make it the first time, we keep trying. Chane, you stay there to anchor the rope on the other side while Ore-Locks comes back for more chests."

Chane nodded once, and Brot'an dropped to one knee.

The master assassin began pulling the disassembled pieces of his short bow from under the back of his clothing. Even as Ore-Locks went to the chests, Chane began searching about the open area around the ledge they were on.

"We cannot see what might await on the far side, or farther on if the tunnel continues over there," he said. "And I see nowhere to anchor the rope on this side. Someone will have to hold it . . . and be left behind."

Leesil clenched his teeth, but everything Chane said was right.

"I will see to the last part."

Everyone turned at Brot'an's comment. His assembled short bow lay beside him as he struck a stiletto's blade against a dark stone in his hand. Sparks flew.

"Begin assembling the ropes," he instructed. "Tear off strips of cloth from lighter clothing, as many as possible."

Again, he began digging into his own clothes and produced a small clay vial.

Leesil eyed the aging assassin. Just how many bits and pieces did Brot'an carry hidden?

After the ropes were tied together and a small pile of cloth strips lay before Brot'an, he tied one strip to each of three out of four short arrows. He then tied more strips together and lashed that length around the final arrow and the rope's end. Last, he poured a sluggish black fluid out of the vial onto the remaining pile of cloth and the strips around the three arrows.

Two strikes of the stiletto against the black stone lit the pile, and Brot'an quickly lit an arrow. Brot'an rose and drew the arrow with one glance at Ore-Locks.

"Go," Brot'an commanded. "Return once you determine if there is a way to anchor the rope on the far side."

Chane hefted a chest. Ore-Locks did the same and grabbed Chane's forearm. Both vanished into the half cavern's wall, and Leesil had more worried thoughts.

What if there was another passage or space beyond the far ledge? And what if there wasn't? There had to be. What if something therein heard an arrow strike or spotted its small flame?

Brot'an fired.

Leesil turned, following the flaming arrow's flicker across the chasm through the dark. It quickly grew small, until he heard it hit. He saw the tiny flicker of flame skitter across stone and then come to a stop. As he was about to turn to Brot'an, another tiny flame followed the first, and then a third one.

Those small flames landing apart showed there *was* a stone floor on the other side.

They waited and watched for any sign of Ore-Locks and Chane.

However long that was, it was too long for Leesil. If no anchor point was found over there, even with both Chane and Ore-Locks holding on to the rope, there was still the question of who would be left behind. That one had to be strong enough to anchor the rope's near end. Ghassan could likely cross the chasm his own way, and Leesil had no intention of staying behind.

"Do not be concerned," Brot'an said quietly.

Leesil looked back and up, but Brot'an merely stared across the chasm. It still unnerved Leesil how often the assassin thought several steps ahead of everyone, but what steps this time?

Chap ranged along the battle's outskirts. The undead he could now see numbered less than the living—but there were still too many to fix on any one. Their presence ate him inside, and it was hard not to cut loose and hunt the nearest one.

The longer Magiere remained in there, the worse the situation would become, yet he was still uncertain how to stop her. Should he run her down or try to reach her through memories? What if both failed and he was left with only one other choice?

Could he face losing her if he had to take her over completely?

No other options came to him.

He readied for the worst and then heard paws and claws closing behind him. Spinning around, he bared his teeth.

Two majay-hì raced in from the south where he had left Chuillyon and Vreuvillä. He watched as they neared and circled him. The large, mottled male passed close enough to brush his shoulder.

An image of the wild priestess erupted in Chap's mind.

All he could guess was that she had sent this pair to him. For an instant, he wished his daughter were here. Shade had spent time among their kind and knew better the ways of memory-speak.

Chap huffed once as the speckled gray female came close. In brushing her shoulder with his head, he called up his memory of Magiere fully lost to her dhampir side. Then he bolted off into the battle, looking back once to see that the pair followed him.

He charged into the snarls, screams, and bloodshed, almost deafened by the noise and assaulted by flashes of combatants half lit by scattered fires. With only two unknown majay-hì beside him, there were too many other *things* all around him.

Chane fell to his knees and dropped his chest as Ore-Locks dragged him out of stone. For an instant, he could not discern on which side of the chasm they had emerged. Though he did not need air, he could not help choking a few times. Then he saw two of Brot'an's arrows on stone still lit.

Sick, weakened, and embarrassed at having dreaded yet another venture through stone, he struggled to his feet.

"All right?" Ore-Locks asked.

Chane nodded and pointed to the arrows. "Wave two of those to let them know we are here."

When Ore-Locks did so, Chane saw Ghassan's crystal light on the chasm's other side swinging back and forth.

"The rope comes next," he added.

Though he listened and watched for anything that might come, nothing did. There was another deeper darkness at the back to this huge hollow on the chasm's far side. The distant sound of a bowstring's thrum pulled him back around.

Both he and Ore-Locks stepped quickly to either side of the half cavern.

Chane listened but heard nothing for an instant. Then came the soft clatter of an arrow and the flop of something far off . . . and down in the chasm below. It was not hard to guess.

The rope's weight had been too much for the shot. Only then did he remember the cold-lamp crystal he still carried.

Chane dug it out and rubbed it between his palms. He heard another bowstring thrum. It took three more shots for the rope-weighted arrow to clear the chasm.

Ore-Locks hooked it with his outstretched sword.

Chane rushed over to pull the arrow free as he gripped the rope.

"Three more chests," he whispered, and, with a nod, Ore-Locks vanished into stone.

Sau'ilahk's wounds still burned inside from Osha's arrows, though he did not know why. He dodged through the chaos as his stick-creature servitors harried and tripped up anything in his way. Another kind of servitor, consisting of gas, wormed through the air above him.

Seeing the battle through the roiling cloud of scintillating mist, as well as with his own eyes, made him nauseated. He had not felt this way in centuries, but this was the only way to navigate and keep his bearings. Somewhere in this madness below the mountain was the reason for why Beloved's forces turned on themselves. More questions tormented him, and he was exhausted from too many conjures.

If the creatures in the horde were Beloved's tools, why had it not seized control of them? Why did it allow them to decimate one another? And why had Khalidah still not answered him?

Perhaps Beloved was not the only one who betrayed him. Whatever caused this chaos was the work of either of his betrayers—or perhaps both. Had Khalidah used him to regain the orbs for Beloved?

And he still had not finished with Wynn Hygeorht.

Through the gaseous servitor's view, something more bizarre pulled his attention. Three majay-hì wove, snapped, and rammed through the battle, and yet others of their kind were nowhere around him. The only others he had seen had retreated to open ground.

Sau'ilahk hesitated, trying to quell wrath and anguish. Why would these three reenter the battle but not stop to finish off any prey?

As he watched them race onward, two of his stick-creature servitors with glowing eyes tore at a goblin in his way. One tried to get at the beast's eyes. As that bristling monster wailed in and tore away that one, he hacked into its skull, double-handed, with his sword.

Sau'ilahk thought of those three dogs as he focused upon his spy above. *Follow them!*

Leesil settled a hand on the rope pulled across the chasm between Brot'an behind him and Chane and Ore-Locks on the other side. All five chests had been taken through stone, and now Ore-Locks and Chane stood like anchors, holding their side of the rope, ready for Leesil to cross over.

First, Leesil peeked over the nearer side into that endless darkness below, and with some hesitation, he looked back to Ghassan.

"You're certain you can get across . . . your way?"

Ghassan sighed with a roll of his eyes. "Yes, if you will get on with this."

At that, the domin took hold of the rope in front of Brot'an.

It appeared that only Leesil would have to cross this way, though Brot'an's way across would be worse. There had been a good deal of arguing about that once he'd finally announced his plan.

How he would survive a swing across, avoid slamming into the far wall, and climb or be pulled up—if he kept his grip—wasn't imaginable.

"Go," Brot'an said.

With little choice, Leesil gripped the rope, hooked one leg over it, and reached out along it beyond the ledge. He pulled himself hand over hand, stopping more than once to rest for the span of two breaths. Still, he crawled as fast as possible so the others wouldn't have to hold him up longer than necessary.

He was never foolish enough to look down.

Looking up into the endless dark above was bad enough. By the time he heard Chane rasp, "You are clear," he was exhausted.

Leesil unhooked his legs, felt with one foot for solid stone, and dropped to his feet. He quickly took hold of the rope in front of Chane, though they all relaxed for a moment.

Ghassan would cross first—at Brot'an's previous insistence.

At first Leesil saw nothing in the dark out over the chasm. All of Brot'an's lit arrows had been extinguished to save them, but Chane had illuminated his own crystal and left that by the edge. Something drew nearer, above in the dark, taking form by the crystal's light.

Ghassan slowly floated toward Leesil, though higher above, and the domin's eyes fixed straight ahead. He never wavered or dropped lower or higher, until he began to descend. As he arced down to alight without a sound upon the ledge, it was as if he had simply taken a stroll in midair.

The domin was about to step into the lead in gripping the rope, but Leesil waved him farther back, wanting to stay at the lead himself as Brot'an made his leap. At one quick whistle in the dark from the chasm's far side, Leesil tensed.

"Brace," he said, tightening his own grip.

The rope went slack, and Leesil's hands clenched even tighter. He watched as the rope dropped down over the edge and suddenly shifted a bit to one side. It then lurched taut in his hands under a sudden sharp weight.

Brot'an must have run to one side and jumped at a tangent, trying to arc around through the chasm to keep from slamming straight into its nearer side.

"Don't pull unless I say," Leesil ordered the others.

If the rope frayed on the ledge, better that it did so in only one spot so that it could be cut and retied. They would need as much of its length as possible—if any of them survived to leave this place.

Weight on the rope increased rapidly in an instant. Likely Brot'an had used his arc to neutralize the collision and was running along the chasm's wall.

The rope finally centered up over the chasm's edge.

"Can you hold?" Ghassan asked behind him.

"Yes," Leesil answered.

The domin hurried around him to the edge and looked down. He quickly straightened and turned around.

"He is on his way up."

Leesil took a deep breath as he waited and held fast to the rope with the others.

Chap swerved as something gray and shadowy scrambling through the legs of the others tried to grab his foreleg with a bony hand. He barely glimpsed its head when it was suddenly stomped to a pulp under a huge booted foot. There had been no time or chance to see it clearly.

He kept running.

More than once he'd had to ram or brush one of his companions to get the male or female to break off an assault upon an undead. Keeping them with him in all this became harder with each panting breath.

There was only one target they—he—had to find. And his hunger was aroused by all around him, everywhere, with so many undead mixed in the slaughter.

Chap barely hung on to sanity, and that was slipping. His instincts nearly overwhelmed him; time and again he fought against turning on an undead that tried to assault him. Too much hunger and too many screams of fury and terror were coming at him from everywhere. Then he was struck by a hunger greater than the others—a hunger for one target. He fought to keep himself from *hunting* that one.

Yet when he sensed it, he clung to it and instantly lost himself. He swerved to seek it out as awareness of all else stripped away.

There was now only the hunt, and Chap had only one prey.

Sau'ilahk wove through the battle in a tangent toward where three majay-hì were headed. He had already lost two of his ground-level servitors along the way. Then his watchful one above showed him the large gray dog bolting in a fixed direction. The other two majay-hì fell behind in trying to keep up.

The battleground was thinning as more combatants fell, not all of them dead for a first or second time as they crawled and clawed across the parched ground. In a cluster ahead, one fought amid others all attempting to get at her. When she twisted to strike out at an opponent with hooked fingers, and follow with a wide and long single-edged blade, in the dark he saw her too-pale face curtained in flailing black hair.

Even among the other undead, he felt her most of all.

The urge to go at her with his bare hands was immediate.

Sau'ilahk restrained himself, fighting for self-control. Why did he feel driven with hunger? Something more was wrong about her, and then he sensed her *life*.

That was impossible for an undead.

Was that why the others went at her with such insane hunger? Her eyes were like nothing living, pure black without pupils, and yet she saw everything.

She had to be the source of whatever had happened to the horde. If so, was this somehow Beloved's own doing? Who else could have done this, controlled this woman?

She nearly cleaved a ghul in half with her broad blade.

Planned or not, if this was Beloved's doing, then that was enough for him. Betrayed again and again, if he could not strike down his tormentor of a thousand years, then he would end any of its tools. And by the way he took her life, Beloved would know who had taken her.

The gray majay-hì broke into sight and charged at the woman.

Sau'ilahk stalled again. Was it enough to simply watch Beloved's tool be destroyed?

No, it was not.

Chap saw only the undead woman; he ignored all others. He broke through a tangle of those killing and those dying and fixed on the one that he hunted.

White face and black eyes were all that he saw. His hackles stiffened upright, his ears flattened, and his jowls pulled back. The need to hunt compelled him. This need fixed upon that one greatest hunger he sensed, even as the tiniest, deepest part within him shriveled in fright of himself.

And still he could not stop.

Some gray thing of slit nostrils and eyes as black as *hers* split slantwise under the strike of her sword. As its halves fell, he leaped through its spattering fluids and hit her straight on before she recovered from her swing.

In that scant moment, he saw only a tall woman's pale, feral face, her fangs and distended teeth, and her eyes as fully black as darkness. Everything in the night tumbled as they both slammed down on the parched earth. He righted himself as she came at him on all fours.

Her hand clamped on his throat, choking off his breath.

With a twist of his head, he bit down on her forearm, grinding on flesh.

When that white face came at him with jaws opened wide, he raked it aside with his foreclaws and then tore at her abdomen, trying to rip through studded armor.

Something else slammed into both of them. He heard snarls, snapping teeth, howls, and screeches that were not his own as he tumbled. His head and body pounded on the hard ground again and again under the weight of others.

Chap smelled—tasted—something that cut through the hunger.

Blood?

Sau'ilahk barely evaded one ghul long enough for his servitors to assault it. When he spun around that tangle, he stumbled into a break in the battle to a sight that froze him.

The woman in studded leather armor rolled across the ground under the assault of two majay-hì, while a third such animal shook itself in trying to rise.

He was close enough to see her more clearly now.

She had the face of an undead—a vampire—lost in a bloodlust madness. But that face was also marred with scratches and claw marks that bled . . . red, not black.

All around her lay dismembered bodies of ghul, other white-skinned men and women, as well as once-living things and other humans. The ground itself was soaked dark with blood and other fluids that stained her and the majay-hì as they thrashed and tore at each other.

She was a living woman who acted like an undead caught in maddened hunger.

That thing—she—had to be the one he sought. Given that she was unnatural in both life and death, nothing natural could have made her that way by birth, so she could have only one maker.

And that was the one who had made—tricked—him a thousand years ago with a wish for eternal life.

He saw in her some little part of what Beloved should have given him, instead of eternity as a fleshless spirit. This woman was the tool of his tormentor, his betrayer. But there were still those majay-hì in his way. He could not face all those at once and alone.

Anguish, hate, envy, and spite became one.

He dropped to his knees, slammed his hands down, and ground his fingers into the hardpack. As he bled away what he had left for a last conjury, Sau'ilahk, once the highest of Beloved's followers, screamed out . . .

"You—you caused all of this!"

That shriek of hate cut through Chap's agony, and he pushed up to all fours with his head aching. He saw a white-skinned woman trying to grab two majay-hì that attacked her over and over. Still he was not certain what he saw. His skull pounded inside, he tasted blood in his mouth, and the scent of it made his head ache even more.

"If not Beloved, then I finish you—tool—to strike our maker!"

This second scream pulled Chap's full focus. What he saw froze him, and that instant stretched out in his returning awareness.

A young man with blue-black hair, tall and well formed, hunkered on the ground with his fingers grinding into the hard earth. His face had a gash in the right cheek, and a like one bled at his left shoulder.

Chap sensed something more as he stared.

Undead . . . another undead.

A memory surged up in the voice of Wynn as his mind replayed something she had told him. That face had a name for a young duke, but someone else hid behind it. Wynn had claimed that Chane destroyed this one, yet here he was.

—*Sau'ilahk*—, whispered Wynn's voice out of memory.

How could he still be alive and whole?

Chap saw things scurry in around the man. Small, with single glowing eyes like balls of crude glass, they were half the size of a dog. Spindly like insects, their gnarled limbs looked like darkly stained wood.

And Chap remembered . . . the prey . . . his prey . . . Magiere.

He gagged on the taste of her blood still in his teeth.

"Before dying," Sau'ilahk went on, "Beloved will suffer as I have, helpless when I take your life. And when you are dead flesh, I will take its precious anchors as well. Tell that to your master when it creeps into your head."

He sounded as if the Enemy *wanted* the orbs brought to it.

Chap went still and cold. Over the last season and before, he and those with him had sought to recover the orbs—the anchors. Had they unwittingly served the Enemy's own wishes? Had he been so easily manipulated?

"Beloved will never be free!" Sau'ilahk hissed.

This recalled the words of Chap's kin in the Lhoin'na forest.

Leave the enslaved alone.

If the Enemy had called the orbs to itself, was it already bound in some way? Had it never left the mountain in all of these centuries? And how would the orbs free it?

Those questions brought blind panic. Could everything they had done here have been wrong and exactly what the Enemy wanted?

His thoughts raced to what he had seen when he had touched the orb of Spirit.

As with the others he had touched at some time, he had felt a presence inside it. The Enemy—the dragon in that placeless timelessness—was a Fay. So why did it want the orbs, the anchors? Did its greater minions—Sau'ilahk, the specter, and others—seek the orbs for it or against it? Did some of them wish to destroy the Ancient Enemy themselves?

Leave the enslaved alone.

The Enemy had manipulated him to bring the orbs together and had done nothing to stop its own servants from the same purpose and worse. Did the ancient one—the Night Voice—want someone to use those orbs to kill it? Why?

Chap looked around at the carnage Magiere had created. Yet nothing had stopped her or the Enemy's forces, as if it were all as desired. And Leesil now had the orbs somewhere inside the mountain in seeking out the Enemy.

The implications were beyond any terror.

Chap had seen five Fay who sacrificed to create Existence. Had one of them sought retreat from that? Was the Ancient Enemy one of those five? If so, what would happen if it vanished from existence?

He remembered the presence he had felt when Magiere mistakenly opened the first orb beneath the six-towered castle in the Pock Peaks. Leesil had claimed he saw a shadow in the shape of a massive serpent with a head that Wynn later claimed was a weürm, a serpentlike dragon.

Leave the enslaved alone.

Chap began to tremble. Caught between bringing Magiere back to herself, and pulling Sau'ilahk down, and finding a way to halt Leesil, he was too late in . . .

Magiere tore loose from one majay-hì. The other was down and not moving. She charged for Sau'ilahk. The earth cracked around Sau'ilahk's hooked fingers as something began to emerge.

Snarling, Chap charged on a line between them.

The night suddenly lit up from the north.

Caught in a chorus of screams all around, Chap stumbled, blinded for an instant.

Osha halted short of the battle and quickly unstoppered the small bottle Wynn had forced on him.

It should not be this way. What it held should have been for her. And what she had asked of him should have never been asked.

He pulled the last two arrows with white metal tips and sank each head, one at a time, into the bottle. After replacing the stopper, he tucked the bottle away inside his tunic. Then he rose and nocked one arrow with the other pinched between two fingers of his hand around the bow's handle.

Still, he hesitated.

If what Chane claimed was true about the fluid affecting the undead . . .

If he did what Wynn asked to stop Magiere . . .

Osha did not want to think of murdering a friend. He looked toward the chaos before him, not hearing the shouts, raging snarls, growls, and screams. All he heard were his own shallow, quick breaths and the hammering of his heart.

Light filled the dark from behind him.

So many out there scrambled to escape, though the staff was too far to burn most of them. As they scattered, he saw so much more.

Magiere rushed at another target, and even from afar, Osha could see her fully black eyes. This time, Wynn's light did not bring Magiere back. The dhampir was all that was left of her. As tears leaked from his wide eyes, he wiped his sleeve across them.

Then he raised and drew his bow, knowing he could not miss his target.

As Chap's sight cleared, his every thought stilled at the sight of Magiere.

She screeched and snarled as one of Sau'ilahk's small stick-creatures leaped into her face. Even as she clawed the thing off, the large male majay-hì rammed her legs from behind. Magiere toppled back and hit the ground.

"No!" Sau'ilahk screamed out. "She is mine!"

One of those glowing-eyed stick things went at the majay-hì as Magiere thrashed over onto all fours.

The ground around Sau'ilahk's hooked fingers began to break apart.

Chap howled as he charged at Magiere's back to stop her before whatever came out of the ground. She spun, and he faltered.

Magiere's eyes fixed on him as if she had forgotten any other target. There was nothing left of the woman he knew, only the dhampir, only a monster out of his worst nightmare.

All he saw was her, just as he had once seen her in that sorcerous phantasm in the forests of Droevinka where everything living around her died.

Was he to die here at the hands of someone he loved?

She charged, and he set himself, ready to lunge.

Magiere's snarl twisted into a shriek of rage—and she stumbled and lurched.

An arrow stuck out through her hauberk between her chest and right shoulder.

Chap saw his own shock mirrored in Magiere's white face.

That face twisted quickly into pain as smoke welled out around the arrow's shaft. Black lines spidered through her face and then her hands, and she dropped the falchion.

Magiere fell screaming and thrashing upon the ground. And there was Sau'ilahk on his feet, staring in shock.

CHAPTER NINETEEN

Leesil crept onward behind Ghassan, who still held his glowing cold-lamp crystal while carrying one chest, as they went deeper into a ragged tunnel they'd found in the chasm's far side. Leesil supported the forward ends of the poles for two chests with Brot'an behind him at the poles' back ends. Somewhere farther back were Chane and Ore-Locks doing likewise.

They did not go far before Ghassan halted suddenly, and Leesil lurched to a stop.

The domin turned about, set his chest aside, and straightened with a finger over his lips. Leesil quietly lowered his poles and only released and set them down once he felt the chests settle.

Ghassan turned ahead once more, and upon stepping forward, Leesil saw the crystal's light expand into an immense cavern of walls that all slanted leftward. The domin halted again, and Leesil stepped up beside him. He was too fixed on what he saw to even notice the others gathering.

There were huge bones spread out in the cavern's rear, as if the creature to which they'd belonged had simply lain down for the last time and never moved again. Nearest was its skull. If he walked up to it, the top would be taller than he was. The rest was just as large.

All of it was darkened and discolored. Some bones glittered, as if ages of dripping moisture had embedded minerals in the crust over its bones.

Fearful of stepping closer, Leesil noticed something else. It had no limbs. Just the spine of bones curled like a serpent too immense to imagine all the way to that skull with three ridges of what might've been horns.

The side rows ran around the back from empty eye sockets big enough to crawl into. The much smaller center spikes started near the bridge's midpoint and ended at the midtop.

"A serpent," Brot'an whispered somewhere behind Leesil.

"No, *gí'uyllæ*," Ore-Locks corrected.

"All-eater," Chane explained, "or dragon."

"I have never heard of one so large in any tale," Ore-Locks added.

Leesil stepped carefully toward it, listening and watching everywhere for anything. More than once he slowed or paused. The skull grew larger in his sight the closer he came to it. Of what teeth were still whole, the longest had to weigh more than two—or even three—of the men who'd come with him. The more he stared at the huge skull, imagining what such a creature would have once looked like, the more his mind rolled backward to a memory.

Below the six-towered castle in the Pock Peaks, Magiere had been caught in a daze when they'd found the first orb, and she had opened it with her thôrhk. In the chaos that followed, as the orb of Water tried to swallow all moisture in that cavern, Leesil had seen an immense shadow coil through the cavern's upper reaches. Like a serpent bigger than any of the towers, its open maw had come down as if to swallow her.

"What is this?" he asked aloud.

In answer, a hiss echoed throughout the cavern.

—Where is my child?—

Leesil retreated from the skull and pulled both blades. He heard the others spread out as they drew weapons, so they'd heard it too, but he kept his eyes on the enormous skull. Had he really heard those words in his head? Hesitantly, he looked about at the others.

Chane did the same, though he was frowning in confusion.

Leesil thought they'd all pulled their weapons. Not Chane, but he did so upon seeing that everyone else had.

Then Leesil saw Ghassan.

A strange manic look covered the domin's face. Was it fear, hate, or both? Wide-eyed, his head rolled about, perhaps looking into the cavern's heights, but then his gaze resettled to glare at those bones.

"It is still here," he whispered slowly. "The bones do not matter. We will set up the orbs and end it here, now."

Leesil felt completely at a loss.

End what? There was nothing here but that hiss, whatever it was. From what he'd once seen when the first orb was opened, opening all of them wouldn't touch anything that wasn't physically here, alive or dead. And the orbs were supposed to be a last resort.

And no one knew for certain what the orbs would do.

—My child . . . where is she? What have you . . . they . . . done with her?—

Leesil went cold.

He knew "child" meant Magiere. This thing—whatever and wherever— might be what had spoken in her dreams, and if so, had it lost touch with her? What had happened to Magiere?

—Then you will serve me a last time—

"Ignore it!" Ghassan ordered. "Get the orbs, quickly, and take off your thôrhks for use."

Leesil looked around, wondering to whom that voice was actually speaking. Was it to him, someone else here, or all of them?

"Why do you hesitate?" Ghassan whispered, rushing two steps toward Leesil. "This is why we came here."

"What is happening?" Chane rasped, making everyone start.

Leesil twisted about and startled Chane in turn. The vampire watched only Ghassan.

—Open the anchors . . . end this now . . . and forever—

"Do you not hear it?" Ore-Locks whispered.

In one glance at the dwarf, Chane's eyes drained of all color, becoming clear in the light of Ghassan's crystal. Chane turned to Leesil.

"Do not listen to what you think you hear!" he rasped.

Leesil's every instinct took hold of Chane's warning.

Whirling in search of the archer, Chap spotted Osha. The young one stood not far off, haloed by Wynn's distant light. And that light glinted too brightly on the head of another drawn arrow.

Osha's large amber eyes streamed tears down his long face.

He had shot Magiere, most likely with a white metal arrowhead from the Chein'âs. Chap could not even guess what that had done to her. Osha's eyes then blinked. Did his aim falter at something else?

Chap quickly looked back.

Sau'ilahk had recovered from shock, and he slammed his hands to the earth again.

Twisting around, Chap shouted into Osha's thoughts.

—*No!*— . . . —*Shoot Sau'ilahk, the duke!*—

Osha's aim shifted instantly, and the arrow released. Chap heard the shriek before he could follow the arrow's path.

Sau'ilahk reeled back on his knees, mouth gaping. An arrow still shuddered from impact in the center of his chest, and he began to shake. Inky lines spread up into his face from beneath a strapped leather collar and then down into his hands as well. Those lines split and bled as smoke rose from the same cracks. He fell back upon the broken earth.

Sau'ilahk's wild thrashing was quickly obscured by the increasing smoke, though his wails and screeches still rose in the night.

Chap bolted for Magiere, lying still and prone, and he lunged past her, planting himself between her and the wild thrashing amid the smoke. Uncertain of anything, he watched the broken ground for whatever might still come out of the earth from the conjurer's touch.

One shriek cut off too suddenly. Not another sound or movement disturbed the billowing smoke.

Chap remained rigid in waiting and watching, even when he heard Osha come running. As the smoke began to thin, he saw something more. The body was still, dead, and the skin was blackened. Chap began to wonder if something more than just Chein'âs metal was at work here. But nothing came out of the earth where Sau'ilahk had crouched a moment ago.

Doubtful relief kept him watching longer. Osha stepped beyond him toward the duke's finally fallen and charred body, at last the corpse that it should have been. Then the young one turned, looking back beyond Chap.

Osha cringed, back-stepped once in visible anguish, and dropped his bow.

No matter what Chap felt, no matter what he wanted, he had no time for Magiere. She would not be the only one to die if he did not reach Leesil, and there was only one way to accomplish that.

Chap snarled at Osha with a snap of teeth and a short lunge.

—*Where is Chuillyon . . . where did you part from him?*—

Osha back-stepped, looking down.

—*Answer!*—

"With . . . Wynn . . . and Wayfarer and Shade," Osha panted out, pointing toward the light.

Chap could not help glancing at Magiere, lying still and black marked. He gave Osha a final command before bolting toward Wynn's light.

—*Pick her up and follow*—

Osha went numb as Chap raced off.

Remaining in place, Osha cringed at the thought of what the elder majay-hì had demanded. He could not bear to look upon Magiere's remains—upon what he had done.

Slowly, Osha crept toward Magiere's body but only looked to her nearest hand. There was no smoke rising from it. He did see the lines in her flesh, as if every vein beneath her pale skin had blackened and swelled. But the skin had not split, bled, or charred as with Sau'ilahk's stolen flesh.

Then Osha's gaze worked upward, first to the hauberk's shredded skirt, then to the sword belt nearly severed, upward to the torso, and finally to where that arrow was still embedded in her shoulder.

Osha choked once and stumbled, doubting what he saw. He dropped beside her, putting an ear near her mouth—and heard a shallow breath.

Quickly straightening, again he hesitated, not knowing if he should jerk out the arrow. That might worsen any bleeding and end what little life to which she clung. Rising to his feet, he cast around.

Most of the nearby fighting had scattered, as even the living members of the horde had fled when the nearest undead had run from the light and tore at anything in their way. Fighting was still intense farther south, and he saw one rider among others harrying everything within reach.

Osha put fingers to his mouth and whistled over and over as loudly as he could.

Finally, that one rider clear of the others wheeled its mount his way. At a distance, he could not tell who it was, even as it charged toward him.

Dropping to one knee, he pulled a knife from a sheath at his back and set its edge low against the arrow's shaft. Using the blade, he snapped the shaft some three finger widths above Magiere's armor. He then slung his bow and reached down to grip Magiere beneath her shoulders.

He had barely lifted her to sitting in a slump when a horse's hooves thundered up beside him, and he looked up into the severe eyes of Commander Althahk. The commander of the Shé'ith appeared little better than Magiere, blood marred, torn, and ragged, with his sword's blade obscured in black and red smears.

"You abandoned your squad!" Althahk shouted at him.

Osha ignored this and pointed down at Magiere. "I must take her north to the light while she still lives. The majay-hì demands it!"

The commander barely noticed the black-haired woman leaning unconscious against Osha's right leg. A puzzled, confused scowl turned to outright fury.

"We have dead and injured scattered everywhere," Althahk snarled. "And more if we do not stop it . . . and you deserted!"

Osha realized there was nothing he could say that would accomplish what he needed. Then his frantic, wandering eyes fixed on Althahk's mount. Froth-covered and stained in sweat and blood, En'wi'rên snorted over and over, watching him.

The Shé'ith did not see their horses as mere mounts but as their allies, their battle mates. Could *she* possibly understand what the commander would not?

He had never learned enough about her kind, but he had no other recourse.

"Please," he begged. "I must do this . . . as the majay-hì commanded."

That did not even make sense to him. How could anyone—even she— understand what he asked? Or understand how different Chap was from even his own Fay-born kind?

En'wi'rên whinnied—and then bucked and twisted violently.

Althahk's eyes snapped wide. He dropped his sword to grab for the saddle's front edge.

Osha almost backed away, but he would not leave Magiere undefended as the horse pranced wildly. The commander's furious shouts were impossible to follow in his strange dialect. En'wi'rên did not relent until . . .

"Bithâ!" Althahk shouted, over and over.

En'wi'rên settled. With a final thrash of her head and a sharp snort, she looked to Osha, and he stared back in disbelief.

"Very well," Althahk snapped. "Osha, get the woman up and over, behind the saddle."

Osha quickly put his hands beneath Magiere's arms. As he lifted her up, he could not help a last glance at En'wi'rên. It was a struggle to get Magiere draped over the horse's haunches, even with the commander's help, but as Althahk reached behind himself to grip hold of her belt, Osha stepped back, at a loss.

There was no space for him to mount as well.

"Grab the stirrup's strap!" Althahk ordered. "And run with her!"

Osha took hold, and En'wi'rên lunged.

Chap's claws scratched hard ground as he ran for Wynn's light. The closer he came, the more he squinted, until he finally could not look at it at all. He heard other paws coming toward him, but when he glanced ahead, he almost blinded himself again.

The sun crystal had never been that brilliant before.

Those other paws grew closer.

Shade caught up on Chap's right side, and he conveyed a message to her with as few words as possible.

—*Osha . . . Magiere . . . behind . . . bring*—

Without answering, Shade veered off, and he ran onward.

Something broke the light's glare, and Chap looked ahead. A tall figure in a long dark robe stood too close to the sun crystal to be an undead.

Chap slowed, panting as he approached.

Even with his hood pulled forward, Chuillyon had to squint amid the bright light as he looked down at Chap in stunned silence. Somewhere beyond the tall elf was Wynn with her staff and Wayfarer as well. Chap could not help wondering again how the staff's crystal had been made so brilliant this time.

Chuillyon crouched down, cocking his head slightly.

—*We . . . must go to . . . Leesil*—

Chuillyon's eyes widened at that demand, hearing the words in his head. In puzzlement, he looked up beyond Chap, perhaps to the mountain.

—Where . . . did you . . . hide . . . the sprout?— . . . *—We must . . . take . . . Wynn . . . and go there . . . now—*

"Does Leesil still carry his branch?" Chuillyon asked.

—Yes—

While reaching for the pocket of his robe, Chuillyon answered. "Then we can reach him from here. I have already retrieved the . . ." He faltered, looking up.

Chap heard hooves pounding closer behind him, and he spun around.

Khalidah faced Leesil as he heard Beloved speak again.

—Open the anchors and break my bonds. Unmake me and unmake existence. My kin will pay, and I will be free. End my bondage—

Is this what his god thought to do, to unmake existence and be free? That would not happen, though certainly Beloved would die. Any nonsense concerning "kin" meant nothing. A new master would take Beloved's place, no matter how many else died for him to become a god.

The lines, symbols, and signs of sorcery took shape in Khalidah's sight.

He turned on Leesil first.

Ghassan heard every word within the prison of his own flesh. He heard the very thoughts of his captor. Wild fear grew in his effort to understand what was about to happen.

The Enemy sought to die and spoke of "kin," and Wynn had let slip enough references to orbs—the anchors. Perhaps some of that had come from the majay-hì they called Chap. A few times Ghassan had seen strange things concerning that one.

Then there was the other black majay-hì called Shade.

Two descended from a Fay-born race, one little renegade sage, a half-blood, and a dhampir—half-undead—had sought out the orbs. A fallen

Lhoin'na sage who traveled via the gift of a fabled tree, supposedly as old as the world itself, had joined them. And along the way there had been too many tenuous connections he had overheard in his prison as those with Khalidah sought to recover all of the anchors . . . of Existence.

Ghassan knew theories of the Elements—and there was one orb for each. If they were "anchors," and even one was opened to free what it anchored . . .

Existence itself—everything—would end.

Ghassan had failed so many times against the specter, even to the loss of his own flesh. It had kept him alive within it merely as a resource, if needed. And he knew what had happened to all other such hosts it had taken.

He could not defeat Khalidah, but he would not need to do so.

Leesil heard every hissing whisper of the Enemy, as if those words had been spoken aloud to echo through the cavern. He was left at a loss for their meaning, and he second-guessed opening the orbs, one or all.

Why would something that thought itself a god want to die? Why would it want them to kill it? While Ghassan appeared lost in some seething thought, Leesil looked from one companion to another. There was only one that he could trust now.

Chane hadn't heard the whisper—because of his ring—and didn't know what the Enemy wanted.

"Chane," Leesil whispered, "don't let . . . anyone . . . anyone . . ."

Suddenly, his voice failed, and he couldn't make a sound.

Chane stared at him. "What? Do not let anyone what?"

Leesil tried to answer but couldn't. Both his hands opened of their own accord, and he dropped his winged blades.

He felt a weight lift from around his neck, and as his hand came up, he was holding Magiere's thôrhk. He didn't even know he'd removed it until he saw it in his hand. He tried to turn but couldn't.

He could see Chane looking away, looking at something beyond him, and still he couldn't turn his head. Instead, he faced the orb chests in the cavern's entrance. As he took a step toward them, he saw Ore-Locks doing the same. In panic, he struggled to look for Brot'an, and then . . .

Chane's face twisted, lips separating over elongated fangs. He half crouched for a rush, then twisted and stumbled back as if struck by something unseen. Again, and again, and the third time, he wrenched backward, toppling and flipping across the cavern's rough floor.

Everything around Leesil became fuzzy, like a half-remembered dream upon waking, as he took another step toward the chests.

Brot'an heard Léshil falter in speech and then saw him reach up blindly to remove Magiere's thôrhk. Instantly, Brot'an fixed on Ghassan, who stood passive, still, and silent. Ore-Locks copied Léshil's every action, as if he were under the same influence.

Chane tried to rush Ghassan and was somehow thrown backward.

As Chane's feet left the cavern's floor, Brot'an flicked loose the tie holding his left stiletto. The blade's handle dropped against his left palm as he pulled the bone knife from behind his back.

Ghassan's head began to turn his way.

Brot'an threw himself back and left over the smaller vertebrae of the skeleton's tailbone looping toward its skull. He ducked and half crouched against the larger vertebrae near that skull. Inside his mind, he repeated a litany:

The stillness of thought is a silence, unheard and unnoticed.

The silence of flesh leaves only shadow, impenetrable and intangible.

Mind and body but not spirit became one with the shadows, and as Brot'an watched, Ghassan's expression shifted to shock.

The domin backed away, spun around, and looked everywhere in trying to find his vanished target. He back-stepped even farther and then turned to reacquire his original targets.

Both Léshil and Ore-Locks faltered in shuffling toward the chests. Chane rose, stumbled, and tried to pick up one dropped sword. Again, at Ghassan's glance, the undead flew backward, and he slammed into the far wall with an audible crack.

Brot'an did not move in thought or flesh. Though shadow held and hid both, spirit alone kept his presence and awareness. Deep within he already knew who had to be saved most of all.

Léshil was somehow the way to kill the Enemy, if it was truly here.

And Brot'an believed it was, for he had finally realized that it had a tool among them. He watched Ghassan without conscious thought. He had set his next action deep within himself before vanishing. He waited in stillness for Chane's next attack to trigger his own reaction. And when that came . . .

Leesil's forced steps faltered just before he heard someone grunt amid a clatter of something striking stone. That was quickly followed by the rough sound of someone falling on the cavern floor.

For that instant, nothing drove Leesil forward, and he was able to barely turn his head.

He saw Ore-Locks do the same with visible effort. His last clear glimpse of Chane had been of the vampire trying to pick himself up.

Leesil knew Ghassan was still somewhere behind him. His body lurched, his hand clenched tighter upon Magiere's thôrhk, and one of his feet slid forward. However he and Ore-Locks were being controlled, Chane was not affected. And the one person Leesil hadn't seen anywhere was Brot'an.

He knew the old assassin's tactics.

Brot'an must have shifted to the cavern's far side and melded into the shadows, but if he even moved, the shadows wouldn't hide him anymore. Unlike Chane with his ring, if the domin fixed on Brot'an, he might be able to use Brot'an against Chane.

There was only one way to give Brot'an an instant to strike.

Chane had to move the other way to draw Ghassan's attention.

Leesil fought to speak, but only two words came out: "Chane . . . orbs . . ."

Chane's head felt as if it had split as he struggled up. He knew he was damaged without feeling for the wound at the back of his skull. The cavern dimmed and blurred again and again, and he struggled to keep his feet. Then he realized both of his hands were empty.

There was something long but blurred near his left foot. That glint had to be his older, ground-down blade and not the mottled steel of his dwarven longsword. When he tried to reach down for it, he nearly lost his balance and stopped.

What had happened with the others?

They had heard something, but he had not. Had it tampered with their awareness? Then Ghassan had focused upon Leesil and Ore-Locks, and both had turned away.

Chane had realized then that Ghassan was the traitor among them. But Brot'an had somehow vanished into the skeleton, and there was no one else left able to stop Ghassan.

When Chane lifted his head, Leesil and Ore-Locks were only blurs in the half-light. Before he had hit the wall, both of them had lurched and shuffled strangely toward the cavern's entrance. He tried to reach again for one of his weapons and heard . . .

"Chane . . . orbs . . ."

He froze and looked. He still could not see Leesil clearly, but it was the half-blood's voice that he had heard. What about the orbs?

He thought he understood, though it was a deadly ploy.

What if even one orb was taken away? Could Ghassan accomplish anything if that happened? However, any one of the orbs' presence had always sated Chane's hunger.

He needed hunger now.

He needed to find a way to call it up.

Chane let himself fall and collapse upon that blur of one sword. As he hunched there, he clawed at it blindly, until he gripped its hilt. He needed to hunt, to feed, and to kill.

Once he had freely reveled in the beast within him—that was him—for the pleasure it had brought. He had given that up, pushed it down, and chained it, in order to be what Wynn might want. Now he had to be that thing—that monster—he never wished to see reflected in her eyes.

And if he did not, and she still lived . . .

Chane loosed the thing chained down for so long within him as he held to only one thought—an orb.

Khalidah panicked for the first time since the dhampir had rammed his previous host out of an empty manor's window back in the empire's capital. The elder assassin had vanished without a trace.

No matter how much Khalidah probed for any presence, he could not find Brot'an. That was impossible. Even though he could not reach Chane's mind, he could see that one. All he could do was drive the half-blood and dwarf, but even in that, he had to split his awareness a third way to remain sensitive to other mental presences that might reappear in the cavern.

Brot'an was still here—somewhere—and would never flee, so how did he evade detection? How? This fearful, irate wondering cost him.

"Chane . . . get to . . . orbs . . ."

At Leesil's stuttered whisper, Khalidah exerted his will to silence the half-blood. He glanced aside, looking for Chane. The undead was on his hands and knees, broken and cowering, so Khalidah looked to the dwarf and then to the half-blood again.

Without warning, Chane lunged from the floor, rushing at the half-blood.

Bending Leesil and the dwarf to his will was nothing to Khalidah, and even splitting his awareness a third time to remain aware for Brot'an was only slightly trying. But Chane, his mind hidden though he remained visible, was another matter.

This time, Khalidah would smash that undead to pulp upon stone.

Chane rushed by the half-blood without pause.

Khalidah flinched at that, focused on Chane . . . and inexplicably blinked.

Ghassan felt Khalidah's shock as Chane rushed for the chests holding the orbs.

Somewhere in the cavern, the elder assassin hid his presence. As Khalidah split his focus again to fix upon Chane, Ghassan struck out with the last of his near-broken will.

All he needed was an instant of control for a breach of focus—just a *blink*.

When it happened, torment followed with the specter's outrage.

You . . . I am done with you! I no longer need even your memories!

Within the prison of his own mind, Ghassan burned as if set afire. In so much sudden pain, he could not even scream, though none would have heard him.

His suffering ended suddenly.

Ghassan floundered in the darkness, but even then, he tried to reach for and hold on to Khalidah's presence yet again.

It took but an instant.

At Chane's lunge and Ghassan's wayward glance, Brot'an sprang and vaulted the skeleton's tailbone. He matched every running step to the sound of Chane's footfalls to mask his approach. In three steps, he reached his target.

There was one strike that might kill quicker than a sorcerer's thought.

Brot'an wrapped his left arm around Ghassan's throat as he rammed the stiletto's tip up into the back of the domin's skull.

*   *   *

Leesil saw Chane rush by toward the chests, and then he lurched to a sudden halt. He almost fell forward and for an instant didn't realize he could move freely. Chane's distraction had worked, and Leesil knew he needed to act quickly.

He dropped Magiere's thôrhk, grabbed up both fallen winged blades, and spun, ignoring Chane. Again he stalled.

Ghassan stood with eyes wide and mouth slack, a thick arm around his throat. His own hands gripped tightly to either side of that arm's elbow, but he didn't move.

"Chane?" Ore-Locks shouted somewhere to the left. "Chane!"

"Stop him," Leesil ordered without looking. "Any way you have to."

Ghassan's head lurched slightly forward, eyes rolling up under his lids. Behind him stood Brot'an with his other hand hidden behind the domin's head, and Leesil knew what the elder assassin had done.

It was over for the moment. The traitor among them was dead.

Ghassan's eyes snapped open, narrowed viciously, and his hands released Brot'an's arm to thrust up and back for the master assassin's head.

Leesil charged while cocking back one blade.

Brot'an suddenly found himself in darkness and silence. He felt numb in thought and flesh, as if he had neither, though he could still somehow look about. Darkness—impenetrable shadow—was everywhere, as if he had sunk into it once more in mind and body.

It had taken the whole world as well.

The cavern, his target, the bones, the others . . . were gone. Never in his long life had he ever been so completely without sound.

"Since you took my flesh, it is only fitting that I take yours." He heard—felt—something barely perceptible shift in the black void.

Someone stepped out of the surrounding darkness into view: a man. He was smallish, bald, and wizened. His eyes were black, and he wore a simple robe. His face shone with hatred.

As that visage closed on Brot'an, he merely waited . . . until it was close enough. The instant was interrupted as something else took form behind the old one out of the pure darkness. Domin Ghassan il'Sänke rushed in without a sound behind the wizened one.

I know you now . . . all that you are . . . by your own thoughts.

Brot'an heard this, though Ghassan's mouth never moved. As their gazes locked, the domin silently clamped his hands over the old one's eyes. As he pulled that bald head back, its mouth opened and its lips curled in a snarl.

"Worm! How did you follow me to new flesh?"

Again, the domin's mouth did not move. *Finish this . . . as only you can.*

The old one's hands clamped over the domin's own. "I am done with you!"

White fire flickered on and within those old hands. It quickly spread into the domin's.

Ghassan screamed as those flames illuminating nothing else in the dark spread over him, even to his anguished face.

Brot'ân'duivé lunged in. Without realizing he could, he clamped both hands around the old one's throat. White flame spread onto his own flesh. There was no wound or agony in his life to match this.

Still he tightened his grip.

There was a third shadow beyond that which took mind and body.

Only if spirit remained could one emerge from shadow once more.

This secret was learned—or not—in the first step upon the path of a greimasg'äh, a "shadow-gripper." Many failed in that moment, which was why so few of them walked among the Anmaglâhk.

Brot'ân'duivé's agony was only a sign that life still remained. Both would end as he let shadow take his spirit and that of all others with him inside his last shadow.

That Léshil—Léshiârelaohk, "Sorrow-Tear's Champion"—survived for their people's sake was all that mattered to the Dog in the Dark.

Leesil rammed his right blade's spade into Ghassan's chest with all of his force and weight. The tip tore through fabric and sank in nearly to his grip as he rammed the other blade in. He wrenched them both out to strike again.

Ghassan crumpled, as did Brot'an, and the first fell across the second, both on their backs.

Leesil dropped atop them, one knee crushing down into the domin's blood-soaked clothes as he raised his right blade to strike for the throat. He hesitated at the blank eyes staring up at him.

Neither of them blinked—not Ghassan or Brot'an. Both stared up sightlessly into the cavern, their faces slack and expressionless.

Leesil pulled, rolled, and kicked Ghassan's body off.

"Brot'an?" he whispered, and then louder, "Brot'an!"

The master assassin didn't move.

"He is gone."

At that rasp, Leesil twisted on one knee to find Chane—and Ore-Locks—standing behind him.

"I would . . . know," Chane added, his gaze locked on Brot'an.

Chane didn't look good. He was shuddering, and his eyes were still colorless. Leesil looked back down.

He didn't know what to think or feel.

Ghassan had turned on all of them, and there was no knowing how or why. Brot'an didn't have any new wounds, and yet he was dead. What had just happened?

—Now you are the only one—

Leesil lurched to his feet, instinctively facing the immense horned skull.

—My death . . . no, my freedom . . . means yours as well—

The Enemy was still here, in some way.

Leesil looked everywhere but saw nothing, not even the shadow of an immense coiled serpent or dragon as in the cavern below the six-towered castle. What little light was present led his eyes to Ghassan's crystal on the cavern floor, likely dropped in the struggle with Brot'an.

He sheathed one blade, grabbed up the crystal, and raised it high, again looking everywhere. Somewhere outside the mountain, the battle went on.

Leesil didn't want to imagine what had happened to Magiere if this unseen thing could no longer find her. Then he felt a light grip on his arm over the branch lashed onto it.

Ore-Locks uttered a sharp exclamation in his own tongue.

"Wynn?" Chane rasped.

Leesil lurched back, pulling out of that grip, and there was a startled Chuillyon quickly raising his hands. Behind the tall elf stood Wynn, still lightly gripping Chuillyon's robe as she looked blankly down at the cavern floor. She had her staff in her other hand.

Chap startled Leesil yet again as he came around from behind Chuillyon.

—Kin . . . treacherous kin of my kin—

Chap froze just short of Leesil as he heard that hiss. Judging from the way Leesil had turned about, he had heard it as well, as had Ore-Locks. Only Chane did not react, and then Chap saw the bodies.

Ghassan and Brot'an both lay unblinking with eyes open. Both looked battered, but only the former was bloodied.

Chap looked to Leesil's stained blade, and yet there was no time to question whatever had happened here.

Chane rushed around him to Wynn. Though she turned at his movement, she did not—could not—look at him.

There was no time for that either.

—And why do my kin send one of their guard . . . dogs—

That hiss sounded—felt—somehow familiar. By the light from a crystal that Leesil gripped, Chap studied the skeleton. Dead for so long, those bones might have almost melded with the stone if not for their size. He looked up to Leesil.

—*Do . . . nothing . . . yet*—

"Where's Magiere?" Leesil asked, quick-stepping in.

"She's with Osha and Wayfarer," Wynn answered, though her eyes focused on nothing. "With Shade and the Shé'ith commander also; they hid her away in the foothills."

—*Enough . . . listen!*—

At Chap's sharp demand, Leesil flinched.

"Wynn?" Chane rasped. "What is wrong? Look at me!"

Before Chap could say anything, Wynn reached out, groping for a grip on Chane's arm.

"Not now," she told him.

—*So, dog, you have power to command the others*—

The tone of that hissing, both in Chap's ears and in his head, was so disdainful. It was also too much like the chorus of whispers when he communed with his kin, and too much like the voices when he had touched the orb of Spirit, though now there was only one voice.

He answered it.

—*No*—

The voice then filled with rage or panic or both.

—*Open the anchors, whelp, or I will summon even more of my servants. And none of your companions, your wards, will ever leave this place*—

Chap tilted his head.

—*There is no one left to call, or you would have called them . . . called her*—

"What's happening?" Leesil asked. "What did you say to it?"

Chap ignored this distraction. It would not be hard to know to whom the Enemy now spoke, though no one else here could have heard his own answer. No one except perhaps Wynn, and she was wise enough not to let the Enemy know so.

A moment of silence followed, and then . . .

—*I can call upon hundreds to hunt you for the rest of your short days . . . and nights. Oh, yes, especially the nights. Even if you are not found, I remain when you are food for worms and then forgotten dust*—

That one word—"forgotten"—lingered in Chap's thoughts.

How much longer than a thousand forgotten years of history had it been since the Fay, the One and the Many, made a world—an existence—to escape nothingness? How many times had all of this happened before, as one of five among those who had sacrificed for the others sought to be free again?

—*Why do you sympathize with those who call you deviant? You and I are not so different in that*—

"Chap," Leesil whispered, "what in seven hells is happening?"

"Leesil, shut up!" Wynn warned.

And yet Chap hesitated.

—*Order the mixed-blood to open the anchors . . . and free me*—

Chap was at a loss. A part of him could feel empathy for the voice, after what his kin had done to him. He no longer believed his losses of memory from his time among his kin had been by his own choice. They had done that to him.

Had they likewise tricked those of their own who had made such a sacrifice for the rest to have an Existence? And still . . .

—*No*—

At his simple refusal, the hiss became pleading in tone.

—*I am weary . . . and wish to* be *no more*—

After all of the hints that Chap had heard and pieced together, he knew the last of that statement was a lie. Destroying the Enemy would mean removing one of what the sages called the Elements from among the other four. To do so would unmake Existence.

Why would it want such a thing?

Chap ground his paws and claws against the cavern floor's stone. He called upon the element of Earth first, letting it fill him. From there he reached for Water from any moisture in the cavern. Then Air, and then Fire from the heat of his own flesh.

He asked: —*Who*—*what*—*are you?*—

With that single question, he began to burn in blue-white flame as he added his own Spirit. This time, no one would see this, for Wynn was blind.

Chap launched his thoughts into the dark. His *self* as a Fay broke loose, and the cave around him vanished. In that darkness, weightless and bodiless, he felt it . . . that other timeless presence, so mournful, spiteful, and chained. And through it, he looked back as far as he could and learned much more than he had forced from his kin.

We will create Existence. We will enliven it with Spirit.

Five distinct and separate presences among his kind could be heard: Earth, Water, Fire, Air, and Spirit. But one of them—Spirit—rebelled, as Chap had in his own way after being born into flesh. It wailed in panic.

Once something is created, there is no power to control it.

Its—Chap's—kin did not listen.

Existence came to be, time itself formed without beginning or end, and Spirit wailed out again.

Less and less can this be controlled. Undo what we have done.

And again, it was ignored. The other four swarmed upon and subjugated Spirit to "anchor" it among them. Eons passed, a world formed, and the first lives upon it were born.

That which grew and that which moved; that which nourished and that which consumed.

The first tree and the first dragon.

So much later came other forms, and then the Úirishg—elves, dwarves, Séyilf, Chein'âs, and the sea-people were born and spread. From their mingling came humans.

But it—Spirit—the Enemy to be—had escaped in part.

Even in that formless darkness, Chap envisioned the bones in the cavern.

Once living, even its unimaginable long life came to an end, for that which consumed was itself consumed.

Spirit could never end this way. That fragment of it in the dead flesh became something other than life, something opposite: a death that still lived as the first undead. And even so, still it was trapped, enslaved, anchored.

Anguish turned to hate. From that, came the thirteen Children such as Li'kän, Volyno, and others. They in turn created more of their kind that mingled among the living as the Enemy gathered its forces.

Lost in the endless memories of Spirit—the Enemy—that voice in eternal night, Chap watched battle after battle. There was nothing else in its memories except for its own anguish and anger. Atrocities of blood and death overwhelmed Chap until he fought and struggled to shut them out.

From spite, the Night Voice used its own forces and found a way to enslave those who had enslaved it, and it trapped pieces of their essences— Earth, Water, Air, and Fire—within stone orbs. It created a fifth for itself as a way to anchor the others to it.

But no matter the destruction and suffering, it could not break free.

It sank into anguish again and slunk away to a hidden place . . . until the next time. And it all began again.

Memories grew vague, and everything went black. Finally Chap could not take any more. He tried to escape as the memories began again. He heard it whispering once more to its Children after a thousand years.

Find the anchors . . .

Chap tried to pull out, to break away, and could not.

Leesil remained still and quiet as he watched Chap. The dog had gone rigid, his crystal blue eyes fixed on nothing, and not once had Leesil heard the hissing voice in his head after that. But the more he watched, the more a soft glow began spreading over Chap's body.

Leesil couldn't hold off any longer. "Chap!"

His oldest friend didn't answer. He took a step and then hesitated. What could he possibly do to stop whatever was happening? He glanced to Wynn, but she wouldn't see any of this, so he turned to Chuillyon.

"What do I do?"

Chuillyon was staring wide-eyed at the dog. He started, as if suddenly awakening, and shook his head once.

"I do not know," he whispered. "Whatever has taken the majay-hì must be broken."

Wynn twisted toward Chuillyon's voice. She took a sudden step and stumbled. Chane grabbed her arm to steady her.

"Do not open the orbs!" she cried. "That is what it wants. We cannot destroy it. It has to be trapped, once and for all, somehow. Even Chap would tell you that is more important than saving him."

None of this was any help to Leesil in trying to help Chap. And even if he helped Chap, how could he or any of them trap something without a body that could reach across the world to anything unliving . . . undead?

He was sick to death of death itself. Two had died here in this place, and how many more had died below the mountain?

"Untie the branch," Chuillyon instructed.

Leesil's mind went blank. He followed the elder elf's eyes to the branch that Wynn had lashed to his forearm. Yes, of course it had been the way for the others to come here with Chuillyon, but what good was it for anything else?

It had been given to him by the long-dead ancestors of the an'Cróan when he'd gone for name-taking just to save Magiere. One of those ghosts had given it to him.

It came from Roise Chârmune in a land where no undead could walk.

"Plant it there!" Chuillyon whispered harshly, pointing toward the immense skeleton.

Leesil never had a chance to respond.

Chap collapsed upon the cavern floor, and Leesil had barely dropped down beside him when he heard the hissing.

—*No! If you wish to end me, open the anchors!*—

Leesil grabbed Chap's head, trying to see whether the dog was all right.

Chap pulled his head free and, after one glance at the branch still lashed to Leesil's arm, he looked up.

—*Set that . . . close to . . . the bones*—

The hiss rose again, this time without words, filling Leesil's head and the cavern with a sound like a whirlwind.

Still Leesil hesitated. By his mother's training as an anmaglâhk, he knew to act instantly. His human half warned caution. Would the branch trap or destroy the Enemy? Was he about to unmake Existence? Had those ghosts known anything when they'd given him the branch and put another name on him?

Leesil . . . Léshil . . . Léshiârelaohk . . . "Sorrow-Tear's Champion."

None of this was enough. There was only one thing he could depend upon now without question—Chap.

Leesil dropped his blade and unlashed the branch. He sprang at a run toward the bones, not knowing how he could plant a branch in stone.

Wynn, unable to see anything, only heard fast footfalls amid the rushing like a wind from somewhere else, for the air around her felt still.

"Who has water?"

She knew that was Chuillyon, but before she could answer, another voice did.

"I do," Ore-Locks called.

"Wynn, I need you to—," Chuillyon began.

"I know," she cut in, and then, "Chane, get out of here."

"No, I am not leaving you," he rasped, lightly gripping her arm. "And there is nowhere to go."

"She is right," said Ore-Locks, his voice now closer, "if I guess correctly at what the elf is up to with the half-blood. Get into the tunnel and stay out of sight of this cavern."

Wynn waited, but Chane did not leave.

"Get out now," she said, "or you will burn!"

"I'll look after her," Ore-Locks said, then added, "I swear."

Wynn felt his large hand press gently against her upper arm, and yet Chane still had not released her other one.

"Go!" she insisted.

His hand was suddenly gone, and Ore-Locks's hand slid around her back. His other arm swept up her legs as he lifted her.

"What are you doing?"

"No time for you to stumble about," he answered.

"Come quickly!" Chuillyon shouted. Then Wynn was bouncing in Ore-Locks's arms as the dwarf ran. All she could think of was whether she had the strength to ignite the staff once more. In answer to that, over the sound of the false wind and Ore-Locks's heavy footfalls, she heard Chap in her head.

—*I am with you, little one.*—

With the branch in one hand and the cold-lamp crystal in the other, Leesil vaulted the skeleton's arced tailbone. As he landed, he felt something like a low shudder building in the cavern's floor, as if that hiss like a torrent of wind was carried within the stone instead of in the air.

He ran on, ducked in near the base of the great skull, and then hesitated. He had no idea what he was doing. He laid down the crystal, thrust the broken end of the branch into the stone floor with both hands, and stood watching it.

Nothing happened—except a crackle and sudden buck of the stone beneath him.

*   *   *

Chuillyon rolled over the tailbone in his long robe, which was not convenient at all. The last time Wynn had lit her staff, it had taken help from the young follower of the priestess to do so.

It was not enough to simply plant the branch.

He had placed similar sprouts more than once before at the great tree's bidding. The branch might hold at bay whatever still lingered in this place, but it could not be held so forever: like its parent—or its grandparent, Chârmun—it had to live and take root.

As Ore-Locks leaped atop the tailbone, Chuillyon regained his feet and did not wait to ask. Spotting the waterskin tied at the back of the dwarf's belt, he grabbed it and jerked it free.

This was only the first need.

Then he felt and heard a great crack of stone. He did not want to see from where that came and ran on, following Wynn as the dwarf dropped her on her feet beside the half-blood.

Chuillyon pulled the skin's stopper as he came in behind Leesil.

Leesil looked up as the others came in around him, but Chane was missing. For some reason, that panicked him, and he looked back over his shoulder. Ore-Locks dropped Wynn on her feet, blocking his view, and then Chuillyon crouched beside him, a waterskin in his hands.

"You must want this," the elder elf nearly shouted, for the noise in the cavern kept growing. "The branch is a living thing, and you are its caretaker. It will know what you *feel* for it."

What in seven hells did that mean?

Chuillyon shoved the waterskin at him. "Take it, for you must do this! That sprout—that branch—was not bestowed upon me."

Leesil didn't hesitate, though he wasn't fully certain what would happen. There was no soil here; only hard, dark stone beneath the branch's bottom end.

Chap shoved his head in and looked up at him.

—*Now!*—

Leesil upended the waterskin, pouring its contents over the branch with his other hand.

Was that all it would take?

Small root tendrils sprouted from the branch's base. They curled like animate limbs. The hissing rose to the sound of a hurricane, deafening in Leesil's ears. A shudder in stone made him lose his footing. He dropped to his knees, holding the branch in place.

"Wynn—light!" Chuillyon shouted.

Wynn understood without seeing, for she had to. She was exhausted and in pain, and hoped Chane had done as she asked.

Something damp and long pushed in under her free hand and licked it.

—*I am still here and will grip the staff to do what I can*—

Wynn felt the staff jostle and jerk slightly, and she gripped it with both hands, hoping whatever Chap did might help.

"Wynn!" Chuillyon shouted.

She whispered the words aloud, hoping that would help.

"Mên Rúhk el-När . . . mênajil il'Núr'u mên'Hkâ'ät."

Chap twisted his head to one side and bit down on the staff. He did not wait for Wynn to begin, and once again called upon all Elements, ending with his own Spirit.

He heard Wynn's whisper, and the staff lit up with the strength of the sun. He shut his eyes tight against the glare.

*   *   *

Leesil flinched as the glare washed over him. He had to duck his head and squint as he looked down, and just before he saw, he heard stone crack again.

The branch's roots expanded and punched into the cavern's floor. As stone cracked, he heard the hiss become a wail, tearing at his ears. Those tendrils from the branch coiled and snaked into fractured openings in stone.

Silence fell so suddenly that every muscle in his body clenched.

"Less!" Chuillyon shouted, and then lowered his voice. "Too much, Wynn, too much light."

Chap appeared at Leesil's side before the light began to soften, bit by bit, and then he realized the next problem. Wynn could not hold the crystal lit forever.

—*She . . . will not . . . need . . . to do so*—

Leesil looked aside, but Chap was only staring at the branch. Other than rooting by the base and tendrils, it looked much the same. Was it truly still alive? Would it grow to something more that would end everything that started here?

And exactly how did Chap think the staff's crystal could go on without Wynn?

Chap turned and was almost blinded by the staff's crystal. Only Wynn's eyes were fully open, for she would never see what was done here. For an instant, this pained him more than he could bear, but she was not the one he needed now. Chap dropped his head, half closing his eyes, as he stepped around behind Wynn.

When he had line of sight to Ore-Locks, the dwarf had one hand raised, shielding his eyes.

—*Can you . . . plant . . . the staff . . . into stone?*—

Ore-Locks's black-pellet eyes shifted to fix on Chap.

—The staff . . . must touch . . . the branch . . . forever—

Then he looked to Wynn, who was always so much easier to speak to.

—Let Ore-Locks lead you by the staff, but do not let go until I tell you—

That Ore-Locks—or any stonewalker—was here at all was blind luck. Then again, how much else of what had led them to this moment seemed that way? The dwarf had been gifted an orb by the flesh descendants of "that which consumes" and befriended by one of the Enemy's tools, an undead. And a half-blood had been given a descendant of "that which nourishes."

There were some things even a Fay-descended would never know.

There were some things he could only hope would work now and forever.

Ore-Locks carefully led Wynn closer to the branch. Leesil shifted where he knelt but kept his grip as he squinted at Chap. As Ore-Locks knelt and slid his grip on the staff down to its bottom end, Chap looked to Leesil again.

—Branch . . . and . . . staff . . . together—

Leesil took a loose hold on Wynn's staff as Ore-Locks set its base against the branch. He watched as the young stonewalker, a guardian of the dead, sank one broad hand into stone along with the staff's base. Ore-Locks withdrew his hand with an audible sigh.

Leesil waited, half looking up with barely open eyes, though he did not look as far as the crystal. Instead, he looked to Wynn's grip.

Chap huffed once—and Wynn let go.

The crystal's light dimmed to a softer glow and held steady.

No one said a word. Everything was too quiet until . . .

"And that is that," Chuillyon half whispered.

Leesil wasn't certain he believed this.

"What about the orbs?" Wynn asked.

Twisting about, Leesil looked toward the cavern's entrance and barely made out the nearest chest. Closer still were the bodies of Brot'an and Ghassan, and somewhere beyond those chests, Chane must have hidden himself in the dark.

Leesil looked back to Ore-Locks.

"Can you sink the orbs as well? Hide them in stone?"

Ore-Locks's eyes widened. He looked down at the branch resting against the staff, and then up again. He nodded once. "Yes."

"Not all of them," Wynn said. "One . . . you know the one . . . should be placed next to the branch, Spirit trapped forever with Spirit."

Leesil didn't understand that and was suspicious for a moment. Then again, he didn't really care. So long as the other four couldn't ever be used again, the one would be close to worthless, and no undead would ever reach it beneath the ignited staff.

"Then I'm guessing Chuillyon can get us out of here the same way you came in," he said.

Chap answered first, before Wynn could speak.

—*Yes . . . he left his . . . sprout . . . with . . . Osha and Wayfarer*—

"We'll need to throw a cloak over the sun crystal long enough to get Chane out first," Leesil said.

No one answered him.

He rose, looked all around, and listened. Now there was no other sound in this place but his own slow breaths and those of the others. It was too quiet and still after so much and so long. He looked everywhere again for the shadow of a serpent or dragon in the air, but there was nothing.

All he wanted was to reach Magiere and never see this place again.

CHAPTER TWENTY

Chane resurfaced at the base of the mountain with Ore-Locks still gripping his arm. After such a long pass through stone, he instinctively gagged and gasped, though he did not need air. His final exit from the cavern had not gone quite as planned, and his mind was churning with all that had happened there.

Back when he had first fled the cavern and down the tunnel at Wynn's insistence, the following moments had been his longest in memory. Fretful for the others' possible failure, he had done one more thing once out of sight of the cavern.

He took the orb of Spirit from its chest and carried it all the way to the chasm's edge. As a result, his hunger vanished, and the beast inside him whimpered back into hiding.

In this way, if whatever was to happen did not work after Wynn lit her staff, and he had to return, he would not have to retrieve that one orb. All he needed to do was shove it over the edge into the deepest depths.

When Leesil came looking for him, obviously he had found one empty chest in passing. He was coldly furious and panicked, though Ore-Locks had harassed him along the way, trying to assure him that Chane would not take an orb without good reason. It was not until Chane led them to the chasm's edge and the orb that Leesil realized and accepted the truth that Chane had been trying to separate the orb of Spirit from the Enemy.

In turn, Chane did not blame him for the need to take it back once Wynn's plan for it had been explained. Ore-Locks had already buried the other four orbs in stone where they could never be found or reached. The three of them returned the last orb to the cavern. A cloak had been thrown over the sun crystal so that its light shone downward. Chane was not burned so long as he kept his distance.

However, even once the orb of Spirit was placed in against the small roots of Leesil's branch, not everything had gone well.

Chuillyon found that he could not transport Chane out of the mountain. Yes, he tried, but it did not work. The bodies of Ghassan and Brot'an could be transported, but not that of an undead. Neither the offspring of the first tree, nor Chârmun itself, would allow this, it seemed.

So Ore-Locks had taken him out through stone.

And now, here Chane was in the dark beneath the stars, still ill from the long passage. He fell to his knees as Ore-Locks released him and, before the young stonewalker could ask anything, Chane waved him off.

"I am . . . all right," he managed. "Give me a moment."

Ore-Locks did, and Chane looked northward. Somewhere out there, Chuillyon had moved the others through Leesil's planted branch to the sprout that the elder elf had left behind. Osha and Wayfarer and Shade had hidden away Magiere with that sprout, and Wynn was now there, still blind.

In the cavern, after everything had ended, Chane had looked into her light brown eyes in her oval, olive-toned face. Perhaps she had known, for she turned away from him. He had felt broken inside in ways worse than wounded flesh, and there was no way to rid himself of that sorrow, for the dead could not weep.

"Are you ready to move on?" Ore-Locks asked.

Chane slowly rose up without answering.

Chuillyon had done his best to describe where he had placed his sprout with the younger trio and Magiere. Finding that place would take only a little effort; reaching it might be more troublesome. With a final nod of agreement, Ore-Locks followed as Chane hurried down the last of the foothills below the peak.

As they neared the open plain, they slowed to a pause without a word, looking out upon the carnage. Both of them could see well at night, Chane more so.

Charred, torn, and dismembered bodies were strewn everywhere; some majay-hì and Lhoin'na lay among them. But as far as Chane could see, most of the horde was dead or scattered.

He spotted a few still moving. He heard the occasional distant moan, cry, or wail. And once, a figure too dark for even him to clearly make out flitted as if running and stopping here and there among the fallen. At least once he heard a scream cut short.

Ore-Locks did not move at these sights or sounds.

Then they heard sooner than saw Shé'ith riders harrying stragglers in flight.

Much as others might see all of this as Magiere's doing, in part, Chane saw otherwise. At the sight of so many dead, he knew this level of frenzied slaughter among the horde itself would not have happened without her. She had ignited it, and as a result, the undead servants had turned upon the horde's greater living numbers.

Without this having happened, Wynn and anyone else out here would not have survived—even with her staff.

"Enough," Ore-Locks whispered. "I have seen enough."

So had Chane.

They turned northward and drew their weapons quietly. Both remained watchful for the slightest sound or movement in the dark. It took a while to search out where the others hid. It was Ore-Locks who first spotted something in the dark, and pointed.

Chane bolted at the sight of shimmering hair near the base of one foothill.

He was still a hundred strides away when that one rose up, drew an arrow in a bow, and then froze. Chane slowed to a quick walk, so as not to startle Osha any further as he drew closer.

Osha—cut and battered—looked stricken sick. Tracks of dried tears striped the grime and dust on his face. Chane could not find any words, though some small part of him envied those tears. Osha turned away into the foothills, and Chane followed with Ore-Locks.

The first sign that they neared their destination was the spark of two crystal blue eyes in the moonlight. Shade wheeled, rushing down the deep hollow's left side, and turned inward ahead of them. Among the huddled forms farther in near the steep back, Chuillyon was nearest and rose up.

"We will wait until close to dawn," he whispered, "before we try to regain the camp or contact any allies still out there."

Osha turned back without a word, likely returning to his place on watch.

Chane agreed with waiting until close to dawn, so long as he had time to reach a tent. He looked upon the others present.

Leesil and Chap sat to one side with Wynn to the other, all looking down and toward the hollow's rear. Chane wanted to go to Wynn, though there was little space. Wayfarer was just beyond them, curled in, half lying, half leaning on one arm, and her head hung forward.

The girl pressed a scrap of cloth around a snapped arrow shaft sticking up from a still form lying on the hollow's most level spot.

Magiere's eyes were closed, her mouth barely parted. Black lines like veins ran through her pale face, neck, and arms as she lay in the remnants of her armor. The cloth Wayfarer held over the wound partway up Magiere's right shoulder was stained dark as well.

More than once, Chane had wanted to finish Magiere. Here and now it would have been so easy to do. Not even Chap or Leesil could have stopped him in time.

But his hunger for vengeance had abandoned him.

Ore-Locks pushed in at his shoulder. "Has she . . . Is she on her way to her ancestors?"

Wynn lifted her head a little at that. "No, not yet, but the arrowhead was Chein'âs metal . . . and had been dipped—"

"In the healing potion," Chane finished.

Osha had done as he had instructed.

Wynn turned her head slightly at his voice. By the light of one dim cold-lamp crystal in her hand, he noticed that she looked better now than she had in the cavern, as if she were no longer in pain, but her eyes still focused on nothing.

"Where is the rest of the potion?" he demanded. "Why have you not—"

"I tried it," Wynn said, "and gave what was left to the others, except Magiere."

Chane took a step, but Ore-Locks grabbed his arm. In hope, he almost ripped free of that grip. One word she had said made him freeze.

Tried.

Wynn looked away—looked at nothing—and the truth left Chane cold. The potion had done nothing to restore her sight.

And now he did not care about anything else. She would never again read an old tome or map, scribble away in yet another journal, or wonder in awe at anything. She would never again look upon him in the way that no one else ever had.

Osha knelt on one knee with his bow in hand atop a low crest overlooking the plain below the mountain. He watched and listened for anything that might come too close in the dark so as to make certain the others were left in peace. He longed to comfort Wynn, to see to Wayfarer and Léshil in their worries and fears, but he could not.

Now as opposed to being lost to herself, Magiere was lost *within* herself.

Her two sides waged war upon each other because of his arrow. Even if one side won, there was still the poison he had delivered on a white metal tip. Since he could do even less for her than for the others, at least he could see they were left in peace this night.

Yet even that was not the full truth.

Osha could not face what he had done to Magiere. Neither could he wipe her black-veined face from his thoughts.

Lingering near his daughter, Shade, Chap was nearly overwhelmed by too much pressing down upon him as he watched Osha walk away. So much had happened to the three youngest ones, though his daughter had somehow survived and kept Wayfarer out of the battle as much as possible. Even a father's pride in a daughter left him knotted inside; he had little to do with who she had become.

There was nothing he could do for Wayfarer as they waited for the sun and to see whether Magiere survived.

He looked to Shade, almost too black to see in the dark. At least with her, he could now speak almost as easily as with Wynn. They shared much of the small sage's voice, words, and memories.

—I must go— . . . *—Signal me if anything happens—*

Shade huffed once, and Chap loped downslope, heading after Osha. Still, he could not stop thinking of much more. Had all of this happened before?

No, not all of it, not Magiere.

The Ancient Enemy, il'Samar, Beloved, the Night Voice, had waged war a thousand years ago. But had this simply happened again and again before that? Only Magiere had been different this time from what Chap had learned, and of course those with her, including himself.

The Enemy had made the Children to recover its tools—the orbs, the anchors—each time it arose again. But this time it had made and used Magiere for that purpose. Had it seen in her, its child, a true escape rather than decimating what its kin had created? To it, the world and Existence were a prison.

Chap had now helped to enslave it again, a final time. What else could he or any of them have done? But it had cost much to do so.

Wynn might never see again. Magiere might not survive. If not, a part of Leesil would die with her, and a part of Chap as well.

Brot'an was gone, and though Chap could not help some relief in that, how it had happened left him suspicious. In what he had gathered from the memories and words of those who were there, the last strike of the assassin's blade should have killed anyone instantly. Yet Ghassan had seized Brot'an's head, and then both had died as Leesil struck.

Or had that been Ghassan il'Sänke at all? In flesh perhaps, but what else? Had the specter truly died in the imperial capital, or had it only let its enemies think so?

Too many losses, not all in death, left Chap desperate.

When Chuillyon had first brought their small group out of the mountain, he had tried several times to reach Magiere's thoughts. What he had found in her was like what had been left in the guide he had possessed in the northern wastes.

There was nothing inside Magiere, not a single thought to be reached.

The longer she lingered, the worse the end would be for everyone. Chap could not save himself or Leesil from that. But he needed to save someone . . . anyone.

As he neared where Osha knelt on one knee facing out toward the plain, he could tell that his approach had already been heard and identified. If not, the young an'Cróan would have turned upon any potential threat.

Osha remained facing out into the night, even when Chap was three steps away.

And what could Chap possibly say? Certainly not that Osha's act had been necessary and the only choice. Osha already knew this.

—*Hard choices . . . are . . . hard . . . to live . . . with*—

Osha did not move or look back.

—You . . . did not . . . choose . . . alone—

Osha's head lowered slightly, but Chap could not tell if he had heard a sigh or a hiss escaping through clenched teeth.

"I had the final choice . . . to act!" Osha rasped too much like Chane.

Chap hesitated. So much had been broken or ruined for Osha.

From the Chein'âs tearing him from his place among the Anmaglâhk to Brot'an's coldhearted training in their exile as traitors, and now to possibly killing a respected friend.

Of course, Osha alone was not wholly responsible, not even for using the potion Chane had given him. In fury fed by so many undead around Magiere, Chap knew even he might have been the one to finish her—or she him. Osha's action had given them both a hair-thin chance to survive.

But that choice had cost Osha too much, and therein lay yet more guilt for Chap.

—And we . . . live . . . because . . . you did . . . act—

Osha glared back over his shoulder.

—Go to . . . the others— . . . *—They . . . suffer . . . too—* . . . *—I will . . . watch . . . here—*

Among all other losses, had the young an'Cróan lost respect for majay-hì, the guardians of his lost homeland? Then again, perhaps it was only Chap whom Osha no longer held in awe.

Without a word, the young one rose, strode back into the foothills, and left Chap with only his discomforting thoughts of Magiere.

By dawn, there might be one less of those who had unwittingly come to stop the end of Existence itself.

Leesil sat with his arms wrapped around his knees as he stared unblinking at his still, silent, and marred wife.

As badly off as Magiere was, they'd decided not to remove the end of

Osha's arrow from her yet. Wayfarer kept applying scraps of cloth torn off her own clothes to control the blood leaking around the embedded arrow. Those scraps came away stained in black, like the fluids of an undead, instead of red. This went on and on so long that Leesil didn't know how much of the night had passed.

If Magiere didn't awaken by dawn, he feared she never would.

He never should've let her come here. He should've just done this without her, no matter how she'd have fought him. It didn't matter what she had or hadn't done, horde or not, undead or not. There could have been another way, even if he couldn't think of it right now.

The sound of approaching footsteps reached him, but he didn't look back. The steps halted, and he heard Chuillyon rise to meet whoever had come.

"No change," the tall elf whispered.

Leesil heard Wynn shift at that, but he didn't look at her either. Likely Chane still crouched behind her. Leesil knew he should feel awful for what had happened to Wynn, but here and now all of his fear was only for his wife.

Wayfarer looked up and beyond him, shook her head once, and he knew Osha must have come back. Still, Leesil couldn't take his eyes off Magiere's marred face. He'd had enough, no matter the risk.

"Move aside," he ordered.

Wayfarer looked his way, and her large green eyes filled with panic by the dim cold-lamp crystal left near Magiere.

"Do not," the girl pleaded. "Please! She might not—"

"Get out of the way," Leesil warned.

"Do not be foolish!" Ore-Locks said. "Whatever the potion on the arrowhead, it is already in her. Bleeding will only weaken her more in fighting it."

Leesil reached out and grabbed Wayfarer's arm. In the last instant, he eased his grip but still firmly pulled her away.

"Please wait," Wynn insisted. "At least until you see some sign, before you risk making things worse."

Ignoring Wynn, Leesil pushed Wayfarer off behind, knelt at Magiere's side, and flattened one hand around the base of the arrow's snapped shaft. Someone behind him—Osha or Chuillyon or maybe even Ore-Locks—took a step.

He didn't think about whom to trust to not get in his way. There was only one person who hadn't shown interest in that.

"Chane," Leesil said without looking, "keep them back."

Another breath passed before he heard Chane rise.

"What? Don't do this!" Wynn begged. "She is too weak."

Whether that was for him or Chane, Leesil didn't care. He only hoped that what little of Magiere remained could still fight to do what was needed. There had to be enough of the dhampir left to close that wound before she bled out.

He gripped the stub of the arrow's shaft with his other hand.

Night came again outside the tent, though a cold-lamp crystal glowed faintly between the bedrolls inside. Next to that were a waterskin, a small cup carved from a goat's horn, and a bit of oiled cloth holding jerked goat's meat and shriveled figs.

Magiere hadn't touched anything but the water.

Outside, she could hear Leesil still pacing.

The voices of the others in the camp were too muted to hear clearly. There was also the soft crackle of the campfire, its light flickering against the tent's canvas, except when Leesil's pacing blocked the light, time and again. Sitting there, looking at her own arms, Magiere couldn't bear to have anyone see her, even in the dark, for while her body had nearly healed already, she knew theirs had not.

She'd taken as many wounds as any of them, probably more. Though Wynn had shared out the last of Chane's healing potion among the others, there hadn't been much to go around. Some would need much more time before the physical marks of what they'd been through finally faded.

Magiere continued looking at her arms.

Closed cuts barely showed at all. There were only hints of yellowing in her pale skin where there had once been bruises from blunt force. Even those would vanish in another day—two at the most.

Not so for any of the others. Not for what she'd put them through. And she didn't even remember what Osha had done.

Magiere pulled down on the jerkin's collar, one that wasn't hers and had been scavenged from somewhere after her own clothing had been cut off her. She lowered her eyes to see the wound—or now scar—from Osha's arrow.

She kept staring, for she'd never seen any scar on her own flesh.

When she'd first awoken two nights ago, she hadn't even known what had happened. She'd simply looked upward into Leesil's panicked, wide, amber eyes, not even sure whom she saw. Hanging over her, he'd suddenly twisted away and shouted—or screamed.

"Chap! She's awake!"

The following moments were still vague in memory.

Something had nearly shredded the tent in trying to get in. A huge furred form nearly knocked Leesil aside in its rush. Large unblinking crystal blue eyes, sparked by some nearby light, gazed down at her over a long and narrow muzzle. And that face dropped too close, too fast, in snuffling at her.

Magiere remembered sucking a breath in sudden panic.

She knew she was awake only when she'd felt something as if inside her thoughts. It was still, silent, and as watchful at those blue eyes staring at her.

Chap almost collapsed atop her as his eyes closed.

She heard his sigh and, even though she'd finally recognized him and Leesil, this wasn't the end of it. Someone else was trying to get into the tent.

"Please wait. Let me."

That rasp of words sounded familiar.

Leesil straightened up, then turned away where he knelt, and she'd realized he was gripping her right arm. He didn't let go even as he reached out somewhere beyond her sight. Chap shifted away a little to her other side as someone else crawled into view down near her covered legs. Leesil guided that one's small hand to contact with her right shin beneath the blanket.

"Easy," Leesil said to the newcomer. "You're right at her feet."

The visitor, smaller than he was, pushed back a draping hood.

Magiere looked upon and even recognized Wynn.

She'd wanted to say something but couldn't. It took every effort just to breathe and keep her eyes open a little longer.

Even back on the first night, it had seemed strange—frightening—that Wynn didn't look at her or Chap or Leesil. The last thing Magiere remembered of that night, when she couldn't keep her eyes open any longer, was Leesil calling out . . .

"Magiere . . . ? Magiere!"

Two more nights and days had passed, and she'd wakened sporadically.

There were times, as she heard bit by bit some of what had happened, that she'd wanted them to stop. She didn't want to hear any more. All of that came after Chap told her that Leesil and the others had succeeded.

—*This time . . . the Enemy . . . will . . . never . . . come back*—

Leesil or Chap, and sometimes Wynn, were always there whenever she awoke a little longer each time. Fragments of memory returned that she'd rather have forgotten but couldn't. They ran backward from a final instant of agony.

She'd nearly turned on Chap—and he on her—and she might've killed him.

She'd snapped the neck of another majay-hì a moment before he'd rammed her.

How many of the living had she killed among the undead that had driven her—the dhampir—into something worse than what it hunted?

The afternoon of the second day, with her one arm in a sling, she decided to try stepping out of the tent, no matter how much Leesil tried to stop her. She didn't see the girl until too late.

Wayfarer nearly knocked her over when the girl slammed into and wrapped her small arms around her. At least Leesil had been right behind to hold her up.

Others around the camp rose, and that was when she saw their state. There were some greetings and good wishes, some questions and answers, but none of that really mattered as she kept looking all ways. Of course, Chane wasn't there, likely hidden from the sun in one of the other tents, but someone else was missing.

Osha was gone.

Leesil wouldn't let her go off and look. Instead, he forced her back into the tent and eventually shooed out Wayfarer, halting the girl's fussing. After that, all Magiere could do was collapse, and it was dark out when she awoke again.

Now she sat up and remained there after rubbing the crystal left by the bedroll. The wound in her shoulder no longer pained her. For any of the others, it would have taken a moon or more for a wound like that to heal over and leave a scar.

She listened to the muted voices outside while Leesil kept pacing, likely caught between looking in on her and not wanting to disturb her rest. Or maybe he was just keeping the others from doing so. Finally, she couldn't tolerate sitting there any longer, though she left the sling in place.

After taking a deep, shuddering breath, she crawled to the tent's flap. She was only halfway out when Leesil stepped in, pulled the flap back, and grabbed her arm. She let him help her up rather than let the others see she was better off than they were.

Again, Osha was nowhere to be seen.

Some fussing ensued when she approached those around the campfire.

Wayfarer wouldn't leave her alone, though she didn't mind. She was too relieved to see the girl was unharmed. And then there was Wynn—blind— with Chane hovering at the small sage's side.

During the time that she'd been recovering, Brot'an's and Ghassan's bodies had been rendered to ash. Leesil and Ore-Locks hadn't cared much about Ghassan's receiving proper rites, but for some strange reason, Chap had insisted. Chuillyon promised to attend to returning their remains to their respective peoples, somehow.

As Magiere now sat by the fire, Leesil began recounting everything that had happened in the mountain. He was just finishing when they heard horses' hooves approaching. Magiere tensed, but Leesil shook his head as he stood. Four Shé'ith riders came upslope out of the dark.

The leader dismounted outside the ring of tents and stepped toward them. He was unusually tall with several wounds on his face and arms. Chuillyon rose, hurried around the campfire, and met him halfway.

"Althahk, I thank you again for your assistance. The Enemy is gone this time . . . for good and always."

The tall one studied the strangely mixed group around the fire and perhaps fixed on Magiere the longest. It took effort for her not to glance away from his severe amber eyes, but he looked away instead of to the others.

"No one is to speak of what happened here—not ever to anyone," he commanded. "We will not risk others coming to see . . . and search."

Such arrogance might've once put Magiere on edge, causing her to verbally take him apart, but not now, not after what she'd done.

Chuillyon nodded politely. "We are all sworn to silence."

Althahk looked about. "Where is Osha? Does he come with the Shé'ith?"

Wynn shifted, turning toward that voice. "I think not."

Althahk hesitated. By the furrowing of his brow, Magiere guessed Wynn's answer was less than satisfying. But if the sage hadn't said so, Magiere would have—and not so politely—for she had something else in mind for Osha.

"What of the Foirfeahkan?" Althahk asked. "I have not seen her since last night."

That seemed to distress him, and Magiere followed his gaze to Wayfarer. The girl lowered her eyes and looked only to the fire. Stranger still, Shade rose up at Wynn's side and growled at the tall Lhoin'na. Chuillyon was slow in answering.

"I have sent Vreuvillä and . . . and her tribe . . . home with their dead."

Magiere knew that "her tribe" referred to the majay-hì.

Althahk remained silent a moment longer. "Then you will do the same for the Shé'ith at dawn."

He turned back and mounted without another word. Those with him did the same, and all four Shé'ith wheeled and left.

Chuillyon was quiet after that. And no one noticed—or at least no one said anything—as Magiere looked about the camp and beyond it. They also wouldn't know how far she could see in the dark, though she wasn't watching the riders.

—He left . . . again . . . upon hearing . . . you . . . rise—

Magiere found Chap watching her.

—Are you . . . well . . . enough?—

She didn't answer, merely got up, and in leaving said, "I need to walk."

Wayfarer grasped her hand, and Leesil was on his feet instantly.

"No you don't!" he warned. "You're staying—"

Chap's sudden snarl cut off everything, and even startled Ore-Locks.

"You keep out of this," Leesil said to Chap.

Magiere grabbed her husband's arm. "I'm all right," she whispered. "Just stay with Wayfarer. Maybe it's time to tell her some things, and I won't be long."

—Find him . . . before . . . it is . . . worse—

At that Magiere sighed in frustration, though she nodded to Chap. On her way out, heading west, she saw something more.

Her falchion lay in its sheath next to one tent. It didn't matter that someone tried to clean the blood and other stains. That sheath would never come fully clean.

Magiere walked on into the dark.

She'd failed to control the horde and had instead driven it into a frenzy around her. That might have kept it from going after the others outside the mountain, but she'd killed more than undead out there. She'd endangered everyone, and what more could have happened if she hadn't been stopped?

Everything that she, Leesil, and Chap had seen in those phantasms long ago in her homeland had been true. It simply hadn't happened the way they'd seen. It hadn't ended the same way either because . . .

Magiere slowed upon hearing someone ahead coming upslope in the dark. And that someone stopped in three steps upon spotting her. Osha backed away and quickly turned.

"Stop!" Magiere ordered.

He dropped his head. She went for him, and when he heard her, he tried to walk off again.

She grabbed the back of his cloak and jerked him to a stop. When he refused to turn and face her, she forgot pretending that she was as unhealed as the others. Throwing an arm around him, she pulled him against herself.

"You listen to me," she began softly.

Back in the camp, Leesil fidgeted and forced himself not to pace again, but he still kept looking off to where Magiere had vanished in the dark.

—Leave . . . her . . . alone—

He turned about to fix Chap with a stare.

—What she does . . . is necessary—

Leesil turned toward the open darkness again, though Magiere was long gone.

—The worst wounds . . . are not . . . of flesh— . . . *—Healing his . . . will heal . . . hers—*

Maybe Chap was right, if she found Osha.

"So, we are done," Wayfarer whispered. "And everyone goes home, at least most."

She sat staring into the fire.

"There is a place for all," Chuillyon said, speaking to the girl, this time with his typical soft smile. "When I return the Shé'ith, I will take you to—"

"No," Leesil cut in, also speaking to Wayfarer. "You're going home, to a real home."

She looked up at him. "I do not have a home anymore."

"Of course you do! You're coming with us."

Everyone around the fire fell silent. Even Wynn raised her head. Shade's ears pricked up, and Chap hauled himself up with a dog's grumble.

Wayfarer's eyes were locked on Leesil.

"If I don't convince you," he added, "I'll never hear the end of it from Magiere. And if you're around, maybe you can keep that mangy mutt clean."

Chap growled and wrinkled his jowls.

Magiere tightened her arm around Osha every time he tried to pull free. He still hadn't said a word.

"You stopped me when no one else could!" she told him. "No one else could've done what you did, made that shot . . . or I wouldn't be here."

She felt him shudder.

Magiere half pulled, half stepped around Osha. When he turned his face away, she took hold of it, though he was taller than she was. She forced him to look at her.

"You saved me," she added, more softly this time. "Don't you ever think of it another way."

There'd been too much harm done because of her. He'd suffered more than most would for skills that no one else had. Certainly Brot'an, if he'd been there, could've taken that shot, but only Osha had done so with any thought for her life.

He'd missed her heart and still stopped her. An anmaglâhk wouldn't have bothered. No matter what he thought he'd lost, he was better than they were.

Osha finally looked at her, his eyes glassy. Before his tears fell, and she couldn't stop the same . . .

"Come on," she added gruffly, "or they'll start talking about us being out here alone so long."

At that, Osha blinked, making one tear, but his eyes then widened in shock.

Magiere sighed. Leesil was the funny one, and she just wasn't any good at it.

"Oh, forget it," she grumbled, jerking him around to push him ahead.

By the time they'd neared the camp, they could already hear Leesil.

"What?" he half shouted. "That is the stupidest thing I've ever heard you come up with."

"It has to be that way," Wynn countered. "We have to be certain."

Magiere stepped around as Osha slowed. Chane stood behind Wynn, dour as ever. Ore-Locks was eyeing Chane, not Wynn, and he didn't look happy. Chuillyon was the only one who appeared to contemplate whatever Wynn had said that set Leesil off.

Strangest of all, Chap was still and silent—and that worried Magiere the most.

"What's going on?" she demanded.

Leesil threw his hands up, bit off something foul before he said it, and coughed an exhale instead. He jabbed a finger at Wynn.

"She wants to stay here . . . in the mountain!"

Magiere stopped in her tracks and felt her own mouth drop open.

"What?" she finally got out.

"I must," Wynn continued calmly. "If the staff goes out, someone must reignite it. That can be only me."

Magiere was still numb, and any outrage wouldn't come out. Leesil got to that before she did.

"You can't stay out here," he snarled. "There's nothing to eat, there's no water, there's no—"

"I'll manage," Wynn interrupted.

"And I will stay with her," Chane added in his rasp.

Another shocked silence came and went, though not without Osha stepping past Magiere to look between Wynn and Chane.

"Oh, that's even better!" Magiere finally erupted, fixing on Wynn and forgetting any sorrow for her friend's loss of sight. "And where are you going to find enough livestock for him if you can't feed yourself? A moon at most, and he'll be hunting again."

Chane's answering rasp was more pronounced. "I have no need to hunt. There is one orb still exposed. It will sustain me . . . as I have not fed—in any way—since before we even arrived in the empire's capital."

"We'll be all right," Wynn said. "What would happen otherwise if the crystal goes out? We must stay to make certain it remains lit. There's no one else who can do so."

Magiere couldn't find another argument, and as Leesil said nothing, he was at a loss as well. Even Osha didn't make a sound and just stood there. But to Magiere, the pain on his face was evident until he looked to Chane.

Everyone knew the unspoken contention between those two concerning Wynn.

Wynn had made a choice. She's chosen to remain here, and she'd chosen Chane.

But in addition to Osha, there was another affected by Wynn's choice.

Magiere carefully glanced aside and found Wayfarer watching Osha. She hoped the girl didn't see this as an opportunity. Leesil would've already told her where she was going, where her home was now—with them. But Osha would not forget this moment for a long time to come.

If Wynn wouldn't be swayed, then something had to be done for her survival. The sage had already lost too much for what had to be done. A few ideas came to mind, though they might involve a small breach concerning Althahk's demand for secrecy.

Still, that would have to wait as well.

Magiere reached out, grasped Osha's shoulder, and pulled him around. "Take the tent with Wayfarer and Ore-Locks."

He barely looked at her, not saying a word.

"Be packed and ready in the morning," she added. "You're going home—to our home—or I'll come after you again."

Osha walked off, and Magiere waved Wayfarer after him. She wasn't certain of the latter choice but didn't want him to be left alone.

"Ore-Locks," Leesil said, "we need to talk about some . . . arrangements in the morning."

"He and I have already spoken," Chane interrupted. "If you have considerations we have not thought of, those are welcome."

Magiere eyed Leesil, wondering whether he'd had notions similar to hers where Wynn was concerned.

"I would appreciate it," Wynn began, "if all of you stopped *fussing*! I am not half as incapable as everyone keeps assuming."

Magiere couldn't remember how many uncomfortable pauses had passed, but there was another one. How they could part this way, even if there were plans as yet so that it wouldn't be forever?

"Chuillyon," Magiere said.

The elder sage, who'd been watching in uncomfortable silence as he sat near the fire, looked up and blinked in surprise.

"You'll be needed in what we have in mind," Magiere added, exchanging a glance with Leesil. "I'll tell you more tomorrow."

Chuillyon frowned in puzzlement. "Very well."

"And Shade," Wynn began, catching all off guard, but then her voice began to falter, "you are going with them . . . little sister."

"Wait, what?" Leesil cut in with a step.

Even Magiere had assumed Shade would stay with Wynn—and Chane. Wynn ignored Leesil, but Shade was already up on all fours, as was Chap.

"You have to go, Shade," Wynn added.

The dog's ears, though pricked up, flattened as Shade gave a mewling growl.

She began barking, even snapping, but Wynn dropped off the stone she sat on and grabbed for Shade's head. Fresh tears flowed down Wynn's cheeks.

"You need to have a life of your own," Wynn said. "It's not here in the heat and sand. Go with Wayfarer and your father. At least, you'll have trees, rain, forest . . . and I believe we will see each other again, somehow."

Magiere then noticed Chane.

He looked down upon Wynn and Shade with an expression she couldn't have imagined on his face, the face she'd see more than once turn into the bloodthirsty monster that he was inside.

Was that sadness?

The sight hit her hard as she thought on how the past few years had changed them all. Here they were at the end of it—the trials and battles they had never asked for, never wanted.

It was finally over.

Shade pulled out of Wynn's hold. A strange mewling whine shook her all over. She turned and raced off toward where Osha and Wayfarer had both vanished into their tent. Chap just watched after his daughter for a moment and looked back to Wynn, who crumpled upon the ground in tears. Chane knelt beside her.

Battles were done, but there were still wounds being inflicted. Hopefully, time could heal those as well.

Chane raised Wynn up and started to see her off to their tent.

Ore-Locks cleared his throat uncomfortably. "I—I will look in on the younger ones."

"I think I shall retire as well," Chuillyon said.

Both went off.

"Come on, Chap," Leesil said, heading for their tent, and then he looked at Magiere.

She nodded silently and turned to follow. Leesil lifted the flap, Chap crept in slowly, and Leesil looked up. Magiere faltered upon spotting something else beside that tent.

"In a moment," she said.

Leesil frowned but nodded and slipped inside.

Magiere stood paused over her falchion. There was no other blade like it for what it could do to the undead. She picked it up, began to draw it slowly, and stopped before a three-finger breadth of the blade showed. Then she turned as Chane was about to duck inside a tent behind Wynn.

"Wait," Magiere called.

Chane froze without flinching, though he eyed the sword and then her. Magiere slammed the falchion back into its sheath and threw it at him across the camp. Stunned, Chane straightened in dropping the tent flap as he caught the weapon.

For a moment, Magiere couldn't speak.

"Just in case," she said finally, "should something come looking for what we left in the mountain. I won't need that blade anymore."

Before he could say anything, she turned and swatted her way into the tent.

Inside, with the cold lamp she'd left there now dimming, Leesil lay on his back upon a bedroll with his head propped against Chap's shoulder. Both had their eyes closed in exhaustion.

If they were actually asleep, she didn't want to wake them, and if not . . .

Magiere dropped and crawled in, putting her back against Leesil's chest and her head up against Chap. Nothing more needed to be said, though she heard Leesil whisper, whether asleep in exhaustion or not.

"Home . . ."

EPILOGUE

Chane stepped to the chasm's edge beneath the mountain peak at the easternmost end of the Sky-Cutter Range. Wall-mounted lanterns with alchemically heated cold-lamp crystals lit the half cavern around him. Their light still could not reach the chasm's far side as he stared numbly along the cable-suspended bridge that spanned the wide breach.

The stench of lamp oil filled the air around him.

On the chasm's far side, along another hidden tunnel, was another cavern where grew a new child, or grandchild, of Chârmun among a skeleton of huge bones. The bridge was not the only transformation made beneath the mountain over the past thirty years. Other comforts had long ago been arranged for the two guardians who lived here—himself and Wynn.

Ore-Locks with his stonewalker brethren, Chuillyon and several more legitimate white sages, and a select few of the newer green order had all contributed. There were gifts and other support from the small number of allies who knew what had happened here.

Ore-Locks had also seen to safeguards for the way in and out of the peak, and there were now multiple, connected chambers nearby, cut into the mountain's stone to serve as a home. The youngest stonewalker had been a good friend, the likes of which Chane never thought he would have.

Tonight he stood alone with Magiere's falchion in hand, staring across the bridge. Since that long-past night when she had tossed this weapon at him, he had never drawn the blade that had once taken his head.

But he did so now and stepped out along the bridge, sword and sheath in his hands.

The rope cabling was inspected and repaired as needed each year. It swayed a little, and yet he did not need to grip the braided rope railings. The earliest nights beneath the mountain were still fresh in his memory, when he had escorted Wynn to check the sun-crystal staff.

On their first visit, she had felt her way onward without him. Without sight, she did not trust just touching the staff to know if the crystal was still lit. She draped her cloak over it and called out to him, and only then did he dare enter.

The sun crystal was still glowing—it was always still glowing.

Over time, they guessed this must have been the influence of Chârmun's child, tree and sun crystal sustaining each other.

After that first visit, Chane remade some physical protections that he had once used—along with a potion to fight off dormancy—in protecting Wynn during daylight hours. With his body fully covered, he could accompany her to check on the crystal. Once they entered the cavern, she still threw a cloak over the top of the staff, as even his covering would not protect him for long. Although Chane knew they did not need to fully enter the cavern to see that the crystal glowed, Wynn insisted on making a full check of the staff and tree. Perhaps it helped her feel she was fulfilling her duty.

It was several years before Wynn willingly missed even one night's visit to the tree.

Over time, the new grandchild of Chârmun grew more and more immense.

Chane could imagine it even now, as he walked the chasm's bridge, though he would not go to see it this night or ever again.

Its branches nearly reached that cavern's walls, though under the canopy it was difficult to tell if it had reached the ceiling higher above. Even while wearing the "ring of nothing," Chane had always felt it prodding him, trying to uncover what he was. Through that tree, all but Ore-Locks and his kind visited this place, and others were brought by white sages of Chuillyon's previous order.

Chane stepped off the bridge into the far half-cavern landing, but he went no farther. Instead, he leaned the falchion and its sheath against one of the bridge's upright anchor posts. About to turn back, he hesitated, peering toward the landing's rear. He barely made out the passage leading to the cavern of immense bones caught in the great tree's spreading roots.

Two cold-lamp crystals were mounted in plain holders on the bridge posts. He took out the nearest above the falchion, rubbed it furiously for light, and replaced it before heading back.

He crossed the bridge again and paused upon reaching the other side, remembering.

In their early time here, going to the tree had always left Wynn somber. On several occasions she had resisted his help in the return and blindly felt for a grip on the braided railing.

Her frustration had grown worse—and dangerous—in that first year after so many visits to the staff. The sun crystal she never saw for herself was what had taken her sight. Perhaps in her blindness, she never knew how much of that he saw in her face.

Chane had not foreseen the lengths to which this would drive her.

Or at least he did not until one night when the white sages had come through the tree to deliver seasonal supplies. As always, they helped him move crates and baskets across the bridge, taking the previous empty containers with them. After a brief parting, he took a moment to assess the stores and discovered a pouch of roasted chestnuts crusted with cinnamon and nutmeg.

At the prospect of anything that might cheer Wynn, he left everything else and hurried off with the pouch.

A short ways up the passage, he had turned into an opening excavated by

Ore-Locks and others. Therein were the chambers he shared with Wynn. They were filled with cushioned chairs, a few orange dwarven crystals for heat, a small scribe's desk for himself and his journals, and shelves with odd things and many books that he read to himself or her. By the end of that first year, they had the comforts of a true home beneath the mountain.

But Wynn was nowhere to be seen that night. Though not exactly worrisome, it was odd. She always settled for the evenings in this outer chamber. He stepped onward toward the back of the room, and as he was about to open the heavy curtain within another opening, he heard the whispers.

Quietly, he pulled the curtain aside.

Wynn knelt on the stone floor at the bed's foot, having pushed aside a thick rug. By her whispers, he knew what she was doing, but he hesitated at breaking her focus. He feared some worse mishap if he interrupted.

What had she been thinking?

Without true sight, how could her mantic sight ever show her even the Elements within all things? The taint in her from a thaumaturgical ritual gone wrong so long ago could do nothing for a blind woman. He had never felt so restrained in helplessness, waiting for her to fail.

Wynn stopped whispering.

She pitched forward, caught herself, hands braced on the floor, and gagged. Then Chane dropped the pouch as he charged for her.

He dropped to his knees, and she collapsed against him, breathing too fast and hard.

"What are you doing? Why?" he asked softly.

Her head toppled back, struck his shoulder, and her eyes opened wide. He watched those brown irises shift more than once, pause, and shift again about the chamber.

She slapped a hand over her mouth as her eyes clamped shut. Her other hand slammed down on his folded leg, and her small fingers ground into his thigh. He felt nothing in his worry—except shock.

In the brief moment Wynn's eyes had opened, they had moved more than once about the chamber.

She had *seen* something.

Her eyes opened again, and he thought she might sicken again. Then she looked up at his face so near to hers.

"Chane?" Wynn whispered.

He should have made her stop then and there, but he could not.

Obviously she had been toying with this in secret whenever he went hunting lizards and desert rodents to supplement their supplies. Or when he was working to improve his meager conjuring, which eventually moved from fire to water for their additional use. Given her loss of sight, he had never thought she would try this, for how could mantic sight work if she could not see?

But it had, and more than this, she blinked twice. For an instant, her expression cleared of sickness, and she smiled at him. It was not the last time he would have that aching joy. So long as he wore the ring, there was one thing—one person—that did make her head ache in vertigo when she looked upon Spirit or any other elemental component of the world.

She would see him, only him, as he truly was.

Even so, he could not stop her from suffering in her tampering. Seeing elemental Spirit in her surroundings was all that she had. How could he deny her those brief moments of independence?

Now, standing at the near side of the chasm—and in that memory— Chane went numb again, and yet he could not stop remembering.

Wynn had found a way to see, now and then, and even for the price, she was much happier. She and Chane had a life together.

At night, they walked out under the moon and stars. In the seasons and years that followed, they studied languages, history, culture, and more from texts she or he requested from visiting sages. They drank tea brought from any corner of the world that sages could reach. They played board games and cards, ones they had always known and even a few new ones.

There were true visits as well—for more than just assistance in maintaining their vigilant existence.

Magiere, Chap, and Leesil came once a year, at least, with the aid of the white sages.

Chuillyon, likely with Leesil's convincing, had planted his small sprout from Chârmun in the royal grounds of Bela in Belaski on the eastern continent. Both were rather discomforted when asked how, and neither was very forthcoming. It was a short journey up the coast from Miiska to Bela, but this would have to be planned for the right time when the white sages came to the new "branch" of the guild in that city. They were necessary to send anyone else through or send them back.

On those visits, Wynn was overjoyed to see her three friends. Chane made an effort to be civil, and Magiere reciprocated. Chap ignored him, and Leesil was occasionally sociable.

After a few years, Chap came less frequently.

Leesil said Chap—and Shade—had moved on to an'Cróan lands to live full-time with the one they called Lily. Both majay-hì had already been going there regularly before then, though Chap still returned to Miiska as often as he could arrange. Eventually, Chane heard that Osha and Wayfarer had followed that way as well, and on that particular visit, both Magiere and Leesil were distant, as if preoccupied.

This had left Chane wondering, considering that both Osha and Wayfarer had originally fled their homeland as traitors and outcasts.

Time changed even more things, though not always purely in partings. A few more years passed to another night that burned into Chane's memories, never to be forgotten. It had started on the far side of the bridge.

Chane had been up and about that night while Wynn slept. He had come down to sit near the closest side of the bridge while working on a journal.

Another visitor came, though at first he had not noticed. He was distracted when one of the cold-lamp crystals on the bridge's far posts suddenly lit up. It startled him, for it was not time for the seasonal supplies.

A lone figure stood there between the far bridge posts.

Likely female by its small stature, it was shrouded in a long robe with a full, draping hood—both a deep forest green. This was the first time he had seen that color of robe.

With one of his many journals in hand, he snapped it closed and rose to his feet. The figure did not move, even as strange noises echoed faintly out of the passage to the tree's cavern.

Those noises quickly turned to a ruckus.

And still the green-robed figure did not move, even when a tiny furred form raced around it straight onto the bridge. And two more—and another— and another, five in all.

Chane stood staring.

The following pair of pups—brown and gray—pounced on and over the mottled one in the lead. He lurched forward a step, fearful that one or more might tumble over the bridge. They did not even slow their raucous, tumbling race until the first skidded onto the landing before him.

She barely pulled up short before ramming headlong into his boot.

Wide crystal-blues stared up him, but only for an instant. The second one rammed into and over the top of her, and that one did hit his boot. He was too shocked at the sight of them to even move, though he quickly curled the fingers of his left hand, checking with his thumb that he still wore the "ring of nothing."

The rest of the tiny pack followed, including the last: a black male stalking slowly in on him. Its ears twitched, flattened briefly, twitched again, and tiny jowls pulled back in a hesitant growl.

Chane did not move, even as a cream-coated little female with bark-colored streaks clawed at his shin in sniffing him. A more distant but sharp bark drew his eyes instantly. Halfway across the bridge, a huge black form with crystal-blue eyes led the green-robed sage.

He would have known Shade anywhere, even for the darkness at the bridge's center.

Shade came in growling at the little ones and trying to get them settled. It was hopeless, since she was outnumbered. And the green-robed sage, the first and last visitor among the others, stepped off the bridge, brushing back her hood.

It was Wayfarer.

Beneath her dark green robe, long but split down the front like Wynn's old travel one, the girl was dressed even more like the wild woman, the Foirfeahkan, called Vreuvillä. Multiple tiny braids of hair to either side of her face had strange wooden charms woven into them. Though one-quarter human, she still physically looked the same, as if she had not aged at all since he had last seen her.

Later would come many questions about green sages—who were not just sages—and how they came to be among the an'Cróan. Part sage by Chuillyon's outcast meddling, they also practiced what Wayfarer had learned from Leaf's Heart. But there and then, Chane looked down at one of the few others he had missed for a long time.

Shade huffed at him and stood waiting.

With the noise of the five little ones, it was entirely unnecessary for anyone to go and awaken Wynn. This was not the last time Shade would come, and after that, green-robed sages were sometimes the ones to bring supplies. But of all memories in a life with Wynn, that night was forever lodged in Chane.

Shade had brought her children to meet her "sister" . . . and Chane himself.

Where else might a mortal sage and a vampire find peace and contentment without judgment? He did not need to feed, with the orb nearby, and she had everything she required. They had each other most of all.

More years passed.

Chane had once imagined a life with Wynn in the Numan branch of the Guild of Sagecraft. This life was close enough—better—but as he now stood staring at the empty bridge, there were other nights he wished to tear out of memory.

The first had not registered upon him until too late.

He had paid no notice to small lines that grew on Wynn's oval face or the few strands of gray that appeared in her wispy brown hair. He knew she would age while he would not, but she had barely passed the age of fifty, and there was so much time left for them.

One night, she did not eat.

When he asked, she told him she was not hungry. He should have listened to the way she said this. In the following nights—and days—she barely ate at all.

The look of discomfort, then pain, began to show on her face.

He wanted to take her to a coastal city for a physician. She was too weak for the long journey. He wanted to take her to the tree in the hope that she might be able to call to someone through it for help. She became too weak to walk that far, and then so fragile that he feared carrying her.

He grew desperate to find some help, and so he dressed to shield himself before entering that far cavern alone. Even protected, he felt himself begin to burn. He threw Wynn's cloak over the crystal for more protection, and then realized he would still have to remove a glove to . . .

When he and Wynn had gone among the Lhoin'na, he had not dared to touch Chârmun.

Would its offspring allow him to do so? Would it affect him like touching the white petals he once used in the healing potion that had stopped Magiere? And even if he could touch it, what then?

He was not a white sage, one of Chârmun's chosen.

By his nature, he was its enemy. If it killed him, Wynn would have no one to care for her.

He stood there in growing discomfort and then in pain, until smoke began to seep out around his clothing. Finally he fled into the passage's dark, out of reach of the sun crystal's light. Frustrated panic drove him back to Wynn, and he desperately hoped that someone would soon come to them.

One night, Wynn could not sit up.

That this happened during another supply visit by white sages was pure chance. Even so, Chane knew it would take a long time to get a message to Magiere, Leesil, and especially Chap.

But he sent a message with the sages. He also begged them to send him a difficult-to-obtain ingredient called boar's bell. They had hesitated to agree until he told them what it was for.

They left.

Chane waited.

Shortly thereafter, Chuillyon arrived and brought two healer sages of the Lhoin'na guild branch. They brought the boar's bell and more *Anamgiah* blossoms, but the blossoms did nothing for Wynn, not this time. Chuillyon took the healers back to the tree and sent them home, though he remained awhile longer.

Chane used the boar's bell to re-create the potion to stave off dormancy that he had once needed to guard over Wynn while they had searched for the orbs. In this way, he could care for her both day and night.

On the sixth following night, just before dawn, Chane lay beside Wynn, their heads on the same pillow. Her eyes were closed, and he thought she was asleep. Then her hand sought out his, though her eyes did not open.

"I would rather have lived my life here with you," she whispered, "than with anyone, anywhere else, in this world."

His throat tightened, and he was about to answer, when the bedchamber was suddenly too quiet. Afraid to even shake her, all he could do was whisper her name, over and over, louder and louder, until his rasping voice tore at his own ears.

The silence had come when Wynn stopped breathing.

He lay there all day and through the next night with his face pressed into Wynn's shoulder. When he finally emerged, Chuillyon was still there in the outer room. The tall Lhoin'na said nothing and only nodded respectfully.

Rather than burn again, Chane let Chuillyon place her body in the cavern with the tree. He gathered stones from outside the peak for the elder sage to mound up her grave cairn. Chuillyon left after promising to look for Magiere and the others himself, though it was already too late for them to come.

Chane now often crossed the bridge to reignite the cold-lamp crystal on the far side—just in case someone arrived. Until tonight, he had not thought of the sword Magiere had thrown at him. Only tonight had he brought it and left it at the chasm's far side.

It was a warning and an invitation.

He had a "life" because of Wynn, but that life was now over.

And yet he would—could—not die with her a third and final time.

All around him the stench of lamp oil was thick. He had spread so much of it that even the bottomless chasm's air had not yet dissipated those fumes. It had taken most of the previous night to scavenge enough for his need. But it would not be enough to be certain.

The presence of the orb beneath the tree's roots would still reach him. Yes, he could have fled the mountain and gotten far enough away that its constant feeding of him could no longer heal his wounds. Even then, he could not be certain that fire would finish him rather than leave him charred to rise yet again.

There was only one way to be certain of following Wynn.

How long did he wait there, sipping from the flask of potion to keep himself awake? How many times did he cross that bridge, now shivering from lack of dormancy, to relight that one cold-lamp crystal at the far side? Was it more than one night, another day, three or maybe four?

In the silence, he heard distant footsteps on stone.

When Chane looked, the cold-lamp crystal at the bridge's far end had dimmed again, but not enough to hide someone standing near it. That someone finally reached down to grasp the falchion's hilt and then strode slowly along the bridge.

She no longer wore the studded leather armor, for that had been lost—cut off her—the morning after all had ended outside the mountain. Instead, she wore a plain shirt beneath a dark brown cloak that she flipped back over away from her sword arm.

Magiere stepped off the bridge's near end. She did not look a day older than the night when she had been struck down by an arrow. Then again, neither did he.

"Wynn is gone," he said flatly in his rasp.

She had maimed his voice, when she had taken his head with that blade once before. And that was the only way to be certain of a final death. But all she did was look away toward the passage beyond him where his home—Wynn's now-silent empty home—lay.

Magiere's eyes turned back on him.

"You knew this would happen eventually," he said. "So do it . . . since this is what you have always wanted."

She watched him with no emotion on her pale face framed in blood-black hair.

"No."

Chane flinched at her one word, suddenly panic-stricken in grief. Where was the monster in her, now that he needed it for the monster in him?

"It's not what Wynn would've wanted," she said, "not for you, not for either of us."

Chane began to shudder, either from too many nights without dormancy or just the despair of failing to follow Wynn.

"I won't come back again," she said. "I am leaving, and I suggest you do the same. That staff will never go out, and now that Wynn is gone . . ."

Magiere dropped the falchion. It clattered on stone as she turned away. She was three steps onto the bridge before he lunged after her.

"You had a life because of her," she said, pausing but not turning back. "Don't waste whatever's left. Don't do that to her. I won't do that to her . . . for you."

Chane stood there, watching her leave. He took up the falchion, prepared to go after her. She never broke stride and never looked back.

"I am nothing without her!" he shouted. "So let me be nothing!"

"And how's that possible?" she said. "You came back—twice. Maybe a monster, and maybe something else, because of her. Would she want that wasted?"

He stood there so long after Magiere was gone. Someone had to be in there, waiting at the tree to take her away. Whoever that had been would be gone as well, unable to take an undead out of this place the same way. But Magiere's words kept burning him.

Maybe a monster . . . maybe something else . . . because of . . . her.

How was he to go on without the one person who had loved him? Yet how could he willfully end the life she had given him?

Chane stared down at Magiere's falchion in his hand.

He threw it off the bridge, though he never heard it hit bottom. He would gather only a few things before leaving this empty place.

Magiere was numb when a white sage returned her to the royal grounds of Bela. Chuillyon had planted his sprout—now a tree—of Chârmun there when they had all returned after those final nights near the peak.

She was still numb at the end of the long ride to Miiska.

There was something that Chane hadn't thought on in the years that had passed.

He had come back twice, but how could this be possible if there wasn't *something* inside him that was able to come back? She was more than the monster she'd been made to be, so why not the same with him? It didn't change any choice she'd made in hunting the undead or in what he'd done before Wynn, but now . . .

But perhaps like her there was more than a monster—there was *someone*—in him.

Magiere reached the stable up the street from the Sea Lion tavern. She left the horse with the young attendant still there. But when she was nearly home—finally—she stalled, thinking of Wynn.

No one should've been out in the trees toward the shore behind her home, but that was where she heard voices she couldn't quite make out. And upon getting closer . . .

"She was your friend as well as Mother's," a woman's voice insisted. "You should have gone. I would have, but I thought to come here first."

"Your mother needed to go alone this time," a man answered. "It's the last time. And you don't know everything . . . about how it might end."

Hearing the voices brought both relief and the grief that Magiere had held off. But she wasn't going to cry for a lost friend—not yet—and she walked off into those trees. She didn't care about being quiet and barely caught sight of a short woman in a long dark robe among the night-shadowed trees near the sea.

That one turned. "Mother?"

A man struggled up from beyond a tree nearer the shoreline, and moonlight across the water haloed him in a glimmer that caught hair once fully white-blond.

"It's about time," he said. "So, is he finally dead or not?"

Magiere closed quickly, right past Wayfarer, and threw her arms around Leesil.

"You know better than that," she whispered, suddenly so weary.

"Still had to ask," Leesil whispered back. "Sooner or later, you and Chane were going to have it out. I knew even I couldn't hold that off."

Magiere leaned back, looking into her husband's beautiful amber eyes. She saw his fright at having let her go alone fade. She also saw the lines in his face, the locks of hair that were now more white-gray than white-blond, and the exhaustion of the wait that she felt herself.

"As long as you came back," he said.

All she wanted then was to go home and stay there with him. There was no telling how long she would have him. Yes, she had grown older as well, but not as much as he.

In the end, how long would she have to live without him? That was too terrible a thought, and she had to look away. And there was Wayfarer, watching her with as much worry as Leesil had.

"Get over here," Magiere said softly.

Wayfarer, still too small for one of her people, slipped in close and wrapped her arms around Magiere. It felt good to hold her again. No matter how often the girl returned now, it was never often enough for Magiere. She didn't even care about those ridiculous little wooden trinkets braided into the girl's dark hair or how much the girl—no, woman—had changed over the years.

"All right, girl," Magiere growled. "Where is that husband of yours?"

Wayfarer hesitated and let out a long, slow sigh. "He . . . could not . . . face it."

"So he's off playing with his deer again?"

The girl's eyes widened and scrunched in a scowl. This was followed by a sigh that was more of a scoff. How much she—all of them—had changed.

"Clhuassas—*listeners*—are not deer!" Wayfarer admonished. "And he is not *playing* with—"

"I don't care!" Magiere released Leesil and grabbed the girl by both shoulders. "You tell Osha we'd better see him by solstice or—"

"Yes, Mother," Wayfarer interrupted, with a roll of her green eyes.

"Here we go again," Leesil grumbled.

Magiere ignored him, finishing, "Or I'll go drag him back here by his hair!"

"Yes, Mother!"

There was silence for three breaths before Magiere straightened with a quick snort.

"Fine, good enough. Now let's go *home*."

She grabbed each of their hands and pulled them along as she headed toward the back door of the Sea Lion's kitchen. The high-pitched squeal of a child rose somewhere upstairs in the tavern.

Magiere stopped in her tracks and let go of Wayfarer and Leesil as she stared up at the windows of the top floor.

A laugh, like from a boy, was followed by the crash of pottery shattering and furniture toppling. More squeals and laughter were cut short by a deep rolling growl—but only for an instant.